ON THE MOB 2

THE CUPPACIO TWINS

LISA AUSTIN

LISA AUSTIN PUBLICATIONS

SYNOPSIS

Jagoda Bay, known for its lavish mansions and flashy mobsters, is currently the city of bizarre problems, erratic decisions, and difficult circumstances thanks to the Cuppacio family and their associates. With only three marriages holding back the Cuppacio men from securing their place in the Rinaldi Mafia, all eyes are on the twins, Renello and Metavello, as they are next to wed their prospective wives.

Twin one, Metavello, unbeknownst to him, has taken a bite of forbidden fruit, and now he wants the whole damn thing. With nothing but Discover and her glorious "center" on his mind, he is determined to remove all obstacles that block her from becoming his forever. But once he learns that the fruit has been sliced not once but twice by people close to his business and his heart, how can he ignore all of the signs leading to a "no" from the Rinaldi Mafia. Now, Metavello must decide if the fruit is as tasty as it was before he learned of all the imperfections at the core. And how can he choose when all he wants to do is take another bite?

Discover has never felt more stuck than she does with the three men currently tapping in and out of her environment. Since moving back to Jagoda Bay to fulfill her commitment to her husband, she has encountered the past, been disinterested in her present, and repeatedly rammed by her future. She left her child's father behind when she decided to raise her daughter alone, and now, at every turn, there he is. Her husband is ready to create an heir, but how could Discover ever split her time with her daughter, Discovery. And her handful of run-ins with Metavello have caused highs and lows that Discover has decided she can do without. All three men are unsolvable issues, and it's literally making Discover sick to her stomach.

Twin two, Renello, wants nothing but to see Pia happy, but only if *he* is the one making her happy. With his actions showing Pia that he wants more from her than the title of "once my cousin, not my cousin, but still maybe my cousin," Renello has no plans but to get money, remove any threats to Pia's well-being, and get married. However, his bridal choice has yet to make any moves to solidify that she will be agreeing to marriage, and this causes Renello to push boundaries until someone caves. And while Renello is known for being solid as a rock, Pia has proven to be made of stone as well.

Pia has made tough decisions her whole life. From being a teen mom to the sole provider for her family, she was once the poster child for struggle. Having Renello come back into her life gave Pia a glimpse of security she had not seen since she was a young girl. Now, she is leveling up again when her long-lost father enters the picture, and she plans to hit pause on anything requiring her to use her decision-making skills. Pause on her nagging baby daddy. Pause on sorting through her past and her future with Renello. Pause on her doing anything except enjoying a season of luxury. But are the pauses helping Pia move forward to find her purpose in life, or is it another excuse for her to avoid her past and her underlying feelings? Can she be okay with her long-lost cousin only being her unrelated platonic friend?

Essex has had love for the Cuppacio family since they forced him to showcase his artistic talents in the form of tattoos. Now, he is set for life as a highly sought-after tattoo artist, and with his current mixtape blowing up, he's adding up-and-coming rapper out of Chicago to his resume. Currently spending more time in Jagoda Bay, his luck continues to rise; from securing Bella as his social media manager to finding his newest freak, Missy- Essex has no plans to check out of his Airbnb anytime soon. But who is this pretty little girl who keeps popping up on his Instagram timeline? And was that his first love at his concert? And why has his baby mama started acting out since his recent success?

What's next when one twin is stuck in the cousin-zone with the love of his life, and the other twin is addicted to a woman who he can't marry and sometimes can't find? The twins, once against the idea of being compelled to secure wives, are now chasing after two women who have turned the obligation into an obsession.

HI!

Hey, y'all! We made it! I appreciate you all so much for following along with this series! Again, I ask that you trust the process with this one. Enjoy over one hundred and twenty thousand words of love, drama, and mobbing.

I love and appreciate you all!

Remember to trust the process of this story!

ORDER OF BOOKS

Humbled on Christmas Day
    Daddy's lil Baby
    Pregnant by a muthafuckin' Don 2
    Pregnant by a muthafuckin' Don 2
    Put it on the mob
    Put it on the mob 2
    Also there is mention of characters from a previous Novella in this text titled Big Boss. You do not have to read big Boss to follow the story. If you would like to read Big Boss here is the link.
    Big Boss

CHAPTER 1
ESSEX

"Is you cool?"

"What the hell do you mean 'is I'm cool'? Essex, don't play with me! You said you were coming home to get your kids three weeks ago, and I hadn't seen you! You all over the fucking blogs and shit-"

"Ahh! There you go. That's the problem. Some social media shit got you tight?"

"How much would you like to load on the Visa card?" the impatient cashier with the dimpled forehead asked. She had about nine other customers in line behind me, who were all mostly old folk. Huffing and puffing wasn't going to do shit for her.

"Visa card? What the hell are you doing, and where the fuck you at?"

Ignoring my baby mama's screams, I replied to the cashier, "Two hunnid."

"I hope you loading that card for your kids!"

"Aye, add me one of these hundred-dollar DoorDash cards."

Pointing at the row of cards behind the cashier, I pinned my phone to my ear with my shoulder and counted the bills to cash out. I'd gotten more than halfway to my destination when I realized that I couldn't show up anywhere empty-handed. I'd planned on giving out cash to the birthday person, but being around them Cuppacio niggas as of late, I realized they did shit big, and I wasn't trying to go in there ghetto as fuck.

Collecting the cards from the cashier, who wanted to be anywhere but here, I tossed her a wink, drawing blush to her slender cheeks. She was about twenty years my senior, but if a smile could remove her sour-ass mood, the least I could do was give her one. My baby mama was still in my fucking ear talking nonsense, and all I was trying to do was make it from the front door of the Dollar General to the driver's side of the Durango truck I'd rented.

"You hear me, Essex? Where the fuck you about to go?"

I waited until the engine turned over and the GPS was back in motion before I answered her while pulling from the parking lot. "To a birthday party."

"I hope not to a bitch birthday party." She screamed so loud that I knew her voice was going to be nonexistent by tomorrow.

Vivianna and I didn't even do shit like this. I used to pride myself on having a cool ass baby mama. Our first son, now four-year-old Elias, was and still is the light of my fucking life. Vivianna and I weren't in a relationship per se, but she was the woman I was fucking anytime I put the ink gun down. Co-parenting had been a breeze with her. I put her up in an upscale townhouse near downtown Chicago that cost a nigga a pretty penny every month. She drove a nice-ass Infinity truck, and I made sure her pockets were laced. All was curiosity of me, so when I wanted to fuck, she let me, and when I didn't fuck, she didn't trip. Shit was good. That's why I wasn't tripping when she popped up pregnant a few months after Elias' birthday. We welcomed our second son into the world, and I didn't think it was possible for my heart to grow any more than it did with Elias, but when Elijah was born, that proved my theory to be incorrect. I loved the fuck out of my sons, and I made sure they or their mama didn't want for shit.

My boys were the sole reason why I hired help at my shop. For the longest time, I was a one-man show. Since I was sixteen, I'd been tattooing niggas until my fucking eyes bled. I would go days without sleep just to make sure I didn't miss out on no fucking money. When my kids came into the picture, I knew time was way more important than money, so I scaled back some, started scheduling appointments-only sessions, and pulled some young niggas out of the hood that was nice with a pencil and taught them the game.

"Viv, I'm going to a fucking kids party. Not no bitch's kid, either. My nigga told me to pull up, so that's what I'ma do. If social media pissing you the fuck off, you need to stay off that shit—I do."

"If you stay off of it... how in the fuck did you make a TikTok and post a whole damn dancing video? You don't even really show your face online, but all of a sudden, you doing the fucking Cha Cha Slide for likes and views."

Before I could stop myself, I tossed my head back in laughter. Viv got funny as fuck anytime she was mad. She didn't even have a right to be mad because, for one, I hadn't fucked her in over a year, and for two, she wasn't my woman even when we were fucking. Right after our second son was born, she started preaching that family shit, and I knew I had to keep my dick out of her, so I did. I wasn't the type of nigga that wanted to create a broken home. That's why I took care of Viv the way I did, but I wasn't going to force myself to be with someone that I knew wasn't the one. Viv knew my sentiments.

Her tweakin' on a nigga was all new.

I'd always been a low-key nigga, and even though my business page and designs were all over the internet and had been for nearly a decade, I stayed off that shit. It wasn't always by choice, though. Most of the time, I was tatting, so when I did get free time, I spent that responding to emails and DMs. Scrolling the blog pages wasn't a luxury I had until lately.

"You wild as hell. My people had me doing that shit. Bella know her shit, too, because my streams and shit have gone up."

I didn't know shit about streams or none of that, but the producer I'd worked with to do the mixtape had it down to a science. Every other day, he was screenshotting me some stats and had put me on to sign up for different platforms so that I could get paid as an independent artist. All this shit was new to me, and even though he spent hours breaking the shit down, I was still unsure like a motherfucker.

"That lil' young hoe just want to suck yo' dick!"

"Aye! You tripping. Ion even look at Bella like that, so cut that shit out. She a fucking baby and ain't did shit to you. Fuck all this animosity coming from anyway, Viv? You know we don't even do that? What's up... you need some dick?"

Viv wasn't a freak, which sucked for her because that's what I liked, but she did have some good pussy. She was a pretty-ass face with a nice little body, so she got my dick hard anytime I was on that with her. She couldn't suck a dick to save her fucking life, but the pussy stayed wet. Aside from her being *okay* in bed, she was a damn good mother to my sons, and that shit was a turn-on. As of late, though, she'd been turning me the fuck off, and I'd been holding back from going in on her ass like I wanted to because I would never disrespect a woman, especially the mother of my child. I hadn't fucked in a while due to her wanting to take it further with me, but if giving her some dick would shut her the fuck up, I would give her ass a sample. It was all she could take anyway.

"You know I need some dick, and you know you not giving it up, so I don't even know why you're trying to tease me." She mumbled some cuss words before switching back to the party. "And, how you at a party without your kids, though? They like cake and shit too."

Pulling up to the big-ass mansion, I shook my head in awe and parked behind a Bentley. When my nigga Ezio told me he had business to tend to in Jagoda Bay, I just thought he was on some lining his pockets type shit. But when I saw his fucking wedding, and then the big, pink-ass house he lived in, I knew that nigga was on more than some getting money shit. These niggas were printing the fucking money.

I'd been around The Cuppacios since we were kids. I had just run away from my situation and was out on the streets. I was trying to sell my drawings and shit when I ran into this light-skinned-ass nigga with colored eyes that had three equally crazy-looking niggas behind him. Those niggas were well put together, so I knew they weren't from the hood. I was expecting them to buy my drawings so that I could get me a forty-dollar-a-night room and some food. When Ezio told me to tattoo him, I must've looked at the nigga like he was crazy.

He took me with them, we watched YouTube video tutorials, and then I tatted that nigga. After that, I never went hungry, and I'd been eating ever since. I knew those niggas had some shit going on when I saw how a bunch of teenagers were running households. When I found out they had been mob-affiliated and the heads had gotten whacked off, I was in disbelief. They were bosses, even back then with the little they had.

We'd all starved together, hustled together, and came up together. If it wasn't for the Cuppacios, there was no telling where I would be. I owed them niggas everything. Seeing

Demise's estate at the Halloween party, this one, and how each of my niggas had come to Jagoda Bay and made a fucking name for themselves was motivating.

The roundabout driveway was lined with six-figure cars, and the house rivaled Buckingham Palace. A manicured lawed stretched for miles, and groomed bushes littered the landscaping. I didn't know what type of child this party was for, but I knew the shit was going to be next level once I stepped inside. This is what I wanted for my children. Big-ass lavish homes, ridiculous-ass birthday parties, private lessons—just the best of everything.

"Damn right, you not getting no daddy dick. You got a whole nigga, Viv. To keep this shit from being so messy, keep that lil' pussy over there. But I'ma fly out soon and scoop them. I want them to feel the city out anyway."

I loved Jagoda Bay from the moment my feet hit the soil. Shit just felt like home even though I'd never been here a day in my fucking life. When I saw Discover's fine-ass in Target, I knew then that I was meant to be here. I hadn't expected to run into the girl who had taken my V-card, but now that I had, I knew this was where I needed to be. Even if she didn't use a nigga's contact, I just knew that seeing her was a good sign. I did hope that her sexy ass hit me up so that I could figure out how in the hell had she ended up here. If I remember correctly, I think she was from here, but my years before connecting with the Cuppacios were a blur. We'd done so much shit and lived so damn fast that by the time I turned twenty, I didn't even know I had made my first million. I called myself depositing all my money in the bank one day, and the adrenaline running through me when I saw the multiple commas matched the adrenaline I had seeing Discover again. She had never really left a nigga's brain, even after all these years. I wouldn't mind linking up with her at all.

"So you moving out there? I thought you were just visiting Ezio and n'em? Fuck am I to do if you're out there? Plus, I hope you're not trying to quit tatting for rapping. That shit is not guaranteed."

It was hard to hurt the feelings of a nigga like me, but hearing Viv say that shit did cause a shift in my chest. I was never meant to rap. It was some shit I did when I was bored, and even then, all I did was write down rhymes. When that nigga Frost all but forced me into the booth after giving his ass a suggestion on a song, I didn't leave that studio until my mixtape was born. *Gunned down* was some real-life mistake type shit. I had no idea it was going to blow up. There were days when I was back home just out and about and would pull up at the red light to niggas bobbing to my shit. They wouldn't even know it was me. Shit was mind-boggling how my music was growing such a large audience in a short amount of time, and just a few weeks ago, Viv's words wouldn't mean shit to me because music wasn't my focus. Now that I'd seen the influence and had my niggas pour into me, I felt like it was possible to really take this music shit to the next level.

"Viv... Ion gon' lie. Yo' energy too fucked up right now. What the fuck I do ain't none of your business. Long as you can keep fucking the next nigga under the roof I pay for and spend my money without a care in the world, you shouldn't be concerned. If I stop doing tats today, you and my kids will be straight until the day y'all leave this world. But I'ma hit you, tho'. Kiss my boys for me."

"Es—"

I disconnected on her ass and snatched the cards up. Vivian was the last motherfucker to tell somebody what they should and shouldn't be doing when she didn't even have a damn job. Her job was to raise my seeds, and when she wasn't doing that, she ran the streets of Chicago. She came from a middle-class family, and since her mama was a housewife, that had always been her goal, even without a husband. This little Instafame shit had her growing a green head, and that shit wasn't cute on her. Shaking her from my thoughts, I hopped out the whip and headed to the front door.

"Who the fuck lives in this bitch? Scarface?"

Ding Dong

Crossing my arms in front of my crotch, I popped my neck while waiting for the front door to open. A balloon arch that went a few feet over my head informed me that the party was for a girl. I remember when Viv was pregnant with Elijah, the doctor had said it was a girl. We had prepared for a baby girl, buying all the dope pink and purple shit. At her last appointment, it was confirmed he was a damn boy instead and pissed Viv off. I was sick as hell for a minute, but when he brought his ass out of the womb screaming, all the pink shit I'd wasted my money on wasn't even a thought no more.

When the door was snatched open, I came face to face with the birthday girl. She had a pin on her pink Prada dress that was overflowing with money, and her long hair was pressed past her shoulders. The glasses on her pretty face was a clear pink, and behind her, the party thrown in her honor was in full swing.

I had the birthday girl by a few feet since I stood at well over six feet, so she looked up at me while pushing her glasses up on her face. We engaged in a stare-off, and I almost turned the fuck around because little lady wasn't trying to let a nigga in.

Immediately, a smile covered her face, and I knew then a nigga was good. Just as I stepped into the extravagant crib, she jumped up, leaving her body dangling straight while her arms were wrapped around my neck. It caught me off guard like a motherfucker because I didn't know this little girl or her people. I didn't know what the fuck to do, so I held my hands up while looking around the party for a savior. She was hanging on a nigga like she was a damn Koala bear, and when I felt her wet tears on my neck, my body stiffened.

"Essexxx! Hey, y'all... it's Essex! The one that sing "*E-Block*" in here!"

I went from having one child dangling from my neck, which she still was, to being surrounded by at least a dozen little kids asking for my autograph. Some were a part of the Cuppacio clan, and the others must've been here in honor of the birthday girl. That's when it dawned on me; she must've known me from social media. Patting her back, I smiled at all the kids while I let her get her tears out. When her grip loosened, I bent over so that her Prada sneakers touched the marble again.

Her face was swollen and red, but she was still the prettiest little girl I'd ever seen.

"I'm so sorry for doing that. It was inappropriate. I'm just... so... happy you're here." She pushed her glasses up on her face and wiped her eyes.

"It's yo' party. You can cry if you want too. I'm glad to be here." I handed her the cards and then went into my pocket and pulled out five more big faces for her to add to her birthday pin. "Happy birthday, pretty mama."

The kids behind her jumped up and down as she held her monetary gifts.

"Nigga, you got the kids out here going crazy. I hate to see how the women react when yo' ass go in the backyard."

Ezio walked up and slapped hands with me. He'd put on a little weight since getting clean, and now that he had a son on the way, I just knew his ass was eating more than Jisei. Eventually, the kids ran off, leaving me with my nigga.

"You trippin'... I didn't even know the damn kids would

recognize me." I shook in disbelief.

"Everyone knows you. From the hoes to the kids to the haters to the real niggas. I keep telling yo' ass—you everywhere now. You need to gon' establish a legit team; manager and shit. Bella told everybody with an ear that she your social media manager, so don't even try to give her job away."

We both shared a laugh. Bella was on top of that shit. She'd been reposting videos, and anytime someone with a name was on live listening to my shit, she was tagging me and screen recording. I wouldn't give her job away even if she didn't mind. Hell, I was even thinking about letting her run the tattoo business page.

"I'ma get on it. This shit just new and instant as a muthafucka, joe."

Ezio led me to the backyard where the party was set up, looking like an extravagant carnival. No one was in the pool since it was now the first of November and a bit chilly, but it was warm enough to lounge outside. All types of food vendors were set up, and life-size emoji balloons floated about. The bouncy houses and rides would have had my busy-ass sons going crazy. Ezio wasn't lying—I guess everyone did know me. I'd had to take pictures for the first hour of being here, and by the time I was able to fire up and chill with the fellas, I was ready to fucking eat.

"Where them twin niggas at?" I asked Shio.

Shio was always on time. That nigga didn't do late, so it didn't shock me to see that he was already here. Ezio, now being sober, married, and such a prominent member of the mafia, had to be on time too. His wife didn't play that late shit anyways. The twins, on the other hand, didn't give a flying fuck. Vello and I had been hanging the tightest since I'd been in the city, and when I asked the nigga if he was on the way, he claimed he would make it before me.

"No telling with them niggas."

I handed Shio the blunt, and he declined. We were far enough away from the children, but still close enough to see what was going on.

"Aye, who party this is? I mean, I seen the birthday girl and shit, but who her people? They mob-tied?"

I was still learning this mob shit, and since I wasn't Rinaldi Mob, there was a lot that they didn't disclose, which I understood completely. The Cuppacios were the only family I had outside of my kids and Viv, but I wasn't blood and understood that some shit wasn't for my ears. Still, my niggas had put me in the loop, and in order for me to even step foot in Demise's home, he had to clear a nigga. I signed an NDA without actually signing the shit. The shit was a street NDA. If I played where he laid his head, he was going to slit my neck, cut off my dick, and nip my arteries. Those were his words. He didn't have to worry about me, though; my street days were long behind me. I had my shit one hundred percent legal with the ink.

Shio looked around before stepping close. "Hell yeah. Remember the other Don?"

"Talkin' 'bout the fag?"

"Yeah, this Don Rio spot."

They'd told me all about Gay Boy Mansion, and now, a nigga had the creeps. Kids shouldn't even be running around this motherfucker with what I assumed went down.

"Shit, speaking of. There he go right there. I can't believe the nigga got a wife." Shio nodded toward the back of the house, across the yard.

I could see the back of Don Rio's head and wanted to at least speak since I was at his house. But the nigga was way across the yard talking to Demise, and the woman on his arm with the fat ass was laughing with Dasani. All these niggas wives were bad. It made me proud to have a badass baby mama because if I had an average bitch, I would have been scared to bring Viv around. I didn't have any plans on dragging her ass up here, but I knew it wouldn't be long. That nigga of hers was too soft because even though I didn't lay my hands on a woman, Viv couldn't have been playing with me like she did her nigga. He knew his bitch loved me, but he still accepted the flirting and shit she did with me.

After eating, getting high as a kite, laughing at the kids dancing to the latest hits, and chopping it up with the rest of the clan, the twins still hadn't arrived. I shook my head, still shocked that my song was in rotation at this party. After jigging to my own shit and declining an impromptu perfor-mance, I had to piss. A bathroom was connected to the pool house, so I trudged in that direction. I hadn't even introduced myself to the man of the house, and I hadn't laid eyes on him again since earlier, so I didn't feel comfortable constantly walking in his shit. Gay or not, he was still the king of the fucking castle.

Stepping inside the guesthouse, the décor matched the main house, and even though it was all too rich looking for my taste, I appreciated the effort. This nigga had long bread. His guesthouse was twice the size of my Chicago apartment and my baby mama's townhome combined. Walking through the living room, I concluded that the hallway to the left led to a bathroom since I could see the kitchen to my right.

The first door I came upon was cracked, but I could tell that it was the bathroom from the white vanity that I was able to see from where I stood. I didn't want to just open the door, so I stood back from view just in case there was a little kid in there who was too scared to close the door. My oldest son uses the bathroom with the door wide open and even tries that shit when we are in public. I knew how kids could be.

"It's your birthday, D-Berry. Please dry your face. I thought you were having fun?"

Hearing sniffles had my ears perking, but I still kept my distance.

"Mother, I don't care about that! I just—"

"You just what, baby? Talk to me... please. What has you so upset?"

Needing to piss bad as hell and figuring those occupying the bathroom wouldn't be coming out anytime soon, I went to the next door. It was a modestly decorated bedroom with an en suite bathroom. After pissing and washing my hands, I trudged right past the cracked door and went back out to the party. This time, where I'd been standing stood both late-ass twins.

"Superstar! You made it, my boy."

I slapped hands with Vello and then Nel. It always tripped me out that these niggas never planned outfits and shit but always ended up being color-coordinated. Today, they were in nude colors, and while their drip was different, the shit was still in the same family. The only way I could tell these niggas apart was because of the tattoos I'd done on them. They had many identical ones, but Nel had that big-ass rose tattoo with Pia's name on display.

"Fuck you niggas was late for? Vello, how I beat you when we were just on the phone?"

Vello shook his head, and I knew his answer before he could tell me. He'd gotten caught up with a woman.

"Aye, where you going?" I cut in on whatever Vello was about to say, asking Nel, who had taken off toward the house's back entrance. The nigga had just gotten here, but we all turned our heads in the direction that Nel ran off in. I'd been in Jagoda Bay for a month, and had only seen him a handful of times. Let Vello tell it, he was pussy-whipped without actually getting any of Pia's pussy.

"Get the fuck off my dick!" was his reply as he stepped

inside the house.

Vello held the middle finger up while Shio shook his head, and I chuckled.

"Where the fuck fav going?" Ezio asked, walking up with a cotton candy swirl in his hand. This was his fourth one. That nigga had been eating so much you would have thought he was the one carrying the baby instead of Jisei. Hell, it was still crazy that his feral ass had tied the knot.

"His kissing cousin must've pulled up," Vello responded with a frown on his face.

They'd told me the story of Pia last night at the Halloween party, and the whole shit was chaotic. Ezio burning her house down had me remembering how we were all young and bad as fuck. Granted, I didn't know them at the time all this shit went down, but if Nel was feeling her on that level, I didn't see shit wrong with him pursuing her. They may have been raised as cousins until elementary but hadn't gone through puberty or anything together. Wasn't shit wrong with them fucking. These niggas knew that too; they just liked to give each other a hard time.

Shio fired up another blunt, and Vello went off to find his twin, more than likely. Shio and Ezio were chopping it up, so I pulled my phone out to check my notifications. My fucking TikTok was blowing up, and I seemed to get a notification every second. Bella's little ass had been on top of it, though. I couldn't believe I'd let her young ass talk me into a job that I wasn't even hiring for. But she knew more about this shit than I did. Speaking of Bella, she'd sent me a text saying she was creating me a personal page. She didn't even give me a chance to respond before sending the name of an email address, Instagram username, and password. I only had my business page and didn't want to merge this rap shit with my bread and butter, so a personal page was definitely needed if I was going to explore this music celebrity lane.

'Preciate that.

BELLA

Log on now. Your followers are climbing by the minute. Plus rapper Flexer sent you a DM.

You didn't respond?

BELLA

No! I was tempted to give him my number but to not make you look like you played for the other team, I stood down.

YEAH, *maybe Bella running my shit wasn't the best idea.*

"I can't believe you 'bout to have one of these running around." Shio choked out as more kids ran past us.

"Shit, me neither. Crazy thing is, a nigga almost had twins," Ezio responded.

"You was almost neck and neck with me," I added while logging into my new page with a blunt in the other hand. By the time I had the password entered, I was passing the blunt. I was high as fuck, so I was done smoking; I would let them niggas finish it.

Bella wasn't lying when she said my followers were climbing. I was already at eight thousand followers. In the right-hand corner, the number seventeen was displayed, letting me know how many DMs I'd received. Clicking the icon, I smirked at the first DM being from girls I'd seen here and there on social media. Bella had added my mixtape cover for my profile picture, and it was the only one on my page. Backing out of my DMs, I clicked out of the app altogether and went to my Photos. I searched my pictures, passing the hundreds of tattoos

I'd done within the last few months, and found what I was looking for. After adding the picture to my favorites albums, I went back to the Instagram page. I was going to add the picture of my sons from the day I brought them to the studio with me. I'd gone in to add adlibs to my track and they sat in awe of all the buttons in front of the engineer. In the picture, they both were in the booth with headphones on their ears, smiling, looking just like their needy-ass mama. Blood tests proved that they both were mine, so there were no issues there; I just didn't have a chance in the gene pool with Viv. They even had her high yellow skin tone. That picture of them would be the first one added to my profile outside of the mixtape cover Bella had uploaded. Before I could upload it, another DM notification popped up at the top of my phone. I didn't like that, and would have to change the settings before this shit disturbed my peace.

BrianaDior: Pull up at my booking. I'll be in your city this weekend.

BRIANA WAS FINE AS FUCK. She was a brown-skinned bombshell with a short pixie cut, which looked sexy as fuck on her. I'd done her tattoos a few times, and even though she tried to put the pussy on me way before this rap shit, I was still going to pass. Briana was a good girl. The only reason she'd blown up on social media was due to her YouTube segments with an ex-boyfriend. I thought she was pretty and respected the fact that no one had really been linked to her outside her ex, but when it came to getting my dick wet, I didn't give a fuck about respect. I liked me a freak. If we got in the room and you were scared to choke on this dick, it wasn't shit moving forward with us.

Skipping past the other two DMs because I knew those two girls too, and they both wouldn't be shit but paying customers to me, I clicked on the one from Flexer. He was a young nigga from Memphis that used to be on some crash dummy shit until he started rapping at the age of sixteen. Now, at twenty years old, he'd made his mark on the industry. He'd booked me on several occasions to not only tattoo him but his whole team as well. I was proud of Flexer. I had no plans to do any inking in the Bay but made exceptions for a few of my folks. He was in that lineup, for sure.

Flexer: So you mean to tell me out of all the times I done booked your ass you didn't think to tell me you could rap? Me: It ain't shit. That nigga Frost pushed me in the fucking booth and I didn't leave that bitch till Gunned Down was born.

"Here." Shio tried handing me the blunt, but I turned it down. These niggas were talking about going out later, and if I got too high, I wouldn't leave the fucking bed. I had an Airbnb not too far from Ezio's, and the owner had it set up so nice that I wanted to purchase that bitch.

Flexer: That's whatsup! I been listening to this shit on replay like a muthafucka. But Ion know what the next week looking like for you, but I want to add you to my show. It's next Saturday. I had Reaper opening but you know what happened to him.

My heart drummed wildly in my chest. Show? Flexer wasn't just anybody. He was on track to become one of the greats, and that nigga wasn't even legal enough to drink yet. That didn't stop his ass from popping bottles and shit on the regular, but still. Him wanting me to open for him was a big fucking deal. Reaper was a young rapper from Jagoda Bay who, like me, had blown up off one mixtape. His tape had been on replay for the last year, and right when he was able to slow down from touring to be able to do his album, the young nigga was gunned down in his own city along with his baby mama in the passenger seat. Jagoda Bay was pretty, but they weren't an exception to the dog-eat-dog shit that went on in every other major city, especially Chicago. Now, instead of reaping the benefits of his instant success, his son had to be raised without a father and a mother.

Me: Ima be honest, I really just hopped in this shit. Ion know shit about performing, but looks like I got six days to figure the shit out.

From years of owning my shop, I was used to dealing with the public. But performing in front of hundreds, maybe thousands of people in less than a week, had me shook low-key.

Flexer: I know you doing yo thang with the tattoos. Shit you really the best to ever do it. But, this rap shit? Easy fucking peasy. It's plenty bullshit that come with it too and

plenty sleepless nights but you done been up three days no sleep completing a piece for me so you not no stranger to long nights. I'm offering you the same thing I did Reaper. Twenty bands to come open for me at the Fall Ball.

I'D HEARD about the Fall Ball. It was a big-ass concert that Jagoda Bay threw every year, and each year, a different rapper headlined it. It was a big fucking deal to just attend, so performing was over the top.

Flexer: Ima send you a couple DJ's your way and some managers. Shit as a matter of fact, Reapers manager may be free.
Me: Say less, send the info. Lock me in.
Flexer: Ayeee! Fuck you tum bout! Ima leave you as a surprise for the opening. They gone love this shit. Fuck it, I'll turn you up even more. I got thirty for ya.

THIRTY THOUSAND DOLLARS just to stand on the stage and rap a few songs for my mixtape? Hell yeah! I ain't never been scared of shit, but I was scared shitless at the thought of being on that stage. I wasn't turning down thirty bands, though. The amount of tattoos I had to do for that type of bread—damn right, I was down.

Me: I need a few passes for my people if that's cool. I can pull up on you this week. I'm already in Jagoda Bay.

I HADN'T TYPED that message, but knew it was none other than Bella's hot ass. I wasn't even going to trip because I would prefer it if my people came through. I didn't want to do the performing shit alone, but I damn sure would if I had to.

Flexer: I got you. Come to the crib tomorrow. I'm here.
Me: Bet.

I DID SEND the last message right as a text message from Bella popped up at the top of my screen.

BELLA

Don't be mad lol. I promise I won't do no weird shit in your DMs I don't even play like that. I need my job. By the way, I need three of them passes and a stack. I need to get my fit together for Saturday.

I RECEIVED ANOTHER NOTIFICATION, and while trying to reply back to Bella, I clicked on it by mistake. Outside of my picture of the mixtape, a video had been posted to my profile. The birthday girl was dancing to my song, doing the same dance Bella had us doing a few weeks ago. You could see the rest of her party friends behind her, doing the dance too. "Gunned Down OUT NOW" was the caption. I must've watched the video at least three times before another notification came across the screen.

Vivtheboysmama: Hmmm. Cute. But upload a video your sons before you upload videos of random ass kids. Crazy work.

I COULDN'T BELIEVE Viv had done some shit like that. When I tried to click on the comment, I received an error message. I was sure that Bella had deleted it.

BELLA

> Aye! You better get yo baby mama! This is business! We not even doing that!

INSTEAD OF REPLYING to Bella about Viv, I sent her two stacks on Apple Pay. I needed to find out how much social media managers received for payment because I wanted to be sure I didn't undercut her. Viv had me heated, though, and instead of cursing her ass out in front of all these folks, I let Shio and Ezio know I was leaving and walked through the side gate to get to my car.

I had never had no fucking baby mama drama, and I wasn't going to let this rap shit turn Viv into an ignorant-ass woman. We didn't even do that type of shit. She had a whole nigga that was fucking her, so what the fuck I had going on shouldn't sway her one bit. That jealousy shit wasn't cute, and her commenting that shit under some kid's videos was foul. I was going to upload my son's but first, I was on Viv's top. With her non-dick-taking ass.

CHAPTER 2
PIA

I felt a ringing in my ears, my heart slammed against my chest, and my mouth had gone dry. I hadn't heard my mama's voice in years. I'd forgotten what she sounded like. But the first time she opened her mouth, it was to ask me words I had never thought would come from her.

"Oh my God, Mama! You talked!"

Pearla tossed her arms around our mama's neck and sobbed onto her chest. Tears burned the rim of my eyes as we all stood under the balloon arch. A black man, who looked too young to be what Patty had insinuated that he was, stared back at me. I could tell he was mixed with something due to his thick accent, but he was definitely black.

My mama rubbed Pearla's back while she continued to gaze at Rio. That was who he'd introduced himself as. On the side of him was a beautiful black woman whose skin tone mimicked mine. I'd never seen this man or woman before a day in my life, but my mom seemed to know exactly who he was. We all stood around, too stunned to speak. The sounds of a birthday party in full effect sounded off in the distance as we all just took in my mom's words and Pearla's sniffles.

"Rio. It's me—"

"Patricia." His accent was heavy, but when he spoke my mother's name, I could tell that his voice was shaky.

So, they do know one another.

I was going to have whiplash with the way my head was whipping back and forth between my mom and Rio. This lady hadn't uttered a word in years, and the first thing that came out of her mouth happened to be a deep, dark-ass secret. Ain't that some shit?

"Patricia."

Rio removed his hand from his wife's and took a step forward. Pearla unwrapped her arms from around our mother. I pulled her to my side and took a quick glance at her face. Her eyes were starting to swell, and her nose was red. The last time she'd heard our mother's voice was probably at an age when she was too young to actually remember it.

My mom reached her hand out and palmed his cheek. A broad smile stretched across her face while shock was still displayed on his.

"Rio," the woman he'd introduced as his wife, Discover, spoke up.

If a woman was on my doorstep touching my husband and saying that he fathered her grown child, I would be ready to lay all three of our asses out. But only confusion was on her face. She watched Rio and my mom without malice, and for her sake, that was good. I was shocked, but a bitch stayed on go. If a hoe even looked at my people wrong, I was on their asses.

Rio didn't reply back to his wife. He just stood in my mama's face with her hand still pressed to his cheek. They were two long-lost, star-crossed lovers while the rest of us stood idly.

"Um, do you all mind if I take him out back with the rest of the party? That way, you all can come in and talk?" Discover asked skeptically. She had a huge-ass rock on her finger, her face was perfectly made up, and the fitted sweater dress she was wearing did her figure right. She was drop-dead gorgeous. Hell, he was gorgeous. They were both just two gorgeous-ass people.

Neltz was standing on the opposite side of where Pearla stood beside me. I'd nearly forgotten my son was here. It was the quietest he'd ever been.

"What? Hell nawl... I'm not going? I'm tryna see the tea like everybody else. Grandma done found her long-lost baby daddy, and ain't nobody told me nothing! I knew I should have acted a fool when you dropped me off to my daddy all them months ago. I missed too much."

Discover all but clutched her pearls. Neltz was so damn embarrassing, it was ridiculous.

"Neltz..."

I didn't have it in me to give him more than that. But he knew by the tone of my voice that I wasn't playing. My son kicked invisible rocks before sticking his hands in the pockets of his Gap hoodie set and followed Discover.

She took one last look at her husband and my mama before grabbing Neltz's hand and disappearing into the big-ass house. Before they rounded the corner, I could see him watching her ass. That boy was going to give me a house full of badass grandbabies. I just prayed he waited until he was forty and married before he started having children.

Now, with Neltz gone, I focused my attention back to my mom and Rio. Pearla was sniffing, but had begun to dry her face. I couldn't even process my emotions. My hands were shaky, and my head was throbbing, but I had to suppress it all.

What the hell is going on?

"Mama... Is *he*... our daddy? I thought... I thought Niccoli was?"

We didn't talk about Niccoli at all, but Pearla did know his name. Outside of that, he wasn't worth mentioning—ever.

"No, baby. He's not your father. He's Natazia's."

I didn't go by my first name, nor did Pearla. We'd always gone by our middle names since birth, but my mama was the only one who would call us by our given names. To me, Natazia although a beautiful name, was too similar to Niccoli.

"Oh... okay." Pearla hesitated.

"I'll gladly take her, though," Rio spoke up, still glaring into my mama's eyes. It almost felt like we were interrupting them.

"Um, Pearla. Let's go into the party."

Rio finally broke his trance. "No. Please... not yet."

I nodded in response.

"I saw where they went off to. I'll catch up with them." Pearla stopped at our mother and kissed her cheek. "Please don't go mute on us again, Mama. I need you."

Those three words broke me. The tears that were threatening to fall finally broke through the barrier and curled under my chin.

My mama winked, and that gave Pearla the assurance to walk into the house. My chest felt like it was about to explode. I didn't know if I was dreaming or what, but if this wasn't real, I was going to be pissed. I knew Niccoli wasn't my father. He'd made that clear that he didn't father Pearla or me on several occasions. I'd never divulged that information to anyone back then, not even Renello. I felt like if I spoke those words, they wouldn't be my family anymore. I loved my cousins so much back then. The best part of my days was when we could all get together. Telling them that Niccoli used to scream he wasn't our daddy from the rooftops wasn't something I wanted to divulge.

"What the fuck going on?" My heart sang with delight as

25

Renello walked up, asking the question in his usual abrasive nature.

Not wasting any time, I tossed my arms around his neck, and his immediately went around my waist. He was so tall that he had to bend so that I wouldn't be standing on my tippy toes.

My mother speaking, her revelation, and him being present in the flesh—it was all just so much. Silent tears fell down my face as the stress of the situation eased up because Renello was there.

"Pia baby, what's wrong?" Renello almost whispered.

"Even when you were children, you two were inseparable. So I assume that you won't be sneaking in and out anymore, Renello?" my mama said, speaking again.

I pulled from Renello's embrace with the same shock that I had when she spoke for the first time. She was still in Rio's space, but her words were clear. She'd known that Renello was back the whole time, and here I was trying to hide it. No wonder she'd been all upbeat for the last month.

"It's good to see you, Ms. Patrice. You look good."

"Ummhmm. You're just too handsome. You look good too, Rio."

Rio blushed like a schoolboy.

"Patricia. You're still the most beautiful woman on the planet. We have so much to discuss. Come... come in."

"Is your wife okay with that?" I asked.

"Trust me... the last thing his wife needs to be worried about is you. I still can't believe this nigga married," Renello said.

Rio placed his hand on the small of my mama's back, prompting her to remove his hand from her face. They walked ahead of us as she placed an arm around his back. They were worse than Renello and I. If this was how we acted, then I could understand why Renello had blurred the lines.

"What the fuck going on, Pia baby?"

We were still following Rio and my mama while I admired his home. I had stepped inside of a plethora of extravagant homes in the span of a month. Who would have known my people were living like this while I was somewhere struggling to make rent? One day, I was a low-income flashlight cop, and the next, I was partying in mansions and being handed keys to Benz trucks. This shit was too crazy. If I wasn't starring in it, I wouldn't even believe this was all my life.

"My mama talked."

That was all I could get out, not even thinking about the fact that Renello had just heard her talk. I was too over-whelmed with emotion. My head was just everywhere.

Rio's home, much like the outside, gave museum vibes. It was beautiful. A DJ speaking over a turntable and multiple bouncy houses could be seen from the room he led us to. The large wooden desk and walls lined with bookshelves led me to believe that this was his office. They'd spent some money on this party. From my view, I could see Neltz talking to some of the older Cuppacio teens, and my forehead began to sweat.

Renello followed my gaze and pulled me to his side with his arm around my neck. "He's good. They ain't gon' let him do nuthin' too crazy."

I wasn't so sure. At the Halloween party, they were getting high as a damn kite. But at least they were sixteen. Neltz was nine, and therefore, should have had his ass on the bouncy houses or the rides with the other kids his age.

"God, Patrice! I should have come and found you."

Rio was pacing. Not only did his home give indication that he was wealthy, but his attire did. He was dressed in a silk two-piece set with designer slide-in loafers on his feet. His outfit fit him just right, showing that he put in work in the gym. If this was my daddy, he was fine-fine. I couldn't even be mad at

Patty for procreating with him.

"No, you shouldn't have. You did the right thing... never came back. They humiliated you time and time again. What they did to you was wrong!"

"Aye... could y'all elaborate on what's going on?" Renello's dark brows were slanted in a frown.

My mama faced us while Rio continued to pace. "Niccoli's and Rio's father used to make us... for a year straight. Then, Pia was born. We were what? Sixteen at the time? Rio?"

Rio finally stopped pacing and looked at my mama. "Yes, my love. God! I can't believe this."

He loved my mama. I didn't know to what magnitude, but he loved her. That much was evident.

"She's yours. It's not much we can do about it now because she is an adult that not only takes care of herself, but me, my daughter, and her son as well. But we can get a blood test—"

Rio grabbed my mama's hands in his. "Patrice. No need for a blood test. She looks exactly like my mother—exactly like my sister, but a darker version. She has my mother's skin tone."

"Hold up. Rio... you like dick, though. Like nigga, you gay as hell. How in the fuck do you got a child... Oh shit! That story you told Ezio. That shit was true? With Pia n'em mama?"

"What story?"

"So, my brand-new ass grandaddy gay?" Neltz, who was just outside, was standing in the doorway with a tall, slim, light-skinned lady behind him. She was drop-dead fucking gorgeous, and the Fendi sweater hanging off her shoulders gave away that she was high maintenance.

"Aht aht. No cursing, Neltz. You said you had to use the bathroom, and this isn't it. Watch your mouth and go in that door behind me." The lady scolded Neltz, and normally, I would say something about someone talking to my child crazy, but I was overstimulated at the moment. Neltz had tough skin;

he also needed his behind put in a child's place.

"Aye, young nigga, what she tell you? And when you done, find your way back outside. She ain't gotta escort you." Renello added to the conversation.

Neltz stomped off. The smile slowly faded off the lady's face, and she stepped into the room in defense mode.

"Brother. You good?"

Brother? So this is my auntie? We look the same damn age.

While her eyes were on her brother, mine was on her. Outside of her slick hair that she had pulled back into a tight bun and her light-skin tone, it was almost like looking in a mirror. She and I were damn near identical outside of her being at least thirty pounds smaller than me and four shades lighter. I used to wish I looked like Pearla and my mama because they looked so much alike. Pearla's looks began to change the older she got, and now, when side by side, the three of us looked related, but Pearla and my mama looked more like mother and daughter than she and I did.

"Arianee. This is my daughter, Natazia Pia. This is her mother, Patrice."

"Ahhhhhhhh!" Arainee's shrills pierced my ears, and her running full speed, only stopping to pull me into a hug, startled me. Even though she scared the shit out of me, her hug felt good. I felt some type of way that I wasn't biologically related to Scarlett and them. We had the most fun at the party, and they felt like family, but knowing I had a blood-related aunt made me feel good. I was still overwhelmed by everything, but she smelled good and looked like me, so I gave into her hug.

"Oh my fucking God! She looks just like Mommy!"

Arianee's big brown eyes glossed over while she looked from me to Rio. The citrusy smell wafting from her pores went well with her natural fragrance. Even her hands smelled good. All I'd put on today was Pearla's One Thousand Wishes lotion and spray. I didn't own a lick of perfume, but with the way all these women I'd come across had been smelling, that was another thing I had to add to my list of upping my game on.

"She looks just like me! Rio! What the fuck?" Arianee stood back but held onto my hands.

"You two are twins, my God." My mother clutched her chest as she watched us with a smile. I was still in utter disbelief that she was even speaking right now. She'd really surprised the fuck out of us.

"Let me let you go. I'm so sorry. But wow! Rio, how? When? But you've never... or so I thought. Mama isn't going to believe this! Ugh, I wish they would have come!"

So, I have living grandparents.

"God! I'm talking too much! I'm sorry, brother! I just can't fucking believe this! I have a fucking niece that looks like she could be my sister."

Arianee hugged me again. She stepped back, snatched a Kleenex off of Rio's desk, and dabbed her eyes.

"We... we have so much to talk about. I've missed so much. How have you been living? Have you been well?"

I opened my mouth to respond to Rio, who looked desperate for me to tell him that I'd been living like a Princess. Sadly, though, that wasn't my reality. I'd struggled. I'd lost. I'd been heartbroken. Now, my finances weren't a worry, and I had my son back, but it seemed like life wasn't done throwing curve balls at me.

"Hell nawl. She haven't lived well. She's gone through some shit. For a while, I thought she was dead. We just found her, and she's good now. I got her."

Renello pulled me into his side, where my body curved next to his without me even having to tell it to. Arianee looked from Renello to me while still dapping her eyes as her lip curved upward slightly.

"Renello. I... this is my daughter. My living, breathing child. Adult or not, she has Mecanio blood running through her. I've missed her life. I don't even know how old she is. I don't know her birthday. She's mine, but I don't mind sharing her. I just want to make up for lost time, and that means giving her everything that I have."

I swallowed a wad of air as Rio poured his heart out. A tear slipped from his eye, and that made Arianee cry more. We'd come here for a party and got an episode of Maury instead.

Turning to Renello, I cleared my throat.

"What? You need me to step out, hunh?" Renello's feelings looked hurt, but this moment wasn't about him and me.

I wanted nothing more than to have my person here at my side, but seeing my father in such a vulnerable state in front of another man didn't sit right with me. I didn't know what type of business he and Renello had, if any, and would rather do this without everyone's eyes on us. I would fill Renello in later *after* he and I talked. We had our own grievances to hash out.

"I'll come find you after. Plus, you need to keep eyes on your junior," I kidded, trying to make light of the situation.

Renello swiped his thumb across his nose and nodded.

"I'll go too. But, Pia! Please give me the chance to talk to you and exchange numbers before you leave. Please!" Arianee begged.

Giving her a small smile, I nodded. She was right behind Renello, and once I was sure they were gone, I faced my mom and dad. That shit sounded so weird to think about—*my mom and dad*.

"Why don't we all take a seat?" I suggested.

My mom and I sat down in the two brown leather chairs near the unlit fireplace, and Rio rested on the desk.

"I should have come back! I know what they were making us do—"

"Wait. Making? Could you start from how you know each other?"

I had an idea, especially with the way Niccoli used to carry on, but I needed to hear it with my own ears.

"Well… dammit, I can't believe this is even real right now. Give me just a moment, beautiful."

My cheeks warmed. I'd never thought I'd ever hear my daddy call me beautiful. Hell, I'd never thought I'd ever see my father. I accepted the fact that he, whoever he was, was dead somewhere. In my mind, I told myself if he was anything like Niccoli, I didn't need him.

"You look just like my mother." Rio chuckled. "But when I was around sixteen, my father used to force me to do things because he didn't want to believe that I was a homosexual."

"So, you're gay. But your wife?"

"She's only my wife on paper. I met Discover when she was barely legal and living in one of my family's shelters. One look at her, and she reminded me so much of your mother… I had to help her. I've been gay for as long as I can remember. I have never laid with Discover. She is well taken care of as my wife, and we only come together for business. She lives in New York but recently relocated here for a business transaction. I love her as a friend. But your mother… she is the only woman I ever *loved*. It's never been sexual; her strength, compassion, and humility inspired me. What I did to her was basically… rape."

"Rio! That's a lie!" My mother shot up from her seat and went to rub Rio's back.

"Patrice… you didn't consent. Niccoli made you, and my father made me just because Niccoli suggested it. It was wrong. Then, it went on for so long. I should have known you would have gotten pregnant." His voice stressed his feelings as his face displayed the stress.

In the span of ten minutes, he looked like he'd aged a few

years. I almost felt bad for even bringing this to his doorstep. He was just smiling and happy when he introduced us to his wife, and now it looked as if he'd been told he had three days to live.

"I told you. I told you when given the chance to never come back. I told you to be brave enough to stand up to your father and live in your truth. You did nothing wrong. Pia and I survived. We escaped. Life hadn't been the easiest, but our daughter made it worth living."

I swiped away at the tears my mother had caused to fall. I'd yearned to hear her voice for so long. Now, here she was, chatting up a storm. This was all surreal.

"I promise, Patrice. I promise... I'm here. From here on out. I'm going to give you all everything. I have to make up for all of this. I haven't seen you in twenty-five years."

Patrice leaned in and kissed Rio's cheek. He was looking at my mother with stars in his eyes.

"I'll let you two talk. Let me go find my grandson and gawk at all these Cuppacios that I haven't seen since they were in diapers. Pia—" My mother pointed at me. "No more surprises." She winked before exiting.

We both watched as she shimmied out of the room. Rio and I were alone, and I could feel him staring at me as I looked out the window into the backyard. Renello had made Neltz get inside of one of the bouncy houses. He was guarding the entrance of it with a scowl on his face and his arms crossed.

"Pia, I'm sorry."

Those three words weren't needed. He didn't owe that to me at all. He hadn't known I'd existed. But hearing him say them healed something in me. For so long, I'd forgotten all about my childhood. Well, according to Pearla, I'd locked them away in order to suppress my trauma. I'd forgotten what it felt like to have a dad because the one I'd been given was mean and cruel. Niccoli was not only disgusting, but racist, and he should have never been granted a black wife or black daughters.

"You don't have anything to be sorry about, but thank you."

"You're beautiful."

"Thank you. You're really handsome too. I can finally see where I get my looks from."

He smiled. "Me and Patrice did good. You've been living in Jagoda Bay all this time?"

"Yes. We fled Chicago when I was like seven, I think. Pearla was a baby. We've been here since."

"You were a teen mom?"

"Yes..." I cringed.

"It's okay. My mother had me as a teen. Sixteen, to be exact."

"Hmm. Runs in the family." I tried making light of the subject and the current circumstances. I was literally standing here talking to my dad, a stranger. "So, what do you do?"

I had to know. He was living way too large, not to mention that rock on Discover's finger.

Rio stared at me long and hard as if he was contemplating whether he wanted to tell me. "I'm head of the Mecanio Mob."

I chuckled. "My mama went from one mobster to another, hunh?"

Rio smiled again. "Something like that. What do you do? Or, what did you do before Renello came along?'

My head tilted in confusion.

"The Cuppacios seek council from me. In turn, I've learned each one of them inside and out. He loves you. Anything a man loves, he takes care of."

"Yeah. Well, I used to do security. That was barely paying the bills, but yes, Renello came back around, and I was able to quit my job. I also moved out of my apartment, and now I rent a house."

"*Rent?*"

"I like my house." I could see the wheels turning inside his head, so I had to shut him down. Just like I told Renello, I didn't mind renting. I loved my house. I liked my apartment before Banger was killed in front of it.

"You shouldn't have ever had to struggle. You shouldn't have ever had to work unless it was something you wanted to do. I was in the same city as you all this time and—"

"It's okay. You didn't know. We can't do anything about the past. But we can move forward."

"We can."

"Yes."

"Can I hug you, Pia?"

I nodded and fell into my father's arms. I let out a cry so deep that it shook my entire body. I bit my bottom lip until it throbbed like my pulse. A raw and primitive grief overwhelmed me. All this time. All this time, I'd lived hard when I didn't even have to. The swell of pain was beyond tears. I was a fucking G, but I'd been crying so much as of late that I swore after this, I was done.

"It's okay. It's okay, my child. I'm going to take care of you. I promise. You'll want for nothing. You, your mom, your sister, or my grandson. No more worries. No more stress."

It sounded good. It all sounded way too good to be true. But swaying in my father's arms, I felt like that little girl in pigtails who yearned for this from her father. I didn't get this, though. The only male figure I'd ever gotten this type of affection from was Renello.

I could feel my throat closing up as deep sobs racked my insides. "Rio?"

"Hmm?"

"Don't leave me?"

Rio kissed my forehead. "Never."

I hoped so bad that this wouldn't be all too good to be true. But God didn't favor me like that. I knew that somewhere, somehow, bullshit was brewing. I just hoped it brewed for as long as possible before he spilled over.

CHAPTER 3
VELLO

When Rio said he was throwing a party that was kid-friendly, he meant it. From the bouncy houses to the face painting stations to the fucking clowns I'd seen fraternizing about, this shit was a child's dream. With the exception of when I came over to visit the other day, and the vendors were setting all this shit up, I'd never seen this place look like anything less than a dick paradise. To see kids running around and smiling like Rio wasn't getting his dick shitted on upon these very grounds was mind-boggling. I was happy as shit that I didn't have a kid because no matter how well this place was cleaned, there was no way my child would be around this bitch jumping and giggling. Don hadn't put little Mafia on the ground once. That nigga had been holding his daughter since he walked in—Matteo too.

I'd been here every bit of an hour and hadn't seen Rio once. I didn't know who or what he was throwing this party for, but I needed to talk to that nigga. He'd spat all that shit to me about being ready to fill the next nigga's shoes when dating his wife, but on foe nem, I didn't give a fuck. I had to have Big Mama. I didn't know how in the fuck it was possible for me to not be able to eat, sleep, or fuck without her ass, and I'd only been in her presence three times—two of which my dick was planted deep in her guts. I'd fucked plenty of women, but none had left a fucking stain on my brain like Big Mama had. Here I was, clowning on Twin about Pia when I needed to snatch one of the red noses off the entertainers walking around the party, making animal-shaped balloons. I felt like Bozo with the way I'd been craving this woman when I didn't even know shit about her. It took a real fucking goofy-ass nigga to fall for a woman he'd just met. I didn't give a fuck, though; I had to have her.

At first, all I wanted to do was fuck. She was too fucking good-looking to not want to bend over. But then, I fucked, and I fucked again, and now, I didn't want to stop fucking on her pretty ass. Women be so quick to say all that men wanted to do was fuck, but how could we not? Women be so fucking pretty. So fucking soft. So fucking feminine. Most smelled so fucking good. That shit was attractive as fuck.

Big Mama had an aura about herself that kept a nigga intrigued. All I knew was that I couldn't go another day without talking to her. I'd damn near used every nigga's phone in the vicinity of me to call her, and she blocked every number. I needed Rio to switch over to Don Mecanio to do whatever the fuck was needed to find her. I was hating like a motherfucker now that I made her ass stop giving out information about herself. Had I just shut the fuck up, I would be able to pull down on her. I'd even driven through the different neighborhoods of the Twin Peak Lakes subdivision and had yet to stumble across her. This shit was driving a nigga crazy.

"And this is my big-headed-ass cousin, Vello."

Bella stood in front of me, lips blue from eating on a snow cone, hand on her little-ass hips with a posse behind her.

"Aye! I ain't in the mood for yo' shit today, Bells."

I was talking shit, but had a smile on my face. A nigga felt like I was dying inside, but I fucked with my fast-ass cousin. She'd talked herself into a job with Essex, and had been doing a damn good job with his social media. I couldn't get on TikTok without someone tagging him in that dance. Ours had the most likes, though. Thanks to Bella, I had so much pussy lined up in my inbox. I wasn't studying any of them hoes, though. My dick couldn't even get hard if it wasn't Big Mama.

"Oh my God! Nel really does have a twin."

One of the two girls standing behind Bella spoke up, and I immediately knew who it was.

"Pearla? You done growed up on a nigga!" I pulled Pearla in a one-armed hug. She'd grown up so beautifully. Nel was a hoe-ass nigga for keeping them away from us. Sensitive-ass nigga.

"You know me?"

Letting her go, I gave her a once-over. I couldn't believe she wasn't a baby anymore. Pia used to carry her ass around like a rag doll. You would have thought Pearla was one of her toys.

"Of course, I know you. Last time I saw you, you were a baby. Yo' mama n'em here?"

Her smile showed off a mouth full of braces with pink bands around them. Just like back then, Pia had been taking good care of Pearla. From the Ed Hardy fit to the fresh hairdo to the all-white Air Forces—Pearla hadn't missed a beat.

"Yes. My mom is over there eating, and Pia is inside." Pearla pointed at her mom, and when my eyes followed her finger, I chortled at my mama all in Patty's face. I could hear her loud-ass Patois over the music.

"Well, you already know Pearla. This is Mahzeyah." Bella was back to introducing the posse members.

Mahzeyah was around the same age as Pearla and Bella,

but she had a thick-ass diamond Cuban on her neck. The Rick Owens fit and sneakers she was wearing cost a pretty penny. Her young ass was flossing. I scanned the party to see who she was a product of, and when my eyes landed on that nigga Million, I jutted my chin up at him. Her dressed the way she was made sense. Her daddy was watching her little ass like a hawk. Being in Jagoda Bay, we'd met most of the key players in the game, and Million was most definitely one of them. He and his partner had a nice underground dog fighting club that Don had dragged us to once, and that bitch was lit. I was going to make it my business to go back.

"Bella, don't be walking around introducing them to everybody. Fuck you is? The host?"

Bella crunched down on her snow cone again while the girls snickered. "See, I only introduced them to you because I just got here, and I wanted to let my family meet my new crew. You used to be my favorite, Vello. Now, you on my shit list. Don't come asking me for tickets to the Fall Ball next week cuz the answer is no."

"What?"

"Essex is opening for Flexer." Bella shrugged like that shit wasn't a big deal.

"Oh my God! *The* Flexer? My mama loves him!" Mahzeyah squealed at the newly revealed information.

"Yeah, it's going to be lit! I can't wait! I'ma be in that bitch so live!" Bella's thin ass dropped down to the ground, leaving the girls to snicker.

"The hell you are—"

"Aht aht. Let's go, y'all. We don't need this negative energy."

"You don't even know them, Bella, while you acting like the damn ringleader."

She tossed up a finger sign and flicked her blue-tinted

tongue out. "I do now. Hater."

Bella and her crew walked off. I had a feeling that all three of them were going to be another problem added to my list. I was happy as fuck for my boy Essex, though, and couldn't wait to curse his ass out because he hadn't disclosed that info when he was just rotating a blunt with a nigga. Either way, I was glad my boy was getting these opportunities. I would be there to support him, no doubt.

Looking around, I noticed all my guys were somewhere spread throughout the party, so it was the perfect opportunity for me to talk to Rio. I couldn't hit up Reuchie or Don to help me find out information on Big Mama because she didn't meet their criteria. When Don said that she was off-limits at the school, that let me know that he already knew she was married. I couldn't stand how those niggas knew what the fuck was going on in our lives before we did. That was one of the things about this mob shit that I didn't fuck with. Niggas had too much fucking insight on a nigga and shit.

I'd walked all around this fucking party looking for Rio, and once thirty minutes passed, and there was no sign of him, my fucking bladder began to scream. Going inside, I headed to the first bathroom on the main floor. Thankfully it was empty, so I pissed, washed my hands, and decided that I was going to continue my "Rio hunt" inside. Unless that nigga was at the bottom of the pool, he wasn't outside, nor was he in the pool house. I needed him to get on top of this business as soon as possible. If he could get me an address tonight, that would be amazing. I was going to pull up, kill her bitch-ass husband if he was home, and kidnap her pretty ass. If our mama's made them Cuppacio niggas feel anything like how I was feeling behind Big Mama, I could see why they'd trafficked their asses. On foe nem, I understood. There was no way I could go another night without either hearing her voice or seeing her face. I didn't give a fuck; I was pulling the fuck up as soon as I had the drop on her ass. She had me fucked up.

Leaving the bathroom, I tried to remember where the fuck Rio's bedroom was. He'd given a nigga a tour once, and the whole time, I was just hoping I didn't see no gay shit, so I was barely paying attention. When I came to two double doors, I pushed them open, and seeing the big circular bed in the middle of the room, I knew I was in the right place. It looked like that was a spot where big-ass orgies took place. Hot-ass velvet covers made up the bed, and I had to swallow back vomit at the thought of what the fuck occurred on those covers.

"Sick-ass shit."

Hearing a toilet flush, I stood where I was. I didn't want to walk in on the nigga doing his business, so I stood near the door, too damn creeped out to walk further in the room. Water from a faucet ran, and I could hear the brushing of teeth.

"Fuck that nigga brushing his teeth for?" I mumbled. I hope he wasn't in there sucking dick.

I was antsy as hell. I'd smoked like three blunts, and my nerves still weren't calm. I needed Big Mama, and I needed her ass pronto. I wasn't taking my ass home until I had her location.

Once the water stopped, I straightened my posture so that I could plead my case with this nigga. Rio was forever giving a motherfucker a speech and shit. I didn't need to hear all that today. I just needed the lo'; that's it, that's all.

"Aye, Rio. Remember that married broad I was telling you about? I need the drop on her. Ion need you to do shit but give me her address. I can handle the rest—"

Rio stepped out of the bathroom, and my words were caught in my throat. Unless Rio had undergone an extensive sex change to look like the woman I'd been searching for, the very person that I'd been tweaking out over stood a few feet away from me, looking sexy as fuck, but annoyed as hell to see me.

"Today got to be a nigga's lucky day."

I took a few steps toward her with my heart racing in excitement. I didn't stop until I was towering over her, and her sweet perfume tickled my nostrils. She was too fucking pretty, and I'd concluded that she was just as fine made all up as she was hair tied and bare-faced. I scanned her critically and beamed approval. I had to fight the overwhelming feeling of putting my mouth on her. I'd never wanted to keep my lips on a woman's pussy the way I did hers. Hell, she had me ready to slurp her ass up.

"Metavello! What the fuck do you want, and why the fuck are you here?" she whispered harshly.

I was so ecstatic to see her that I'd forgotten all about where we were. She was asking me what the fuck I was doing here when I needed to be the one asking her that shit. My dick was hard as a motherfucker, and my heart was jumping for joy. She was looking at a nigga as if I was the scum of the earth, but none of that shit mattered.

"I should be asking you that, but I really don't even give a fuck about the logistics of it all. Where yo' phone at?"

My gaze dropped from her eyes to the creamy expanse of her neck to her covered shoulders and then down to her breast. The sweater dress did her body so fucking right.

My dick was harder than Mandarin Chinese. Big Mama was pretty as fuck in her fall dress and shit. Her hair was parted down the middle in a short little bob, and I loved it on her chocolate ass.

She looked like she wanted to say something smart, but her eyes scanned over to the dresser next to me, where a phone rested. I snatched that bitch up just as she was about to grab it.

"Metavello. Give me my fucking phone. Now!"

I held the phone above her head and held my forearm out to create some distance.

"Ion know what the fuck yo' beef is with me, but you had no business blocking my fucking number. You had me calling from all these niggas numbers, putting them in my fucking business and shit. Fuck you got going on, Big Mama?"

Her titties bounced as she tried to reach up and grab her phone. She was too fucking sexy, even being upset.

"If you don't know why I'm mad, then I don't know why I'm mad either! Give me my phone! Now!"

The last time I'd seen her was when I was wiping my nut out of her pussy, and at the time, we were all good. Now, she was acting as if I was her worst enemy. Shit didn't make sense.

"I'll break this shit. On foe nem, I will. Aye!"

Lowering my forearm, I used my body to back her sexy ass into the wall that was covered in some type of gold wallpaper. Rio's house reminded me of the beauty and the beast. Shit had the same aesthetics.

Her chest heaved up and down as I pressed my dick into her abdomen.

"Get off me." She gritted while attempting to shift herself from between me and the wall.

Sliding her phone into my back pocket, I grabbed her around her neck, applying just enough pressure so that she could get a little bit of oxygen. Placing a kiss on her plump lips, I moved my lips to her ear.

"You got three seconds to tell me what the fuck I do to you, why the fuck you won't pick up for me, and why in the *fuck* are you in this nigga's bathroom before I crash the fuck out."

I could feel her body temperature rise. I loosened the grip on her neck just enough so that she could talk. I deliberately shut out the awareness around me. If she was in Rio's bathroom, that had to mean something. It implied something that wasn't good—something that I wouldn't have believed in my wildest fucking dreams. Still, I needed to hear it from her.

"You act like you didn't—"

"Unh unh. Start with why the fuck you in this nigga's room. Make it quick because I'm 'bout to turn this fucking kid's party into a massacre."

"I'm... he's... he's my husband!"

The blood in my temples began to pound. I stiffened, momentarily abashed, as I repeated what she'd said in my head. I was angry at myself for being embarrassed. Beads of cold sweat formed on my forehead as I swallowed down the spit that had gathered in my mouth. My world spun. My fucking world was spinning as panic clawed my throat. Words ain't never caused me to shed a tear. As a matter of fact, I hadn't fucking cried since I was a damn kid, but here I was, ready to ball up on that nut-filled bed and cry a fucking river. I was ready for Rio to give me the location so I could kill Big Mama's husband, and that nigga *was* her husband. Ain't this some fucking shit!

"Aye! Pack yo' shit up. Let's roll."

I didn't know what the fuck the plan was, but she was coming with me. All this fucking time I'd been losing my mind over this girl, and her ass was married to Don Rio Mecanio. I didn't just fall for another nigga's bitch; I fell for *that* nigga's bitch. Don and the mob was just going to have to be mad at me because that shit was dead. This was my hoe now.

"Metavello, move! This is Discovery's party! How can I just run off into the sunset with you? Hunh? How? Plus, you just acted like you didn't know me when you were at Target with Essex. He and I talked, and you told him to get his hoe." She used air quotation marks when she said hoe.

I didn't know what the fuck she was talking about, but she

wasn't making her case any better.

"Man... how the fuck you know Essex? And why the fuck you was in Target talking to him?"

It was like the more this girl opened her mouth to reveal some shit, the sicker I felt. My fucking stomach was in knots. She was turning my world upside down, and she didn't even know it.

"Get the fuck off me! How I know him is not yo' business."

Discover tried pushing me away, but I was frozen in place. She'd just dumped this shit on me and was acting normal. I wasn't normal. This shit wasn't normal! A gay nigga had my hoe! I was ready to go against the mob to snatch her ass up and she was already wifed up by a Don!

"Aye! I'm 'bout to tweak the fuck out! Big Mama! Answer the fucking question! How you know Essex?"

"Okay, okay! We grew up together! I haven't seen him in years!"

"I grew up with Essex, and he ain't never mentioned yo' ass. But I'ma let that shit ride. When this party over, you bringing yo' ass with me. Ion know the ends and outs of divorcing a Don, but you need to figure the shit out. I been 'round this bitch going crazy, and you sitting up here married to Rio?"

"Nigga, I been told you I was married!"

"You didn't say to who, though!"

"You told me to stop giving out all that information! Remember?!"

We were in this bitch screaming like we didn't have no damn sense. This girl had me too heated. How the fuck did she know every single person around me, but I didn't know her ass?

"Where was all this energy in Target, Metavello?"

"Man, I wasn't in no fucking Target. If you saw a nigga in

Target, that wasn't me! That had to be my brother! I got a fucking twin."

Big Mama drew her head back like I'd slapped her, but I didn't let her neck go.

"A twin?"

"Yeah. A fucking twin." I mimicked her voice.

"Uh... oh... okay."

"Nah. Ain't no fucking okay! Fuck I look like ignoring you? Matta fact, bend over. I need to taste that pussy."

I loved eating on her. Big Mama had the cleanest-tasting pussy I'd ever put my mouth on. I could tell that she not only took care of herself, but she also placed the right foods in her body. As wet as that pussy was, she had to have been drinking all of her electrolytes and shit.

"Metavello.... noooo. I don't feel good. Plus, Rio is too good to me for me to do him like this in his room. I'll go with you. I'll go with you, but not tonight. It's my baby's birthday. I'll meet you at the same hotel this weekend. Let me just get some things in order."

"Big Mama..."

"Discover. My name is Discover, for the record."

I knew her fucking name. It came up on the caller ID when I called her, but Mecanio damn sure wasn't her last name. At least, not on her phone records.

"Big Mama. If I have to come find you—"

"You won't... you won't. I promise! Just give me the week. I promise."

"Ion believe you."

Lowering to my knees, I kept my hand around her neck. I didn't give a fuck about her not feeling good. I needed to taste this pussy. She'd dropped a big-ass bomb on me! I needed some pussy to ease my mind. With my free hand, I pushed her dress up, slid her panties down, tucked them in my pocket, and came face to face with her bare, wet pussy. I was going to collect her panties like Pokémon cards. When I got finished with her ass, she wouldn't have a pair in her drawer. The floor was hard as shit underneath my knees, but again, I didn't give a fuck. I had a date with this pussy, and I was thirsty for that shit.

Looking up at Big Mama, her chest heaved as her eyes examined the door. I'd never been more grateful for long-ass arms until this moment. I applied pressure to her throat as I draped her left thigh over my shoulder.

"He... he may catch us." She rasped as her eyes shifted to me.

"Well, you need to nut fast then."

Tired of being too close to her pussy without it in my mouth, I latched on to her bud, and her juices burst on my tongue.

"Fuuuuck!"

I loved pussy. I loved the way it smelled, felt, and tasted. I didn't give every woman the privilege of seeing what my head game was about, but when I came across one that I didn't mind licking on, I took advantage. Before Big Mama, I hadn't eaten pussy in a minute and forgot how much that shit turned me on.

Big Mama's eyes rolled to the back of her head as she tried gripping the wall with one hand and grabbed my locs with the other. Her secretions were running down my chin as I lapped her up. Her silky folds twirled around my tongue as I drank up all of her fluids. My dick was damn near bursting out of my jeans.

"Metavellooooo—"

Saying fuck it, I stood, pulled my dick out, and slammed her back into the wall. I'd only planned on eating it, but one week was too long. In one motion, I was back inside my new favorite place.

I bit down on her chin as I slid in and out of her. Her pussy was so fucking wet and had a death grip on my dick. It made sense that Rio was her husband. That nigga didn't like pussy. I'd been thinking that Big Mama's nigga hadn't been fucking her right when, in reality, he hadn't been fucking her at all.

Looping my arm around her waist, she crossed her legs behind my back as I drilled into her center. She was so fucking soft. So fucking feminine. So fucking pretty. This was, for sure, the best pussy I'd ever had. I didn't even feel bad about wanting to crash out behind this pussy. Pretty-ass pussy attached to a pretty-ass bitch with a pretty-ass name. Yeah, it was up about her.

"Oh my God!"

Reaching in, I stuck my tongue in her mouth, and we engaged in a sloppy yet passionate kiss. My dick throbbed, but I was holding out because I wanted her to get hers. She'd already cum in my mouth, but I needed her to buck on this dick.

"You think I give a fuck about you being married to that nigga?"

I increased my pace, fucking her faster and harder than I ever knew I was capable of.

"I... I knowww! I know you don't careeeee!"

My dick had never been so fucking wet before. This girl had me so aroused that it was pitiful.

"Well, why in the fuck you try to deny me my pussy? Hunh? On God, I'll kill that nigga right now!"

Her pussy was sucking my dick in and spitting it back out. There was no way this girl was this tight. I'd never felt no shit like this before. She had that rainwater in between her fucking legs. Ain't no way I was giving this pussy up. I didn't give a fuck who it belonged to.

"I... I knowww!"

"Stop fucking playing with me, gur! Shit."

I looked down at her pussy creaming all over my dick as her legs tightened around my waist.

"Fuck!"

Hot semen shot from my dick and sprayed her walls. Just as I'd been collecting her panties, she'd been collecting my nut.

Leaning in, I latched on to her lips again, damn near sucking her whole face in my mouth. Every part of this girl tasted good. She had my fucking heart pounding, head throbbing, and body tingling. Just the thought of not seeing her until the weekend made my fucking stomach queasy. This shit didn't make no sense.

She winced as I slid my dick out of her. I pecked her lips repeatedly as I helped her stand. I hadn't even stopped pecking her lips as I tucked my dick in my pants.

"What are we doing?"

"Us."

I pecked her lips several more times before backing out of her space. She went to walk to the bathroom, and I grabbed the back of her dress, pulling her into me. This girl had my fucking mind gone. Burying my face in her neck, I placed my arms around her stomach.

"I gotta clean up, Metavello." She moaned as she squirmed in my arms.

I didn't want to let her ass go. I wanted to be everywhere this fucking girl was, even if it was here at the Gay Boy Mansion. I'd never felt so attached to a person a day in my life. Just the thought of her had my fucking heart fluttering. She felt so good in my arms and even better on my dick. I couldn't get enough. If this was what it felt like to be sprung, I was glad I hadn't felt this shit earlier in life. I was down bad behind Big Mama. I was fall-off-the-bone tender behind her. A whole fucking chicken tender.

"Metavello..."

"I want you so fucking bad, Discover."

Her breathing hitched as I sucked on her neck. Her pussy was still on my breath, and I was ready to eat that shit again.

"You... you got me, Metavello."

"Gimme a kiss."

She turned her head, and I sucked her tongue out of her mouth. The kiss was even nastier than before, and my dick was back standing at attention.

"Ummm. Stop. Your nut is running down my legssss."

"Good. That's how I want you always."

Finally, I let her go. Slapping her ass, I watched as she walked into the bathroom. It took everything in me not to follow her. Instead, I pulled her phone from my pocket, unlocked all twelve numbers I'd called her from, and left it on the dresser. The water from the faucet began running and I knew that was my cue to leave.

"Aye! You better fucking answer when I call."

I didn't know how this shit was about to go, but I did know I didn't want nobody but Big Mama. If Rio and I had to shoot it out, then that's what it was. I tried not to keep up with the rules too much, but I did know one of the most abided-by rules in the mafia was that you couldn't marry a woman who was already married to a neighboring mob. Fuck them rules, though, Discover was mine. Now, I had to call that nigga Essex to see what the fuck she meant by they grew up together. I see now I was going to have to lay all these niggas down behind my bitch.

CHAPTER 4
NEL

These old-ass mob niggas were freaky as hell back in the day. Rio's ass was Pia's fucking daddy. Niccoli's sick ass used to pass Patrice's pussy around so much that it wasn't far-fetched that Pia belonged to that nigga. I fucked with Rio, though, so him being her father wasn't an issue to me. It was the fact that I didn't know what the fuck it meant for her future that had me around this bitch smoking three blunts in one hour and on edge.

I was trying not to think about the shit too much, though. If Rio came with that weird shit with Pia, I was putting his ass in the dirt. She didn't need to be tied into any familia plans he had. He could pay his back child support and keep his ass over there getting his dick eaten up by the chipmunk boys.

Don had the bright idea to call a meeting early the next morning as if we hadn't all been at the party past midnight. Them fucking kids were still running around after twelve, lit on sugar candy and shit. Rio knew how to throw a kid's party, I tell you that much. I had a nasty-ass attitude that I had to carry my ass home last night because I didn't want to wake Pia up by going to training at three in the morning. I could barely hold my eyes open by the time we were done, so I had no choice but to take my ass back to my own house, wash, and hop in the bed. I'd been getting some decent sleep when I felt an annoying-ass presence standing over me.

"Aye. When I move, please don't move near me no more. You worrisome as fuck."

My eyes were still closed as Vello walked around to the opposite side of my bed. When I felt the mattress dip, I sighed. All I needed was about one more hour of rest, and then I was headed to Pia's. This nigga and his bullshit wasn't on the agenda today.

"Twin. I need you to get the all-black out. We got a nigga to kill."

My eyes shot open because malice was in my brother's tone. I was the certified crash-out twin. I wasn't even aware that Vello had some static in the streets, but even if I was still a little bit mad at the family, I was riding for my brother.

"Fuck we doing then?"

I was laying on my stomach while Vello had his back against my headboard, dressed in his fucking outside clothes. He was looking straight ahead at the TV that was powered off, and it looked like he wanted to fucking cry.

"I done fell for another nigga's bitch."

"She a stripper?"

Vello snapped his head at me with a snarl on his face. "Why the fuck do you think she's a stripper for?"

"Cuz nigga, you love the strip club. Them hoes get all yo' fucking money. I thought you was ready to die 'bout that for sale-ass pussy."

Sitting up, I stretched my arms above my head and yawned. I picked my phone up from my nightstand and saw that I had twelve missed calls from Pia.

"Fuck." I cursed under my breath.

I hadn't told her that I wasn't coming over. I wanted to give her time to talk to her mama. Hell, she'd put my ass out of the room when she talked to Rio, so I felt like she wasn't trying to rap with my ass.

"Well, no. The fuck. This don't got shit to do with no stripper." Vello spat, not noticing I was ignoring his ass.

I called Pia, and she sent my ass to voicemail. It was seven thirty in the morning, so I knew she was up. Today was Neltz's first day of school, and she'd said she was dropping him off. I tried calling three more times and got the same result.

"Okay. Who the fuck we gotta kill, Vello? Ion want to hear all the extra shit."

I continued to try and dial Pia, and her petty ass kept pressing ignore. I had my own shit going on, and Vello was up in here on his Keith Sweat shit.

Vello looked upside my head in disgust. I tossed my phone back on the nightstand, frustrated as fuck. Pia and I hadn't had words, but I knew today was the fucking day. I should have just taken my ass over there last night.

"See. That's the fucking problem right there. We not in tune with each other's feelings. We supposed to be able to talk with each other about everything."

My mind was on Natazia Pia. That's it, that's all. But this nigga wouldn't leave, so I couldn't leave until I heard him out. "Who is the bitch?"

"Nigga! Don't call her no bitch!"

"I'm just repeatin' after you!"

"It was a figure of speech!"

"Okay. What's going on, dear brother? What nigga we gotta kill? Cuz I'ma need you to ride when I bury Rio. That's Pia's daddy, and ion know what the fuck his intentions with her are. These mobsters like to marry their daughters and sisters and shit off for the sake of business, and if he thinks that shit gon' fly over here, I'm bodying all his shit."

Pia didn't need no fucking daddy—especially one over a mob. I would bet every dollar I had in the bank that Rio already had his mean-ass daughter's husband lined the fuck up, and she ain't know shit about shit. Rio had me fucked up.

"Shit, say less. That's the nigga I want to kill," Vello grinned.

"Wait. What, nigga? Gay Rio?"

"Hell yeah."

"Man, get the fuck outta my bed. Fuck you mean you fell for his bitch? You like dick now? I shol' seen sum'n on TikTok that said in every twin set, one is gay. I should have known we weren't the exception."

"Nigga, what? Fuck wrong with you! I ain't gay! Don Mecanio got a wife, and that's my bitch. I want her. I got her."

"Wait. His fake wife that we ain't never seen before?" Ain't she like 40?"

"Nigga, no! She's our age."

"Still. He forty. How long they been married? He on the same shit the Cuppacios were on?"

"Ion even know. To be honest with you, I am my daddy's son. I'm ready to snatch her ass up and lock her away, only bringing her out when I want to fuck. On foe n'em, I'm ready to die about that pussy. I need you to bring that black out. We either need it for a mission, or for my funeral. Ion give a fuck no more."

This nigga had hit me with a fucking double whammy.

"Wait, wait, wait a damn minute." I didn't mean to laugh, but this shit was too funny. What were the fucking odds that Vello's laid-back ass had gotten himself in a pickle like this? Nigga swore he could never be placed in a jar.

"You laughing, but I'm deadass serious. One of us gone

die."

"Hell nawl. I ain't dying. Don't wish that shit on me."

"Nigga, I'm talking 'bout me or Don. But I thought we said whoever died first, the other was gon' join?"

Picking my phone back up, I tried to call Pia again but she was continuing to send me to voicemail.

"Nah. I changed my fucking mind. You get yo'self killed out there, all I got for you is flower bringing and slow singing, my guy. I'll ride with you, but I'm taking my ass home to Pia. Period."

"You sound like a girl... talking about some fucking 'period.'"

"And you sound like a nigga that's 'bout to die behind some pussy that's married to a gay man. I hope you strapped up."

When Vello went mute, I knew it was my cue to get the fuck up out of here. Maybe his being with a stripper didn't sound too bad. I would rather his ass get a bitch that sold ass than the shit he done got himself into.

"Look, I gotta pull down on Pia. Just let me know what the fuck you wanna do and when you wanna do it."

"You just saying some shit so I can leave."

"Nigga, when have you known me to lie about riding for you? I said I got you. I got shit to do right now, though, so if you not trying to get this shit popping today, I gotta go, my boy."

"I'm sick behind that lil' pussy too. I can't even fucking sleep." Vello whined trying to prolong the conversation.

"Aw shit.... come on now, Vello. I can't do this shit with you today. Call Ma! She don't have shit else to do today."

"I'm for real, Nel." Vello grabbed his stomach.

"Aye, I'm for real too! Why the fuck you bending over like that for? Don't yo' love sick-ass throw up in my bed!"

"I can't help it! I been so sick lately. Help me, brother!"

Vello began dry-heaving, and I hopped up. "What the fuck am I supposed to do? I said I would slide! Take yo' ass to the love doctor or some shit! I gotta go!"

Vello, still with his stomach clutched, looked at me. "Who the fuck is the love doctor?"

"Shio."

"On God, brother, I can't even talk about you no more. I got it bad. I got it fucking bad. Ion even want to eat unless it's her pussy on a platter."

"Okay, first off, ew. Secondly, who the fuck is this girl? She better look like Teyana Taylor for all this shit you doing!"

Vello started dry-heaving again. If he threw up on my mattress, I was shooting his ass. This was the nicest thing in my fucking house outside of Ma's bedroom that she had the nerve to keep locked.

"You seen her before. You the reason she not fucking with me. She saw yo' ass in Target with Essex. Oh shit, Essex! I may have to kill that nigga toooo." Vello heaved again, and now I was the one about to tweak out.

"Fuck you mean—" I thought back to the day I let Essex talk me into going to Target with him. He spent most of the time signing autographs and shit. I was too annoyed. "You talking 'bout the girl that was buying the pregnancy test?"

If I remember correctly, ole girl was on the aisle with the feminine products. Yeah, she was because I'd bought Pia some wipes and tampons to keep at my house whenever she came over. I spent most of my time at hers, but if it ever came to it that she wanted to spend the night and she needed some feminine products, I would have her covered. Those shits were underneath the cabinet in my bathroom.

"Yeah... hell yeah. She was buying a pregnancy test, fasho. Essex said he didn't mind playing stepdaddy too." I instigated and Vello's eyes ballooned.

"Pregnancy test! Stop fucking playing with me, broth—"

Vello hopped up this time, actually having to throw up. He ran full speed to my bathroom, and when I heard all the waffles and shit of whatever he'd consumed enter my toilet, I gagged myself.

I barely looked at the girl that Essex was talking to that day, so I couldn't remember if she was worth all this shit Vello was doing. All I knew was that the bitch was looking upside my head and shit. I may have talked crazy to her, but shit, I talk crazy to everybody.

"On foe n'em, this bitch got me fucked up." Vello cried into the toilet.

I was over his fucking antics for the day. "You doin' too fucking much. She not even worth all that."

"I know you saw me calling yo' fucking phone, Renello!"

Aw hell.

Groaning, I pinched my tear ducts before turning to face Pia. "I called you right back, too, Pia baby."

My eyes landed on Pia, who had a bonnet on her head, a T-shirt she'd more than likely slept in, and biker short style leggings. She had on a jacket zipped up to her neck, and the shirt was so long that it hung beyond the jacket's hem. She hadn't even put lotion on her legs. I knew Pia didn't have much and had to make do with what she had before I came into the picture, and to this day, that shit fucked with me. However, this look right here was on some other shit. I knew her ass hadn't planned on going into Neltz's school looking like this, and if so, his ass was guaranteed to get to fighting on day one.

"Fuck, bro! You got a toothbrush in this bitch? *Blarggggggggghhhhh!*"

Vello was still hurling his fucking insides out in my toilet. He had to fucking roll. I wasn't cleaning up after his ass, either, so I hope he knew he was bleaching my shit down before he left.

"Pia... I had meetings this morning. You already know anytime I have training, I come to the crib."

Pia's eyes twitched as her hands were balled up and hanging at her sides. "Okay! So, yo' fucking phone don't work? You heard that nigga say he was my fucking daddy! You was supposed to be at the house so I could talk about the shit! The fuck! I thought you was supposed to be my person!"

Pia was loud as fuck. She didn't even like loud-ass noises in the morning, so I knew she was on one.

"Pia... come rub my stomach, cousin. I'm sick." Vello came out of the bathroom, rubbing his hand down his chest as sweat beads lined his forehead.

He'd had a long conversation with Pia at the Halloween party, and now he was acting like no time was lost between them. He'd even exchanged numbers with Pia with his lonely ass. I needed to slap the shit out of him because he was the one to invite Pia to the fucking birthday party where she ran into her long-lost-ass daddy. He was in here sick as fuck, but he was the reason for his own misery. Had he never gone to that party, he would have never known he was fucking Rio's wife. This was all on his sour stomach ass.

Pia turned her nose up at Vello. "What's wrong with you? Matter of fact, don't answer that. I called yo' ass too, and you didn't answer either," she said with venom laced in her tone.

Towering over Pia, I grabbed her wrist just in case she had a mind to swing on a nigga. I was still learning the new Pia—the adult Pia. She'd called me more times than she should have, and my ass was in here sleep, slick in my feelings because I didn't like not knowing shit. I did know how this mob shit went, though, and there was no telling what the fuck Rio's secretive ass had going on.

"Let me go, Renello! You got me driving way over here, and y'all ignoring me like that shit cool. Why you didn't come home last night?" Pia's expression softened, and when her eyes glossed over, my stomach turned.

"Yeah, nigga! Why you didn't go home last night? Pia... he really mad cuz you met yo' daddy, and he think you gon' push him to the side. He say I got separation anxiety, but it's really him." Vello's sensitive stomach ass cackled. He must have laughed too hard because he burped and grabbed at his mouth. Before I could turn my focus back to Pia, I watched my goofy-ass twin pull a pair of panties out of his back pocket and sniff them.

"Yo'... what the fuck? Can you get the fuck out? I told you I got you on that. Gon' and take them crusty-ass panties with you and go get yo' own shit together."

Instead of following directions, Vello leaned against the dresser with a grin, tucking the panties back inside his pants pocket. He was just in this bitch crying, and now he was ready to see if Pia would rock my shit. This nigga was so fucking messy.

"Really, Renello?" Pia cocked her head in disbelief.

Rubbing my hand down my face, I tried to ignore my racing heart. This was not how I thought my fucking morning would go. Now, Pia was going to be looking at me on some insecure and controlling type shit.

"I just had to come home and get some rest. That's it, Pia baby. I was about to get dressed, grab us some breakfast, and head yo' way. All the think pieces this lovesick-ass nigga putting in the air is false."

"Oh really, Twin?"

Vello had thirty seconds before I laid his crybaby ass out.

Squinting her eyes, Pia looked from me to Vello before snatching her hands from my grasp. I went cold immediately.

There was a nurturing warmth anytime we were in each other's space, and when it was removed, that shit had me feeling like a fiend. The only reason I slept halfway decent last night was because a nigga was dead tired. If it wasn't for that, I would have been up half the night thinking and channel surfing, until I gave in and went to her crib. Exhaustion and stubbornness had me staying put, and I guess that shit made me the bad guy because I didn't want to share Pia.

"Next time, bring your ass home. If you got training, cool... at least call me. I just knew I was going to have you to talk to, and you wasn't even there. Ion like that, Renello," Pia said and then exhaled.

"I know. That's my fault. It won't happen again. I got you."

"Man... you don't got sh—I mean, nothing in the refrigerator." Neltz walked in with a scowl on his oily-ass face. His mama had him ready for his first day of school, for real. His evil ass kept a mug on more than his mama and me combined. His hair had a fresh chop and was pulled into his signature bun. His new school was public, so he was able to wear his regular clothes. Pia had him in a grey and white Jordan graphic tee, black Jordan joggers, and grey and white Jordan 3's. She may have walked around looking homeless at times, but she kept Neltz and Pearla on point.

"Renello Jr. What's good, young nigga?"

Renello looked over at my brother, and his frown deepened. "And it really is two of y'all. Mama, really?"

"What you mean... *Mama, really*? What that got to do with me?"

Neltz shook his head at Vello. Yesterday when he'd gotten a glimpse of my brother and me, he'd damn near tweaked out. He was mad and fascinated all at once.

"I heard twins hereditary. If y'all have a kid, and it's two of 'em at the same time, I'm moving back out. On foe nem."

"Boy! When you start saying some foe nem? And we not having no kids together. We—"

"Yeah, yeah. Cousins. Y'all ain't no cousins, Mama. Maybe y'all thought y'all was, but you just met yo' real daddy yesterday. You look just like that man. Grandma don't got no family, so if you was kin to these niggas... it would be on the daddy side. I fool with the other Cuppacios, though. They ain't my real cousins, and I ain't ever claiming that. I'm tryna get at Bella."

Vello tossed his head back, and a deep laughter erupted from his weak-ass soul. "Man... Pia, where the fuck you get this spawn of Satan?"

"Same place yo' mama got you, nigga. But then again... nawl, she didn't. Cuz we ain't birthing no twins 'round here. Matta fact, my mama not having no mo' kids." Neltz chopped his hand in the air as if he were laying down the law. He shifted his attention from Vello, who was still cracking up at me. "You may as well go get nipped and tucked. It's ova wit, Daddy Number Two."

This young nigga here.

"Aye! What the fuck, Pia? This youngin' too turnt."

"Neltz! What the fuck did I tell you about speaking out the side of your neck?"

"Ma! I'm for real, though. We don't have time for no babies. Grandma just started talking, you got a rich gay daddy, and we in a new house. We gotta soak all this in."

Pia grabbed the back of her neck. I pulled her into my chest and hooked my arm around her neck, tugging on her bonnet.

"See! That right there is what I'm talkin' 'bout. He too infatuated with you, Mama. That ain't healthy."

"On foe nem... it ain't, nephew." Vello was still cackling.

"Neltz! Go to the car. I told you to stay there, anyway. I'm about to take you to school."

Neltz eyed his mama but tried to keep his expression neutral. "Okay, Mama."

Vello and I knew what his look was about; Neltz knew his mama was about to have him late to school.

My annoying-ass brother kicked himself off my dresser, making it shift. He knew my shit was cheap, but insisted on slamming against it and shit. "Nephew, I got you. Come on," Vello said, volunteering to take him to school.

"Nigga! Ion know you."

"Ion know yo' lil' ass, either. We can get Chick-fil-A, though, and I'll let you drive half the way."

"Vello! No!" Pia's body stiffened against mine.

"Okay, Unc. I'm down!" Neltz's fake ass smiled.

Vello tossed his arm around Neltz and smirked. "They lame anyways, nephew."

Pia tried to go after Vello, but I held her against my chest. If he wanted to deal with Neltz's badass, he could. I was ready for Vello to leave any fucking way. If Neltz was the way to do it, then adi-fucking-os.

"Aye." Grabbing Pia's chin, I lifted her face so that I could look into her deep brown eyes. Even in the morning, she was so fucking pretty.

"Hmmm?"

"Didn't I tell you I would always come back?"

"Yes."

"Well then. You know where I stand, Pia baby. I'm just waiting on you."

Her thick lashes swept against her plump cheeks as she blinked rapidly. Reaching down, I cuffed her ass, being sure to graze her pussy. Her hooded eyes remained calm, but her cheeks turned a deep plum color as she gasped.

Leaning down, I nipped at her ear. "I'm on yo' time. I know you gotta process this shit, but I'm letting you know now... it's only one outcome. That's us walking down that fucking aisle. I told yo' ass I gotta get married, and I would rather it be you beside me."

It would only be Pia at the altar with me in a perfect world. But if she refused, that was cool too. I would just do what Vello claimed he would at first and buy a bitch. I'd send that hoe off like Rio did and live happily ever after with Pia.

"Let it go."

Pia exhaled slowly as I placed kisses on her ear, trailing to her neck.

"If I don't want that with you? Then what?"

"Then, my wife just gotta accept you as my mistress."

Pia pushed my chest. I stumbled back a bit, but only because I was laughing.

"Let me stop bringing up marriage. I only told you that shit the other day just to fuck with you. I ain't thinking about that."

"But you do gotta get married."

"I'm not worried yet, Pia baby. C'mere."

I snatched her to my chest again. Instead of grabbing on her ass, I stuck my face in her neck and inhaled her Dove scented skin mixed with whatever products had been used in her hair.

"This is all so much."

"You smell good."

"Renellooooo..."

Her whining made my dick hard. I know she felt it, but she didn't have to worry about me taking it that far. I wanted to stay smothered in her neck, but I knew what she needed.

"Aye..." I removed my face from her neck and grabbed her chin. Even with that big-ass bonnet on her head, looking like somebody's project-ass mama, her ass was beautiful. "Come ride my face real quick."

Her chest swelled. A look of uneasiness appeared right

before her cheeks flushed plum even more. She looked ashamed, but I could feel the heat radiating off her body.

I'd already brushed my teeth when I got up for the meeting this morning, so I knew my saliva wouldn't fuck up her PH. Instead of waiting for Pia to make her mind up on whether she wanted a nut, I reached down and pulled her bottoms down. When they gathered at her ankles, I grabbed her hips, walked backward until I hit the bed, laid back, and pulled her ass upwards. The big-ass shirt she was wearing covered my face, but it was cool because it was probably best if she didn't see me anyway. With her thick thighs on both sides of my head, I stuck my nose in her shaved pussy and took a long whiff.

"Oh God."

Pia smelled so fucking clean. Her arousal was my favorite scent. She tried to play that family shit, but all damn day, her little ass was stimulated by me. That shit turned me on in the worst way to know I brought those emotions out of her. My dick was on brick as I slurped her clit in my mouth while her ass rested on my chin.

I expelled my breath in a gentle, steady hiss as I sucked down on her nub. She was so fucking wet that her pussy was a slippery mess. Once she bucked on my face a few times, I flicked my tongue on her clit, feeling more heat rush from her body.

"Stop being shy, Pia baby. Ride my face."

"Unh unnnnh!"

She was being stubborn. It was cool, though. The aromatic waves of pleasure spewing from her pot let me know that she loved the way I was making her pretty ass feel, even though she was barely sitting on my face. I didn't have her pinned to me; technically, I wasn't even touching her. She had the ability to get up at any time if she wanted. Yet, she stayed planted right on my face.

"I... I'm 'bout to come!"

Those words ignited a fire that I wasn't ready to put out. I went into a pussy eating frenzy, sucking her entire mound into my mouth. Her body thrummed as she cried out, "I'm coming!"

Desire flushed through me as I drank her ejaculation. Every hair on my scalp stood to attention, every skin cell tingled, and every neuron fired as she shook and shuddered atop my face. Warmth spread across my chest while I listened to Pia's erratic breathing.

Pushing her shirt from over my head, I caught her licking her lips with her eyes shut. Now that I wasn't blinded by darkness, I stared right at her pussy, which was still in my face. I pecked it. Once, then twice, then thrice, and those pecks turned into me French hissing her pretty and creamy-ass pussy.

"Sttttt-stop," she moaned out, and that shit didn't do anything but turn me on even more.

Giving my favorite meal one more kiss, I lifted her from my face so she could put her leggings back on. She'd left what I was claiming as her new favorite seat wet and smelling like her gushy sex. Clearing her throat, she snatched her leggings off the ground and ran into my bathroom. Sighing, I swiped the residue of her pleasure from my face.

Pia wasn't ready for me. She was still trying to process our lack of kinship and shit. But not me. Ever since I heard Ezio tell Shio he'd burnt their house down because Niccoli got that DNA test, I knew I loved her beyond that of family. Call it weird, gross, or whatever. I think my heart always knew Pia and I weren't related. I've loved this girl for as long as I can remember. If I ever got the chance to stick my dick in her, it would have to be on her terms because if I pushed it, that shit wouldn't even be fair. Pia was tough, but my dick was tougher.

I wouldn't even be able to finish the job from feeling so bad. Fucking her before she was ready would only leave her more confused. For now, I would settle for just being in her space.

I only ate her pussy again because I knew that she needed that release. She'd just discovered her pops, she had a badass child, her mama talked after a muted decade, her weak-ass baby daddy was tripping on her, and I'd come in and turned her life upside down. That nut was warranted. But, going forward, I wasn't making any more moves on an intimate level. If she wanted me, she would have to be the one to initiate it. I didn't want to feel like I was taking advantage of her ass. If she wanted me, she could take it. Tasting her pussy the second time was better than the first time, though. It would be hard for me to keep my mouth off her, but I had to try.

"You hungry," I yelled over the faucet water.

"I am."

"Aite. I'm about to get dressed. Then, we can run by the mall and grab you some shit and talk about this Rio nigga over breakfast."

Standing, I headed to my closet as Pia cleaned herself in the bathroom. The more time I spent in this damn room, the more I despised it. The furniture was so damn small, fifteen people could probably stand comfortably in my room.

"But the malls not open, Renello. I can just go to the house."

I groaned. "The malls not open for regular folks. Give me a few minutes, Pia baby," I replied, snatching a jogging suit down from the hanger.

I would keep my hands to myself when it came to Pia, but everything else was a go. I was about to spoil this girl so fucking rotten. She deserved that shit. If Rio thought he was about to come in and step on my toes, he had another thing coming.

I didn't lose. Ever. Especially when it came to Pia.

CHAPTER 5
DISCOVER "BIG MAMA"

With my first pregnancy, I experienced a little bit of nausea, and that was it. This new baby, though, had been taking me through the wire. The fatigue made it extremely hard to get out of bed, so I'd been rotting on my mattress, day in and day out. The nausea had my dark skin ashy, and looking in the mirror scared the shit out of me because I looked like a walking corpse. When I woke up this morning around three to pee and felt intense cramps, I got excited. Four pregnancy tests had already confirmed that I was expecting, but feeling the cramps led me to believe that I was getting my period and those tests were all flukes. By the time I got up and dressed my daughter for school, my period was still nowhere to be found. I wanted to cry. The only thing that was on the tissue when I wiped was milky, odorless discharge.

Forcing myself out of bed, I snuck off to a small medical center up the street, where I'd paid cash for my visit, and a blood test confirmed that I was indeed pregnant. I'd already known, but there was a small delusional part of my brain that was hoping that I wasn't. I still needed to get an ultrasound for an accurate due date, but there was no need. I'd only had sex with two men, and the first one hadn't touched me since I was a teen. This was Metavello's baby.

Seeing him at my daughter's birthday party was the last thing I expected. When my husband begged me to let him throw Discovery's party, I was skeptical. When he said he wanted to throw it at his home, I wanted to scream, hell no. I knew what the fuck went down over there and wanted my baby to see no parts. But then, I also knew what type of man Rio was. He wouldn't dare have any foul shit going on with us present. So, since he had the family and friends, I folded and let him throw the party. Did I expect to see Metavello? Fuck no. Did I expect that Metavello would be a twin? Fuck no. Did I expect that Essex would be at the fucking party? Fuck no. Luckily, he didn't see me and had left hours before it was over. Both my baby daddies and my husband under one roof was too much to process.

When Metavello revealed that it wasn't him at Target, that shouldn't have made me as happy as it did. I wanted to jump for joy. I'd just known Metavello was a flaw-ass fuck boy for having his face in my pussy one day and acting like he didn't know me the next. His twin, though, was still on my shit list because he was rude as hell.

Now, here I was, bed rotting. I was sick to my fucking stomach with the confirmation of pregnancy papers resting at the foot of my bed. Discovery would be out of school in less than thirty minutes, and I hadn't decided if I wanted to tell her. She had a moment at her party where she wouldn't stop crying, and even though I hadn't gotten down to the bottom of it, I wanted to tread lightly with her. Maybe she was over-whelmed with gratitude. I felt like shit, though, because the person she wanted more than anything was at her party, and I was too chicken to even make the introductions. I mean, what the fuck would I say? I was pregnant when you left Ms. Maeve's house, and this is your baby?

I couldn't deal with that right now. As selfish as it sounded, I was happy that the party was over and that Essex went undetected. I didn't know that man. I didn't know if that was someone whom I even wanted in my daughter's life because I didn't know his character. What if he already had kids? What if he had a wife? There was no way any bitch on this earth was going to be treating my baby any kind of way. I would go to jail if someone ever treated mine with anything less than love. My daughter was not only kind and intelligent, but she was special. She was one in a fucking trillion when it came to daughters. I wasn't ready to share that with anyone, and that was why Rio and I worked so well. He was always nice to my baby, but he let her be mine. He didn't force his way into her life, and I loved him for it. He wasn't her father, and I wasn't going to pretend he was. D-Berry was mine, and I didn't want to share.

Deciding that today wasn't the day that I let my daughter know she was being promoted to big sister, it took all the strength I had to swoop the papers from the bed and stuff them in my nightstand drawer. I'd been dry-heaving for days. I couldn't keep shit down and couldn't even remember the last time I had food that stayed in my stomach. This was not how I imagined the pregnancy would go. I didn't know if I could do this shit. I'd thought about getting rid of the fucker altogether, but I thought about how my life would be had I gotten rid of Discovery. She was my entire world. She was the one thing in my life that made perfect sense. I had so much love for my daughter that I wasn't even sure if I had enough room to love another child in the capacity that I loved her. But an abortion just seemed so wrong. Here I was, dreading coming back to Jagoda Bay to have a baby, and now that I was pregnant, getting rid of it was the last thing I wanted to do. I wanted to have Metavello's baby more than I wanted to breathe, and at the same time, I hated the day we met. Still, getting rid of this baby was the logical thing to do.

A notification popped up across my phone, and I saw that it was the camera. Discovery was walking in with the house-keeper behind her. Josephine carried a paper bag full of groceries. She was a Godsend. I felt bad that she'd followed us here, leaving her grandchildren in New York, but she assured me it was fine. I told her they could come down and visit anytime.

I could hear the padding of Discovery's sneakers as she ran down the hall. When my door burst open, she dropped her backpack and came to the side of the bed.

A frown covered her gorgeous face as she reached up and placed a palm on my damp forehead. "You have a fever?"

"I'm good, baby."

I loved seeing Discovery in her blazer with the school's emblem and plaid skirt. Her hair was still pressed fresh from yesterday's birthday style, and pink glitter speckles were still on her eyelid, even though we'd done her skincare routine twice last night.

"You've been sick for over a week, Mother. Have Rio send the doctor over."

"Okay, I'll call him," I lied.

I hadn't heard from Rio and was praying he didn't call me. I didn't want to hear anything about this baby he planned on having me impregnated with because that was out of the ques-tion. I was already pregnant, and the moment his doctors examined me, they would see that. There were so many things swirling through my mind in regard to my marriage. Rio had been nothing but patient and loving to my daughter and me, but now that I'd gotten pregnant by another man, I was scared of what that meant for our future. Without Rio, I had nothing. Yes, I had commas in my bank account and cards with no limits, but he had the power to take all of that away. I didn't need shit. I have lived without for most of my life and could surely do it again. However, I was afraid for my daughter. She said she didn't care about any of this lifestyle, but it was only because she'd never had to starve before—I had.

"Do you think you'll be well by the weekend?"

Sitting up in the bed, I placed my back against the headboard and had to fight a wave of nausea.

"Of course, baby. I'll be well. What you got in mind? We could take a flight. I know we said no birthday trip this year, but we could go home and have a sleepover with your friends."

I missed New York, but the thought of all those smells had me ready to barf. I didn't want to go back there right now, even though if you asked me that question last week, I would have been ready to haul ass. But, if the birthday girl wanted it, she got it.

"Hmm. Tempting. But no. Plus, this is our home now."

I swallowed hard as my baby smiled. I didn't know what the hell it was about Jagoda Bay, but she loved it. Maybe there was some type of attachment to it since she'd been born here, but hell, I'd been born here too, and I dreaded this place. Yes, the city had improved, and it was beautiful. But I just didn't want to be here—well, a few weeks ago, I didn't.

"Okay. What do you have in mind? Mexico? Jamaica? Oh, we could—"

"I want to go to the Fall Ball!"

What the hell is a fall ball?

My brows shot to my dry hairline as Discovery's bright eyes gleamed. "Hunh?"

"It's like this big concert. I want to go. Pleaseeeee! I was on Ticket Master during free period, and I saw that they have some front-row tickets available for twenty-six hundred with the taxes and fees and everything! That's for two tickets. You know Josephine doesn't like loud noises. So it would be just the two of us." Discovery pushed her glasses up her face.

A concert was another one of those places where I didn't want to be, but how could I say no to my baby? She hadn't asked to go to a concert since JoJo Siwa's D.R.E.A.M. Tour three years ago. Outside of catching frequent Broadway shows, we hadn't been to a concert. Well, we've been to hers at her school, but that was it.

"Okay. Send me the link, and I'll get them. How was school? Come here. Give me a hug."

Discovery jumped up and down while clapping her hands.

My heart seemed to turn over, witnessing my daughter in delight. Most people claimed their children were their whole world, but Discovery was mine for sure. I would do anything to see that glow of hers, even at the expense of my own misery. I was in no position to be going to a concert. Not only was I pregnant, but I was as sick as ever. Still, I would put on a smile and rock out with my baby girl. It was her world; I was just living in it.

"Yesss! Thank you so much, Mommy! I love you! And uh—" She took two steps back. "School was great. You are sick, so I can't hug you. I'll go to the kitchen and help Josephine. She's making you soup. Again, Mommy, you're the best. I love you!"

Discovery gave me air kisses and was on her way. Whatever my baby girl wanted, she got. Anytime one of our birthdays rolled around, we were usually on somebody's plane headed to somebody's island. Everything was already starting to feel so different about our lives, and we'd only been here a few months. I missed our old lives. We were secluded, there was no threat of another parent, and I wasn't an adultery-committing hoe in our old life either. Fear settled in the pit of my belly, overshadowing the nausea that seemed to never go away. What would happen when Rio found out about this? What would happen if he divorced me and took away the only life my daughter ever knew? I had no fucking life skills outside of being a mother. I was a fucking trophy wife. As a matter of fact, if you looked up the definition of trophy wife, you would see my picture. All I did was play dress up, take care of my appearance and health, and raise my daughter. The only reason I had a high school diploma was because Rio pushed me to take online courses to get it. Other than that, it was all I had to my name that wasn't attached to my husband. I should have looked at Metavello and let his ass go on about his business. Letting him not only fuck me, but fuck me raw, was my gravest mistake, but there was a part of me that yearned for that man.

I had to be dick-whipped. That was the only answer. I didn't need the baby, but I imagined what the hell our combined looks would create. Then I thought about what having his child meant for my daughter's future and got mad all over again. I'd been in this bed, letting my thoughts get the best of me, and if I didn't stop, I was never going to get better. I had to come up with a solution eventually, though. Aborting the baby was the only logical thing to do, but then, I would still have to get pregnant right after that. It was all just a lot to process.

My phone vibrated somewhere in the bed, so with my eyes closed, I felt around in the covers for it. When it was located, I went to my text messages and saw Discovery had sent me the link to the tickets. I didn't even know who was performing. At this point, I didn't even give a damn. I was just going to purchase the tickets and pray to God that this damn dot in my belly would cooperate so that I didn't barf on the artists or on the stage.

Discovery had not only sent me the link for the tickets, but she'd logged into the Ticket Master account that I forgot I had and already had the tickets in the cart. A fifteen-minute countdown indicated that if I hadn't purchased before the allotted time clock, the tickets would be removed from my cart. I started to add another ticket for Arianee, my sister-in-law, but if I got sick at the concert, I didn't want her catching on to me.

"These damn tickets are twenty-six hundred dollars. This girl better be glad I love her,"

I mumbled as I added the insurance to the tickets.

Before I could check out, my phone rang. I was about to get annoyed, but the name *Eater* displayed on my screen made me remove the bonnet from my head. I knew my hair looked crazy underneath, but I'd rather him see my hair than a bonnet. He'd already seen me that way once.

Sliding my finger across the screen, I cleared my throat and waited for the call to connect. Dark skin, thick brows, a sharp nose, and broad lips were all attached to one sexy-ass man who appeared on my screen. Damn.

"Aye." Metavello had a blunt to his dark-hued lips and blew out a wad of smoke. Everything this man did turned me on, and turned on was the last thing I needed to be in the state I was currently in.

"Hi." Oh God. I sounded like a fucking child and looked a hot ass mess. It was too late for all that now, though. I swallowed hard and continued, "I'm glad you called. I gotta cancel this weekend."

Metavello's expression didn't waver. His demeanor was calm, but it could have been because he was smoking. I didn't smoke but knew enough to know weed relaxed you. He was just ready to not only expose me but kill Rio, which I doubt he could do with all the power Rio had, and now he was docile.

"Big Mama... I ain't tryna hear all that. Stop playing with

me, girl."

The blunt dangling from his lips sparked bright red at the tip as he inhaled and blew smoke directly into the screen. Everything this man did soiled my panties. How could one person have you ready to risk everything that you prayed for? That was Metavello, and I needed to stay far away from this man, but there was a part of me that couldn't.

A warning voice whispered in my head to hang up. Instead, I bit my bottom lip and looked away briefly. "Seriously... Discovery has me taking her to some Fall Ball. As a matter of fact, I was checking out the tickets just before you called."

Remembering I was on a countdown, I swiped out of the FaceTime screen and went back to the Ticket Master app. Not seeing his face for a few seconds would do me some good.

"Aye..."

"Yes?" I answered, clicking away on the screen.

The tickets were still there, and I had five minutes to complete my purchase before they were removed from the cart. I was surprised that front-row seats were available with the concert being less than five days away, but they were resale tickets, so that explained not only the availability but also the price.

"I'll take y'all."

I paused on checking out and went back to Metavello and I's video call. "What?"

By now, he'd put his blunt out and was walking through what appeared to be a home. Smacking his lips, his face soured. "That weed tastes funny as fuck."

I didn't know if it was his space or not, but I caught a glimpse of the interior. Jealousy surged through me. He had to be at a woman's house, or one lived with him. From what I could see, the home was immaculate. I had no reason to be jealous because my ass was married. He'd never even answered

77

me when I asked him if he had a girlfriend the night after we had sex in his car outside of the club. Surely, a man like Metavello was taken. He was too good-looking and too hung not to be.

"I said I'll take y'all. I gotta get Lil' Chef a birthday gift, anyway."

"She wants front-row seats. Why? I don't know. So, that's okay. I got it."

I wasn't expecting him to spend damn near three thousand dollars on concert tickets for my daughter. I had the money to take her and would do so comfortably.

It was hard to focus on anything with this man's face staring back at me. I watched his lips as he stated, "If I said I got it, then I got it."

"Metavello—" I started, shaking my head to remove the arousing thoughts about what else his lips could do.

"I done had my dick so far in yo' fucking guts that the least a nigga can do is take y'all to a fucking concert. That's nothing, baby."

My whole face heated, and I started to pout like a scolded child. "I'm just trying to be considerate. You really don't have to do that."

His face went out of view, and I could see he was in a bathroom. My eyes had never scanned an area so fast before in my life. I was trying to peep women's products on the vanity. Nothing was there besides soap dispensers. When the water sputtered, I knew he was turning the shower on.

"Do you be being considerate when you be spending that niggas bread?"

I shook my head no.

"Well, then. I ain't no broke-ass nigga, Big Mama. It ain't shit but a concert."

"Okay."

"I'ma send you my address. I want y'all to pull up over here and ride with me. I know yo' scary ass don't want me to pull up at Gay Boy mansion?"

"At what?"

Metavello smiled that beautiful smile of his.

I was so fucking infatuated with this man. I not only stayed on the phone while he bathed, with him placing the phone somewhere in the corner of his massive shower as I watched him wash his body, but I let him convince me into locking my door while we had FaceTime sex. It was funny how I was always too sick to do anything until Metavello popped up.

Lord, help me.

"YOUR HOUSE IS REALLY NICE, METAVELLO."

My palms were sweaty, my heart was thudding out of my chest, and my stomach was doing flip-flops as I sat in the passenger seat of Metavello's Porsche. This was the Porsche that he'd fucked me senseless in, and my daughter was in the back seat just smiling. I'd played that night over in my mind too many times to count. Shaking the nasty thoughts from my brain, I turned in my seat to look at my daughter. Metavello was zooming in and out of traffic, and I'd almost driven myself crazy looking through the side mirrors to see if I could detect my husband or anyone connected to him. It was days like this that I was glad I only had a detail when Rio deemed it necessary. I still hadn't heard from him since the party, so he had no idea what the hell I had going on.

"You look pretty, D-Berry."

My daughter insisted on dressing herself at the last minute. My feelings were hurt because I'd ordered her a Moschino outfit to be expedited and thought the pink dress with the brand's signature bears all over it was too cute. I thought the outfit was girly and fitting for a concert, and Discovery acted as if she loved the look too. Imagine my surprise when I came out of my room from doing my makeup, and she had changed. I was feeling some type of way, but we were already running late and had to drive twenty-five minutes to the address Metavello had sent us.

Now, looking at her in the back seat, I see that her outfit choice was the better option. She'd put on a black Off-White top that was cropped at the belt line. The black jeans were distressed and had Off-White running down the outer seams. She finished the look with some Off-White sneakers, a matching crossbody bag, her signature strawberry perfume, and the Virgil Off-White prescription shades that rested on her head. My daughter was too fly for her own good.

"Thank you. You look good too, Mommy. Don't even look sick."

My eyes bulged as I hurriedly turned back in my seat, adjusting my seat belt. I could feel Metavello's eyes on me, but I ignored them like I had been since we'd pulled up at his house. As always, he looked fucking good and smelled even better. At this point, I wanted to see inside his closet. If it was anything like that pretty-ass home that we'd pulled up to minutes earlier, I knew it was immaculate. Discovery and I took an Uber to his house. Rio wasn't the type of man who paid attention to where I went or what I did, but I had to be cautious. Hell, he could have a tracker on my car for all I knew, so an Uber was the best option.

"'Preciate that. You fly as fuck, birthday girl," Metavello said, looking in the rearview mirror and grinning big at Discovery.

I could feel Discovery smiling from behind me. She'd convinced me to get her hair pressed again. It was parted down the middle and hanging down her back. She was looking like the cover of a perm box.

Metavello turned the radio up, and Future blared through the speakers. The ginger candy resting underneath my tongue had kept my nausea down for the last two days, and I hoped it would stay consistent throughout the show.

"You look good, baby." Metavello licked his lips as he bobbed his head to the music and switched lanes. The three of us in the car felt so right, but the shit was nothing less than wrong. When I'd told Discovery that Metavello was taking us to the concert, I'd expected her smart ass to ask me a series of questions. The only thing she did was smile. I didn't know what had gotten into my daughter as of late, but Discovery used to be the child who had to know the details about everything. She knew that Rio's and I's marriage was everything but normal, but she rocked with it. Me popping up with the man we'd seen at Walmart, and him popping up at her party hadn't even parted her lips. She hadn't said shit, so I wasn't saying shit. Hopefully, when she had questions, I would have answers for her, but at this point, I was just taking everything day by day.

"Thank you," I whispered, knowing he couldn't hear me over the music. I wanted to relax, but being in Metavello's presence was anything but relaxing. I became more uncomfortable by the minute as my apprehension grew. I needed to tell his ass to pull over and call my daughter and me an Uber back home, but I was already in too deep. Plus, Discovery would be crushed if we didn't go to this show.

At least I was looking cute, though. You wouldn't have even thought I was sick with the way I had pulled myself together. I was in a Versace Towel Stitch Jacquard short-sleeved red and pink mini dress, Red Chanel sneakers, and the matching Chanel Boy bag. I must've had my seamstress take the dress in too much because it felt like it had been sown together on my body. I was still comfortable but the look was giving date night instead of concert attendee because of how tight the dress was. I'd gotten my hair freshly done with Discovery and had it styled in Chinese bangs while the rest of my neck-length hair was bone straight. I was sure if Metavello leaned forward and looked over, he could see the black boy shorts I was wearing.

I was scared shitless at the thought of being in a public place with Metavello. But, again, logic was never present where he was. They couldn't co-exist with one another. I didn't know who was performing; I just knew my daughter wanted to go, and Metavello wanted to take us, so I was game. Josephina was meeting us at Metavello's house to take Discovery back home after the show, and my pussy thumped at what was to come after this concert. At some point, I had to stop fucking on this man and talk with him. There were so many questions that I should have been wanting to ask him. How did he know my husband? What was their affiliation? What did he want with me? And who the fuck was he? Yet, I didn't even care enough to know the answers. I just knew the man beside me made my body feel way too good, and for now, I was leaning into that feeling. I would worry about everything else another day.

Traffic laws didn't exist to Metavello. He'd broken them all and gotten us to the venue ten minutes before the show was set to start. When I thought he was parking across the street at the parking garage, he surprised me by pulling behind the arena and down a steep paved road that led to what looked like underground parking. His engine echoed in the tunnel, over the loud music, and when tour busses and black trucks came to view, I gasped. He'd fooled the hell out of me because it was clear that he knew someone performing or connected to this concert.

I could feel Discovery sitting up in her seat, her own curiosity piquing her.

Instead of parking in the lot, Metavello parallel parked behind a black G-Wagon, and only then did he kill the engine. His fingers tapped my forearm, which was resting on the middle console, and that motion sent chills all over my body. Lifting my arm, he pulled three lanyards from the console, a knot of money, and a gun before shutting it back close. He was discreet as hell with tucking his gun so Discovery didn't see it, which I appreciated, but I knew there was no way he could get past security with it.

"Birthday girl!" Metavello looked over at me as he spoke to my daughter, and all it took was for him to lick his lips, and my floodgates opened a little bit more. I was so happy that I'd put on a panty liner because I definitely needed it fooling with him.

"Yes!"

"How do backstage passes sound?"

"Are you kidding? Do we get to meet all the artists?" Discovery was losing her shit with excitement.

"Yeah. But after the show. Come on... my homie opening, and ion want to miss him."

Metavello cut his eyes at me again, but this time, his brow had risen. I didn't know what that look was about, but I waited in the car as he hopped out and opened both our doors. He walked straight through the back door like he was the fucking president, and he didn't even have his lanyard on his neck. Discovery and I wore ours proudly, and I tried hard not to act too excited for the VIP treatment. We were led down a set of stairs as Discovery and Metavello talked like long-lost best friends, while I was just happy and scared at the same damn time to be along for the ride.

Our seats were deadass in front of the center of the stage, so I had to take a picture of my baby in front of the stage while we waited for the DJ to stop playing music and for the show to start. I'd never been to the arena before because it was one of those new features that came along while I was living in New York. It was nice, though, and packed to capacity. Everyone looked good, but all the different smells had me reaching into my bag and popping another ginger candy in my mouth.

"I thought yo' ass wasn't gon' make it upset stomach-ass nigga."

A voice damn near sounding identical to Metavello's caught my attention, and seeing him slap hands with the person that had his whole face had me nearly choking on my candy. Now that they were next to each other, his brother was the one I'd seen in Target. Metavello had a faint scar above his brow that his brother didn't have, and his brother had a big-ass tattoo across his neck. Other than that, they were identical. When he moved aside, I saw the girl Rio claimed to be his daughter, and that choking came to fruition. I didn't know why in the hell I hadn't thought this shit through more precisely. I didn't expect to see her ass here, that was for damn sure.

Panic rioted through me. I gasped, panting in terror, as Pia's eyes raked my frame. She seemed shocked, and as she began putting two and two together, she turned her head to focus on Metavello's twin. This shit was a disaster, and the show hadn't even started.

"Mother, are you okay?" Discovery pulled her shades down on her face, like the diva she was, and reached to rub my back.

Metavello and his brother eyed me, and the double-trouble shit was almost too much. His brother was fine as hell, just like Metavello was, and the right type of bitch would have a grand-ass time with them both on a freaky-ass night. Lord, let me stop. I could barely take Metavello's dick, and here I was, lusting over a two-for-one.

"Aye... you good?" Metavello's hand was still locked in his twin's, and if I knew better, I would say his twin's eyes were on my belly.

"Um... yeah. Hi, y'all." I was already caught. There was no sense in me acting weird. I didn't know if ole girl was going to tell her daddy on me, but there was nothing I could do about it but pray and try to enjoy the show. Maybe she wouldn't remember me.

"Hey... Discover. Right?"

Swallowing hard, I nodded. So much for her not remembering me. Here I was, married to her father and out with another nigga. This shit was too messy. Hell, I didn't even know if he was her father for real, but with the way she was the dark-skinned version of Arianee and looked exactly like Rio's mother, there were no fucking doubts. Rio had a child the same age as me. That was crazy.

"Pia? I think that's what I heard."

I assumed Pia and Metavello's twin were together because not only were they both dressed alike, but he also had her name tattooed big as hell on his neck. This shit was too out of line.

"That's me." She looked at Metavello and smirked, and all his ass did was throw his hands up.

"You niggas are wild. Let me find out, Renello." She wagged her finger at the twin she'd come with.

Renello looked like his brother, no doubt, but there was an almost crazed look about him. He was staring at Pia like she would get up and fly away, and I knew then that man was head over heels in love. I didn't know much about love where a man was concerned, but my eyes knew what the fuck it looked like.

"Pia baby... don't start."

She shrugged. "I ain't said nothing. And I remember you, birthday girl. You are too pretty. See, I knew I should have

85

brought Neltz."

"Hell nawl, you shouldn't have brought his ass. Teacher done called twice this week, and this was his first damn week. He'll be aite," Renello grumbled.

"Man... my twin, cool. You definitely should have brought him, ole strict-ass nigga. I'ma pick him up for school Monday."

"Vello, no. Because soon as he try to sneak one of me or Pearla's keys, I'ma beat his ass."

I assumed they were talking about Pia's son, who looked just like Rio to me. Genetics were a crazy thing because that boy was a spitting image of his grandfather.

What the fuck?

My husband's daughter had really caught me out with another man. I prayed she was a girl's girl and didn't rat me out. I had to sit my ass down somewhere after this, though. I was still getting my dick tonight. Shit, I was already pregnant and caught up. It wasn't shit else that could be done.

"Jagoda Bay! Put ya muthafuckin' phones in the air for the first artist to grace the stage tonight!"

We all faced the stage as the lights went low. Metavello came and stood to the right of me. Discovery was to the left, and to her left were Pia and Renello. My baby had pulled her phone out and went straight to her camera. She looked like a real big girl, and just watching her made me extremely emotional. It was either this baby in my belly, the fear of what was to come, or the excitement of being in the moment that had me on the verge of shedding tears.

"Jagoda Bay! I am DJ Wreckless! I want to formally welcome you to the Fall Ball!" The crowd went wild.

Metavello draped his arms over my shoulder and leaned over to my ear. "I'ma fuck the shit out of you tonight. I been craving for a taste of that pussy."

Fuck.

I looked over at my daughter to see if she was paying us any attention and was relieved that she wasn't. She was completely locked in on the stage, ready to record the whole damn show from the looks of it. She had her portable charger in her purse, so she was ready.

"And I'm real street nigga... ain't no hoeing me!" A raspy voice spat over the horns and gun sounds while screams pierced my ears. Still, no artist had taken the stage yet. Lights began flashing, and a beat dropped.

"I'ma real street nigga... ain't no hoeing me. When she look... that ass took it... ain't no slowing me." Everyone rapped word for word, and for the second time tonight, my whole world ended.

Discovery was screaming and jumping up and down while recording as Pia laughed at her. I couldn't control the spasmodic trembling within me. My ears were hot, my stomach was boiling, and I became extremely light-headed. I felt as if a hand was closing around my throat. There was no way in hell that my baby wanted to come to this concert. Plus, when in the fuck did Essex start rapping?

Vello still had his arm around my neck as he rapped along. Everyone was enjoying the moment, and I was fighting hard not to pass the fuck out. Essex looked just as good as he did in Target and at the birthday party last weekend. Ironically enough, he was dressed head to toe in black and white Off-White, matching Discovery to a T.

What in the hell?

Looking at Discovery, I had no idea she knew his music. She had to have seen him at her party since she was this much of a super fan. But she hadn't mentioned seeing him, though. I mean, my daughter liked all genres of music, but I had never even heard of any of these songs that everyone seemed to know except me.

Essex had always been fine. It was one of the reasons why it was so easy for me to hand my virginity over on a silver platter. Time had been good to him. His smooth peanut butter skin was covered in tattoos, and we were so close that we could see the sweat that the bright lights had conjured up on his hairline. While the twins were dreaded up, Essex had seasick waves that faded on the sides and were edged by a crisp line. He wore one diamond necklace that danced under the lights and an iced-out watch on his wrist. He reminded me of Vello in so many ways. It was a given that they hung out because they had similar demeanors. They damn sure both looked the part. Hell, it seemed that Metavello was surrounded by nothing but fine men because, at every turn, I ran into one at the party.

Glancing from Discovery to Essex had me growing sicker by the minute. Clenching my hands until my nails pierced my skin, I had to chill out before I drew blood. I used to feel like my baby looked like me, but she was her daddy's fucking twin. Seeing them side by side was astounding. They shared the same milky brown skin, short forehead, long chin, and wide mouth. Even their short, stubby noses were the same, reminding me of an oval-shaped button. It was damn near the same double-take as Renello and Metavello, except it was between a nine-year-old girl and a twenty-six-year-old man. It was scary. It was cruel. It was a slap to the face.

How in the hell could all three of my situations be all together yet again? I didn't know if Pia would rat me out. I didn't know if Metavello would press the issue of Essex and I's relationship. I didn't know a gotdamn thing. What I did know was that if we put these backstage passes to use, I probably wouldn't even make it. I would pass away from cardiac arrest because someone would figure me out. How could they not? These two were standing here looking like twins. All it would take was for Essex to see Discovery and me hand in hand, and he would start counting back the years.

Essex's segment seemed to go on for hours when, in reality, it was probably no more than thirty minutes. Three more artists had come and performed, and they were a complete blur to me. By the time they called for the intermission, I was ready to get the fuck out of there but knew that wasn't an option, so I settled for a bathroom break instead.

"Discover! We been calling your name for a good three minutes."

Thankfully, since we had VIP passes, we had access to private one-stall bathrooms, bars, and concessions that were only available for the exclusive ticket holders. Now, being out in the hallways, the buttery smells of what appeared to be popcorn and pretzels tickled my nostrils. I heard Pia calling my name since the lounge wasn't that packed, but I kept my back to her. I was trying my hardest to hold my composure, but I was slowly losing it.

"Mom, do you still not feel good?"

Using my thumb, I dabbed the corner of my eye and blinked a few times to dry my orbs. When I felt like my face was clear, I turned to face them. Sometime during the concert, Pia and Discovery had become the best of friends. They were dancing and singing together, so Pia holding her hand while standing in front of me wasn't surprising. I was a terrible concert pal because the whole show, I'd been in shock and had barely moved a muscle.

"Yes, D-Berry. I still don't feel good. Do you have to use the restroom?"

Discovery bobbed her head. With how she'd been carrying on, you would have thought that her hair would have been sweated out by now, but it was still silky. Her beautician had done her big one. We'd been using some lady that Rio had connected us with, and she hadn't disappointed yet. Usually, when I looked into my daughter's face, I saw nothing but love, joy, and me. Staring at her now, I still felt the love and the joy, but she was her father's daughter for sure. It almost pissed me off how I had missed the resemblance, but then again, I hadn't seen Essex in years.

Pia gave me a once over, and the thought of her telling her father about me had me sweating bullets. Anxiety spurted through me. I was in a moment where too many things were affecting my mental at once.

Essex. Rio. Vello. This baby.

There was conflict with all three men, and shit, I didn't know which problem to solve first.

"There are the restrooms right there." Pia pointed.

Grabbing my daughter's free hand, the three of us went to an open door. There were about six personal bathrooms, and three of them were available. I stuck my head in the door of the one we approached to make sure it was clean, and when I gave it the nod of approval, Discovery ran in, locking the door behind her.

"I love your daughter. She's so pretty and intelligent. Well-behaved too. Don't get mad if I steal her," Pia said chuckling.

I gave her a tight smile. Everyone who came across Discovery had the exact same sentiments. There was a light around her that was so alluring that it made me want to keep her all to myself—and I had.

Pia took a step toward me and cleared her throat. "I just found out Rio is my father. But that don't mean I'm a rat-ass bitch. I don't even know the man, nor do I know what you and Rio have going on in your marriage. I've known Metavello and Renello all my life, so they have my loyalty by default. I'm not going to say shit to him. You can relax."

Pia didn't know how badly I needed to hear those words. Before I could speak, the toilet flushed, water ran into the sink, and Discovery reappeared.

"I'm having so much fun! Best day ever!"

Pia gave me a knowing look, and I smiled at my daughter. "I'm so happy you're enjoying yourself, D-Berry."

"Girl! You are the life of the party. I need your energy. You gotta come to all the concerts with me now." Pia cheesed while rubbing her shoulder on Discovery's.

"I'll be ready too!" Discovery scanned the concession line that had gone from two people standing in it to now about a dozen, and then focused on me. "Go sit over there. I'm going to get in line to get food."

My daughter didn't wait for my reply before she sprinted off toward the line. A bar top table was nearby, so Pia and I naturally walked over and took seats as we watched Discovery.

"I… appreciate you."

I didn't know Pia, and Pia didn't know me. But my daughter loved her, and she agreed to keep my secret. The least I could do was give her a bit of the backstory.

"Your father is the most important man in my life. He and I have never been on a… romantic level. He was one hundred percent upfront with me about being gay. He wanted to help me out, and to this day, I don't know why he had the urge to do so. He made me his wife to ensure I would get all the benefits and perks in the instance something happened to him. The only thing I had to do in return was give him an heir."

Pia swallowed but didn't interrupt me. I had diarrhea at the mouth but felt comfortable telling Pia my business. I didn't have girlfriends. I didn't have any family. I felt a sense of relief with each word spewing from my mouth.

"I met Metavello in Walmart. After I met him that one time, I kept running into him, and well… I guess being lonely affected me more than I let on. We had sex—more than once. Now, I'm… pregnant." I sighed. Saying it aloud made it real. I was in deep shit.

Pia gasped, confirming the deep shit I was in. Telling her I was carrying another man's baby before either of the men in my life knew was stupid, but I needed to get this out.

"I live in New York. Well *lived*. I came here to fulfill my promise to Rio. We were supposed to do IVF treatments so that I could conceive..."

"But now you're carrying Metavello's baby. And you want to keep it."

I nodded. Was it that damn obvious?

"Okay... damn! Okay... this is a lot, girl. But before I say what I have to say, let me ask you this. How do you know Essex?"

I drew my head back.

"Girl... when he came on that stage, you looked like you saw a ghost. Before you answer my question, let me just put out there... I do not know that man. I met him at the Halloween party, and my son has been playing the hell out of his music as of late. He's childhood friends with the twins, though. I do know that."

Running my tongue across my teeth, my eyes swept from Pia to my daughter, who had moved up in line.

Pia's eye doubled in size. "Girl! Wait! You fucked that fine-ass nigga too? That's Discovery's daddy, hunh?"

"It wasn't even like that. He was my first. I was a teenager. Nothing more. I haven't seen that man since I was fifteen."

Discovery still had four people in front of her, and the DJ could still be heard hyping the crowd, meaning the show hadn't started back.

"When I gave birth to my daughter, she was all I had. I was content with just her and I. I knew that even though I didn't have anything, I had Discovery. Looking for someone to share the responsibility of her with me isn't something I ever sought out to do. She'd asked about him for years, and now, with everything going on, how the hell am I supposed to face this man and tell him I have his daughter? I have enough going on. I don't even have the mental capacity to add Essex in the mix."

I was flustered. I was frustrated. I was nauseated. I was stressed the fuck out. The cramping I'd been feeling in my lower abdomen since Essex popped up on the stage was an indication that I needed to take a fucking chill pill. If I kept stressing, there wouldn't even be a baby to worry about.

"I'ma be honest with you. My life... my life is a hot mess, too, girl. My mom went from not saying a word for years to hopping up every day with somewhere to go and something to say. I got a long-lost daddy now, my son is bad as hell, my baby daddy is the baby daddy from hell, I don't have a job or a high school diploma, and the person that I love most, outside of my kid, wants me in a way that I don't want him."

If she was talking about Renello, I would have never guessed that because they looked pretty comfortable the entire concert. That man looked like he was ready to drop down and propose to her, and here she was saying it was platonic between them. It was a story there, and if I wasn't so deep in my own shit, I would have loved to ask more questions about it. Instead, I just listened and took what she was willing to give.

"What I'm saying is... you not the only one who has some secrets in the closet. Shit gon' work out. It always does," Pia said, attempting to assure me.

Discovery had paid for her food with the Apple Pay feature on her phone and was making her way to the condiment stand. I could see chicken tenders, fries, and a green smoothie on her tray. Only my daughter would come to a concert and get a green smoothie.

"Listen... why don't you head home? I can tell you're not

feeling good, and the stress can't be good for the baby. I have a son and a sister that I raised from birth, so your daughter will be fine with me."

"I—"

"Before you say no, I'm just trying to look out. When the show is over, we are going to Essex's dressing room. With you present, he will put the pieces together. You'll eventually have to face him, but let's just not make that day today. Okay?"

Under normal circumstances, I would have never left my daughter with anyone. But today, I felt like I couldn't fucking breathe. I was suffocating. I needed to get the fuck out of this venue and soak in the tub. I didn't want to stop Discovery's fun, though. My daughter walked up, sipping from her straw, and I hadn't seen her this excited in a while.

"Hey, boo. How you feel about letting your mama take an Uber home? You can stay and turn up with me at the concert, and then we can do the meet and greet. I'll take you home after."

"Ohhh! I think that is a *fantastic* idea! Mom... say yes, please!"

"Okay. You can stay. But Pia, her nanny will pick her up from the concert. If you can just wait with her while she pulls up, that will be fine."

Pia stood and pulled her phone out of the back pocket of her jeans. I cringed internally. She looked good, but with the way I'd been feeling lately, I couldn't even imagine wearing jeans, and I loved me a good pair of denim. Now, I despised the thought. It just felt like they would be uncomfortable. It took all the strength I had to even get dressed to come to the show today. These days, all I wanted to do was lay around in bed and pray that I kept my food down.

"That's cool, girl. Us teen moms gotta stick together."

After our numbers were exchanged, I ordered an Uber,

kissed my daughter bye, and headed out of the venue. Having Metavello's dick in my guts was the plan tonight, but I just needed some time to myself to process everything. I would have to treat Pia to lunch as soon as I got this sickness behind me. She'd just come and saved the day, and she didn't even know it. Thank God for my stepdaughter.

Oh my... this shit was so weird.

CHAPTER 6
PEARLA

"Mama... I love you so much!" With my arms around her small waist, I laid my head on her shoulder and took in her cinnamon scent as we lay in her bed watching Lifetime together.

Whatever lotion she'd used after her shower smelled heavenly, wafting from her pores. My days from this past week pretty much went just like this. I would come home from school and get into my mama's skin. I wasn't a stranger to lying with my mom. It was the one way I'd been able to bond with her since she didn't talk growing up. She would stare off into space while I talked her ears off or braided her hair. I was elated that she'd finally spoken, but it was rather odd seeing her out of her room more. It would take some getting used to having her around the house doing things like decorating, cleaning, and cooking. Granted, she'd always cooked and cleaned, but she usually only cleaned her room and the kitchen when she was in the mood to cook. The other day, I caught her getting out of a nice-ass car with shopping bags. She had everything from home décor to designer items for her girls and grandson. I wanted to ask so bad where she'd been, but I was too scared that she would shut down on me again. My mama already had her some motion and had only been talking a week.

"I love you too, prettiest Pearl in the clam."

She rubbed her fingers through my braids, and it was much appreciated because I'd just gotten them done after school yesterday. Pia had given me money to go to the Africans. When I counted out four hundred dollars, I knew off top the style I was getting. After searching TikTok, I found a new salon up the street from our house, and they hadn't disappointed. I went straight to the beauty supply store, grabbed a pack of water wave human hair, and got small knotless braids.

"Is there anything I can do to make sure you don't... you know... go back to not talking?"

As happy as I was that my mother had been talking for the last week, I was equally afraid. I didn't want her going mute on me again. After hearing her thick, raspy voice, I couldn't take it if she closed herself off to me again. I loved my sister dearly. Pia is my best friend and the best sister a girl could ask for. But her ass is tough as nails. My mother, though? She's so delicate and soft and nurturing. I needed her. I need her.

"Pearla... sit up. Look at me."

Lifting my head from her chest, my braids fell into my face as I sat up. Tossing them behind my head, I looked into my mother's gorgeous profile. Patrice was such a beautiful woman. At one point, all I wanted to be was my mother. With her peachy, high cheekbones, flawless tan skin, and naturally arched brows, she was breathtaking. She didn't even look like she had a grown daughter and a teenager. I loved this woman so much.

"I don't know why I stopped talking, but I'm so sorry that I did that to you." My mother had apologized to me more times than I could count in the last week. Her going mute weighed on her shoulders like dumbbells. While I appreciated her apologies, I didn't want her to go back to not talking. That would crush me.

My mother moved a braid out of my face while she held my gaze. "It was like one day... I woke up, and the words wouldn't come out. All I wanted was to be left alone and to sleep. It was selfish. It was so wrong for Pia to have to figure things out on her own, but I couldn't help it."

Placing her lips to my forehead, she held them there as I closed my eyes and took in the feeling. I don't care how old I got; I would always need my mama. It would hurt me so bad if she went back into her shell.

"I promise... I won't go mute anymore. Okay? I was just dealing with some things. I've even been looking online for jobs. I want to help Pia out as much as I can. Plus, you have one more year until you're a senior and off to college, so I need to start stacking my coins." My mother laughed as my phone vibrated in the sports bra I was wearing. She pecked my forehead again and then stood to stretch. My mama had a body that most women killed for. It was crazy because all she'd done was be holed off in a room for the last decade, but she looked like she took daily runs.

BELLA

Get dressed looser. We are going out.

"Who is that that has you smiling? I hope not that boy on your screen block," my mother asked as she stood with a frown on her pretty face and her hand on her sharp hip.

Whereeeeee?

BELLA WAS that long-lost cousin who had me asking myself how I'd even survived so long without her. She walked up to me at the party, asking me if I was the long-lost Pearla and the rest was history. She introduced me to Mahzeyah, and she was just as cool as Bella. The three of us had a ball at the party. I had so many cousins, both girls and boys. They were all cool as hell, and I even smoked for the first time. I hoped Bella had weed because I wanted to get high again. It wasn't even peer pressure. One of the guys asked me if I smoked; I lied and said yes, and went into a coughing fit. I needed that blunt more than I knew because once one of the boys coached me on how to stop choking, I had no worries. My mama talking and revealing Pia's long-lost daddy wasn't even on my mind as I danced with the clouds. Yeah, I needed that again.

"What, Mama?" I lifted my head from my phone, and she still looked pissed about the picture on my screensaver. "Mama... it's called a screensaver. But no, I am not texting him. I don't even know him. It's just a picture." Shaking my head, I went back to my text thread.

THEM GIRLS

Okay I had to add both y'all to the text thread. But y'all like Flexer?"

WHO DIDN'T like Flexer's fine ass? He was one of the hottest rappers out of Memphis. I had no plans on going anywhere today because I had nowhere to go. As much as I loved laying under my mama, it would be cool to get out in these Jagoda Bay streets and have some fun.

Clicking out of the text thread, I went to my home screen, swiped until no more apps were visible, and all but drooled at the picture. I was such a thirsty-ass girl for even having that boy's picture for my screensaver. It was just something about it that I liked. I'd only taken the picture to show my nephew that I had someone changing my tire. I had no idea I would find myself visiting my photo album multiple times a day to study the picture.

Since the day he changed my flat, he'd been on my mind. The way he jumped into action and changed my tire in brand-new clothing was so attractive. His braced-faced smile just added to his cuteness. He was rough around the edges, even with his handsome features, and him taking the time to fix his smile said a lot about him. Veneers were at an all-time high these days. Especially with these certified hood veneer techs floating around. There were days I hated these wires on my teeth, but they were so sexy on him.

His braces had to come off soon because his teeth were perfect. I'd hoped I'd run into him again. Now that I lived way out here, there was a slim chance that I would see him outside the dental office. Hell, with the way he was watching his surroundings, I hoped he was still breathing and free.

We'd lived in or near the hood most of our lives. I knew men like him. The ones that couldn't take two steps without looking over their shoulders. The ones that couldn't sit in one spot for too long. The ones that needed to face the exits at restaurants just so they wouldn't be caught slipping in case their opps wanted to up the score. He was that exact type. Even in the live picture, in one frame, he was in a squatting position with a wretch in his hand while looking behind his shoulder. I hadn't seen the gun when he was in my space, but on camera, it peeked from under the Burberry collared shirt.

He was cute to look at, but I had no space of place for him in my life. Even though my sister seemed to not give a damn, Banger entered my mind way too often. That street shit got him killed right in our apartment complex. My sister didn't think I knew, but that man left behind a woman and several kids. Now, they had to be the ones to suffer. I didn't have the time or energy for a man in the streets. I was going off to college, being somebody in life, helping my people, although it looked like they didn't need future me at all. My future wouldn't be filled with worry, graveyard trips, or jail visits.

"He's cute, though. Too cute." Mama scoffed as if she was mad that he was nice-looking.

My phone vibrated, prompting me to go back to my messages.

THEM GIRLS: (MAHZEYAH)

Hell yes! My mama loves his ass! I told her she had to fall back because that is going to be her son in law one day.

THEM GIRLS: (BELLA)

You better be glad I LOVE you. I'll let you have him. I think ima get me an athlete anyway. 😒

He is fine. Get him, Mahzeyah. What time y'all getting dressed? Who driving?

MAHZEYAH HAD A BENZ, and Bella had a Maxima. Both of their cars were shitting on mine, but I hoped they weren't in the mood to drive. I wanted to put my baby on the road tonight as we cruised the town. I used any excuse I could to drive. I loved my car so much.

THEM GIRLS: (MAHZEYAH)

My mama is not going for me driving to a concert. So, I'm out.

THEM GIRLS: (BELLA)

I'm most definitely not driving. I can get us a ride though. We can ride with Italian.

ITALIAN WAS my cousin who had handed me the blunt. He was fine as hell, but I still looked at everyone as cousins even though we weren't related by blood according to whoever my father was. I'd gone too long without family to blur the lines. Plus, everyone treated me like blood, and I was cool with that.

I'll drive. What y'all wearing tonight? What's the vibes?

I WAS SO happy to have a girl group. The girls at school were cool, but I never really clicked with anyone. I didn't have shit in common with their summers in the Hamptons asses. Bella and Mahzeyah, though? In just one week, we had grown thick as thieves. A few times, I'd nodded off in class due to being on the phone with them all night.

THEM GIRLS: (BELLA)

I'm doing true religion studded jeans and the matching crop top with the new J's.

THEM GIRLS: (MAHZEYAH)

I can do true religion too. I'll have to run to the mall. But I want to wear these red bottom sneakers that I been dying to put on.

WHEN I OPENED my door this morning, there was a Foot Locker bag waiting on the outside of it. I didn't know if it came from Pia or Nel, but they were nowhere to be found to thank them. I also had two brand-new True Religion outfits. I was happy as shit when I saw they came in plus size. Pia copped the sets last week on our shopping trip before the party.

I have the new Js too. I'm ready. What time I need to get dressed?

IT WAS ALREADY FOUR. I'd been to a concert before and loved it, but I knew that you had to get to the venues beforehand to be able to make it to your seat. Parking, the traffic, and taking pics were all tasks in themselves and could very well make you miss half the show.

THEM GIRLS: (MAHZEYAH)

See now I gotta cop. Ya'll not about to outdo me.

THEM GIRLS: (BELLA)

Baby wear them red bottoms. If I HAD EM I
WOULD. Oh and we got backstage passes.

"Pearla."

Snapping my head from my phone, I smiled at my mama. "Yessss?"

Gently grabbing my chin, I locked my screen, looked into her brown eyes as she sighed. "I know I'm asking a lot, especially with the way I've been carrying on these last few years, but I need you to hear me... and hear me good."

I remember days when I wished my mother would scold me. I just wanted her to talk. It didn't matter if she was yelling or nagging at me. But, I got nothing. Now, hearing the warning in her tone, I held my breath, wondering what she was about to say.

Please don't ask me to stay in. I'm trying to be outside tonight.

"No babies."

Well, I wasn't expecting that.

"I want you to get a good education and be somebody in life, and only *if* you want to be a wife can you let a man make you one. After enjoying your marriage and traveling the world, then you welcome babies. I know that sounds too traditional or lame, as you all call it, but it's worth it. That funny-looking Hobo made your sister a baby mama, and you see the way she struggled over the years. I didn't want that for her, but I am mostly to blame. I don't want that for you. Do things differently. Do things right. God has a plan for you, baby; don't stray off course. If he really cares about you, he will respect the fact that you are worth more than being a baby mama. Okay?"

It was so strange hearing my mother lecture me that I was

becoming emotional. She was right; my sister did struggle. She struggled and went without for so long that she deserved all the good. The house, the truck, the money; she deserved it all times ten. I loved children, my badass nephew included, but I wasn't having any children. If I did, I was going to be one of those geriatric pregnant women because I wasn't popping one out until at least forty. Most people were scared of the boogie men or the police; I was scared of being a single mama. I was good on that.

"Mama, it's so crazy hearing you talk, but I got you. I'm not even sexually active at the moment, and I don't have a boyfriend, so I have no plans to even be doing the nasty. School is my main focus. I'm going to a concert with Bella, and I'll be right back home."

My mama searched my face, I guess looking for the truth. When she found what she was looking for, she kissed my forehead and then let me go.

"I remember when that girl was a baby. She still as pretty now as she was back then. She was sassy then, and I see she is still sassy now. You two be careful, and watch your surroundings. Also, keep your phone charged and stick together."

I talked with my mama for a few more minutes and then ran to my room. I loved having a bathroom to myself. It wasn't attached to my room, but it was all mine. I didn't have to worry about sitting on top of a ring of piss when Neltz called himself being lazy and not letting up the toilet seat. I was a neat freak, so my bathroom was clean and smelled good at all times.

Once I had my shower, skin moisturized, and teeth brushed, I called myself having a Flexer concert in my room. I let the time get away from me and had to rush to get dressed. The True Religion number and Jordan's looked good on me. I took a few pictures in my floor-length mirror and a cute little video for my stories. When I woke up today, I didn't think I would be headed to the biggest show of the season, but I wasn't complaining.

"Where you think you going?"

Clutching my chest, I snapped my head around. "Boy! You scared the crap out of me!"

Neltz was standing in my doorframe with a frown on his face. "That mean you not living right."

Shaking off the fact that he'd startled me, I walked over to my desk and snatched my purse up.

Lip gloss, keys, money, license. It was all there.

"Where you 'bout to go?" Neltz asked again.

I didn't even know he was home. His dad had come and picked him up yesterday after school. I guess he was trying to get a rise out of my sister. She didn't even look Hobo's way as he took Neltz. Now, my nephew stood in my room with a crisp line, the same Jordans that I was wearing, and a red and black Gap joggers set. He was looking handsome as always, even with the frown on his face.

"Your auntie grown, baby. Just know I'm outside tonight."

Neltz smacked his teeth as I stood over him with my hand on my hip. "You not grown. You seventeen." Neltz's eyes swept over my attire. "And your skirt too damn short!" He spat.

"Watch your mouth, lil' dude. Just tell your Tee-Tee she look good. It won't kill you to be nice. I tell you all the time when you look good." I fake pouted.

Neltz smacked his teeth again. "Man, your outfit too skimpy. You would look straight if it wasn't for that. You must be going to the same concert my mama going to."

I didn't know Pia was going to the concert, but it made sense. Renello was friends with Essex's fine tatted ass. Hell, Bella was his unofficial social media manager. I looked forward to all the perks that position was going to grant us. I know summer just left, but I couldn't wait until next summer.

"I haven't talked to your mama, but I guess so. I'm going with our cousin, Bella."

"The fine white girl that wanna be black so bad?"

That made me laugh out loud. "Boy, she is not white. She's Italian... just like you are, apparently."

Neltz mugged me and grunted. "I'm a nigga. You see how black I am? How black my mama is? We ain't no Italian. As far as Bella, she not even family for real. She can get it, though," he said with a smirk.

"Man-Man! It's nothing you can do with Bella! You need to be looking at girls your own age. Matter of fact, don't be looking at girls at all. You already do too much. We don't need to add girls to the mix."

"Give me a few years... she gon' be begging for me, and depending on how I feel at the time, I'ma pay her pretty as—I mean, self, dust."

"You gon' think Bella old by the time you get grown." I laughed.

"You might be right. But, it's kinda early for a concert, ain't it?" Neltz pulled his phone out and began scrolling.

"Boy! Get out my business! You had fun with your daddy?"

Neltz didn't pull his head up out his phone as he shrugged so hard that I thought he was going to pop his shoulder out of place. "It was aite. I was ready to come home, though. I figured y'all was over here talking my grandma's ears off."

"And have. But, look... I gotta go. If you come in my room, make the bed back up, Neltz. I'm for real. I want to come home to neat sheets." My nephew loved hanging out in my room when I wasn't home. He'd been that way since he learned to walk and liked to act like he was never in there.

Pulling my phone out, I went to send the girls a text letting them know I was on the way. This shit was about to be so lit. I couldn't believe we were about to see some of my favorite artists perform.

"Man, you still got that nigga's picture on your phone?"

Looking up, I blurted out laughing at the scowl on Neltz's face. You couldn't tell him he wasn't a grown man. He was forever trying to regulate what it was that I did. Oftentimes, he forgot who was the auntie and who was the damn nephew. He rode me harder than his mama.

"Man-Man. Remember... my business? It's mine for a reason."

"Nah. You need to change it before you leave. You going to a whole concert. What if somebody looking over your shoulder, and boom, it's his baby mama. Then she want the smoke with you about his baby and how he not paying his child support."

"Boy! Not you making up scenarios! If a bitch wants to check me over my phone, then cool. She not gon' whoop my ass. That's for sure."

The thought of Baby Shower Shirt having a baby mama caused envy to course through me. I didn't know why in the hell I was having all these thoughts and feelings about a boy who had only changed my tire. This crazy shit was hereditary because I got it straight from my sister and mama, and so did my nephew.

"Won't be no ass whooping going on! I fight girls too! Fuck you mean," Neltz's yelled out of nowhere before pointing at my phone. "But change that picture."

Rolling my eyes, I hit the light switch and kissed my nephew's forehead. "Remember what I said about my bed. And watch your mouth, Man-Man. See you when I get back."

I walked right past him and didn't even stop by my mama's room. I'd checked on her before I'd gotten dressed. I wasn't sure if she would say anything about my outfit even though I didn't think there was anything wrong with it.

"And bring your butt straight home! Tell her, Grandma!" I heard Neltz shout as I walked out the front door. He wasn't talking about nothing. I was on whatever my girls was on.

WHEN BELLA TOLD us we were going to the concert and had backstage passes, I thought she was bluffing. The lights, the singing until we grew hoarse, and the fine-ass artists—a time was had! There were so many pictures and videos on my phone that I couldn't wait to upload. The final picture that we'd taken backstage with Flexer was so lit! He was so down-to-earth and sexy. Mahzeyah must've known she was his type because she talked about him all night, and once he finally laid eyes on her during the meet and greet, he'd been eyeing her all damn night. I never wanted to be a groupie so bad until tonight. Fuck being a psychiatrist. The backstage tour life was for me. It was so fast-paced and turned up. My adrenaline was so high that the chill from the night as we walked from the venue to my car didn't even bother me. I was sporting a black and red long-sleeved True Religion fitted dress that stopped about three inches under my butt. I wore my black and red scrunch socks with my black and red Jordan 12s to complement the dress. We all looked so cute in our True Religion and Jordans that Pia almost teared up seeing me with the girls. She was getting soft on me.

"Unlock this door, Pearla! It's too cold!"

Bella's ass was always cold. Hitting the key fob, I unlocked the door as she slid into the front seat, and Mahzeyah hit the back. Cranking my car, I blasted the heat. We'd stayed behind about an hour after the show ended, just kicking shit and smiling in rappers' faces until Renello's brother kicked us out. He threatened to tell Mahzeyah's father, and that had us hauling ass out of there. We literally ran from the back all the way to the car.

Jerking my car into the traffic that was starting to dwindle, Bella pressed buttons on my radio to connect her phone to Bluetooth.

"I just had the time of my freakin' life! Oh my God!" Mahzeyah squealed.

"On everything I love... Flexer was on your bodyyyyyyy," I added.

The city was lit up, and music could be heard from everyone's car as they drove like bats out of hell through the traffic. I could hear a different song from each of the rappers who performed each time I drove past a different car.

"You think so? He looked so damn good y'all! O.M.G."

"Hell yeah, he was on you bad, friend! Did you see his bitch with the stank face? I double-triple dared that hoe to run up!"

Bella, as pretty as she was, had no chill. She reminded me so much of Missy and my sister. They were quick to fight. Bella had her hair in its natural soft coils, and every time I looked at her, I thought of Alabama Barker. She didn't look anything like her, but the way her ass was full-on Italian but acted like a straight-up black girl was funny as shit. What made it even funnier was that it wasn't an act.

"Girl! She didn't want this shit at all! I was going to show her I'm Avenue's daughter and mop the backstage with her ass. Everybody and they mama know Flexer a hoe. It's my turn with the hoe, though, so she just going to have to figure something out."

We all laughed. Flexer was fooling with Jawn, a YouTuber. I liked her channel or whatever, but I was riding with Mahzeyah.

"Ohhhhh! This is my song!"

Bella turned the knob up to the max as PARTYNEXTDOOR

blared through the speaker. I'd gotten put on to him by TikTok and hadn't stopped listening to him since.

"Never tried to waste your time... you never tried to waste mine... noooo," Bella sang.

"Can't wait to take you down in private.... you know my deepest dark desiressss," I sang off-key as hell.

We hadn't gotten far from the stadium and still had a few miles of traffic to get through until the expressway, but the car concert was going to get us through.

"Your part coming up, Mahzeyah!"

"My bae got diamonds on her arm... diamonds in her ear... she even worked at Diamonds for a year. I'm tryna treat you speciaaaaaal!"

Mahzeyah pointed to the diamonds in her ears and held her wrist up, which housed a diamond bracelet. I was amazed earlier when I pulled up to Bella's two-story, four-bedroom home that her mom owned. Bella's yellow and black bedroom was even off the chain. She'd done my brows and lashes, and I didn't know how to act. But when we pulled up to Mahzeyah's house, I couldn't believe my eyes. It wasn't as big as Pia's new daddy's, but it was still unlike anything I'd seen before. Mahzeyah's daddy was fine as hell, and her mama was super pretty. Mahzeyah's room, though? Her people had her spoiled as fuck because she'd had a whole master bedroom that was all white with hints of light pink. I couldn't wait until we spent the night next weekend. I loved our new house and my new bedroom, but my girls' rooms were goals. Mahzeyah was rich, though. She was iced the hell out, and I was loving it for her. I was glad that she'd chosen to wear her jewelry because Flexer knew he would have to come correct behind her if they went that far.

"To me you are the star of the show still! Even though I got yo' pretty ass from out in mobileeee," we sang in unison.

RING RING

Bella's phone ringing interrupted our karaoke session. "Who is this? I don't know this number."

"Let me see..." Mahzeyah leaned up from the back seat to look at the display since Bella's phone was the one connected to my car.

"Hold up. That's my sister." I recognized Pia's number immediately. I connected the call using my steering wheel.

"Hello... Pia. What happened?"

"Why you not answering yo' phone? I called it like ten times, and it's going to voicemail." I could hear the panic in her voice. She'd left thirty minutes before us after getting the little girl Discovery in the car with her nanny.

Traffic had begun to move, so I looked in the rearview mirror at Mahzeyah. "Hand me my phone out my purse, please."

She nodded and picked up my purse from the back seat. "It's not in here."

"Shoot! I left it on that table that was in the hallway near where they were shooting dice. Pia... let me call you back, sis. I'm good. I have to go back and get my phone."

"Okay, let me call Vello. He's still there and can grab it."

I disconnected the phone, and Bella immediately dialed my number. She called it twice, and it went straight to voicemail. I pulled into the McDonald's parking lot to my right and prepared to make a U-turn. Bella dialed my number again, and this time, it rang.

"It's ringing!" Mahzeyah spoke from the back, stating the obvious.

I held my breath as it rang. It went to voicemail, and I cursed. I did not want my sister to have to make an insurance claim on my phone. True, she had money now, but still. This was an unnecessary expense.

"Fuck it. I'm 'bout to call again. Somebody got it for sure because it was dead. They had to have charged it."

My stomach churned with anxiety and frustration. Something always had to happen to ruin a good-ass night. I had never in my life had this much fun in one day. A night full of celebrities and VIP treatment. Driving my new friends around in my brand-new car. Now, my phone being stolen was trumping all of that. My sister did enough for us. I tried to at least be responsible and take care of anything she gave me. Not too long ago, she was making sure I had, even when she didn't. Until a few days ago, she was still using a cracked phone that was three versions older than mine.

The ringing of the phone through the speaker and our anxious breathing were the only sounds in the car.

"Wassup?"

I drew my head back and crinkled my nose. Mahzeyah placed her hand on my seat as she sat up. Bella was already rolling her neck, ready to go off, as the unrecognizable voice greeted us from my phone. This girl had a mouth so lethal. She'd cursed plenty of guys out backstage, not caring if they were famous or security. She didn't give a damn.

"Wassup? Ain't shit up. You got my cousin's phone, nigga. That's wassup!"

The background was quiet, and it almost sounded like the other person was either smoking or breathing hard. "Where yo' cousin at?"

"What?" I mouthed. Did he seriously ask where I was all casually like he hadn't stolen my phone *and* answered it?

Mahzeyah tapped my seat so that I could speak up.

"Um... I'm right here. I'm on my way back to the stadium so I can get my phone. Where 'bout you at?"

Please, Lord... let this person give me my damn phone back.

"I ain't at the stadium. Pull up to the Bricks."

"What the fuck is the Bricks?" Bella inquired.

"Girl... where the hood niggas be at!" Mahzeyah laughed.

"I know exactly where it is. I'm on the way. Wait. What part of the Bricks?"

It was around the corner from our old apartments, but the Bricks had several sections. It also wasn't the place you wanted to hang out at night, but I needed my phone.

"The middle. When you pull up, you gon' see me."

Click

"I got my mace, so it's all good. Plus, my daddy got my location, so if them niggas on some shit, we covered."

"That nigga sound ugly too. Bitch-ass nigga was probably gon' steal it and sell it. Fuck you take it for and not just leave it with the staff? Roguish-ass nigga make my ass itch!" Bella complained.

We were downtown already, so we weren't too far from the Bricks. I started over No Chill and made the ten-minute drive. Two karaoke sessions later, and we were pulling up.

"Oh, shit. It's live as fuck out here." Bella removed her seatbelt and sat up in her seat.

I hadn't been in the hood since we moved, so seeing all the people and the thriving apartments sparked some excitement in me. I was uneasy about coming out here to get my phone, but I was still on a cloud from the show.

Mahzeyah's phone rang. She sighed. We already knew it was her daddy. "Yes, Daddy?"

"Why y'all out that way, baby girl?" Her father's deep voice boomed through the speaker of her phone. That was a fine man right there. I hated to even say that about her daddy because I didn't even look at grown men like that, but damn.

"Somebody took Pearla's phone. We picking it up and leaving right after, Daddy," she replied sweetly, batting her lashes.

Bella placed her hand over her mouth to hide her snicker. Mahzeyah had her father wrapped around her finger. For so long I didn't too much care about having a daddy, but that was the energy I'd missed growing up. I was smart enough to know that every father wasn't like that. I hoped my sister could at least get it with her new daddy.

"Okay. I got some folks out that way, so you good. I'll have 'em looking out. What time you coming home?"

Mahzeyah's dad was cool as hell. Some days, I wished like hell I had that. She, on the other hand, wishes she had a big sister like Pia.

"We hanging out a bit and getting food... if that's fine." She closed her eyes and crossed her fingers. The diamonds on her wrist lit up the car, reminding me that we were surrounded by some niggas that would rob us blind and not feel bad about it. I had to get my phone and get the hell out of the hood. I would feel awful if something happened while Mahzeyah and Bella were in the car with me.

"Yeah, it's cool. You young ladies, dinner is on me. Have fun, baby girl."

"Girl! your fine-ass daddy so cool," Bella blurted as Mahzeyah tucked her phone in her purse.

"Aite now, Bella! Don't make me get on your ass about my husband!"

Bella and I gasped. We'd thought Mahzeyah had hung up the phone, and apparently she did too with the way she was scrambling trying to pull the phone back out of her Gucci bag.

"You know I'm just playing. I love youuuu, Avenueee."

"Ummhumm. Mama, bring your ass home at a decent hour. Your daddy not talking about shit."

Now, with the phone in her hand, Mahzeyah rolled her eyes and then smiled. "I love you too, Mommy. We still going to the jeweler tomorrow?"

"We will see, lil' girl. It depends on how well you follow instructions and get home at a decent hour. You not twenty-one. I keep telling you that."

"Yes, Mama. I'll be home."

"Bye, Mahzeyah."

This time, she hung up, and we all laughed again.

"Let me stop playing with your mama. I'm scared of grown-ass niggas anyway. Damn! It's lit out here," Bella said, turning her attention back to the Bricks.

I drove to the section the phone thief had instructed us to. There were kids outside like it wasn't late as hell, crackheads running about, a loud-ass radio playing, a grill fired up, and tenants dancing. You would think it was broad daylight with the way everyone was carrying on. But, that was the Bricks for you.

"It's lit, but ion see nun I like, though. These niggas and bitches look rough." Mahzeyah frowned.

"And do," Bella cosigned as we all looked out the windows.

I was sure by now that Neltz had viewed my location and was ready to suit up and fly to the Bricks. Man-Man was probably at home losing his mind because he wasn't Superman. I laughed internally at how protective he was. I'd sent him plenty of pictures and videos before losing my phone, so he knew I was alive, at least.

Pulling up to the section, I saw a dude standing on the curve, grey sweatpants slightly hanging off his waist.

"Is that the dusty-ass nigga right there?" Bella pointed.

"Ion know. Call the phone," Mahzeyah urged.

Bella dialed the number again. I could see him reach into his pocket and answer, but his back was still facing us.

"Wassup?"

"Yeah, nigga... we here."

Bella was something else. She hung up the phone, flipped

down the front visor, and added gloss.

"You shol' doing the most for dusty niggas!" Mahzeyah teased.

"Ugly niggas got mon—damn, he fine!"

The dude that had my phone turned around, and it was at that exact moment I went to meet the Lord. My heart fluttered wildly, all off rhythm. Then, it completely stopped in my chest. When I came back to life, I felt as if my breathing had been cut off. I watched with bulging eyes as the muscles beneath the sleeves of his crisp white tee hardened. He wasn't dusty. He wasn't a thief. He wasn't a stranger. I knew him. As he walked toward us, looking over his shoulder every so often, I must've had three more heart attacks. There was no way! The same guy who had changed my tires was looking fine as hell as he walked to my car with my phone in his hand.

"Oh my God! Y'all... I'm 'bout to drive off!"

I could drive off. My car was heavily tented, so I knew he couldn't see inside. I could drive off and save myself not only embarrassment but my dignity. I should have listened to my nephew and changed that damn screensaver.

"Wait, why? Bitch... you better get his number! He look good."

"He shol' do! And he not even doing too much. Crisp V-neck, grey sweats, and white forces. He fine, friend."

He was staring directly at me through the mild tent, and I found it hard to catch my breath.

"Bitch! Why the fuck is you breathing like that? You got asthma or some shit? Here! You can use my pump."

I didn't have asthma, but I took Bella's pump and inhaled deeply. Three pumps later, I wasn't calm, but I could breathe.

"He... he is the dude on my screensaver!"

"Bitch, what! Baby Shower Shirt?"

"Ohhh, hell no! Yes, drive off. I'll have my daddy buy you

another phone. I can't let you go out like this, friend!"

Before I could reverse, his stomach was at the mirror.

Tap Tap Tap

He tapped the window with the back of his hand, sending me back into overdrive.

"Too late! Okay... let me think of some shit. Look at me." I turned to look at Bella, and her ass put gloss on my lips. "Just roll the window down and play it cool."

"Play it cool? Bella! That man doesn't know me, and I have his picture as my screensaver. He probably thinks I'm crazy as hell!"

"Girl, fuck that! He should be glad a bad bitch admiring him. Roll the window down. If he talks crazy, I'll have the guys my daddy have out here handle him." Mahzeyah added her two cents.

Knowing that sitting here having a conversation with my girls made me look even crazier, I pressed the button to let the window down. Weed, his cologne, and only the smell that the hood had poured into the car.

Lord, ole Lord, help me!

This was going down as the most embarrassing thing that had happened to me.

"Wassup." He leaned down, cutting his height in half. He looked exactly like I'd remembered. His teeth were perfect underneath the silver wire, and his minty breath tickled my nostrils. He searched my face while I stared at his. He was so handsome. His brown skin, bare face that didn't even have a mole, and crisp lineup was all so alluring. His fresh scent was driving me crazy. "We meet again. You good?"

I didn't reply. I stared into his face, getting lost in his dark brown eyes that were alert, unlike the rappers and crew members back at the concert. Everyone was high on something. He wasn't, though—at least he didn't look it or smell like weed.

Bella failed miserably at discreetly tapping my thigh so that I could talk back.

Clearing my throat, I spoke up. "I'm good. Are you good?"

Swiping his tongue across his bottom lip, he looked as if he was staring through my soul.

Oh God.

"I'm breathing." His eyes briefly scanned my car. "Wassup, y'all?"

"Um, hey."

"Hey."

He focused back on me again and then looked behind him. You would think this man was on the run because he had to constantly watch his back. I didn't like it. But, damn, I liked him. I let my eyes wander toward the direction he'd been looking in. The apartments were swarming with people, so in this case, I couldn't blame him for staying on alert. Placing my attention back on him instead of the business around us, I gasped. He was fucking handsome.

"Aye... step out real quick. You good over here. Y'all can get out too."

Bella and Mahzeyah didn't waste any time getting out of the car. The men were already looking and choosing.

He opened my door as I stood out on shaky legs. My hands felt so good in his calloused ones. I could hear my girls snickering behind me while I struggled to keep my breathing under control. A warning voice whispered to leave, but I ignored it while watching him eye me.

"Your keys in the car?" I nodded as Bella and Mahzeyah looped arms, still giggling. "Aite. Stand right there. I'ma turn your car around."

Again, I followed instructions.

"Girl, that boy is fine as hell. Even the way he hopping in

the car look good."

"Yeah, he look way better than the rest of these crazy-looking niggas over here." Bella turned her nose up as the guys eyed us all like prey.

"Hey, baby! Y'all come over here and get something off the grill," an older lady yelled, and Bella and Mahzeyah wasted no time going.

I wasn't even hungry anymore. I was focused on the bright lights of my brakes as he backed in front of the large garbage dumpster. I heard the car shift in park, and when he hopped out, the hairs on the back of my neck stood. Nervously, I bit my lip as he approached. He looked so good. That talk I had with my mama went out the window because I could already imagine what our daughter would look like. She would have his block-shaped head and brown skin with my high cheekbones. Yeah, I was ready to bend it over and spread it or whatever else I knew I wasn't supposed to be doing.

"You good?" He towered over me, even with me standing on the curb. His intoxicating scent took over my senses again, and I had to fight hard not to close my eyes and take him all in.

"Yeah. I'm good."

He looked behind my shoulder briefly and then pulled my hand. He didn't stop until he was sitting on the hood of my car while I stood between his legs. The big-ass garbage can was the view straight ahead, but thankfully, it didn't stink. It must've been emptied recently.

"You enjoy the show?"

"Ye... yeah. You?"

Licking his lips, he smirked. "I missed most of it. Truthfully, I was only there to support my boy."

"Your boy performed?"

His eyes darkened, and if I knew better, I would say it darkened with pain. "Nah. He had a tribute, though."

There was a tribute during Flexer's set. It was a tribute to the rapper Reaper. I remember when his mixtape dropped, he had the world on lock. When everybody found out that his lyrics weren't just lyrics but real life due to them digging up his old tweets from years ago where he'd all but confessed many of his crimes, his fanbase really shot up. He was a hell of a rapper, and all of his videos were shot right here in the Bricks. I didn't recall Baby Shower Shirt being in any of them, though. I would have remembered if I had. He had the type of face that stayed on your mind.

"So, the funeral you went to?"

"It was Reapers. Me and that nigga came up in diapers. He was the closest thing I had to a sibling. Niggas caught him slipping." He chuckled, but I knew he didn't do it in a joking manner. He was trying to hide his anger.

"Well, I'm sorry for your loss. I really did love his music. Also, I'm sorry for judging you the day you changed my tire. You know, thinking you'd come from court.... I swear I'm not even judgmental. I was just living in the hood not long ago and had done so all my life. I'm on a scholarship at my school..." I rushed out. My cheeks burned crimson. I had no business asking if that man had come from court. That was stupid as hell and had to have been something that rubbed off on me from my peers.

"I ain't tripping on that."

"You should. You don't deserve for anyone to judge you."

He rubbed his hand down his fade, and that had my center throbbing. "To be honest, you most definitely should use discernment with niggas like me. I didn't take offense to what you said. Coming from a funeral or court, one ain't better than the other. It's niggas that walk in court and never walk back out. Shit, damn near the same as dying."

His words made me feel sad. The system failed our black

men—like Reaper. He'd made it out and still had fallen victim to the streets.

Hearing loud laughter had me turning my head. Bella and Mahzeyah were dancing in the courtyard with older women, a crackhead that I recognized by the name of Bobby, and random children. They didn't know it yet, but Bobby was going to give them a run for their money. That man never got tired and had some moves on him.

"Bobby's ass gon' have them tired as hell." His deep voice had me turning my attention back to him. Every time I looked at him, I had to fight hard not to reach out and touch his face. I wanted to know his skincare routine so badly. I bet all he used was soap and water. Here I was, having to see a dermatologist and go through an extensive skincare regimen in order to keep clear skin.

"You're so handsome." I shocked my damn self with my confession. With bucked eyes, I placed my hand over my mouth.

Grinning, showing slight dimples, he reached up and grabbed my wrist, pulling my hand down. "Whatchu acting shy for?"

Shrugging my shoulder, I looked past him but was met with the trash can. It was then I put it together that he'd backed in by the trash and chose to sit on my car because he didn't have to look over his shoulder with the big-ass can behind us. What the hell was going on in his life that caused him to be so cautious?

"You the star of the show. No need to be shy. You look good, too, baby."

Oh God.

"Thank you."

Stroking his chin, he stared intently. "You're welcome."

"Um... can I address the elephant in the room? Or the

elephant in the Bricks?"

"We got some gorillas, some lions, tigers, and bears out here. Even a few hyenas, but ain't no elephants, shawty." He chortled.

"The screensaver, I—"

In an instant, he grabbed my waist, flipped me around so that I was sitting on the hood in between his legs, pulled my back to his chest, and held a phone above our heads. When he swiped to the camera and our faces came into view, I erased the shock from mine and tried to play it cool. With an arm draped across my chest, he snapped a few photos. I was cheesing in all of them, looking like a hyped-ass, crazy woman.

"Ain't no elephant like I said. Now, you can be on my screensaver."

I was sad when he let me up, but was glad to be looking in his face again. He flipped his phone around to show me that he'd indeed changed his screensaver. We looked good together.

"I don't even know your name," I revealed.

"It damn sure ain't Baby Shower Shirt." He grinned.

Lord, his nosey ass had seen a message. My phone had been locked, but I was sure when he charged it, the messages popped across my screen.

"I'm just fucking with you. But, Grind."

"Grind?"

"Yeah."

"Grind?"

"Wassup, baby?"

"Why have I never seen you in any of Reapers' videos?" I was genuinely curious, and I'm sure it showed on my face.

"Ion need my face all over the internet."

"So... what you saying is, you not living right?"

"I'm saying... ion fuck with the media."

I swallowed hard.

"I like you, Pearla. That's yo' real name?"

My cheeks flushed again at him admitting he liked me because I liked his ass too. A whole lot. "It's my middle name. Is Grind your real name?"

"Nah," he said, then paused while grinning. "Yo' school. You like it?"

Well, okay then. I guess I wouldn't be getting his real name today. "Yeah. It's cool. I already have college credits, so I'll only have to do three years at JBU. It has its perks."

'What you wanna be?"

"Psychiatrist?"

"Yeah, that's hard. I fuck with it."

"You in school?"

"Nah. I graduated last year." Grind's conversation was light, but his eyes kept scanning me, from my face to my waist. "Ion think the college thang gon' happen for me."

"What you wanna do?"

"Get the money, baby. That's it... that's all."

"You live out here?"

"I'm wherever the money at, baby."

"You have a girlfriend?"

"Nah. You must tryna change that?" His steady gaze bore through my silent expectation. Something tense flared through his entrancement. My heart jolted, and my pulse pounded.

Hell, yes.

"I... uh—"

"Stay where it's safe at, Pearla."

"And you not where it's safe at?"

Licking his lips, he looked up and down my body. "Nah."

I didn't know if he meant safe as in danger or safe as in what he carried in between his legs.

"It was good seeing you and shit, but it's time for y'all to go."

Grind reached into his pocket and handed me my phone. I'd forgotten that this was the reason why I'd come out here. He stood, and since I was still in between his legs, our chests brushed. I wanted to bury my face in his shirt, and I got my wish when he wrapped his arms around me. I felt him touch my ass, but it was actually him stuffing something in the back pocket of my skirt.

"I'ma fuck with you, Pearla. I added my number to your phone. If you find yourself needing your tire changed, hit me up."

I laughed because what I needed help with was *under* my hood. "But... what if I want more than the tire?"

Still locked in his embrace, he walked us to the driver's side of my door. "Stay where it's safe at, Pearla."

"I'ma text you."

He reached down and opened the door. "I'ma text back. Get in. I'll go get your friends."

Sitting in the car, I felt a knot on my bottom. "Grind?"

"Wassup?" He leaned in the door since he'd already closed me in.

"Be careful."

He nipped my chin with his finger before tapping my roof. "I'll try, baby. You be good. Aite?"

I watched him as he swaggered off toward Bella and Mahzeyah, who were now laughing in some boy's faces. I didn't know where they had come from, but they were actually cute from what I could see. They weren't out here when we first pulled up. While he talked with them, I reached into my pocket and was shocked at what I pulled out. There was a small knot of money. Outside of my sister, no one had ever given me anything. Dalton's ass damn sure hadn't given me anything, even after I gave him my virginity. It was pathetic because his parents were loaded. Taking the time out to count the twenties, tens, and fives, I had a final count of three hundred and seventy dollars. I was too geeked.

"Girl! We gotta come back!" Bella opened the door, and I tossed the money into the armrest. I didn't know why I was hiding it, but I felt like Grind and I's interaction was for me and him only.

"Hell, yes... we do! That smoked sausage was good as fuck. Here—" Mahzeyah handed me a plate. "Your man told us to give this to you. Baby, you got you one!"

I didn't want to tell Mahzeyah that Grind had basically shut down the possibility of us being anything, but I kept it to myself. Instead of loathing on the what-ifs, I took the plate and inhaled the charred grill smell.

"Aye!" Grind was back standing on the curb, looking at the car. He couldn't see me but was looking right at me. "Pull off."

"You heard the man. Take us back across town to boring land," Mahzeyah stated while groaning.

Putting my car in drive, I drove us back to our side of Jagoda Bay. Grind, and the hood stayed on my mind the entire ride.

Damn, he is fine!

CHAPTER 7

ESSEX

It had been a minute since I pulled out the pencil and sketch pad. Most of the time, when I did a tattoo, people came in with a picture of what they wanted. Other times, I freestyled. Either way, my work didn't require me to bring out the three-hundred-dollar pencils and white paper. Last night, though, I had this inkling to draw, and I'd been doing it for the last five hours. I was supposed to be asleep because my day tomorrow consisted of me being on the go. I couldn't sleep, though. My heart had been heavy as hell and had been for the last week or so.

At first I thought it was because of how everything had been playing out in my career. Then, I thought it was because of the blogs that had been getting on my fucking nerves. When I concluded that neither of those had been aiding me in feeling down, I felt the pull of my pencil. Now, here I was, running on zero hours of sleep, but the picture in front of me was all worth it. I didn't know where it came from, but the details on my view of the world looked as if it had been printed off NASA's website.

Brr Brrr Brr

My alarm vibrated my phone that was on the nightstand charging. I'd set an alarm so that I wouldn't oversleep, but there was no need for it. I hadn't closed my eyes once, and thankfully, I wasn't tired. Standing from the bed with a stretch, I silenced the alarm and went into the closet where my bag was packed. Taking one last look at the drawing, I smiled in satisfaction before stuffing it in the bag. I didn't know what I was doing with the picture just yet, but I would figure it out soon enough.

Emptying my bladder, I turned the shower on, and while I waited for it to adjust to my temperature, I handled my face and teeth. I'd checked out of the BNB near Ezio's home and booked a new one. This Airbnb was equipped with everything I needed. It also helped that it was downtown and close to everything, like the studio I'd booked to work on some more music. I still hadn't figured out what the fuck it was that I was doing with this music shit, but performing in front of thousands of fans that were rapping my shit word for word did something to a nigga. It was like an out-of-body experience commanding the stage. I was out of breath like a motherfucker when I got to the third song and was regretting like hell that I'd smoked that blunt in the dressing room, but there was no greater feeling than people showing you love for just doing some shit that felt right.

The highlight of my night was the meet and greet. When Flexer came into my dressing room and let me know that there were fans ready to meet me and take pictures, I was speechless. I was just a fucking orphan from Chicago. Nobody had ever loved me like that besides my kids and them Cuppacio boys. There were women crying, hyperventilating, and fighting just to get a damn autograph. I hadn't even practiced a fucking autograph prior to then and just had to fucking go with it. Still, with all that love showed immediately after the show, some shit just didn't feel right.

After being on such a natural high from the Fall Ball and coming off that high immediately after, I figured I needed to be grounded. What better way to get centered than to link up with my sons? So, I booked a flight to Chicago, and thanks to a nigga being up all night, I was going to be chugging down energy drinks to try and keep up with Elias and Elijah. Once I was dressed, I grabbed my duffle bag that I was taking as a carry-on. I had my jewelry locked up in the safe, but I changed my mind at the last minute. I didn't want to catch a charge if the owner of the Airbnb decided to come back and raid my shit. I had the place booked for another month, but I still didn't trust that shit. So, I had my jewelry with me and had already made a deposit for ten of the thirty grand Flexer had paid me to open the show. I kept ten on me and had the other ten tucked in the duffle.

My phone chimed, letting me know that my Uber Black was outside, so I turned off all the lights as well as the heat and made my way outside. I'd turned in my rental yesterday and was going to get another one when I came back to the city. I was only staying in Chicago for two days maximum. I needed more time with my sons, but I had to be here in time for the studio sessions I'd booked. The producer I was scheduled to work with was a busy-ass nigga, and I didn't want to fumble my opportunity just because I was fucking off in Chicago. I had it all planned out. I would pull up at Viv's spot, kick it with my boys, and then go check on my business.

The tattoo shop basically ran itself. I didn't have any issues with the men not paying their dues at the end of the week, and the manager was this gothic white boy that didn't play with their asses. He had some nigga in him, so he made sure he made all the deposits, kept the shop clean, and had all the bills paid on time. The way my tattoo shop was set up, that's how I wanted this rap shit to go. I knew with rap, I would still have to be the one doing the butt of the work with making the appearances, putting in time at the studio, and performing. But I was done hustling. I've tatted until the fucking sun came up. I've chased down customers and begged for work. I've dodged unpaid bills. I was done living like that. I wanted people handling all of the business side of this shit so that way, all I had to do was show up and do what the fuck it was I had to do. Flexer was sending managers my way, and Bella had been doing her thing. So far, it was looking like if I took this shit seriously, it wouldn't be too stressful.

"How you doing, man? Headed to the airport? Delta terminal?"

Climbing in the backseat, I replied, "Yup, yup." to the Uber driver.

I must've spoken Braner's ass up because the driver looked like he could be his fucking daddy or uncle or some shit. He shared the same spiky haircut as my tattoo manager and big-ass loop earrings that he liked to wear in his ear. I started to mention the resemblance, but the scenery outside the window stole my attention.

I wasn't even ten minutes into the nineteen-minute drive, and my stomach had started growling. If we didn't run into any traffic, I would have an hour to spare once I went through TSA. I loved Jagoda Bay's airport because that bitch had all the good eats in it. I wasn't going to splurge on the food, though, because there was no food like Chicago food. I hadn't decided yet if I was going to get some hot lemon pepper mild wings, pizza puffs, or pull down in the hood and buy a plate. Whatever I did, I knew the food was going to be hitting. Jagoda Bay had decent food, too, but it wasn't shit like home.

After getting through the airport, eating, drinking two

energy drinks, and sleeping on the plane because those energy drinks weren't shit, the flight attendant was nudging me awake. I was the last motherfucker left on the plane, and being that I was in first class, I could imagine how everyone had been looking at my ass once they got off. Grabbing my bag from the overhead, I proceeded to exit the plane when I was approached by two more stewardesses. They were blocking the exit, and by the bashful looks on their faces, I knew what it was they wanted.

"Wassup?" My voice was raspier and deeper than usual because I still had sleep in me. That was my last damn time wasting my money on energy drinks because my body still felt tired and sluggish.

They both were around five feet tall; one was thick, the other was petite. Still, they were beautiful girls, and the thought of fucking on a plane had my dick waking up in my joggers.

"Umm, are you Essex? The rapper?" the thick one with the dark skin and short pixie cut spoke up. Ms. Petite looked on with stars in her eyes. Flashing both ladies a Colgate smile, I nodded.

"I am."

"Oh my God! Bitch, I told you!"

They both looked so poised, so I didn't expect the slim one to curse. The shit caught me off guard and had me rumbling in laughter.

"I'm so sorry, but I knew that was you. Can we please get a picture, and then we will let you leave? I love your music! I play it all day!"

"Yes! Her little ratchet ass is who put me on to you. You up next, for real! I'm glad you bringing real rap back!"

The pair were comical as hell, so I chopped it up with them for a bit and even shook hands with the captain, who was a black man too. Once I took pictures with what I assumed was the whole crew, I was let off the plane. The smell of home hit me dead in the face and some of that heaviness I was feeling immediately lifted. I still had my mind set that I would make the transition to living in Jagoda Bay, but I would make as many visits as I could to see my boys and just love on my city. A whole bunch of good shit happened to me out here, but also a lot of bad shit too. Truthfully, it didn't feel the same without them Cuppacio boys reigning terror. I had to be with my family, and I was going to make it my business to split my time so that my role as a father to my two boys wouldn't be affected. Viv was going to lose her shit when she found out that I was moving, and that's why I wasn't telling her until after the move was complete.

Instead of getting a rental, I grabbed an Uber to my apartment to get my own car and headed straight to Vivian's. She didn't know I was coming because I wanted to surprise my boys, and I would hope that by her seeing my face, she would stop tripping on a nigga. Vivian had no reason to trip because she wasn't mine, but with my name popping up everywhere and women staking their claim, she was growing envious. I had to shut that shit down, though, because I wanted this rap shit to go as seamless as possible. I wasn't the type of nigga that did loud and extra shit, so her arguing with fans on the internet wasn't some shit that was about to start. All she had to do was raise my sons and fall in line.

Driving through the city was nostalgic as hell. The last time I was here, my mixtape had just begun to buzz. Now, I have a growing social media platform and an inbox full of not only blue checks but also women begging to get next to me. I'd never had a problem getting women and had been turning them down since I was a young cat but seeing women I literally used to fantasize about fucking blowing me down was a boost to my ego. I wasn't on that, though. Pussy was handed to me on a platter, and sometimes, you got to act like your belly is full even when it isn't. I wasn't the type of nigga that liked to run through women; I got one and stuck to fucking on her alone, and that was how I ended up with two by Viv. I was good on all that for now, but when I ran across the one that held my attention, and that could take all of me, I wasn't opposed to keeping her around. I wasn't a cocky-ass nigga but many women couldn't handle me in the bedroom, and over time, I got used to not fucking as much as the average man because of that reason. When I met the lady that could swallow this motherfucker whole and do tricks on my shit without all that whooping and hollering, I was welcoming her with open arms. However, that woman wasn't my baby mama.

I'd stopped at Walmart before heading to Viviana's and grabbed a few toys for my boys. Even though I took damn good care of them, I didn't like to show up empty-handed. Ringing the doorbell, I stood back while waiting for Vivian to open the door.

"Who is it?" I could hear her house shoes flopping as she walked to the door.

"It's me, Viv."

"What the—"

The locks turned, and then Viv snatched the door open. She'd just gotten out of the shower and was wearing a short black silk robe. Her Caress body wash traveled up my nose. Viv was not only a beautiful woman, but she had a sick-ass body. I used to love watching her naked and putting my mouth on her. Now, my dick didn't even get hard at the sight of her. It wasn't because she was a bad person, but it was because I wasn't on that type of time with her.

"Wassup, Viv?"

Folding her arms across her perky breast, she scanned me

from head to toe. Since I had just been traveling, I was dressed comfortably in a dark brown Essentials jogger set and brown and white Dunks.

"Look who the wind done blew in..."

"Man, move. It's cold as fuck out here, and you standing in the door in a robe." Pushing past her with a smile on my face, I grinned in anticipation of seeing my sons. I couldn't wait to love on them. I'd missed them but didn't know how much I really missed them until I touched down. "Elias and Elijah! Where y'all at? Daddy home!"

I walked to the stairs, jogging up to their room. Peeking my head into the cars-themed bedroom that the two shared, I was met with unmade beds and tags from whatever they'd worn today on the floor. Vivian had the place clean, as she always did, but my kids weren't in their room terrorizing the space like they always were.

Going to their beds, I made both, placed their toys on top of them so there would be no confusion about who got what, scooped the tags off the floor, and headed back downstairs. Viv was leaning against the door frame of the living room when I made it back down.

"They not here. You should have called me before popping up instead of ignoring my calls."

"Where they at?"

"Gone to get haircuts. They should be back soon if you want to wait."

I wanted to voice that Viv didn't do shit all day but sit on social media, so she could have taken my boys to get a haircut herself, but I refrained. I wasn't here to argue, and again, we didn't do shit like that anyways. Grabbing the remote from the coffee table, I put the TV on Sports Center. "Okay, cool."

With my eyes glued to the TV, I could feel Vivian's burning a hole in the side of my face. Chicago wasn't the city where you sat in your car, but if she popped shit, that's where I would be waiting on my sons at.

"So... this rap shit. That's what you doing? You just gon' say fuck the tattoos stuff?"

"Why, Viv? Why do that matter? As long as I take care of you and my kids, how I get my money shouldn't matter," I stated calmly. Despite that heaviness lingering, I was in a good-ass mood and didn't want my baby mama to ruin my current vibe.

Vivian scratched her black and blond tresses while peering at me. "I don't like all them bitches fawning over you, Essex. I don't know what they think this is! It be hoes all in Celeb Gossip comments, talking about how they want to have your baby. We not accepting no more baby mama applications."

"You need to stay off the internet, man. People can say what the fuck they want. That don't mean it's gon' be true. But, a daughter don't sound too bad." I teased to lighten the mood.

"You got me so fucked up, Essex!" Viv stomped in my direction, standing over me. Since I was sitting, her pussy was practically in my face.

"Viv, back the fuck up. Why you trippin' on yo' baby daddy for?" Using my forearm, I gently shoved her out my way, but her ass wasn't budging.

"Because! All them hoes trying to take my baby daddy!" She stomped like a child.

"Man, we not even together, Vivian." I laughed because she looked ridiculous. The shit was funny how this little fame had Viv acting because we didn't do shit like this. I didn't even know what to make of it.

"I'm good to you! I raise your kids, and I don't give you any problems. I make sure all their dentist and doctor's appointments are up-to-date, keep them fresh, and make sure they are in school. Why you do me how you do me? Hunh? You didn't invite us to your show or nothing! Your sons should have been at your first show, Essex! It was kids there taking pictures with you and everything, but not your sons! You do me so wrong! I don't even have you on child support!"

Running my hand down my face, I was regretting like a motherfucker coming back home already. She'd already been blowing up my phone about every little thing she saw on social media, so I had to silence her notifications.

"Listen, Vivian. That show was last minute. The week leading up to the show, I was busy rehearsing, securing a DJ, and paying for my stage set. It's a lot that come with this shit. Y'all will be at the next one, aite?"

"No, fuck that! You need to leave that rap shit alone. All rappers do is get killed anyway! Plus, I heard it's no real money in it. You better off sticking to tattooing!" This was Vivian's second time telling me not to do some shit that brought me joy. Her words were fucking with me just as much as they did the first time. Still, I shook the shit off and thought of how I could get Viv back to the old her.

"Viv... what you want? Why you tripping on me? What you want? Some dick?"

Her body stiffened at the mention of me giving her what she wanted. I could smell the pheromones leaking from her pussy. Reaching up, I pulled the tie from the robe and watched it gap open. Her pussy was freshly waxed, and the tattoos she had on the sides of her belly that I'd done looked good up against her light skin.

"Come on... sit on it," I said, motioning to my waist.

Pulling my dick out of my pants, I grabbed a Magnum from my wallet and sheathed it. Vivian's eyes lowered with lust, but she wasn't moving fast enough. Grabbing her waist, I turned her around and pulled her down on my dick so that her back was facing me. Gripping her ass cheeks, I spread them until I could see the pinks of her pussy and thrust her down on my dick.

"Ahhhhh! Hold up! Hold up." She reached back and clawed at my chest while my dick filled her wet walls. She wasn't sloppy wet like I liked it, but no foreplay occurred, so that was on me.

Grabbing her around the waist, I held her in place while her walls hugged my dick. I pulled her hair back so that my mouth was to her ear.

"Hol' up, Essex! Wait! Go slow!"

"I'm not even fucking you, Viv. You been tripping on a nigga lately and ion like that. Just like you say... you good to me, I'm good to you too. You don't get no reward for being a good mother, but still I applaud you."

"E—Essex! Take it out some!"

"Shut the fuck up! I take care of yo' ass. You don't gotta fucking work, but you walking around this bitch in a nice car and got a laced crib. I gave you the fucking cheat code to life, and you arguing with me about some social media shit that don't concern you."

Vivian's pussy choking my dick felt good as fuck, but I wasn't about to pump in and out of her. This wasn't that.

"Just because you don't want shit out of life don't mean I gotta settle. This rap shit? If it can take me to the next level, then I'ma do the shit. As much as you keep your hand out, you should be pushing me to get more bread."

"Okay! Okay! Fuccck... your dick so big."

"You want to know why I don't fuck you? This one of the reasons. You can't take dick even if your livelihood depended on that shit. I need a big girl, baby. One that can handle daddy dick. You stick to spending my money and taking care of my fucking kids. If that shit becomes too much for you, I can always take them with me."

Letting her hair go, I removed my arm from her waist, and she wasted no time hopping up. I stood so that I could wipe my dick off and dispose of the condom.

"Go put on some fucking clothes!" I called over my shoulders as I walked with my dick in my hands. Grabbing one of the decorative towels she had hanging, I wiped the little juices off that she did get on me and flushed the condom down the toilet. Viv was a pretty girl, but fucking her made my head hurt. I used to be sore as fuck after fucking Viv. I was cool on that.

"Aye, what the fuck wrong with you and why your robe open?"

Hearing that my boys had gotten back, I washed my hands and walked out of the half-bath with a smile on my face. Ignoring Vivian's nigga, I scooped up my sons and planted kisses on their faces. These boys looked so much like their mama, it was crazy, but they did have hints of my features. They were mine, though, so who they looked like didn't matter. I could smell the product the barber had used, and once I confirmed both their shit was cut with precision, only then did I give Viv and her nigga some attention.

Elias climbed on my back while Elijah clung to my front like they always did. I loved the fuck out of their little busy asses. Vivian was still trying to fix her robe while her whole face was red. Her nigga had his face balled up, waiting on her to answer. I wasn't saying shit, though. That was on her for fucking with me. He ought to be glad I didn't fuck his thirsty-ass woman.

"Daddy! We go with you?" Elijah cheered.

"Daddy! I heard your song on the radio," Elias followed up.

"Yeah, y'all coming with Daddy."

Feeling no need to size up Vivian's nigga because it wasn't

that deep with me, I reached in my hoodie and grabbed the ten racks I'd traveled with. Tossing it on the coffee table, I glanced at Vivian. "For child support."

The lust in her eyes returned, but I wasn't fucking with her ass. With my boys in tow, we headed out the door so that we could start our day. "Daddy, can we eat?"

Placing them both in their car seats, I knew exactly what their asses wanted to eat. I should have named their asses after the Ninja Turtles with how much they loved pizza.

After getting stuffed on the best pizza in the fucking world, let alone the city, I went a block over so that they could grab their favorite snacks and I could grab some woods. I was going to go by my shop and ink myself and wanted to be high while doing it. While Elias and Elijah ran to the candy aisle, I went to the small automotive aisle because I needed a new iPhone charging cord. I wasn't worried about nobody fucking with them because Chicago was home for me. I was known for being the tattoo nigga with money, but the terror I'd reigned in the streets with them Cuppacio boys had me certified. Those days were long behind me, but niggas knew not to try me.

"Aye, Julio! Nigga... you need to upgrade yo' iPhone stock!"

I couldn't find what the fuck I was looking for, and that shit aggravated me because I didn't feel like stopping at another store. I had backup chargers at the shop, but there was no telling who had taken them. I didn't leave my room locked up. I had that shit open because anything that belonged to me, them niggas holding my shop down, was welcome to it.

"We have chargers! Look behind the Android one!" Julio, the store owner, yelled back at me.

Removing the Androids products, I located the last three-foot charger for iPhones. I didn't want one that long, but it would work well for when my kids used my phone in the back seat, and it needed to be plugged up to charge. They acted like it killed them to let the phone charge and shit before they jumped on ABC Mouse. Having what I needed, I stood straight to head in the direction where I knew my sons were picking up more candy than they needed. Vivian wasn't strict with their diet, but Elias has an appointment coming up where his ass is going to get a mouth full of silver due to all of his cavities. Their asses didn't need any candy, but what they wanted, Daddy provided.

"I knew that was you!" I had heard those words more times than I could count all damn day. While I usually followed up with a smile or a head nod to be polite, this time, all I had on was a mean mug. She didn't seem to care that I was looking at her as if she had shit on the bottom of her shoe because she continued to smile with her hand on her wide hip.

"So you gon' look at me like you don't know me?" She giggled and then continued, "Essex, I raised you—"

I cut her off by stepping back as she tried to reach for a hug. I wish I didn't know her. I hadn't seen her ass since I was sixteen. I walked out of that fucking dump of a foster home and didn't look back. My leaving happened so fast that I didn't tell or say goodbye to anybody. One random night, I decided I was tired of watching my back and losing out on sleep, so I figured I would do better on the streets. Looking back, I thanked God I gambled on myself because a nigga was self-made like a motherfucker.

The smile on her face dropped once she realized I wasn't gung ho or jolly to see her. I wanted to lie and say time had been kind to Maeve, but that would be a lie. She looked every bit of the sixty-year-old woman that she was. I could tell those state checks were still rolling in because her wig was in pristine condition, and she was rocking a Tommy Hilfiger set with the matching shoes on her one-hundred-and-forty-plus frame. The only thing youthful about Maeve was her shape. She was still stacked, and at her big age, had no problem flaunting it. However, her face gave great grandma. Maeve's skin was saggy and wrinkling, her nose was three sizes too big for her face, her thin lips were covered in red lipstick, and those burgundy nails that only older people rocked adorned her elderly-looking hands. She wreaked of White Diamond perfume and cigarettes, and her attitude still gave me the creeps.

"Maeve, you didn't fuckin' raise me. If you call what the fuck you was doing raising, you need to look up the fucking definition."

I'd been with Maeve seven years before running away. I didn't remember much before getting with her. Still, I knew I had better living conditions with the previous families.

"So, you mean to tell me... I didn't treat you right? I was good to you! You had a roof over your head, clothes on your back, and food in your belly. It wasn't my damn fault you ran away."

I didn't know what the fuck it was with women telling me how good they were to me, like being so-called good to me hadn't been beneficial to them. Maeve got a fat check for me being in her care, and I didn't see a damn dime of it in the seven to eight years I lived there. We wore each other's closed, prayed the food stretched long enough for her to get off her back to go shopping, and she did shit that could get her locked the fuck up.

"Maeve, you were fucking the little boys."

"What?" She drew her head back like I'd slapped the shit out of her.

"You heard me. You were fucking the boys. You treated the girls like shit, letting them roam and do whatever the fuck they wanted as long as they left you alone. Them girls thought you treated the boys better cuz you gave them more attention, but you only did that because you was fucking them. The moment any of the boys hit puberty, you was on they dicks like flies on a shit pile."

I dared her to deny it. Jeremy, one of the boys who was a year younger than me, used to brag about it. I thought he was lying until I'd seen it with my own eyes. I went into her room to ask her if she could sign some shit I needed for school and caught her ass bouncing on one of the boys that I knew had just turned eleven. I wanted to beat her ass, but I didn't want to land my ass in jail. So, I left. I wasn't about to let her bribe me into sticking my dick in her sour-ass pussy. That shit was dead.

"Essex! How dare you? I loved all of my kids! As a matter of fact, you turned out just fine! I see you on the internet and hear you on the radio. Don't you think you owe ya mama something?"

My mama was dead. This old-ass woman had lost all her marbles if she thought I was giving her anything. That heaviness I'd been feeling came back, and all of a sudden, a thought crossed my mind. "Aite. I got something for you; if you can tell me what happened to Discover?"

The smile on Maeve's face diminished the moment my first love's name parted my lips. Discover kept mostly to herself. She'd come in from Jagoda Bay, and I thought she was the prettiest thing. I used to fucking daydream about her anytime she wasn't around and did anything to be in her space. We were two fucked up kids placed in unfortunate situations. We bonded over dead parents and unfortunate situations. I took her virginity on a day when the house was quiet and Maeve wasn't walking around demanding shit from the girls while flirting with the boys. We were both underage, but Discover took dick better than Viv's ass as a virgin. That day went down as one of my favorite memories of Maeve's house. However, after we had sex, Discover started giving my ass the cold shoulder. I tried talking to her ass for a month. When I finally got the hint that she didn't want my ass, I caught Maeve on her child molester shit and dipped. I would have loved to take Discover with me, but shit, I could barely do for myself. It damn sure wasn't nothing I could do for her. She never left my thoughts and prayers, though. Seeing her in Target after all these years was refreshing as fuck.

"How the fuck am I supposed to know what happened to her? That bitch left too!"

I didn't need a location on Discover because I knew she was in Jagoda Bay. She hadn't used my number yet, but she'd been on my mind. As a matter of fact, right after the show, I began thinking about Discover because I could have sworn I saw her ass in the crowd. Right after that, the downcast started. Something within me told me that I needed to talk to her. I didn't know what it was, but I felt something weighing on me regarding her. Shit damn near was spooking a nigga.

"I'm saying, though... did she run away too?" How the fuck did she end up back in Jagoda Bay?

"Discover? Hell no, she didn't run away. I almost wished she had, though. The streets of Chicago would have eaten her little black ass up and spit her out."

The way Maeve disliked the girls was sad as hell. All these years later, she was still jealous of one of the kids she was so-called responsible for. I would hate for her ass to see Discover now. Even though the attire she had on looked to be thrown together for running her Target errand, she was a sight to fucking see. Maeve would kill her fucking self if she could see how pretty Discover was, and she had a big-ass rock on her finger. I wonder if her pregnancy test was positive? I wonder if she's going to abort that motherfucker if it was? I meant what I said when I said I wouldn't mind playing stepdaddy. Then again, I wouldn't mind giving her ass a baby. She looked like she would make a pretty-ass daughter.

"Ahh! You got me!"

Turning my head, I could see Julio had come from behind the counter and was wrestling with my kids. Maeve followed my line of sight, and before she could lock her perverted-ass eyes in on my kids, I cleared my throat. "Okay? So, what happened to her all those years ago? Why did she leave?"

"They yours? Cute little boys."

"Maeve... don't get yo' wig blew back, love. Answer the fucking question."

Maeve smirked while crossing her arms over her wrinkly breast. Cold as it was outside, she had her cropped jacket unzipped to show cleavage. "Look! The little bitch got pregnant!"

Drawing my head back, I processed her words.

Pregnant?

"What you mean pregnant?" I asked to be sure. Discover— the sweet Discover who let me pour my heart out about my folks—couldn't have ended up pregnant.

"Didn't your lady have to get pregnant to give you those boys? I know you know what *pregnant* means. Discover stomach just got big out of nowhere. I took her ass to the doctor, and they confirmed she was big and pregnant. I put her ass in the car and dropped her the fuck off in Jagoda Bay."

I had sex with Discover. But right after that, she cut my ass off. Plenty of the kids in the house were fucking each other, and I wasn't saying that she fucked other boys after I left, but it wasn't shit else to do in that house but fuck.

"Okay... around when did you find out she was pregnant? How long ago after I left?"

Maeve squinted her eyes and then grinned. "Oh. Y'all fucked under my roof?"

"Aye, Maeve—"

"Okay, okay... damn! You don't gotta worry. That shit was so long ago, but I think it was a year or two later after you left." She fanned her hand as if to dismiss the topic.

Looking at her, I tried to pinpoint if she was lying or not. She was eyeing a nigga like I was her next meal, and that shit disgusted me. This lady was old enough to be my mama and my grandma too. That was why there was nothing in this world to get me to do some illegal shit. If something happened to Viv or me, I didn't have a family to step up for Elias and Elijah. Viv had a family with a little bread, but those mother-fuckers were so selfish, I wouldn't put it past them to leave my kids in the system. I refused to let my kids fall victim to a lady like Maeve.

Getting what I needed from my old foster parent, I walked around her so that I could pay for my items and head to my tattoo shop.

"Hey, you can break me off with a lil' change! You said—"

"Man! Suck my dick," I called out right before approaching my boys. They both had arms full of candy.

"Just let me know when and where, Essex! With yo' fine ass! I love the tattoos on your face! Make you look all gangsta!"

I didn't even look back at Maeve as her ass went into a fit of coughs and giggles. Scooping my boys up in my arms, I reached into my pocket, but Julio stopped me.

"Your money is no good here, Essex. Just keep making us proud. I remember you used to stand outside my store and sell your drawings. Now, you're on the charts. Keep making Chicago proud, baby."

Chicago.

This city had made me and damn near broke me. Now, I had the world at my feet, and being back in this city had opened my eyes to two things. One, I was never residing in this fuck-ass city again. I would keep my shop and apartment for visiting purposes, but I couldn't live here anymore. There was too much pain attached to this place. Two, I knew what tattoo I would be getting next. The one I stayed up all sketching. Hopefully, Discover would leave my thoughts after I experienced some needle pain.

I was looking her up as soon as I got some free time in Jagoda Bay. My mind kept telling me I had to talk to Discover.

About what, though?

CHAPTER 8
PIA

"In the case of Natazia Pia Chvesky, Rio Mecanio... you are the father! Damn, I always wanted to say that shit." Missy giggled in my ear whileI held the phone in place with my shoulder.

I'd gotten the email with the results last night and was too damn chicken to open them myself, so I forwarded them to Missy. She was working when she got them, so I sent her a text to call me after she got her rest the following day. I needed to do something with my hands, so I was folding laundry, and thankfully, I'd just folded the last of Neltz's underclothes at the same time she read off the results.

"For real, friend... how you feeling?" Missy inquired as she breathed into the phone. She must've still been lounging in bed.

How was I feeling?

That loaded question had multiple answers. On one hand, I'd already accepted the fact that he was my father. Rio, being the only person who had Patty speaking, verified paternity. Still, I wanted proof. After everything I'd been through in my life, I wasn't up for building relationships with anyone temporarily. Allegations of blood relations were serious; I needed to know for a fact if Rio was my father or not, and by Missy confirming it, I couldn't help but wonder where the hell this would go.

"I really don't even know how I feel." I sighed.

Removing the stacked pile of clothing from my bed, I placed them back in the laundry basket that had seen way too many laundry days and walked into Neltz's room. He seemed to be having a better week since it was already Wednesday, and I hadn't gotten a call from the school. His first week of school was hell, and I was hoping he was finally settling in well. All I wanted for my boy was for him to make friends and not look at everyone as an enemy. Neltz was a natural loner, though, and I was to blame for that. Hell, I still held Missy at arm's length sometimes.

"I've never heard you talk about your other family, friend. As a matter of fact, all I knew was Patty and Pearla before my Godson came along. When you invited me to that Halloween party, and I witnessed you around people that loved you just as much as I do, a bitch got real emotional."

Placing the clothes in Neltz's underwear drawer, I decided to go ahead and make his bed since he'd neglected to do so this morning. Some nights, he stayed up past his bedtime, sneaking on the game. It would have him moving slowly in the mornings. Pearla didn't miss a morning making her bed up, though.

I opted to not respond to Missy because there was so much I wanted to say. However, the words were all jumbled, and I didn't know how to get them out without saying too much. I didn't know the rules of the mob. I didn't even think I would be tied back up in the mob. I didn't know how many times I'd told myself that this was a lot, but it really was. I loved Missy with everything in me and owed her so much for holding me down, but I didn't want to be telling secrets that weren't for me to tell. Still, I had to give her something; after all, I'd let her read the DNA results.

Plopping down in Neltz's game chair, I spotted a bag of half-eaten Cheetos underneath his entertainment center, so I grabbed them. I was going to end up putting my foot in his ass about eating in here. I refused to have roaches.

"For a long time... my son, mama, and sister was enough. Then, I linked back up with my other people and was mad that I hadn't done so sooner."

Noticing that the Airwick in Neltz's room was empty, I stood and went to the hall closet, where I stored the supplies used for cleaning the bedrooms, and opened a brand-new pack. The vanilla and caramel scent was seasonal, and the moment I saw that Walmart had stocked them, I grabbed the entire row. Weeks ago, I couldn't imagine spending two hundred dollars on plug-ins, but it was my favorite scent. I knew after December, I wouldn't see it in stores until next fall. I found myself thanking God for the simple things like that. The me, before Renello came along, would have to wait until I did a job for Daylani's company or wait until I got my income taxes to buy the necessities in bulk. Now, I was buying out the entire row. Fuck the truck and the bags—this was luxury to me.

"Okay, so what's the problem with knowing you have a daddy? It seems to me that your life has gotten so much better since linking with your family. Bitch, you're pushing a new Benz truck, got a new house in the 'burbs, you aren't complaining about no money, and you calling me more. That lets me know you're happy. Talk to me, friend?"

Once the wall plug was changed out, I went back into my room and plopped down on the bed. Renello's Cuban necklace caught my eyes as the blinding diamonds danced while it rested on the nightstand. My pussy thumped in my underwear, and the moment it did, I had to fight back a groan. I didn't like the way my body was starting to react when he wasn't in my presence. I craved his nearness and had to fight the urge to not act like a crazy bitch anytime he didn't answer the phone. He wasn't my man. He could never be my man because I didn't look at him like that. But my body heating at the thought of him said otherwise. I hated it.

Thinking about what I was going to tell Missy, I had to choose my words carefully. At the same time, I was hoping this was the last time I had to tell this story. I had only told Pearla about it because everyone else already knew. I was tired of reliving the past, though, so this was it.

"I was born a Cuppacio. They were a group of sick men, and they are all dead now. We originated in Chicago, but my mom left before the men were killed. I was close with all of my cousins back then, but I was the closest to Renello. We were inseparable as children. He's the one who found me after all these years. I'd unknowingly waitressed at my cousin Ezio's wedding back in September, and Renello spotted me. All of our fathers were related by blood. My father—the man Patty was married to against her will—used to force her to sleep with other men. They were a sick bunch. So, technically, the Cuppacios aren't related to Pearla and me by blood."

I could hear Missy's breathing while I toyed with the loose string on the comforter. My story was so damn bizarre that it would go crazy at the box office if it was written and produced.

"I'm not going to lie, friend... I been stripping in Jagoda Bay for a long time. I done fucked a whole lot of niggas and worked beside a whole lot of bitches."

"Oh my God! Girl, stop. You have not fucked that many niggas." I protested.

"You so sweet... but, friend, I'm a whole hoe. It's cool,

though, because your bestie is a paid hoe. The pussy still tight even with the thousands of miles on it. I keep my oil changed and tune-ups up to date. Anyway..." She popped her lips. Missy was a hot mess in the best way. "I said all that to say, niggas and bitches talk. Not only that, it's my job to know the money-getters in the city. From the men to the women, if they are attached to money and power, I pretty much have heard of them, fucked them, or saw them in passing, whether in the club, the malls, or the restaurants. When I walked into the Rinaldi mansion, I knew you were tied to the mob. Jisei is his baby sister. I didn't know that until the night of the party, but I pointed out his wife right away. Then, when we went down with the men, I recognized damn near all of their faces."

"So, what you saying is, you done fucked the crew, friend?" I kidded.

"Girl, no. You know I try to stick to the white-collar men. Mobsters are just like the NFL, NBA, and rappers. Niggas that get too much money—I steer clear from. Give me a few that make a couple hundred grand a year, and I'm good. Them millionaires be too cocky. Have I danced for 'em? Fuck yeah. But them type of niggas don't pay strippers for pussy like that no way. If they do, they not going after me. They go after the innocent-looking ones that they think are just stripping to pay off school. Only if they knew... them be the ones that live in those backrooms, slanging that throat and pussy."

"Oh, wow. You hell, friend!" I cackled.

"Passion is hell; Missy just be calling it like it is. Anyway, I knew you were tied to the mob. I can imagine there is a lot you can't tell me, and I get it. You know I'm a nosy bitch, but not a prying one. Mecanio? I heard of that name. I can't remember to what capacity, but it's a powerful name in the city. Not saying everything is about money, but you see how much of a differ-ence your well-being makes when you have no money problems? Take this as a blessing. If this man—your father—wants to be in your life, hell... let him. He is rich, ain't he?"

"So much for not prying, hunh?"

"Girl, boo! You know you want to tell me. Hell, who the fuck I'ma tell besides you? Ion fuck with these hoes."

"You might tell Railroad..."

"Ummm. His mouth somethin' serious, friend. I never met a man that makes me vibrate off the head alone. So, you might be right. He just might make a bitch pillow talk."

"Ughhh! And next week you gon' be saying his dick too small for all the lying he do."

"Next week? I'm saying that now! I told you about that gender reveal shit! I'm still trying to get to the bottom of that. Anywayssss. Do you have a Daddy Warbucks, or what? Damn! I may have to skip my rich nigga rule and get at yo' daddy. My Patty gon' have to be mad at me."

Tossing my head back, I barked out a laugh. "He's not going to want you, friend. But, yes, his home is the size of Demise Rinaldi's. He's handsome too. But no, friend. Just stand down."

"Girl! This pussy talks! I walk my thick, young fine ass in his mansion, and he'll be handing over all of your trust fund, friend. I'm not a shady bitch, so I'll at least split it with you."

"You ain't shit! But no, friend. Rio is... gay. I haven't seen him in action, but he voiced that off-top. Plus, he's married to a woman around our age. You don't want to be tied up in that."

"Oh, my shit. What the fuck kind of shit you mobsters got going on? That nigga take dick and in a lavender marriage? Whew, shit. I need some popcorn for all this piping tea."

"Girl! I am not a mobster!"

"John Gotti n'em ain't got shit on y'all. You a mobster, friend. But reach out to the man. Let him get to know you. Money aside, all girls need their daddy. I miss mine every single day. If I could go back just for a day with him, I would give my left leg. And you know I need my left leg to swing across that pole, friend, so what that tell you."

"Bwahaha! You don't need a leg to strip. Hell, you just might make double what you making now, hopping around on a peg leg. I can see you now."

"Yeap! Still flexing on them tired-ass hoes with half an arti-ficial pussy. They know wassup."

Letting Missy read the results was the right thing to do. She'd put a smile on my face when I was feeling uneasy about the whole situation. I didn't know what I would get out of meeting Rio, but even if it was closure and some insight about where I really came from, that was enough for me.

"But for real. Take it from me... let the man in."

I didn't know to build a relationship with Rio, but I was definitely going to give it a shot. He had one time to piss me off, though, and I was done.

"Hold up! So, you named my Godson after the cousin you're close with? Y'all not related, so... is he stepdaddy or what?"

My face burned thinking about how Renello turned his mouth into a vacuum both times. The first time he ate me out, I was shocked. Then Neltz's badass walked in on us. The second time, though? The second time was so good that I hadn't stopped thinking about it. It's gotten so bad that I find myself just staring at his lips mid-day, and then I feel bad right after. Thinking about Renello in a sexual manner literally makes my stomach turn. But then, I act a whole damn fool when I go too long without seeing him. I was so confused.

"That's my cousin, Missy. It's nothing like that."

"Umm. I guess. I say fuck him. He's fair game, and you need the cobwebs knocked off that coochie. You gon' make me put my strap on and come handle you one time, for the one time."

Clutching my stomach, I let out a deep laugh. Missy did too much. She didn't even have a fucking strap. She wasn't *that* gay.

"Friend, no, thank you. I'm cool. Renello and I have a bond, but not one on that level," I lied. I didn't know what the fuck it was that we had.

"Ummhmm. I'ma let you go because this nigga beating on my door like he the police. And I don't want my neighbor calling the real police on his ass. I gotta take his name off the concierge list."

My antennas went up as I sat up in the bed. "You cool?"

"Girl, yeah. His soft ass not about that life. If I need ya, you know I'ma call you, Laila Ali. Oh, and bring the fam to the club Friday. We supposed to have a performer. Carlo's bald-headed ass being all secretive about who it is, but I got a booth. I won't be dancing that night because my fucking knees been hurting. I deserve a night off. You know I got the big booth too. Ya'll deep as shit like Mexicans. As a matter of fact, I just might need to dance. Bring yo' gay-ass daddy too—"

"Bye, Missy. That's why I ain't telling you shit else!" I could barely contain my laughter. This girl did way too much.

"I'm just playing! I love you! Friday! And you better put that shit on too! You got it, Mob Princess! Show these hoes who really 'bout to be running the city!"

"I love your crazy ass too. Bye, girl."

Hanging up the phone, I went to my call log and noticed I had three missed calls. I was stumped because the phone hadn't beeped.

I didn't recognize the number, but the half-moon shape at the top of the screen educated me on why I hadn't been notified of calls. My phone was on Do Not Disturb. I'd change the mode right as Missy called. I didn't want to be interrupted as she read off the results. My mama was out doing whatever her all-of-a-sudden talkative ass did these days. I'd already talked to Renello, and it was rare that he called while he was out making money anyway. Sometimes, it made me antsy, but again, I tried to keep my audacity at bay. Besides, after I pulled up at his house last week, he brought his ass home even if he had a meeting. The only other person who could have called while I was getting the results was Neltz's school, and since his weak-ass daddy had been sniffing around, he could handle it. I still didn't understand how, all of a sudden, he'd taken residence in Jagoda Bay. His wife had to be the dumbest bitch on the planet. But then again, look at Banger's wife. These hoes put up with anything just to say they had a man. A nigga could never leave me home with the kids while he laid dick. I used to think it was the worst thing in the world when Hobo dropped my ass like a hot potato, but looking back, it was a fucking blessing. I was popping a nigga dead in the mouth anytime he thought he was going to play with me on that level.

Putting my phone in normal mode, it rang not even a second later. It was the same number that was on my missed calls log. I answered in a hurried voice because if they'd rung me a fourth time, it had to be an emergency. My mother was out and about, and didn't have a car or a cell phone. It could be someone calling about her or Pearla. If it was Neltz's school calling from a different number, I was taking his game for a week.

"H—hello?"

I stood from my bed. I needed to sit just in case the person on the other end told me some shit that would have me passing out, but my anxiety wouldn't let me.

"Pia Mecanio?" the thick Italian accent replied.

"I... That's not my name." Great. The first words to Rio, as my officially confirmed father, would be disrespect.

A loud chortle filled the line. "Oh, but it is. Had the change made this morning, *mia figlia*."

Swallowing hard, I plopped back down on the bed. "You got the results?"

Duh, Pia! Didn't you get yours?

"I've had the results for days now. I was just waiting for you to receive yours. I wanted to give you some time to take it all in. If it were up to me, you would have found out when I did, which was the day you showed up on my doorstep. I didn't need the test. I strictly had it done for your assurance, and so I wouldn't be—you know what? That doesn't matter. Are you free?"

"Uh. Right now?"

"Of course."

It was a breezy Wednesday and around twelve in the afternoon. Neltz wouldn't be getting home from school until four. Pearla made it home before he did to get him from the bus if needed, and if Mom wasn't back by the time the kids were home, there was food stocked in the fridge and pantries, plus Pia had money. I could make myself free, but still, I wasn't sure if I was ready to be thrust into his world again.

"Yes, I'm free."

My brain and my mind weren't on one accord. I shouldn't have made myself so easily available. But I was a stay-at-home mom now, and as much as I despised going to that sour-ass nursing home, I found myself growing bored when I was the only one home. I kept telling myself I was going to join a gym or get a hobby, but my days consisted of bed rotting and catching up on all the Netflix shows that I was too busy to watch back then.

"Great! A team should be pulling up right about now."

Ding Dong

The door bell sounded off and the Ring camera alert had me pulling the phone from my ear. The same glam team from

Dasani's home stood there chatting, each of them carrying black suitcases.

Oh my God.

"How do you know where I live?"

"Daughter, you will come to find that there isn't much I don't know. Especially when it comes to my child. When Chimo, Lunar, and Bruno are done, a car will be sent for you. See you soon."

What the hell have I gotten myself into? Patty, you shol' know how to pick them.

EVEN THOUGH I was uncomfortable as hell with the glam team showing up at my house, I ended up having a great time. Chimo fixed me a flute of Champagne as he fixed my nails to help me loosen up. Listening to the details from the latest world tour that they'd just come from was comical. I was sure they'd signed an air-tight NDA, so they weren't disclosing too much, but for a minute, I envied them. To travel the world doing what you love and meeting people that one would only dream about sounded like goals. I'd never had time to sit down and think about what I wanted to do, but traveling was at the top of the list. When I did those two events for Daylani out of state and got to see those cities and the luxury that came with that lifestyle, I craved to see new places. I tucked it in the back of my mind because not only did I have a mother to take care of, but a sibling and son too. Now, though? I could explore my options. Not the travel part, though, but I could do more than before.

By the time the team was done, the car had pulled up. I didn't even get to see myself as Lunar rushed me out of the house. He assured me he would lock up behind himself.

Outside my house was a fancy car with a tint that was impossible to see inside and a driver holding the door open in a suit. I'd opted for some fancy-ass sandals instead of heels since the flowy, silky dress that had the girls on display in a tasteful manner didn't show my feet. My nails were the shit. I started to go simple but remembered how much I used to love Missy's junk nails. I didn't know if I knew how to navigate long nails, but I decided to go with it for the hell of it. I let Chimo freestyle, and I wasn't disappointed. The dress I let them choose since I was undecided on all the options they presented was seashell-colored. I didn't see myself, but looking down, I saw that the dress fit like a glove.

Even though it was early November and the leaves were no longer green, today's weather was a whopping seventy-eight degrees. Tomorrow, it would be in the low sixties and would drop from there. That was Jagoda Bay. The dress was long, but the open back and open bust worked for the season because it was warm. Otherwise, I would have flu up the ass.

As the driver hauled me through the city, I admired the bay area. I rarely came to this side of the city because it was out of my league. It was where the rich and famous frequented. Even the grocery stores were out of my budget. Not now, though. Since I had a little something in the account and time on my hands, I would start coming over here, even if it was to people-watch.

My phone vibrated in my hands, and it was Pearla Face-Timing me. Sliding my thumb across the screen to answer the call, I waited as it connected. This new phone was three times bigger and three times heavier than my old phone. It took some getting used to, just like these long-ass Swarovski crystal nails would be.

"Ohhhhh! I been waiting to run to the bathroom to call you when I saw you on the Ring camera. Excuse my French.... but bitttttch! You look *the fuck* good! Where the hell are you headed?"

Pearla's eyes scanned my face, and at the same time, I all but gasped, looking back at myself. The squad had done their thing. My makeup didn't have me looking so different that I didn't recognize myself, but I damn sure was enhanced. Now that I was able to see the top half of myself, the cleavage wasn't as bad as I thought. It was sexy yet tasteful. Lunar had added a few clip-ins to my already lengthy hair and pinned it to one side using a hair broach with seashells and rhinestones. The beaded seashell clutch they forced into my hands matched it perfectly. He'd also added soft, beach wave curls. I was looking gorgeous. I never was a fan of makeup because I didn't go no damn where to wear it. I didn't know how to apply it either unless Missy was begging me to do it, and now, I wanted it done every day after having it done twice. Hell, even if I learned to do my brows like Bruno did and add lashes, I would be good with that.

"Thank you, sister girl. I don't know if you had plans after school, but I need you to get Neltz off the bus, please. Also, if Mama not back, go and get you and Neltz some food."

"You know I got you. But you and Mama showing out! She done got her voice back like her name is the Little Mermaid. You got your grove back, and a father and ain't sat down since."

There had been a few days I rode alongside Renello. It was only if he was picking up money and not drugs, but besides that, Pearla was exaggerating. I had my ass in the house outside of the concert that she, too, was at and the Halloween party.

"Girl, please!"

"You look so pretty! O.M.G. I want to cry! Now, where you going?" Pearla was fanning her face. She was more dramatic than Missy, and that's why I hadn't planned on calling either.

"I don't know. Rio summoned me." I looked out the window and saw that the fancy homes and businesses had faded. There was nothing but sparkling lake water. "I'm somewhere on Bayside."

"Well, I have your location, so have fun! Oh, be still. Let me screenshot." Pearla added gloss to her lips and then took a few screenshots.

"Tag me too." I winked.

"Oh, so now, since you got a rich and famous Daddy, you want to be active on social media? You so aggy!"

My curls cascaded down my shoulder as I laughed. "You do too much."

The car stopped, and I tore my eyes away from Pearla, who was still snapping pictures. White yachts that looked like luxury homes on the water stared back at me.

"Rich? Yes. I don't know about the famous part."

"I gotta go before these teachers try to take my phone. You know, us fatherless children still got school." She playfully rolled her big-ass eyes.

"Awww, boo. You can share my daddy. He already said he got you. But with the way Patty set up, yo' daddy might be the damn President of the United States."

"Or he a bum-ass nigga somewhere. Or dead like Niccoli. Ugh. Never mind, I'm good on a daddy," she said with a frown.

I laughed again as the driver tapped the window. "Call me if y'all need me, okay? I love you...." I cooed.

"I love you too. Again, you look freakin' amazing. Wait! Nel let you leave the house like that?"

"Who the hell Renello is? Not my daddy!"

"Yeah, okay, boo. I gotta go." Pearla winked and disconnected the call.

I placed the phone in my clutch and knocked back on the

window since I knew he couldn't see me. The door opened, I was helped out, and the mild ocean breeze tugged at my curls and kissed my skin. I could almost taste the salt water as I gasped. The boats tied to the docks, rocking on the dark blue water was a sight to see. When Rio asked if I was free, I wasn't expected to be treated like Cinderella and brought to a yacht dock.

"Right this way, Ms. Mecanio." The older black gentleman gestured what direction to walk in. He helped me down the stairs, and when my feet hit the bottom dock, I had to fight my intrusive thoughts that were telling me to jump into the water. I hadn't swam since I was a teen at the local community center, but I knew it was just like riding a bike. We were only inches away from Jagoda Bay's famous lakes. The city was built around the water, and I had never been this close to the bay. It was crazy how trying to survive had you not giving a damn about what the city had to offer. It seemed like the more we walked, the bigger and more grander the yachts got. This was some shit you only saw on TV, and here I was, close enough to reach out and touch it.

"Here we are." I was led to one of the smaller boats in the line-up and had the nerve to be disappointed. It wasn't tiny, but it couldn't hold any more than ten people.

Fuck it, at least I'm on a boat.

Just a few weeks ago, I had a car that didn't open from the outside on the driver's door. I couldn't afford to be ungrateful about the type of boat Rio was meeting me on. But, damn, my ghetto ass would have loved to tour one of these big-ass ones.

After being helped on the boat, I took a seat since that was all I could do, and then the boat pulled off. I tried to remain calm as I saw the driver stand on the dock, talking into a walkie-talkie. Rio was nowhere in sight, but the view as the boat ventured deeper into the water was a beautiful distraction. I was uneasy and clueless, but as my hair danced in the wind while the boat sped at what had to be about fifty miles per hour, I thought about how peaceful this shit was. I pulled my phone out and recorded because there was no telling if I'd ever get on a boat again. I wanted to capture as much as I could. I went to my Instagram page, switched to selfie mode, and recorded myself as if I were one with the wind. I must've watched the video ten times before I posted. I looked like one of those girls on those vintage boats they road in Italy on Instagram and TikTok. But my ass was right in Jagoda Bay. I'd even added the trending song "Je Te Laisserai Des Mots" by Patrick Watson. I didn't know what the hell the song said, but it was fitting for the navy blue waters in my background. One look at my video, and you would've never thought I was just a broke-ass baby mama with twenty-seven dollars in my account a few weeks ago. I guess that's why they said social media was not real.

"What in the—"

String quartet, chatter, and clanging of wine flutes could be heard as the small boat I was sitting on sped through the dark waters. But it wasn't the sounds that had my eyes bulging; it was the massive ship on which all of this was taking place that had me stunned. Yes, ship, because the word yacht wasn't fitting for it, and I didn't know what to call it. It was more than three stories high, had a futuristic, sleek design, was a pearl white color, and was swarmed with people. Here they were, floating in the middle of the ocean, where there weren't people for miles, and having a whole-ass dinner party.

The speed boat I was on stopped close to it, and on cue, sailors or crewmen or whatever they were called tossed a rope and pulled the boat in. It was then that I noticed that I was in the boat alone, beside the driver, who was still talking into the walkie-talkie. This damn tugboat was driving itself. The crew parted, and Rio appeared. The entire party stopped, even the orchestra, who I hadn't laid eyes on yet.

He reached his hand out and took mine in his. He helped me up the five stairs, and the moment my sandals hit the wood, he cleared his throat. "You are stunning. My beautiful creation. *Mia figlia.*"

Rio, as handsome as ever, looking just like my son, kissed the back of my hand. "Everyone... I would like for you to meet Natazia Pia Mecanio. My daughter."

Claps, cheers, and whistles went off around the boat. I was overwhelmed and stunned but appreciative. I'd never been celebrated in my adult life. "What is this?"

"This, my beauty... this is your introduction party. I want everyone who's anyone to know that you are my daughter. My legacy. My heir. This party was thrown in your honor, and what better way to do it than on your boat."

"My... my... my boat?"

Rio took my hand and led me down the side, by passing people who were complimenting my beauty. We strolled to the rail, and he pointed down. Splashing against the water, *Pia Mecanio* was engraved in gold on the boat. Clutching my stomach and my mouth, I stumbled back.

I had a fucking boat?

"This is mine?"

"My darling, it's all yours. Everything down to the hair on my chin. You don't ever have to ask because it's yours."

"Wha-what does this mean? What do you want from me?"

"Pia..." He looked around us as people were staring. It was as if I was on display, and even though I knew it was harmless, it caused my stomach to turn. I didn't like being the center of attention, especially to strangers in fancy clothing, nibbling on fish eggs, and drinking liquid gold.

Is this real?

Rio's cool hand on my back was an indication that this was indeed real. He gestured for me to follow him around to the back deck, where it was empty. "Do you need to take a seat?"

I shook my head no.

Rio was my daddy. He didn't look a day over thirty-five. With the way these men were out here aging like milk, he could probably pass for thirty. Money must come with the fountain of youth because I hadn't come across one person who had it that looked their age. Even here on the boat, everyone looked like stars. They were gazing at me when I was really the one staring at them. I'd stepped into a world I could only imagine myself dreaming about. This was all surreal. I needed to pinch myself, but I was too scared that if I did, I would wake up in that fucking apartment still needing that one hundred dollars to pay the rent man. I wanted to be here— on a fucking boat that there was no telling how many millions it costs. I didn't even own a house yet, but I had a damn boat.

Rio rubbed his hand down his goatee. There wasn't a hint of salt and pepper. Not only was his long ponytail sleek black, but his facial hair was neatly trimmed. The cream pants set he wore fit him like a glove, and his pants stopped right above his ankles and hugged his calves. There was a thick gold Cuban anklet around one of his ankles, and the loafers, I didn't know the name of, looked as if they were explicitly crafted for Rio and his outfit. I didn't know what a million dollars looked like, but if I had been asked to give a visual representation of it, it would be Rio.

"Your father is... somebody. Not just anybody. You're my heir. What that means is you can either follow the line of succession, or you can live out your days existing in whatever your dreams are."

"My dreams..." I whispered.

What were my dreams?

For so long, all I wanted was money left over until the next paycheck, and to be able to afford my bills without having to be charged a late fee. My dream used to be to have an exit plan out of struggle. My dream used to be for my mama to talk again. Now, I have all of that and some. What else could I want?

"Yes. Your dreams. I don't think you understand what being my child means. Your life will never be the same, and I am hoping you see that as a good thing."

I was okay with my life not being the same. I didn't want to go back to forced sex just for a little bit of money. I didn't want to break my back at a job that was barely paying me. I loved seeing my sister and son more than comfortable, but a knowing in the back of my mind knew it wouldn't be that simple. It was something that Rio wanted from me—something he hadn't told me. Nothing was free; even being a niggas kid came with a price. I just didn't know if I could afford to pay it.

"I... I don't know if it's a good thing. I'ma be honest with you, Rio. While I appreciate the boat, this isn't me. I don't know what it is that you would want from me in return because I don't have shit to give."

I loved Jisei, and I loved her for Ezio, but my story would not be hers. My father wasn't going to marry me off to a nigga for the sake of strengthening his organization. Jisei got lucky because she actually loved Ezio. What if I was whisked off to another country? Most of these motherfuckers on the boat looked like they had been flown in from the wealthiest parts of the world with their cultural clothing. Most of these people were dazzled in gold, emeralds, rubies, and diamonds. It was so many fucking diamonds. If pirates were a thing, they would come the fuck up if they raided this boat.

"My child..." Rio kissed the back of my hand again. "I am

only interested in getting to know you right now. At first, I wanted a child strictly because it was required of me. I didn't care if it was a boy or a girl; I just wanted a healthy baby. Now that you've come along already as an adult, I'm sad that I missed out on your life, but I'm happy that you have gone through life and were able to experience living outside of this. You know who I am, mi amour. I was born into money. My organization didn't become this grand until I took over. My sister, as I told you, was not cut for this life—she never wanted it. But you're not like her. You're a survivor. A fighter. When the time comes, I'm going to give you two options. Option one, the one that my parents didn't give Arianee, is that you can spend your days on the boat, exploring crystal blue seas, on and off the jet going to countries that can't be found on a map, eating the most delectable meals, and shopping the rarest of jewels and clothing. You can see life in a way you never thought imaginable. Not a grain of soil is off limits to my princess. You can start today if you'd like. "

Wow. I was just saying I wanted to travel, and here, my father was telling me that I could go anywhere I wanted to go. But that was just option one.

Tearing my eyes away from his, I walked to the railing, dress blowing in the wind, and looked over the waters. This was such a fucking dream. Rio appeared beside me with about as much difference as a fingertip.

"Option two?"

"Again, this isn't a decision you have to make today. As we speak, bank accounts and trusts for my grandson and Pearla are being set up."

"Oh, wow..." I hated to see Neltz with money. If he found out he had trust funds, we wouldn't hear the end of it. He would really be around here knocking folks upside the head.

"Brother! You hogging my niece!" Arianee looked just as

pretty as she did the day of the birthday party. She was wearing an eggshell-colored, long-sleeved bell dress that hugged her frame and flared at the ends like a mermaid. Her hair was in natural coils, and her soft makeup glowed underneath the sun. While she was beautiful, it was the lady on her arm that had me drooling. She had Arianee by at least a foot, and her slender frame in the long, red, thin-strapped dress was runway-worthy. Her skin was so dark that it was almost purple, and the gold highlight on her super-high cheeks agreed with her look. Her hair was in an afro that was so big that it flowed down her back. She had to be an international model. She looked so familiar, though.

"We just stepped aside to get some air, sister. Did I tell the both of you how gorgeous you look?"

"Only a thousand times," the model spoke. Her voice was even sultry. I loved to see dark-skinned, confident women killing it. I'd always loved the skin I was in, even on those days that I had wished I looked more like my mother. I never cared to have lighter skin, though, and I was ecstatic when I had my chocolate baby, Neltz.

"You are beautiful," she faced me and acknowledged.

"Thank you... so are you. Both of you." I blushed.

"You look so good. It's like looking at Mommy in the mirror, but the younger, finer version. Ugggh! You are too pretty! This is Miyo."

"May I hug you?"

It was odd that she asked me for permission, but looking at Rio, it seemed I was responsible for breaking the awkwardness. I leaned in and gave her a hug. She smelled like sweet cherries dipped in Godiva chocolate. I had to stop myself from nuzzling my nose in the crook of her neck before she thought my ass was gay like my daddy.

"You look so familiar." I let my inner thoughts slip out.

"I heard that my niece Mahzeyah went to a concert with your sister. You more than likely saw her, and since we have the same face, much like you and Arianee here, that's probably why."

Miss mamas had politely told my ass that we don't frequent the same circles, so you couldn't have seen me, but with a smile and in a polite tone. I could tell she didn't mean anything by it, but the crazy in me liked to analyze everything and turn it into shade.

"I just wanted my girl to see my new bestie-niece. I will leave y'all to it. Mama and Daddy gon' get you for not inviting them. Come find us when you finish talking to your daddy, Pia. Damn... I can't believe my brother got a child."

"She looks more like his sister."

"Girl, wait until you see my great nephew. Her son looks *just* like Rio. Anyway, let me go find my husband before one of these emperor hoes or princesses try to fuck on him. I ain't above tossing a foreign hoe in the deep blue sea."

"It's a lake, darling." Rio laughed.

"Potato... potatoe... a hoe gon' be swimming with the piranhas behind Solid. Let's go, Miyo, in case I need backup."

Miyo laughed but followed Arianee, who hugged me before she walked away.

Rio held his arm out. I hooked mine in his and slowly walked along the opposite side of the boat from where we came.

"Who are all these people?"

My cheeks were already hurting from smiling and saying thank you for the many compliments I received, and we hadn't even made it to the front of the boat.

"These are some of the people I do business with. They are anything from royalty to cartels to politicians. We even have a few former U.S. presidents aboard."

"Wow. And they all came here for me?" I was trying hard to wrap my mind around it all. I was just a girl from the hood, and now I was amongst the world's elite. They were celebrating me for being Rio's daughter? Why was that important to them?

"Yes. They all came here gladly for you. Some traveled days just to lay eyes on you and to possibly get on your good side." He laughed, but I didn't understand the humor.

"But why would they need to get on *my* good side? I'm not nobody. I don't even have a high school diploma," I fussed. If it was one thing I was insecure about, it was my lack of education. But raising a baby and trying to hold down a family while being a teenager myself was too much. I always said I would get my GED, but I never had the time to do it. That was why I did whatever to make sure Pearla stayed at that private school. I didn't have an education, but she damn sure would. No matter how much money the men in my life threw at me, my sister wouldn't let that steer her off course. The end goal was those degrees. That wasn't changing.

"Pia... you are somebody. As a matter of fact, you are one of the most important people in the city, if not the most important. You're just as worthy as the princesses, duchess, and queens amongst us. You want a diploma? Okay, it's done. You're so much more than you think, and I can't wait until the day you realize that."

Rio stopped, turned us so that we had a view of the lake, and jutted his head. My father was so handsome and held so much youth in his face. It was almost insulting for anyone to call this man a grandfather. But, then again, my mother was the same way. Her not talking kind of aged her a bit in my mind. Not physically, but it was easy to put the grandma title on her due to her temporary disability. Now that she was around here talking and running in and out the door, she didn't look like a grandma either.

"You see way over there?"

Squinting my eyes, I tried to make out what he was pointing at. "The back of the eighteen wheelers floating on the water?"

"Those are trailers. Yes. That. Across the water is the port station. It's one of the largest ports in the South. It controls what comes in and out of Jagoda Bay and surrounding cities and states. Things are shipped from around the world and come right here to Jagoda Bay. That is why people are wanting to get next to you. If you choose option two, what comes and goes will be your say."

So, I would be the Don of merchandise and shit? I wasn't dumb enough to think that household goods were the only things being shipped. If kings and cartels were here, that meant drugs, money, gold, and diamonds were in a few of those containers.

Oh shit! What if people are being shipped too?

"What if... what if I don't want either of those options? What if I just want to get to know you?"

A hearty laugh escaped Rio—my father. "You're going to get to know me, anyway. That isn't up for debate. You're stuck with me, and option one is also non-negotiable. If you decide against option two, though, I'll still love you the same. I will just keep myself healthy until Renello Jr. is of age and present him with the same options, and we both know what his answer will be."

I shouldn't have laughed because this shit was serious business, but I couldn't stop the laugh if I wanted to. Renello's badass was probably born for shit like this, and I hated to say it. I used to blame his behavior on his weak-ass daddy, but maybe, he got that shit from the Mecanio side. I, too, had a temper that I'd learned to control with time, while Pearla and my mom were both mild-mannered. This shit was hereditary.

If me stepping up wouldn't allow Neltz to join until his ass was at least forty, then I definitely would entertain the idea. I think I would have to talk to Renello to see what he thought about me possibly running an entire organization. If he wasn't with it, then that would pose a problem for me. I hadn't heard from him and knew he was probably worrying sick. I hadn't felt my phone vibrate, so it probably meant I was out here without cell service.

"Again... just think about it. No pressure. Right now, we will get to know each other. I still have a few more years left in me. Just know that you will never be sold or bought. You'll never be forced into something you don't want to do. You will marry for love if that is what you desire. I'm the man people come to when they want to strengthen their organizations— not the other way around. You're not a bargaining chip. You're my daughter, and you will be handled with delicate hands. Anyone who doesn't understand that, don't deserve the hands they have; and I love removing what a person doesn't deserve."

Rio's smile dropped, and his words shouldn't have made my heart flutter. My daddy wasn't playing about me. Period. "Now, let's go find your beautiful mother and let a few of these people plead their case to you." Rio winked.

Missy's words from earlier played over in my head like a broken record. That girl needed to go buy a lottery ticket or something because, little did I know, Missy's words may be true.

Hold the hell on. My mama was here?

Patty done started talking and was suddenly every damn where.

CHAPTER 9
NEL

I complained about my brother having my code, but I was low-key geeked that we all had access to each other's homes when needed. From the moment I keyed in the eight-digit pin and was granted entry, I wanted to turn right back the fuck around. Some loud-ass shit was playing on what sounded like a piano, and it wasn't even English. It was always some shit anytime I came over here, but this nigga was the only level-headed one in the crew, so I needed his ear.

"Man! What the fuck is this shit playing, and where the fuck is this shit coming from?"

I walked through the well-decorated home with envy because my shit looked a damn mess still. I'd been at Pia's house every night. I was scared to even go home to start removing the bullshit my mama had designed my space with. I wasn't scared of Pia at all, but I didn't have time for her little ass popping up in that bonnet with the Seed of Chucky behind her, acting a damn fool. That girl was a pit bull when she wanted to be; she was also my sole reason for this visit.

I was too damn tired to be walking through his house, so I

stood in the middle of the living room, pulled my phone out, and dialed him. I'd been running the streets nonstop and sitting in stupid-ass mob meetings with the other trainees. This shit was the longest orientation period I had ever heard of in my fucking life.

"Yeah?"

"Don't 'yeah' me, nigga. Where the fuck you at? And why the fuck you got this bullshit playing like you the fucking Godfather?"

Looking around the space, my face contorted into a deeper frown as I ogled the well-placed vases, floor-to-ceiling curtains, and odd paintings. This shit was dope. I couldn't even lie, though; I was hating like hell.

"I'm in my book room, Nel."

Hanging up, I trudged in the direction of the book room. It didn't take me long to get there, and as I stood in the doorway, I was able to see where the bullshit music was coming from. A vintage record player with a disk spinning on top of it blasted as the lyrics talked about some shit that we knew nothing about.

"And what the fuck is this nigga doing here? Damn! Can I do anything alone?"

Vello was sitting on the opposite side of Shio's desk and turned in his chair with a childish-ass smile on his face. He didn't look like himself, probably from all the throwing up he was more than likely still doing. The nigga had a whole potential baby on the way, and you would think he was the one carrying it. Well, I think he had a baby on the way. The bitch he was knocking did have a pregnancy test in her hand a few weeks ago in Target. I didn't know what the fuck my brother had going on these days. I had my own shit to worry about than to be coddling niggas.

Shio had his glasses resting on his nose as he wrote in a

notebook. I didn't know if this nigga was acting as my brother's counselor or what, but they were going to have to pause their shit because I had some shit to say.

Plopping down in the tan leather chair next to Vello, I appreciated the shape. It was sort of oval and looked good with all of the browns in his office-library. I frowned at all the books that were stacked up to the ceiling. Shio even had them bitches color-coded. Then, he had the nerve to have a ladder. If this wasn't the most hoe shit in the world? Every day these niggas acted more and more like Rio. Next thing I knew, they were going to be sucking dick like him too.

"Hey, Twin."

"What the fuck is you doing here, Vello? I wanted to talk to Shio about some shit in private."

Vello reached over and slapped my chest with the back of his hand. I shoved his arm so hard that I'd hoped I knocked that bitch out of place. He did too much. "I came here for the same reason as you. You changed your code on a nigga, so I can't come vent to you. Ezio and Jisei always fucking and eating, and I damn sure can't keep no food down, so Shio was the next best thing. Big cousin always gives the best advice."

Shio paused his pen and looked over his glasses. I didn't understand why this nigga was so adamant on looking like Dr. King. That shit wouldn't get him no pussy at all. He may as well hop in the pulpit with his stepdaddy.

"You niggas don't want no advice."

"Well, what the fuck we here for then?" That twin shit kicked in as Vello and I spoke the same words at the same time.

"Y'all want for a muthafucka to tell y'all what y'all want to hear, and I'm not up for coddling y'all tonight. As you can see... I'm busy." Shio eyed us both before scribbling again.

"You only saying that shit because I walked in. What the fuck you was doing before? Writing this nigga's problems down and shit? You think because you got your degree and shit, you certified for this type of shit. Newsflash, an associate's degree in welding don't count."

Shio continued to write. "You a hating-ass nigga, Renello."

"It did give hater, Twin." Vello tried tapping my chest again, and I pushed his ass off once more.

"*It did give hater...* shut yo' side-jumping ass up. But anyway! I came here for answers, and I'm not leaving until I get 'em. So, you better make room in that handy-dandy notebook for my shit." Crossing my arms, I gaped my legs and sunk deeper into the chair, making myself as comfortable as possible.

"You niggas. Okay... go ahead, Renello. I'm listening."

"Man! We both got the same dilemma, and we want that shit eliminated," Vello said, butting in.

"Speak for yourself. We may have the same DNA, but we are not the same. I'm not fucking a married man's wife."

"And I'm not fucking my cousin! You just said you had my back, nigga!"

"And I do. I also told you when you ready to ride... I'm holding the reins. You ain't spoke on shit yet." I gritted, "And I ain't fucking my cousin!"

"Yet." Vello snickered.

"You do know we share the same DNA, so that baby that man's wife is carrying is mine, too, if we being technical."

"You do know when you and Pia have a baby, that baby mine too. And he or she will be my nephew-niece-cousin... if we being technical. Pussy."

Shio tossed his pen down and sat back in his chair. "So, you want to kill a nigga over some pussy that is theoretically his and not yours." He pointed at Vello before turning his head to face me. "And you?"

"Man, Pia on some other shit."

"See! You got bitch problems just like me." Vello grinned.

"Anyway, that Rio nigga done threw Pia a party, introducing her as his daughter and shit. She hasn't even talked to me about the party, and it's been a full day. I was shooting dice when the shit was going on, so by the time I looked at the Ring camera, her ass was back in bed, tucked and tipsy. Plus, she got picked up by the nigga's car service today." I was stressed, and I'm sure they heard that shit in my voice.

Pia had been getting up every day with a smile, dressing up and shit. She never told me where she was going. She would just hit me with a "see you later" and be on about her business. She could do what she wanted. I wasn't no controlling-ass nigga, and what went on between her father and her was their business. I had no right to clock her, even though she clocked me down to the fucking millisecond. I just didn't like not knowing what the fuck his intentions were. Dons were slick, ruthless, and calculated as fuck, no matter what fucking region they were from. Rio had me fucked up, though.

"Okay, that's her father from what I was told, right?"

"What's yo' point?"

"Yeah, nigga, what's yo' point? You on that nigga, Rio, dick?" Vello backed.

"Man... look, I ain't on nobody's dick but mine. See, I told you niggas! Y'all don't want advice. You just want to vent, and unfortunately, Shio's venting hours aren't in service at the moment."

"But you not doing shit but writing in that book!"

"In my own house, minding my own business. Y'all came over here fucking with me."

"Aite, cool. Tell me I'm wrong for not feeling that Rio nigga."

"Man, fuck Rio!"

Shio eyed Vello before shaking his head. "Let me guess...

the wife you fucking is, a.k.a. the forbidden woman Don was talking about in that classroom, a.k.a. Rio's long-lost wife?"

"And if it was?"

"Then meeting is adjourned. You two niggas gotta be the most goofiest niggas on the planet if you think I'ma entertain you going up against Rio for dumb-ass reasons."

"You the scariest Cuppacio. Get your head out the books and stop scribbling chicken shit," I spewed, and the words felt like venom coming out of my mouth. Shio's nonchalant attitude had me pissed.

"What Twin said! Fuck is you writing anyway?" Vello plucked the notebook from the desk.

"*Walk on the river. A city of her choice for forty-eight hours. Visit the winery. Take her to where I come from. Church date. Dinner at*—man! What the fuck is this bullshit?"

Vello tossed the book back on the desk, and Shio scooped it up, returning to his page. "None of your fucking business. You like to copy and shit. Back to what the fuck I was saying. You niggas may be different in a lot of ways, but one thing y'all have in common is lack of communication. Pia don't have to tell you shit. She's now the heir. If he is following the line of successions, she is next in line for the throne. Mecanio Mafia may be small, but they are mighty. You know how this mob shit go. Most shit she can't discuss with you because you not her fucking husband. You the play cousin that want to be her man, but too scared to voice that shit." Shio smirked, and I wanted to toss his ass in the fire that was cackling next to the bookshelf.

"I ain't scared of shit!"

"Oh, yeah? Well... why the fuck you still in the cousin zone?" It was so quiet you could time the milliseconds between the crackles in the fireplace. "Exactly." He focused back on Vello. "I told your ass from the jump what the fuck came with taken pussy. Now she pregnant?"

"I don't know. This nigga claim she is, but she ran off before I could get to the bottom of it and blocked me. At this point, taking Rio out is the only option."

"Fuck outta here! Rio would eat your ass for breakfast and dinner. I can't understand why the fuck is y'all plotting against that man when he has shown nothing but respect. Y'all up in this bitch upset about shit that belongs to him."

"Pia do not belong to that nigga."

"She don't? Cuz Dana says she come from his nut sack."

"Man, fuck that." I wasn't trying to hear none of this shit.

"Look... the best thing I can tell ya is communicate. You say ole girl blocked you? Do like Don said, and use your fucking resources. Find out where she lives and have a conversation with her. Get to the bottom of this baby situation. Rio has an heir now. He may just turn her over to you. I don't know the details of the marriage, and barely even knew the nigga was married, but I could imagine it being a business transaction since he don't like pussy."

"Pia ain't no heir." I couldn't stomach Pia belonging or being obligated to anyone but me.

"She is. Again, it's nothing you can do about that. It's her fucking birthright. The best thing you can do is talk to Pia. She may not be keeping shit from you; she is probably just unsure of how to approach you about it. Y'all lay beside each other every night. What the fuck do y'all talk about?"

"Nothing! This nigga giving back and foot rubs, praying Pia lets him get to third base when he still in the dugout!" Vello cackled, and I swear I was about to call Mama to cuss his ass out. This nigga was forever switching sides with his fake ass.

"Had your tired-ass been in the dugout, giving back rubs... you wouldn't have a possible baby floating out here."

Shio sighed at our back and forth. "Y'all need to talk to the women in your lives and Rio. That nigga controls the ports. How the fuck we gon' make money if we don't have access to the ports? We got a whole generation to feed. I'm done talking, though. I got Bible Study. Sit here and plot on your own death all you want, double-mint twins. We gon' put y'all away real nice."

Shio's hating ass wasn't talking about shit. I wasn't wrong about how I was feeling. Fuck Rio. He had some shit up his sleeve when it came to Pia, and I was going to eliminate his ass before he completed his task. She didn't need no fucking daddy. She'd gone seventeen-plus years without one and could go a lifetime more.

Pia ain't no fucking heir.

CHAPTER 10
MISSY

"Passion, I told you I don't have no baby on the way. That was my sister."

If I had a dollar for every time a nigga told me that, I would be rich as fuck by now. I was going to start a collection jar and fine these niggas every time they lie about babies and shit. Instead of calling him out and letting him know that one of the hoes in the club had already put me up on game about Richard and his sixth baby mama-to-be, I continued to entertain his lie. Hoes can't stand to see one of the moneymen give you attention because they felt like it took money out of their pockets, so they made it their business to snitch. They would tattletale in hopes that I would cut the nigga off, but I was the type of bitch that didn't cut a nigga off unless he handed me the scissors, rather it be voluntarily or involuntarily. All in all, bitches didn't move me.

"You listening to me," Richard asked as he stuffed his feet in his work boots. They'd seen better days. I didn't know if the brown color was from dirt or wear and tear. Had I seen the condition of his boots last night when I let his ass in after popping up over here unannounced again, I would have made him leave them bitches outside—where I should have left him. He'd better be glad that my car note and insurance were due, and I needed my pussy stroked. If it wasn't for those three things, he wouldn't have gotten past the threshold.

Folding my arms across my chest and making my short silk robe loosen, I ran my tongue across my top teeth. "Unh hunh."

I heard what he said, but I wasn't *hearing* him. I'd made it up in my mind that this was the last time I let Richard in my pussy. He'd already sent the Apple Pay, so his services were no longer needed. Granted, I didn't need shit this nigga had to offer because I worked my ass off every other night swinging my legs around the pole. Letting niggas play in my pussy was annoying as fuck at times, but it paid the fucking bills and had a bitch living good. Richard and his twenty-eleven baby mamas had no place in my life. None of them hoes had stepped to me. I was guessing because they didn't know he liked to take their kids formula, diaper, and shoe money and spend it on pussy, but I was just over his ass.

"See, that's why I rock with you, baby. You don't never give a nigga no back talk."

Richard looked up at me with a toothless grin as he double-knotted his boot. The nigga had woken up at the crack of fucking dawn, knowing a bitch like me didn't get up until noon. He made me get up because he thought he was about to get some more pussy. After realizing that was not happening, he made my bed, showered by his damn self, and was now about to carry his ass into whichever one of his baby mama's houses with my body wash on him at five in the morning. Niggas were stupid as fuck.

They didn't know how to come get the pussy right after work, then do some shit like go grocery shopping, grab flowers, and go home with a smile on their face. Women were so simple to please. All most of us wanted was to feel seen, heard, and for our nigga not to share his dick. At least a nigga that was sharing dick could do was cover all his damn tracks. If I was a nigga, my hoe would be around this bitch skipping because she was so happy. I would be a dog in the streets but would have my shit so air-tight that she would never even catch the fuck on.

Richard, sitting on the side of my perfectly made bed, patted his pockets while eyeing my frame seductively. I guessed he was trying to make sure I didn't clip his ass for that five hundred that was in his wallet. I may have been a lot of things, but a thief wasn't one. Did I go through his pockets on some nosey shit after putting his ass in a pussy coma? Absolutely. He was in my damn bed, in my damn house.

Once he was content that he had everything, he stood and pulled me to his chest. My hardened nipples brushed up against his navy Dickies work shirt. I wasn't turned on in the slightest. I was just cold as hell. My pussy was sore, too, and I was ready for this nigga to get the fuck on.

Staring in Richard's nutmeg-hued face, he had a boyish charm to him. We damn near stood at equal height, and that was with me only having on house shoes, so when I was in heels, I had him by a few inches. He could use a haircut, but his low cut still looked groomed. He'd been working seventy-hour weeks at the railyard, so I was guessing that he didn't have the time to go get a cut. Ugh. See, I knew too much about this nigga. He had friendly pockets, decent head, and every now and then, when he was trying to prove a point, he put a hurting on my pussy. Now, I had to go soak in some episome salt when his ass left because I had work tonight.

Richard, or Railroad as Pia called him, pecked my jaw like we were passing out church hugs, which was fine by me. I found it comical, though, that this nigga would put his entire head up my pussy but dodge my lips at all cause. How in the fuck you thought my pussy was cleaner than my mouth was beyond me? Plenty niggas could say they fucked, but not many could say they had my lips on any part of their body. More bitches knew what this mouth did than niggas, but go off, Railroad. Taking the initiative, I grabbed his hand and dragged him through my apartment. The sun wasn't out yet because it was four-thirty in the morning, so I walked through my apartment off memory. When I made it out of the darkness and into the living room, the lights from the buildings in the distance gleamed through the space. I opened the door and waited for his ass to walk out. Walking past me, he made sure he slapped my ass, and the nigga must've used all his strength because that shit echoed in the hallway and stung.

Hiding my irritation, I gave Richard a strained smile that probably had me looking like a crazy woman.

"I'ma be back through here this weekend. Ain't they doing sum'n at the club?"

And that was another reason this nigga was getting cut off. He kept up with my shit too much. This nigga even knew my fucking period and ovulation cycle. I knew because, magically, his ass had always tried to slide in it without a rubber when I was ovulating, and that shit was out of the question. He made good money at the railyard, but not enough to be making me baby mama number fifty-two, or whatever. That was the downside to me not fucking with wealthy niggas. Regular niggas sometimes had too many bills and shit. Granted, they made sure I was etched in their budget as one of their bills, but still, he didn't have enough to take me out of the game like that.

Richard liked to come home with me on the nights he knew the club was loaded with niggas that made his one hundred and seventy thousand dollars a year look like chump change.

As a matter of fact, many of them threw that in the club. Still, I didn't look at them outside of my money for the night. I didn't fuck with rich niggas.

"Richard, have a good day at work, baby. You not coming home with me this weekend. I'll call you when I want some more of *your* dick."

The grin on Richard's face dropped. "Man, what the fuck—"

"Excuse me? Are you okay, darling?" Mrs. Covington, my eighty-eight-year-old neighbor, cleared her throat behind us. Richard still had a scowl on his face while I, too, had dropped my smile and was ready to match his fucking energy. "Should I call the police?"

Richard looked me up and down, softened his face, and then took a step back. "No, ma'am... we good."

"Well, leave. You got what you came for, anyhow. Get on."

Chuckling, Richard all but ran down the hall. When he stepped onto the elevator, I glanced over at Mrs. Covington. At four-thirty in the morning, she was fabulous in a long, sparkling emerald, green dress, a thick, waist-length mink coat on her arms, flawless makeup on her Botox, wrinkle-free vanilla skin, large rollers in her grey hair, and a cigarette at the tips of her red nails. She'd been living here since way before I had, and I had a love-hate relationship with the old bird.

"I don't want to hear your shit today, Mrs. Covington."

Placing the Virginia Slim to her plump lips, which looked slightly bruised, more than likely from another round of Botox, she lit her cancer stick and inhaled deeply. Mrs. Covington was the closest thing I had to a grandmother these days, and she was my biggest hater. I fucked with her because she always came through on shit like packages and stalkers, but sometimes, her judging eye and smart-ass mouth wasn't warranted. At first, I thought she was racist because the bitch never would speak, but one day when I brought Pia over and fell asleep on her, I woke up to her and Mrs. Covington cackling like old friends. Pia had opened the door for our DoorDash order, and Mrs. Covington was out there, so they talked until our damn food got cold. Pia wasn't friendly at all and was as black as me, so I figured that I was the problem. We became cordial after that.

Blowing out a wad of smoke with the side of her mouth, Mrs. Covington kept her eyes on me. She didn't like to smoke in her apartment. Her home looked like it was straight out of the eighties, but that shit was glam. I didn't know what the fuck she did for a living in her past life, but her shit was nice and her ass was always dressed up anytime she left the house or came to the door. Old-ass classic cars that looked to cost a fortune were forever picking her up too.

"I have nothing to say, Hot Pants Number Two."

She always called me that shit. At first, it would piss me the fuck off because I felt like she was calling me a hoe, but then I remembered that I was indeed a hoe and let her make it. Plus, she was old as fuck, and old folks were always talking shit.

"Um. Okay, have a good day."

Prepared to close my door, she shook her head. Groaning, I slammed the door, snatched my purse from the bar, grabbed the pre-rolled blunt, and marched back outside the door. Standing across from her, I leaned against my door. Mrs. Covington tossed her lighter to me, and I lit my blunt. Instead of giving her the gold bedazzled lighter back, I held on to it. It was heavy as hell but pretty. Her nicotine, mixed with my exotic weed, created a funk in the hallway that I was surely going to be sent to the office. I needed to be high to deal with Richard and Mrs. Covington in the same hour.

"If you must know, I'm cutting his ass off. He too fucking clingy and got too many hoes."

Crossing her arm so that she could prop her elbow on her fist, she tapped her cigarette with her index finger to let the ashes fall. "He had no business spending the night in the first place. That's why he's clingy."

"Mrs. Covington, I got this." I took another pull from the blunt.

"Honey, you don't have the slightest clue what you're doing."

"What?"

Who was this old-ass white lady to tell me I didn't know what the fuck I was doing? I'd been stripping for over eight years, kept a brand-new car, lived in a lavish apartment, and shopped when I wanted to. I got a new wig every week, and not on no TikTok shop shit. I paid light bill money for my nails and had my way with these niggas. I'd been selling pussy and shaking ass for a long time. Hell, this pussy had been for sale since before I was legal. Was I on the corner with a sign? No. Did I let every nigga with a dollar hit? No. But, if I deemed you worthy, I would let a nigga pay to play.

We both continued to smoke our stress relievers of choice. Not only did this lady have fifty-plus years on me, but we also lived totally different lives. I was sure when she was my age, she was drinking from the whites-only signs and pouring milkshakes on the blacks that sat at the white-only diners. I could tell that she grew up with money. While I didn't grow up poor, I had it hard when my daddy died since my low-down-ass mama didn't want to do shit for me. Mrs. Covington was clearly living in retirement off her family's money, or maybe she'd married wealthy and was now a fabulous widow. What-ever the case was, she couldn't relate. We didn't have shit in common.

"I said, you have no idea what you're doing. That dwarf has not only spent way too many nights at your house, but I'm sure you aren't even charging him an hourly rate."

Choking off the smoke, I patted my chest, stunned at what this lady had just said. "Wh... *cough cough*... Hol' up... *cough cough*... What you tryna say?"

"So, you're hard at hearing, and you don't know business? Got it. Makes sense." This lady was on a roll, and I was ten seconds from sending her old ass to her grave that I was sure had already been paid for and dug. It was just waiting for her body to fill it. "Do you see yourself making this your long-time career?" She looked me up and down. "Because I don't."

"Hol' up—"

"No, you *hol' up*."

No the hell she didn't.

"Selling pussy is an art. While you have the sex appeal and the attitude, you don't have the heart for it, darling. You want a man. As much as you tell yourself you don't, you do. You know how I know?" She pointed to the elevator with the cigarette. "Every time one spends a little harder than the next, you let them come in and out whenever they feel like it. You tell yourself it's because they are spending the money, but there is a bigger part of you that believes they care about you for real, so you give them your version of boyfriend privileges."

My mouth was on the floor. This old-ass lady had read me the fuck down, and all I could do was stare. We stood in stunned silence before I mustered up the courage to challenge her statement. "You don't know shit about me." I spat.

"Oh, but I do, Hot Pants Number Two. You have one leg in the hoe life and another in the possibility of a domestic one. You're confused, and that leads you to put your mouth on women's lady parts. You don't even like women, for real. You want a man, but a man, or men, have hurt you. With the way you treat me, I think a woman has hurt you, too, somewhere along the line. Let me ask you this—"

"Oh, now you want to ask me some shit, old-ass lady?" I was heated. I glanced sharply around, eyes blazing like anyone else was outside listening to this embarrassment. The weed couldn't even calm my racing thoughts. My angry gaze swung over at Mrs. Covington, who seemed to not care at all that I was about to knock her the fuck out.

"Yeah, actually, I do. What do you think I do for a living?" she quizzed like I gave a damn.

"Besides being on your way to the grave?"

"Hot Pants Number Two, with the way that man just eyed you, I just might *outlive you*. Now, answer the question."

Shrugging my shoulders, I rolled my eyes.

"Okay, you're upset. But I don't care; you need to hear this."

"I don't need to do shit but stay black and die."

"You need to keep your pussy in your pants. You're not getting what it's worth, anyway, but that's neither here nor there." Mrs. Covington waved me off. "I have several acres of land in several parts of the U.S. My real estate portfolio is more than a mile long; this little apartment is just one of many. I've really only been here as long as I have to watch you."

I drew my head back. "Watch me?"

Oh, shit! I got an old-ass white lady stalking me now too.

"Hot Pants Number Two, no. I don't like no one's pussy but my own. But, over the years, I have done extremely well for myself, and you know why?"

"Nah. But I'm sure you about to tell me."

"Me not letting men spend the night is the reason."

"Hunh?"

"Male companions fund my life. I've been ticketing this kitty for over sixty-five years, and not one man can tell you they've spent the night. I also haven't had to deal with hundreds of men to earn the millions that are in my bank account."

Tossing my head back, I barked out a laugh. "Wait! So you telling me, you tricking niggas, Mrs. Covington?"

"I have companions that spend on me, yes. More than a few of them have been Negros.

'Hold up, now. You doing too much."

"I wasn't about to use the term... you did, but you get what I'm saying. A man like short guy would have never even been able to tell you what color my pretty little panties were, let alone dipped his stick in me. I can tell you that much."

I couldn't believe this shit. Here I was, thinking my neighbor was a damn trust fund baby, and she was a whole hoe. I couldn't wait to tell Pia.

"Spending money, though, is the least a man could do for me. I prefer assets for my time. I've been written in wills from prominent figures ranging from movie directors, CEOs of Fortune 500 companies, and presidents... with an S."

"I know you fucking lying. Put me in the game, coach. Not you the real-life walking Marilyn Monroe." My irritation turned into curiosity real quick, and now my eye was twitching at the thought of having all that Mrs. Covington alleged she had by selling pussy.

"Oh, honey... you're more like Ms. Monroe. She used to fall in love too. Me, though? I could never."

This lady was a hot-ass mess. But I was intrigued like hell and had so many questions. "If I wanted rich men, I could get them. They come with too much. They act like paying for pussy is a crime in public, but be all for it behind closed doors."

"And what's wrong with that? That's what I prefer. They don't ever have to acknowledge me. As long as I'm getting the assets, I can be a ghost in their world. I've never dealt with a scorned wife, a bitter ex, a prowling, jealous mother, or any of the sorts. Just A-list dinners, movie premiers where I come and go alone, acres, properties, and shopping sprees."

"You crazy."

"No, you're crazy. You end up with stalkers because you make yourself too accessible. Now, watch how hard it is to get rid of that poor chap. You said rich men like to do things in private like he isn't creeping out of here to go to an entire family. What's the difference? If you're going to sell it, you need to be getting the bang for your buck. Have you ever even seen me bring a man to my home? Besides, you wouldn't be mad about him waking you up from your sleep had he not spent the night to begin with."

I shook my head.

"The well very much still works. After they have given me the proper assets, I make them purchase a property for me, and only there is where I let them bed me."

"This is crazy! I can't believe you used to sell ass, Mrs. Covington."

"Used to? I told you it still works. I still have a fella or three I let keep me company. I have not only been able to take care of my entire family, but I've buried them all thanks to my companions. If you're going to get in the game, you have to be the best player on the team because, trust me, you won't be the only one on their roster. You care too much about other players, and you want to lock down the coach; that's your problem."

"I really don't."

"You do. That's why you won't let him come back this weekend. You figured him out when you shouldn't care to begin with. You care too much about what men think of you and not enough about what's in their bank accounts. So what if they don't want to kiss you? Yes, I see the way you look when they don't want to place their lips on yours. You shouldn't yearn for that anyhow, especially not from a half-ass paying customer. But you feel how you feel because you aren't recruiting within your league. Stop cutting these poor men off because they don't want to make you their wife. You don't want to be a wife to a barely-making-it man. If that's your prerogative, you want to be a wife to the richest grape on the vine."

"I cut all my niggas off, and it had nothing to do with them not wanting to be with me. It had everything to do with their turn being over. Richard was the last to go," I stated matter-of-factly.

I most definitely cut everyone off but for reasons different than what I told my high-class prostitute of a neighbor. Pia has a new status now. When I walked into Demise's mansion, I already knew I was in a different world. I was shocked that he'd even given me the okay. A hoe like me was so beneath them and their women. I could guarantee almost all of their wives had been virgins or close to it with no more than five partners. I've lost count of the men I'd fucked. But, for Pia's sake, I knew I had to calm that shit down. I didn't want her father or the other men in her life to think because I had a price on my pussy that I was low-hanging fruit.

Damn, I'd just proven this old bat right.

Mrs. Covington gave me a knowing look before letting her eyes drift down to my pussy area. She glared at it for a while, even though it was covered by the short robe, and then traveled back up to my face. "You cut them off, good. Leave them cut off. Hoeing isn't for you. And stop letting them fuck you like they're a jack rabbit. I know he isn't even toting that much down there to have you walking like that. He knows it's small, and that's why he tries to drill you through the mattress."

This lady had no filter at all.

"It's no man on earth that I have come across that I want to marry. Hoe is life, boo. Look at you; I think I'll be alright."

"You just haven't met the man to lock you down yet. But

you will."

"But you haven't met your man yet, Ms. Portfolio and Acres?"

"No, because I'm not a lover girl. I love properties. I love land. They aren't making land anymore, but men are born every second."

Well, damn.

"Well, help me find him then. Since you know what I want."

"You seem to like them a tad bit off-brand. But when you bring the right one around, I'll let you know... Anywho, I have a prime minister who has been trying to fly me out, and I couldn't because I've been looking out for you."

"Yeah, whatever." Pushing myself off the door, I typed the code to enter my apartment, leaving my neighbor in the hall. I would finish my blunt in the comfort of my home that these low-budget niggas had paid for.

"Hot Pants Number Two? It's *Ms*. Covington. I've never married any of these bozos."

Slamming the door, I added the chain and lit the blunt using the lighter I'd stolen. Instead of plopping down on the couch, I went into my bedroom and did not stop until I got to the shower. Turning it on, I took a choke from the blunt as I went into my closet while my water got up to my desired temp. Standing in the middle of the walk-in, I eyed the selection to see what I wanted to wear. It was barely five in the morning, but I was wide awake after that damn talk.

My eighty-eight-year-old neighbor had more motion than me, and we did the same damn thing for a living. She allegedly had properties and had been left in wills just by being a hoe. Then here I was, and all I had was an apartment I was renting, a car note, wigs, and a couple pieces of designer. It was crazy how one person's words could knock you off your damn pedestal. Regardless of *Ms.* Covington's observations, my niggas were staying cut off. I cared more about my friendship with Pia than I did dick and money. It would crush me if she had to choose because, as much as she loved me, I knew she would choose her family. My friend had always been about her family, which was one of the things I loved about her. I wouldn't let her choose me over her family, even if she had only recently been connected with them.

Deciding I wanted to look like a bad bitch even at the crack of dawn, I snatched down a pair of jeans ripped at the hips, a long-sleeved, sporty crop top, and would pair it with Travis Scotts. By the time I finished this blunt, I wanted to be able to eat good, and breakfast was on my taste buds.

Dropping my robe into the hamper, I took another pull from the blunt before putting it out in the sink and stepping into the shower. Grabbing my loofah, I frowned when I felt that it was already wet from this nasty-ass nigga washing his ass with it. I tossed that motherfucker over the glass door. That was too damn nasty. Who the fuck washes up with someone else's shit? Not letting the thought ruin my morning, I used the dry washcloth that I had provided him to scrub my body down, and thirty minutes later, all remnants of Richard were down the drain.

After washing my face and brushing my teeth, I moisturized my body and slid on a pair of Savage Fenty cotton thongs and the matching bra. I usually went for lace, but the cut of these underwear where high enough that they wouldn't show through the slits of the high-waisted pants. I gave myself the munchies and was too lazy to do my skincare, so I snatched my bedding off the mattress and headed off. I would wash it when I got back. I don't know why Richard liked to play with me. There was no fucking way I was not washing my sheets. He just wanted a man to smell him on my bedding or find that

Lifestyle wrapper that he thought I didn't see him toss under my comforter. He did too much, and that's why it was over with him.

Looking through the peephole to make sure the coast was clear, I jetted down the hallway to the elevator. I couldn't deal with any more of Marilyn Monroe today. By the time I was behind the wheel of my Benz, I had an idea of where I wanted to eat. There was a cute diner in the heart of downtown that was only open until two in the afternoon. Usually, when I went, there were only Caucasians there. Say what you want, but anywhere the white folk packed out usually had good food. We had them on the cooking, but they had us on the taste in restaurants.

The diner had its own parking, so after finding a spot for my car, I grabbed my shades from the compartment, slid them on my face, and placed my Louis bag on my shoulder. The leather on the strap was starting to peel from wear and tear since it was my everyday bag. Another item to replace—too bad I had no more niggas to replace it.

A bell dinged above my head once I entered the buzzing restaurant, and the smell of buttery pancakes and sweet maple syrup filled my nostrils. I was about to smash so hard.

"Welcome to Sunrise Farmhouse! Just one?" The cheery hostess with blonde hair, ocean eyes, and rosy cheeks grinned.

"Yes, just—"

"Nah... make it two."

The hairs on the back of my neck rose as the cashier's eyes traveled from me to behind me. I could feel the deep voice a little too close for comfort, even though he wasn't actually touching me. His voice wasn't so deep that it sounded like the damn boogie man, but it had baritone. His cologne overshadowed the tantalizing aromas spewing from the kitchen. Judging by the way the hostess's eyes lit up and cheeks brightened, he had to be nice-looking. Too bad I wasn't on hoe shit no more. He wouldn't be joining me for breakfast— not now or ever.

Finally wanting to get a look at him, I turned so that I could curse him out in front of these white folk but paused. Him. Brown skin covered in tattoos, bulky arms underneath a sweater, a blinding necklace, and white teeth made up the person smiling at me. Gotdamn. I'd been seeing him more and more in the media lately, and I was embarrassed at how many times I'd watched his performances. When Pia told me she'd gone backstage, it was the first time in my life that I'd ever been jealous of my bestie.

Instead of cursing him out as I'd planned, I turned back to the hostess to confirm our seats. She fumbled with the menus and silverware but eventually led us to our booth. I imagined we looked out of place, walking through the restaurant, but no one gave us funny looks. I wasn't paying attention anyway; I was concentrating on tossing this ass as I walked. I slid into the booth first, and once he sat across from me, I had to gain my composure.

Stop acting like a groupie, bitch.

"I am so sorry to do this," the hostess said just as he started to get comfortable. Her face now matched her cheeks. She pulled out a pen from the pocket of her uniform top and snatched a napkin from the syrup caddy next to the window that the table was pushed against.

"Can I please have your autograph, Essex?" She held the napkin and the pen out for him to sign. This girl looked like she listened to nothing but Taylor Swift, and she was fangirling over this tattooed, iced-out black nigga.

"I hope you don't mind. Oh my goodness! I can't wait to tell my boyfriend, *the Essex* is in my dad's restaurant!"

Chuckling, Essex signed the autograph and passed her

back the pen. "Oh, she don't run shit. You ain't have to ask her permission," he said as he smiled, and it made my already sore pussy thump.

"What's your name, pretty?"

"Oh my goodness! It's Haley!"

"I'll take a picture with you after I fill this fine-ass woman's belly, Haley. Cool?"

"Yes! Thank you! Okay, I'll stop being weird now." She scurried off, and I couldn't help but laugh.

Essex looked so damn good and smelled even better. The tattoos on his face should have made him look like a madman, but instead, it did the opposite. They were perfectly placed.

"So, what do I owe the pleasure of a rap star wanting to eat with me?"

"I ain't nobody, baby. Just a nigga that was doing some shit in the studio, and real niggas fucked with it."

"From the looks of it, more than niggas fucked with it." I tossed my head to a jittery Haley, who was stealing glances at us.

"I see," he added, and we both chuckled before his chuckle turned into a smirk.

Picking up my menu to escape his death stare on me, I scanned it, hoping that I wasn't appearing like Haley. I was nervous as hell and didn't know why. I'd met all types of niggas. I may not have added them to my roster, but I'd danced for plenty of famous niggas. Still, this one in front of me that had only been famous a week, it seemed, had me shaking like I was in church.

By the time I picked out what I wanted, he was still staring. "You not gon' look at the menu?"

"Nah, I come here all the time. Plus, what I want ain't printed on it."

Folding my arms on the table, I leaned in. "So you telling

me you want to smack on this pussy?"

One thing about the business I was in, all it took was for me to be in a man's presence for a few seconds, and I knew if he wanted to fuck or not. Some men came to the club strictly for a dance, others came just for an escape and didn't want a dance, and then there were some that were ready to pay whatever to get that nut up out of them. Essex wanted to fuck me. I knew he did the night of the Halloween party when he was all dressed up in his vampire attire.

His lids lowered as he ran his tongue across his bottom lip. "You know what the fuck going on."

Essex was fine, no doubt. Rapping was extremely fitting to him because he for sure had the aura of a rapper. Not one of those obnoxious, sixty-chains, skinny jean-wearing rappers either. He was laid back with his shit, almost like a young Method Man. However, niggas loved to say they wanted to fuck, but when I had my hands out, it was a different story. This man didn't know me, so I was pretty sure he didn't know what I did for a living. I'd never seen him in the club. I'd only seen him on social media and at the Halloween party. That was it.

I didn't normally talk to men unless I bagged them at the club. That way, they knew exactly what it was they were getting. Even if I did get a man out in public, ten times out of ten, they'd already seen me in the club. Outside of Essex being on my no-fuck list due to his new rising fame, him being oblivious to my tendencies had me ready to hop up out of this booth and go to Waffle House down the street. But he looked good, smelled great, and Ms. Covington's words telling me that I was selling pussy to the wrong group of men kept me planted in the wooden booth. Our waiter showed up, and we placed our drink orders, which were orange juice for me and water for him.

The silence was killing me, so I finally spoke up. "You might not want to pay to play, baby. Plus, I don't do famous niggas."

Essex was slumped in his seat across from me, and his long legs brushed mine ever so often, leaving me to fight the urge to shudder. "I ain't famous."

"Upcoming... same thing."

"Nah. It really ain't," he spoke dryly. Either this man really didn't give a damn about being posted on every blog recently, or he was one hell of an actor. Either way, I was turned on.

We were served our drinks, and I wasted no time removing the paper from the straw and gulping down my juice. Our silence was comfortable, but I was almost embarrassed that I didn't know what to say around him. On one hand, I wanted to treat him like a customer, but on the other, I was enjoying him in my space. Him not knowing what I did for a living was almost refreshing. Any other man would have brought up me dancing for them within the first two seconds of us co-existing. He did say he wanted to fuck, but hell, I wanted to fuck, too, so it was what it was.

"So, what you doing up so early, Missy? You look and smell too good, so I know you haven't been out all night."

"I was woken out of my sleep and couldn't fall back to sleep. So, here I am."

"And that nigga couldn't wait until the sun was up to leave?"

"I guess not." I shrugged.

I was trying not to go ballistic over the fact that he knew my name—my real name. My tricks didn't even know my name. Hell, I had bank accounts that they sent money to in Passion's name since it was an LLC. Yes, I paid my taxes with this pussy. I knew he heard one of the ladies call my name at the party and wondered if one of the men had told him my business. Hopefully, the mob didn't gossip like bitches.

"Are you two ready to order?" The waitress showed back up with her pen and pad out.

"I'll take the chicken and waffles with a side of spinach and cheese eggs." I handed her my menu with a smile.

"I want the steak, medium rare, with breakfast potatoes and an egg white veggie omelet." Essex passed his menu to her as well. Once she had our orders, I took another sip, wishing it was his cum that I was drinking.

Stop being a freak hoe.

"No pancake or waffle?"

"Nah. Ion too much fuck with sweets like that."

I don't think I've ever encountered a man that didn't like sweets, especially those that got high. I loved me some sweets. I didn't function well if I didn't load up on them when I was on my period and ovulating. I needed to get my ass in somebody's gym ASAP because all that sleeping late shit and eating breakfast after work was going to catch up with my ass one day.

"So you gon' let me when we leave here?"

"Let you do what?"

"Pay to play."

Oh, he's serious. "Even though another nigga just climbed out of it hours ago? You sure you want to spend your money here?" I cocked my head.

Even my hoe ass had my limits. I tried not to fuck back to back like that. To be honest, I did more dancing than I did fucking. Every trick had their turn. Random niggas just weren't running in my pussy night after night.

"What the fuck that got to do with me? I'm just tryna get in where I fit in, sweetheart."

Oh, he's a charmer. "Um. Okay... we shall see."

"OH, FUUUUCK! WAIT, ESSEX! WAAAAAAAIIIIIT!"

Bent over on the king-sized bed of the condo he dragged me to after he stuffed my stomach with eggs and waffles, I reached back to push Essex back some. His hard body was behind me while his dick was digging my guts out as if he was digging for gold.

"Move yo' fucking hands, sweetheart." He gritted and gently grabbed my hand. I didn't expect him to place soft kisses on my knuckles as he kept on banging my back in. My pebbled and pierced nipples brushed up against the sheets, creating a beautiful friction. Letting my hand fall, he slowly pushed his palms down the dip of my back. The way he was handling my body versus the way he was poking my pussy didn't match at all.

"Hold up! I'm sorrre! I'm so sore, baby," I cried out.

When Essex brought me to the condo that was only about five minutes away from the restaurant, I wanted to turn the fuck around after seeing what he had tucked in his boxer briefs. His dick was so pretty and brown. The fat mushroom tip oozing pre-cum had me dropping to my knees and taking him down my throat. Minutes later, he was bending me over the bed, and here we were.

Using his large hands to split my ass open as far as it could go, he pushed inside of me with full force. Railroad had already hopped around in my pussy, and now, Essex was murdering my shit. He pulled his dick in and out at a pace that was just right, causing the pleasure to be pure and explosive.

"Do it look like I give a fuck about it being sore? You wet as fuck, sweetheart. The pussy not complaining. Shit tight too! You done letting little niggas get up in here?"

"Ummmmm, Essex!" I had never been vocal during sex. As much as I got fucked, I was usually silent, with a moan slipping out here or there. The men were typically so happy to be fucking a fantasy that they talked enough shit. Now, here I was, acting like I was being killed. Shit, it felt like it.

"Want me to lick on it, sweetheart? Want me to make it feel better?"

"Fuuuuuck!"

Essex pulled his dick out, flipped me around like I weighed nothing, and my eyes instantly went to his sheathed hanging muscle. My mouth water just thinking about how I'd gagged all over it minutes ago.

Grabbing his heavy dick, his sexy ass dropped to his knees and buried his face in my pussy.

"Shit!" Propped up on my elbows, I tossed my head back as he munched on my box. His thick tongue swiped over my entire mound before he sucked on my clit. "Ahh shiiiit! Don't stop!"

Pinching my nipples, I bit down on my lip as he stared a hole into me. The way our eyes were locked in, I could feel the fucking souls tying a fucking knot. Essex's body was a work of fucking art. His tattoos covered damn near every inch of him. I bucked my body in his face and grabbed the back of his head as I rode his mouth. Yes, the dick was huge, but I was a nasty bitch. I could match his fucking freak any day of the week.

A moan of ecstasy escaped my lips as he lapped up all of my juices. I said Railroad had good pussy eating skills, but Essex was proven to be a fucking A-plus student. Fuck that, he was the professor.

My whole being flooded with desire as I felt my stomach cramp. "I'm 'bout to come all over your face! Ummmmm!"

Shaking his head did it. He moved his tongue at unnatural speeds, causing me to become undone.

"Ohhhhhhhhhhh! Eat this pusssyyyyyy!"

Essex slurped me up like a milkshake as I creamed all over his tongue. He made sure to lap it all up, and as I was catching my breath, he grabbed my waist as if my thick ass weighed nothing, stood straight up, and slid my throbbing womb down his dick.

Placing my legs around his waist, I locked one arm around his neck and used my other hand to grab my titty. When I let my long tongue travel down and lick my own breast, his brows furrowed. Licking my titties was one of my specialties in the bedroom. I only really did it when I was with a woman, but Essex was special.

Our bodies were in exquisite harmony with one another, even though his dick was hurting the fuck out of me. The pleasure outweighed the pain, and each time I heard his raspy voice, I got wetter.

"Damn, you doing it like that? You taking this dick, too, sweetheart. I know he big, but you got it." His cocky ass smirked. Standing in the middle of the room, he held my waist as I rode him like I knew he'd never been rode before. Showing his strength, he hooked one arm around my waist and leaned back a bit. "You a fucking beast, baby."

Sweat trickled down my face while I jumped up and down on his dick. Essex was sporting a growl on his handsome face that had me resisting the urge to kiss him. I wanted to suck his lips so bad, but instead, I kept pleasing my titties. I knew how men were about their mouths and strippers. He didn't know I was a stripper, but I was still a hoe he didn't know.

"I'm 'bout to bust sweetheart," he moaned, and that shit was the sexiest thing I've ever heard.

"This dick hurt so bad!" I screamed out.

Electricity seemed to race through me as I came again for the second time. Essex lifted me from his dick, snatched the condom off, and nutted all over my abdomen. That wasn't good enough for me, so I hopped down, letting my knees hit the floor, and relaxed my throat as I received all of his warm semen. You would have thought he ate pancakes the way his cum was so sweet.

"Fuck, sweetheart! Swallow all this fucking nut!"

With tears in my eyes, I peered up at him while draining him dry. When his eyes rolled to the back of his head, I knew I had him. Grabbing the back of my head, he snatched me off his dick and made me stand. Pushing his body into mine, he bit down on his bottom lip and backed me into the bed.

"You can keep up with this dick, hunh?" he asked while lying on top of me. I was trying to catch my breath, but if he wanted another round, I was on go.

Grabbing my throat, he crashed his lips into mine and sucked my tongue into his mouth. Caught off guard, I kept my eyes open, and his crazy ass did too. We were tongue-wrestling on the bed while staring into each other's souls. He was too fucking dangerous.

Drawing his head back, he pecked my lips twice more before flipping us around and scooting up to the headboard. He was too damn strong. After pulling the comforter up around our bodies, I lay on his chest and listened to his heart drum. This man had fucked me senseless.

"I can leave. I don't want you to get in trouble."

I knew he had a woman—he had to. With dick like this, he had to be attached to someone. My legs were way too weak to be tussling with a bitch. I needed a good eight hours of sleep and a long bath before I was good for a fight.

"Man, you gon' lay your pretty ass right here. I'ma grown-ass man. I don't get in trouble. Plus, I'm single."

"Not according to the blogs." I was talking too damn much and sounding like an entitled groupie.

"Aye..."

Angling my head, I looked up at Essex. My pussy thumped, and she knew damn well she couldn't take him again, at least not right now. His brown skin was covered in a sheen of sweat that made him glow like a Greek God.

"I'm single. I got one baby mama. I got two sons by her. They two and four named Elias and Elijah. I'm not fucking her, either. I'm just out here visiting my people, but I'm a Chicago nigga. I think you just gave me a reason to hang around a lil' longer, though."

"You full of shit!" I giggled.

"Nah, but for real, I like it here. I like you too," he confessed.

"I'm not nobody to like," I shamefully admitted.

Grabbing my ass under the cover, he placed a kiss on my lips. "Shid, you a lot to like, baby."

I loved the fact that he didn't handle me like I was a fucking animal. He was firm but gentle. He didn't slap my ass or act like he was about to choke me to death. Other men I'd been with were way too rough. Just because I danced didn't mean I didn't want to be handled with care.

"I know one thing, though, I'ma have to caution myself with yo' ass, or you gon' fuck around and give me a daughter."

Before I could reply, he reached over into the nightstand and pulled out a fat knot of money. I could see the hundred-dollar bill on top but didn't know if it continued throughout. Niggas were known to flaunt. It could be ones underneath the rest of that.

"Ion know about the daughter part, baby. I'm just here for a good time," I let his ass know off the rip. Ms. Covington probably was right about me being a lover girl in a sense, but baby mama me? I might have entertained the idea with a few tricks I'd fallen in like with over the years, but I wasn't that type of hoe. I knew girls that would be jumping up and down at those words because popping babies out of their pussies for rich niggas was their hustle. Not me, though. I wanted the money without the baby.

"Now, who not ready to pay to play? But you sore, though, so I ain't even gon' get the chance to empty my safe in the closet."

Grinning, I licked my lips and slid down his body. In an instant, his dick was hitting the back of my throat while his toes threw up gang signs.

"Fuck! You *my* bitch now. Tell them other niggas it's a wrap. I'm ya fucking sponsor baby. Use a nigga up. Shit! Swallow that dick, Missy!"

Sore pussy and all, I needed that nigga to empty that fucking safe. With a dick that could rearrange my insides tickling my esophagus, I reached down and toyed with my pussy. Rap niggas weren't so bad after all.

My roster has room for one, right?

CHAPTER 11
VELLO

The weather continued to drop in the city, but no matter how cool it was, I was always hot. I'd gone from walking around with sweaters on to now, at the head of November, in shorts and short sleeves. Today, I had no choice but to put on clothes that were appropriate for the weather. I had only been dressed for thirty minutes and was already burning the fuck up. The sickness, though? The sickness was worse than the fucking hot flashes. I didn't know what type of fucking illness that had climbed up in my stomach, but I was blaming Aerie. Ever since she had given me that dry-ass head, I hadn't been feeling right. I should have never taken my ass over there to begin with, knowing children were germy as fuck.

To add more to my already fucked up circumstances, I was spitting all the fucking time. It had gotten to the point that I was now walking around with a fucking spit cup. I'd gone from having a red cup full of drank to a red cup full of saliva. This shit was ridiculous. I hadn't even had time to dwell much on Big Mama's ass. She'd run out of the fucking concert and shit. I knew it had to do with her and Essex's past, and I knew if I dug deep enough, I would end up finding some shit that I didn't like. I'd planned on getting up with her ass, though, because if she was buying pregnancy tests and shit, we had a lot to discuss.

"Name?"

The big nigga guarding the door at the dungeon got on my fucking nerves. He knew my fucking face, knew my fucking name, but always liked to test my fucking gangster anytime I was here. Then when I got down to the bottom, either the nigga teleported down there and would be on the same shit, or his twin was just as much of an asshole as he was. Here I was, standing outside this secluded-ass place, dapper as fuck in a suit, dress shoes, iced the fuck out, but looking dead as fuck in the face with a spit cup in my hand.

A wave of nausea hit me like a tsunami. Closing my eyes, I took a deep breath and counted to ten. Usually, my nausea lasted ten seconds. I was now able to distinguish between having to actually throw up and just being nauseated. When my mouth became overly watery and the nausea didn't subdue, I knew it was time to throw up. When the nausea did subdue and my mouth became overly watery still, it was time to spit. Knowing it was spit time, I opened my eyes, held the cup to my lips, and hawked in it.

"You know my fucking name. Unless you want me to toss this cup of spit in yo' fucking face, let me the fuck in, big-ass nigga. I ain't in the fucking mood."

I wasn't even a rude-ass nigga. That shit was my brother's personality. I wasn't feeling good, and hadn't been feeling good for weeks. My dick was hard constantly, but I was too damn sick to even get some pussy, and my bitch that wasn't really my bitch, was on the run. I wasn't up for this shit at all.

This wide nose, meaty forehead-ass giant pressed down on

his earpiece, whispered some shit, and then stepped aside to let me in.

"Should have done that shit in the first fucking place."

Bumping my shoulder against his forearm since the nigga was taller than me, I tried to break his shit. I'd only made my own shoulder burn in the process, but I shook it off. As I stepped into the building, the dark coldness of it took over, and usually, the creepiness of it all fucked with my mental, but I was too sick to give a fuck. These days, I was too damn sick to do anything. I was too sick to eat, too sick to wash my ass, too sick to fuck Big Mama, and too sick to even fucking breathe. Everything had me hurling over the damn toilet. If it was up to me, I would be in the fucking bed, but I had my meeting with Reuchie and Don today and didn't need to hear them niggas mouths if I didn't show the fuck up.

By the time I made it to the end of the sixteen hundred steps, I was drenched in sweat, had spit three times, and was now thirsty as hell. I couldn't even keep fucking water down but still forced myself to drink it. Hell, I wasn't eating shit, so without water, I would bend over and fucking die. I had no fucking idea that a weak-ass stomach virus would be the thing that took me out. Looking it up online, I saw that it was contagious and being the considerate-ass nigga that I was, I came prepared. Pulling the light blue medical-grade paper mask out of my suit jacket, I placed it on my face. Thankfully, giant number two wasn't guarding the door to the conference room, which was at the opposite end of the casino, so once I had my mask in place, I pushed open the double doors.

"I thought we was gon' have to send some niggas to come find you."

Don, Reuchie, Rut, and Matteo were sitting in seats at the round table that had maybe about fifty chairs pushed up to it. The table was huge in circumference, and I knew it was Don's idea to even get some shit like this customized. I'd never even seen fifty niggas at this table at a time. Usually, when all the mobs met, we did so at the warehouse. The dungeon was normally reserved for underground fun. But, here I was.

"Nah. I adhere to my promises. I didn't know I needed the whole mob for my meeting, though."

Nudging my head at everyone to speak. I took a seat, creating equal distances between all of us, and sat my cup on the table in front of me. If I wasn't down so fucking bad right now, I would smile at the way all of us black niggas were in here looking dapper as fuck. We had that shit on. Granted, Don and Reuchie were always in an expensive-ass suits, but Matteo in one was a rarity. Even though that nigga looked like he didn't want to be here, but shit, that was all the time for him, he looked sharp as fuck. That nigga hated us all, though. He only fucked with his wife and his daughter. He fucked with Don a little bit and Lorenzo a little bit more than Don.

Reuchie eyed my cup, and Don looked at me as if I had shit on my face. Rut was the only one sitting back cool as a cucumber; the rest of these niggas seemed to need pussy just as bad as I did.

"Nigga, if you sick, you could have rescheduled this shit." Matteo frowned.

"I got on a mask, got hand sanitizer in my pocket, and it's a six-foot distance between us all. I think you'll be fine." I smiled behind my mask.

Matteo just stared at me, and I stared at his ass right the fuck back.

"It's good to see you, Vello," Reuchie greeted.

"Likewise. I didn't know all of you would be present today, so I'm a bit skeptical, but I ain't been doing shit, so let's meet."

Don turned his head so hard that I heard his neck pop. "Did this nigga just say he ain't been doing shit?" He pointed and was looking at Rut, but I knew the question was rhetorical as fuck.

"That's exactly what the fuck I said." These niggas knew by now I wasn't no non-confrontational motherfucker.

I knew Don was owed a certain level of respect because this was his shit, but I wasn't up for any bullshit today. Shio had already told me I would be in for a rude awakening when it came to this meeting, but in all honesty, as long as I was able to walk up out of this bitch, I could handle it.

"You know... every fucking day I ask myself if I should have killed you lil' niggas too. Since y'all have come into my organization, y'all have been a thorn in my fucking side. But, fuck all that! You absolutely right. Y'all love to say... *y'all ain't been doing shit*, and that is the fucking problem!"

"Nah, Don, them niggas do shit. They just do the *wrong* shit," Matteo added.

Holding my left hand up, I gave Matteo the middle finger. My mouth watered, so I removed my mask and spit in the cup. This time, frowns were etched on everyone's face, while Reuchie's was one of pure disgust.

"So..." Don sat back in his leather chair. "You finally figured out who the fuck it was that you been fucking, hunh?"

My ears became hot, and all of a sudden, this itchy-ass suit felt like it was too tight. I thought about Discover way too fucking much. She ran the fuck out of that concert, leaving her daughter like I was the damn babysitter. Technically, Pia had Lil' Chef, but still, it was the principle. I didn't know if she had run back home to her dick gobbling-ass husband or what, but I was liable to do her ass dirty when I saw her, and I wasn't even on no shit like that. It wasn't my fault that she was married. She should have never given me the pussy.

Oh, shit! What if she gave me something she caught from that nigga? I hadn't been sick until I met her.

"You know this is prohibited, right?" Reuchie asked.

"What's prohibited?" I feigned ignorance.

"You're fucking Don Rio Mecanios' wife. His fucking wife! This is the same man who has given you loads of information, game, and connections for nothing in return, and you use his wife as a cum rag? All of the bitches in this city, and you go after her?" Reuchie was so mad that he was spitting. He needed to be the motherfucker in the mask.

"Man, look. How the fuck was I supposed to know that she was his wife? Y'all acting like I was on a mission to purposely seek her out. I haven't proposed to the girl or shit. I fucked a couple times, and dassit. I haven't even talked to her," I lied through my fucking teeth. I'd called her ass so many fucking times that her number was the only one in my call log on all of my phones. I was fucked up behind Big Mama and her tight-ass pussy.

Don twisted his lip, calling my ass out, but I waved him off. "Look. We didn't bring you here to clock what you do with your dick. Don Mecanio is an essential part of this organization. His wife? She's off-fucking-limits! You need to schedule a sit down with him ASAP and hope and pray he hears you out."

Removing my mask, I spit again. "I'm not doing shit. Fuck that nigga. Me and my brother will go up against that nigga if he wants smoke. I respect all y'all, so I'll remove myself from this organization so that your business with him won't waiver and handle my business."

Don looked amused and pissed. "So, you mean to tell me, you by your fucking self gon' go against a Don? Not only a Don, but a Don that runs the fucking ports?"

"I won't be by myself. My brother not fucking with that nigga either. He got me."

"Wait. These niggas really is dumb as fuck! You and your lovesick-ass brother want to go up against one of my biggest allies because of pussy that belongs to him and pussy that came from him?"

"You can put it however you want to put it, but yeah."

Don slapped the table and barked out a laugh. "These niggas stupid. But you want to crash out? Cool. I'ma do you one even better. I'm giving you the chance to sit down with Rio. You and your brother. Discover does not meet the criteria Reuchie has set for the requirement of wives for many reasons, but... if you can sit down with Rio, apologize to him for fucking his wife, and convince him to hand her over to you, then she can marry into us after divorcing him." Don reasoned.

"Man... I ain't sitting down with that nigga. I fucked that girl, and it's over with."

"Nigga! That shit ain't over with! You didn't just fuck! You left your mark, nigga! Why the fuck you think you spitting in a cup and shit! Matta fact... take that mask off, goofy-ass nigga! You not sick; you just got that bitch pregnant!"

My stomach dropped at Don's revelation, but I tried to keep my cool. My brother had already said she was, but that nigga said anything to piss you off at times. I'd only fucked that girl three times, so how in the fuck did I have her pregnant? I've fucked plenty of bitches and never had a pregnancy scare.

"You dusty-ass Chicago niggas will not bring my shit down. I done had to kill my family and y'all's, do harsh-ass time in the Feds, and shake hands with muthafuckas I don't respect, not even a little bit, for this organization. I refuse to let niggas that don't know how to pull out fuck me over. First ya other cousin damn near kill my sister, and now you and ya brother trying to play with my money. You niggas need to make it right with Rio! Y'all think y'all more ignorant than me? I'm Demise Rinaldi! The Don of all fucking Don's! Nigga, I invented the word crash-out! I can guarantee you that you can't get up with me on your most stupidest day. Make this shit right! And relay the message to ya brother because ion feel like seeing your face twice. Get the fuck out!"

Standing, I knocked over my cup and bubbly spit in clear and yellow mucus spread across the table.

"Oh, shit. I'm going to be sick!" Reuchie stood, clutching his stomach, and ran out of the room.

"My bad. I'll clean it up—"

"Nigga! Did some panties just fall outcho ass?" Matteo asked, causing all of them niggas to lean in their chairs to look toward the floor. Sure enough, Big Mama's panties from the night we fucked in the car lay to the right of my chair on the floor. Bending down to grab them, I stood back up unashamed. I never gave a fuck about these niggas opinions, and I wasn't going to start now.

"I don't even wanna know. Just get the fuck out, bruh."

Shrugging, I grabbed my cup, made sure the panties were back in my pocket, and made my fucking exit. Don and Matteo's mixed-breed asses looked like they wanted to gun me the fuck down. Them niggas weren't talking about shit. I had a handle on my shit. I wasn't sitting down with Rio's ass. Their allegiance didn't have shit to do with me.

Pulling my phone out, I texted one of the other mob recruits as I waited for the elevator. I wasn't taking the fucking stairs to go back up. My fucking chest was hurting on the way down here. When my phone dinged, I grinned. This nigga claimed he could get anyone's information, so I was about to put his ass to the test. I wasn't going to go see, Rio but it was time for me to face his wife. Talking about she fucking pregnant. Who the fuck gets pregnant that damn fast? Why in the fuck wasn't she on birth control any fucking way?

Let me find out my little soldier foolproof.

CHAPTER 12
ESSEX

Ever since the trip to Chicago, a nigga has been living in the studio. My mixtape, that really started off on some I think I can shit, has been keeping a nigga busy as fuck. In the span of a few weeks, I now had an official deejay. Bella's ass was on my fucking nerves, but she was a beast at the social media shit. I'd been receiving a plethora of calls and messages from everyone between labels and managers. Thanks to Bella conducting interviews, we found the perfect manager: an African by the name of Ekon, and he's only twenty-three. He was the one who had been managing Reaper before he was killed. I was skeptical about his ass at first because he was young as fuck, and hell, look at where Reaper was at.

Yeah, that nigga Reaper was getting buzz, but apparently, he wasn't busy enough because he was posted up in the hood when he was gunned down. I'd even thought Bella had only hired him because she was being fast, but he'd been on his fucking zoom. He was showing and fucking proving. I had seven shows lined up starting the week of Thanksgiving that won't finish until the second week of December. On day one,

214

he was on his shit. I didn't know if it was because he wanted to be sure I wouldn't end up like Reaper, so he wanted to keep me booked and busy, but the nigga hadn't let up. He didn't have to worry about that, though. I didn't know the last time I'd done some ignorant, young nigga shit. I used to do missions with the Cuppacios strictly for survival in the beginning, but had long transitioned from that. I was a businessman now.

Ekon had not only set up the shows, but he'd scored me courtside seats at a few games just so that my face could be plastered on the jumbotrons. This week alone, I not only had photoshoots but also two interviews for viral podcasts that I had to fly out for. In the morning, I had a meeting with a lawyer to see if she was a good fit for the team. This shit has been happening so fucking fast that I barely had enough time to breathe and take it all in. As soon as I landed back in Jagoda Bay this morning, I'd planned on going back to the condo that I'd just signed a six-month lease on in the same building as the Airbnb and rest, but Ekon was calling my ass with a last-minute booking. So, here I was, surrounded by pretty naked women with the mic in my right hand and a stack of ones in my left. I must admit, this was by far my favorite booking.

My manager explained to me not to rap because the promoter had only paid for an appearance, but somehow, they'd brought the mic to my booth, and I was rapping as pussy was being popped in my face. My niggas were to my left and my right, and behind them was a cameraman snapping pictures that would be all over the blogs before I walked out the door and called it a night. I could see why they called this shit the fast life because mine hadn't stopped moving since I did the Fall Ball concert.

"I like a freak bitch
One that's gone get sloppy on the meat
Not no neat shit

Tell me you can take the dick
And I'ma keep yo' secret
Baby daddy blowin' up yo' phone
He's a weak bitch
I'ma real street nigga
Always on some G shit
Suck the dick, slurp the balls
Yeah, you my freak bitch"

"Freak Bitch" was one of the last songs I put on my mixtape. I wasn't a fan of calling women bitches and didn't want to make the shit a habit in my music because I mostly liked to rap about what the fuck I'd been through and where I'd come from, but this has been a song trending on social media lately. The kids were wild as hell these days because there was no reason for them to be running the streams up on that song, but they have. As fucked up as it was, I appreciated their young asses for keeping me in rotation, even though they needed to be listening to some fucking Kids Bop or something. I made real nigga music; it just so happened that everybody fucked with it.

When the song ended, I handed the mic to Shio, and he handed it to security. I did two songs on GP, took plenty of pictures with fans and strippers, and now I wanted to sit back and vibe. My body was sore as fuck. I was the type of nigga that would stay up for days doing tattoo sessions, but the constant traveling, never having enough time in a day, and always being in demand was getting to me. I told myself that these days were far from being over because I was starting to see that with rap, I had just gotten started. Still, I was grateful. I'm a fucking hard body. I know what it felt like to not have shit, and I was determined to never feel that again, nor let my boys ever experience it. Growing up in that orphanage, I ain't have nobody. The only family I had was the niggas that were surrounding me and the two I'd created with my baby mama. I vowed to never let them down, even when I was too tired to go on. I would always push the fuck through.

Speaking of my baby mama, she'd still been on my ass. I thought letting her weak pussy ass sit on the dick would be enough to humble her ass, but nope. All it did was make her crazier. I finally gave in and told her she could fly the boys out here the second week of December, but her worrisome ass would have to stay with them because I would be in and out doing shows. I enjoyed the weekend I spent with my boys when I was in Chicago. They were getting so big and had told all their mama's fucking business. Apparently, her boyfriend wasn't the only nigga she was entertaining. I didn't give a damn, though. Better them than me. I was so caught up in the moment that this paper was all I was worried about. I couldn't believe this was my fucking life right now.

Maeve's sick ass had me grateful that I'd walked out of her shit. She looked fucking terrible in that corner store, and with the way she was coughing up her lungs, I knew her days were numbered. I was still feeling a sense of heaviness periodically, and now, urgency had made its way into the mix. I didn't know what the fuck these feelings were about, though.

"Essexxxx! Can we get in your section! Essexx! You so fine! Esexxxxx!"

I smiled at a few fans who were surrounding the booth. They acted like I'd licked their pussies with the way they were shaking and shit. Being a laid-back nigga that liked his privacy, all this shit took some getting used to. Getting attention from the opposite sex had never been a problem. Even when I didn't have shit, I got pussy and plenty of it. As the money increased, so did the quality of women. I used to have women coming to get tatted just so I could play in that pussy. But the way this little fame had brought in pussy was on a whole different scale.

I told myself that I would sample a few when time permitted, but had only hit one. She'd made a fucking lasting impression, too, because, baby had been on my fucking mind like an aneurysm.

I'd been in the studio and had gone by my favorite breakfast spot that I'd been frequenting that past week. As I was parking, I saw an ass that was out of this fucking world. When I got up on her, I realized I recognized her. She was the junt from the Halloween party at Don's estate. She was bad as fuck in the Cinderella costume and was even finer with the black hair on her head and jeans on her waist. When I joined her for breakfast, I knew I was going to hit. I'd spent so much time people-reading and had learned how they thought without them saying anything. The moment her ass hit the booth, I knew I would be going into the afternoon being deep in her fucking guts. She didn't disappoint either. I've fucked plenty of thick, pretty women claiming to be able to take the dick, but most of them were all body and face, no pussy. Ole girl, though? I should have named my fucking song after her. Not only was she soaking wet, her pussy was gripping, and she was nasty as fuck. She'd swallowed so many of my fucking kids that I knew it was a whole daycare sitting in her gut. I'd planned on asking my folks about her, but God was on my side because I'd seen her pretty ass in the booth next to us that housed all my folk's women, but now that I was done rapping, she was gone.

"Aye, aite now... it's time to go wash y'all's pussy!" Renello stood, snapping his fingers and forcing the girls out. They were going off on his ass but grabbing their money in the process so that they could take their leave. That nigga had been giving them hell all night.

"Bruh, just leave them hoes alone. They just tryna make their money." Vello waved. My nigga hadn't been himself and had been spitting in a fucking cup all damn night. He claimed he loved the strippers, but he'd been on the couch, barely attempting to touch one of these big booties.

"Bruh, shut yo' fragile stomach ass up. Fuck you in here for, anyway? Take yo' ass home to Ma and nurse a bowl of broth or some shit!"

When the girls were gone, Renello set his sights back on the booth next to us. It was comical as fuck that these niggas had their girls next to us because they were either watching them or trying to cop a feel without getting caught. I didn't understand why we weren't in a booth together. The shit was big enough, but Demise explained that his wife wanted one for herself. I was even shocked that that nigga had come out. Every damn body that was at his Halloween party was here at the club. I appreciated the fuck out of them for coming through just as they did for the concert. For these niggas to be important as fuck in the world of organized crime, they showed up for me, and that shit had me feeling like a bitch. The Cuppacios had been a blessing in my life since I was a teen, and now the Rinaldi's were earning a space in my heart too.

"Aye... my nigga! Get yo' Team Jordan wearing ass back! She taken!" Renello jogged down the steps as some nigga was in Pia's face.

The story of him and Pia was crazy as hell, but as fine as she was, I couldn't say I blamed him. The men took that as their cue to file out and join the women's booth, too, since the pussy was gone. Wanting to give them niggas their privacy, I stayed behind with Vello and the other single men. Nodding my head to Future, I opted out of alcohol but puffed on a blunt. I still had a few stacks of ones that needed to be disbursed, and when the girls came back, I would do just that and take my ass to the crib. I already received my backend and sent my manager his fee via Zelle. Tomorrow, I would pay Bella, and the moment I locked a lawyer in, I was going to find out how much I should be paying her. I paid Bella well, but I was certain I was underpaying her for the work she did. That girl was on my socials day in and out. I needed to make sure she wasn't falling behind in her work at school too. She was family and young as hell, but that didn't mean she didn't need to be paid fairly, nor did it mean she needed to fall behind on getting that degree. She was damn good at her job, though, and before Ekon, she'd been wearing many different hats.

Looking over at my dawgs, who were in the next booth booed up, I smirked. I knew those niggas were rich as fuck, but it didn't matter to me. No matter how high up I went with this shit, I was bringing my dawgs with me. I wouldn't have even been in this position if it wasn't for the Cuppacios. It was still hard to believe that we were no longer those knucklehead-ass niggas that did whatever to eat. We'd come a long fucking way.

Pulling my phone out, I chuckled at all the notifications across my screen. I was shocked that Bella hadn't already checked them. She must've had her ass out doing some shit she didn't have no fucking business because usually, she was all up and through the comments and the tags. She kept shit cool and didn't reply back to anything unless it was business, so I let her rock. When she told me she didn't mind the DMs of ass and pussy, she wasn't lying because she wouldn't even open those. She'd gotten good at knowing which of my messages were business and which were those of pleasure. She did tell me to get on my baby mama's ass because she'd been going overboard in my comments, staking her claim.

Viv had gone from a nobody to a whole Instagram influencer in the span of two damn weeks. The shit didn't bother me, though. I would just delete her reckless comments and keep it moving. I wasn't about to cause a scene on social media because Viv and I didn't even move like that. I'd even seen the niggas that would comment on Viv's photos and shit. I'd hoped she'd find a new nigga to harass. I was going to have to remind her ass what the fuck it was with us if she kept on with the bullshit. My doing one dick thrust in her guts wasn't enough. I was going to have to curse her motherfucking ass out. We ain't never been on no beef shit. We raised our kids, and I made sure she was straight. This fame shit had gone more to her head than it did mine. When she brought my boys to Jagoda Bay, I was going to have to have a *real* sit down with her. She had a whole nigga, plus a sneaky link, and even if she didn't, we were over. She had better chances scooping one of those lame niggas on the internet.

"Passion, they don't want no dancers in the section right now," I heard one of the guards tell a dancer. I still had my face in my phone, and the blunt to my lip getting faded, so I didn't even look up. The strippers were cool, but I damn near had to strong-arm one when she tried to take my dick out of my jeans.

"Nigga, don't play with me. You know I'm not even in the same category as them hoes. Now move."

Pulling from the blunt, I tuned the argument between the security and dancer out. If she was able to get up, I would give her the rest of the money I had and take my leave. I was ready to get my ass in the bed. Going through my tags, I liked the ones that weren't too crazy. Bella had been on my ass about what I liked on social media. Last week, I liked a tag from another rapper baby mama, and that shit was all over the blogs. They'd claimed I was fucking the niggas' bitch and some more shit, all because she asked for a picture at one of the podcast interviews I did. I didn't even read her caption when she tagged me; I just liked the picture. Apparently, she was trying to get back at her man because the caption read *"I can pull your favorite rapper."* Bella wanted to clear the shit up formally, but all did was comment on Celeb Gossip with *"Ion even know shorty.*" That apparently caused an uproar too. So, now, I had to be careful with what I liked. Shit was crazy as fuck.

Dberrylovesart: My birthday was so much fun!
Dberrylovesart: Treacherous lil twins.

I HAD BEEN TAGGED in two photos from that same username. I clicked on the second photo first that was captioned treacherous twins. It was backstage at the Fall Ball. I had taken a picture with the little girl that was with the twins and Pia. I remembered little mama matching my fly. She had no business liking my music, but again, the kids had been making my shit go viral. We took a couple of photos, but I had so much going on that I barely paid her any attention. Now, looking at the photos, something pulled in my chest. That heaviness was in overload, and I'd even begun to sweat a bit.

What the fuck was wrong with me?

Dberrylovesart: Treacherous lil twins.

I READ over the caption again before backing out of the photo and going to the next one. I tried to ignore my racing heart, but some shit didn't feel right. The other photo was of me kneeling beside the birthday girl and all of her friends at the party Vello had invited me to. Her hair was different from the concert, but it was the same little girl. I didn't realize it then because I had way too much going on, but it made sense that she was at the concert with the twins since Vello was the one who invited me to the party. But who the hell was she? I don't know why, but I went back to the picture of us at the concert and commented on it. I didn't know how in the hell blog's knew anytime I liked or commented, but they knew that shit in real time.

EssexChi: La Twin 🤍

AFTER COMMENTING ON HER PICTURE, I went to her profile. She was following me, but I wasn't following her. She had ten thousand followers, which was a lot for a child. Clicking on the third picture on her profile, I saw her sitting at a piano. She was performing at a concert. Going further down her profile, I concluded that his damn child was a protégé. Not only did she horseback ride, but she also danced, played two instruments, and painted. Her art was off the fucking chain. Outside of the two pictures of her and I, her face wasn't showing on any of the other pictures on her profile. It was always the side of her face or the back of her head. All of her photos were showing her in action in her element. I always knew how to draw, but she had me beat at her age. She could make some real money off this shit. I tried to find a picture of her parents, but came to the conclusion that there were none. That house I'd gone too was big as hell, and I concluded that she was of some kinship to the gay don. I didn't know if he had a child, so she could have easily been his niece or some shit. But damn, it was some-thing familiar about this girl, and I was hoping it was just the blunt making me feel like that.

"So, you got all this pussy in your face, but got the nerve to be on a child's page?"

Snapping my head up from my phone with a snarl on my face, my expression softened when I saw the sexy being in front of me. I didn't play that weird shit, so I was ready to give the person a piece of my mind, but seeing the smile on her face had me coming off the edge. Missy's fine ass had changed out of the sexy dress I saw her in earlier and was now in dancewear. The high-cut shimmery black one-piece she was wearing left nothing to the imagination showing the side of her smooth chocolate waxed pussy, plump titties, wide hips, and fat ass. The heels had to be at least six inches tall, and I knew if I stood up, I would still tower over her. If my mind wasn't preoccupied, my dick would be begging for her throat.

Running her tongue across her lip, she took a seat in my lap from the side and tossed an arm around my neck. Her titties was now right in my face, and her warm, soft body smelled and felt so good. Thinking about how she was able to lick her own nipple piercing had me gripping her hips. I'd fucked plenty of women, but Missy had been the first that matched my fucking freak. It had only been a couple days since I fucked her after breakfast, but the few hours I spent deep in her stomach and throat was enough to know that she was the best that I'd ever had, and that was saying a lot. Wasn't shit inno-cent about Missy. She was a walking fucking seductress. It wasn't no shy in the streets and freak in the sheets with her. You knew she was a freak when you approached her, and she backed that shit up behind closed doors. It was sexy as fuck, if you asked me. I loved a hoe.

"She's cute."

"Yeah."

I leaned in and pecked Missy's lips. I saw a few camera flashes, but I would deal with that shit later. I was a single man, but I had to be mindful of the narratives they liked to paint online. If I was going to do this rap shit, I was going to do it my way. I wasn't going to let no weak-ass blogs fuck me out of deals and shit because of the lies and clickbait that kept their bellies fed. They weren't going to hoe me, either. I was playing by nobody's rules but my own. I was a street nigga turned businessman through and through, and I was going to go at this shit being me. And right now, *me* liked Missy.

Missy ran her thumb across my lip to wipe off her lip gloss. Her nails were long as hell with all types of jewels and shit on them. My dick felt so good in her hands the other day, and her nails didn't even get in the way. It made sense that her ass was a stripper. She was a natural at bringing niggas to their knees.

"I didn't know you had a daughter. That's yo' twin."

Shaking my head, I continued to glance at the little girl's photo of us at the concert. Missy had just backed up the caption at the concert. Treacherous twins. She looked so much like me that if this was a coincidence, it would be a wild one.

"Wait..." Missy took my phone out of my hand, and I didn't protest. Bella had been the only other female that had touched my phone, and that was because it was on some business shit. My baby mama had tried to go in my phone once, and I damn near broke her wrist trying to get it back. That was a long-ass time ago, though.

"I know her. She's the little girl that was at the concert with Pia! Yeah. Her mama is Pia's—" Missy looked at me with a funny face and then handed me my phone back.

"Aye. What? Why you stop talking?"

"Nigga, because I'm not no talking-ass bitch."

"Nawl. What you was finna say?"

Missy touched her forehead, whispered some shit under her breath, and then turned to me. "Who is that little girl to you?"

Looking back at her picture, I knew I didn't know her, but

my heart felt like it did. "To be honest, I don't know her. But I feel like I do, though."

"Um."

"*Um*, what? Talk to me, baby," I pleaded.

Missy leaned in and placed another kiss on my lips. Kissing a stripper wasn't smart, but this girl's whole body had been in my mouth, including her lips. I wasn't worried about what she did for a living back at the diner, so I definitely didn't give a fuck now. She had great pussy, immaculate head, and our vibes were off the charts. Fuck all the formalities.

Missy looked back at the booth were Pia and n'em were. She then looked at Vello who was still spitting in the cup and not paying us any attention.

"All I know is that the little girl's mama is Pia's stepmama. That's it. Anything else, you gon' have to find out on your own. You got good dick and all, but not enough to make me pillow talk."

Hearing that the little girl was Pia's stepmama had me locking my screen. Pia was a grown-ass woman, so her step-mama had to be in her late forties and up. I knew damn well I hadn't fucked no old-ass woman. I liked my women not too old and damn sure not young. I stuck to my age.

Gripping her inner thigh, I felt the heat of her pussy, and then, my dick got hard. Missy was so fucking sexy. She was easily the baddest stripper in the fucking club.

"Why you dancing tonight? You was just over there vibing with your girls."

"From the looks of my bestie over there dry-humping her supposedly cousin, I probably should have stayed in my clothes."

We both looked over and saw Pia bent over, twerking while Nel tossed money at her. We both bust out laughing. That nigga looked happy as shit.

Missy's smile faded, and I locked my eyes on her plump lips. They were so perfect around my dick. This girl had the power to turn my ass every way but loose, so I had to watch myself around her pretty ass. Women didn't know how much power they had over men. The ones that knew, though, were dangerous, and Missy just so happened to be the head honcho in charge.

"Missy—"

She placed her finger to my lip. "I'm Passion here."

Passion. Shit was fitting.

"Okay, *Passion*. Why the fuck you leave your people to dance tonight? Didn't I leave you straight? I know you not hurting for no bread. You emptied my whole fucking safe." I smiled as I reminisced on the way Missy rode my dick mid-air.

Missy's pussy was so sore and sensitive as we fucked, but she was determined to let me pay to play. I know her ass had gotten me for thirty grand the other day. I wasn't complaining, though. I'd never spent that much on a woman outside of my baby mama, but I wasn't protesting and was damn sure ready to spend it again—on foe nem.

She shrugged. "It's too much money in the house and not enough girls, so the boss put my ass to work," she spoke dryly.

"Tell that nigga he gon' have to recruit from down the road somewhere. You don't dance when yo' nigga is performing unless you on stage with me."

Missy tossed her head back in laughter. "Nigga, you funny! So, you my nigga now?"

Creeping my hand up her oily back, her silky strands brushed my skin. I wrapped her expensive weave around my hand and yanked her head back. I could practically hear her pussy creaming as she moaned. Placing my mouth on her neck, I bit down on it.

"Fuuuuck, Essex. I'm at wooork."

"Ion give a fuck. Get yo' money, but not when daddy performing. What the fuck I just say?"

The two melons on her chest rose and fell repeatedly as I sucked down on her skin. "I don't dance when my nigga is performing unless I'm on stage with him."

Sticking my middle finger past the thin fabric of her uniform, I stroked her slopping pussy.

"Damn, Essexxx!" She hissed as quietly as she could.

"Good girl. Now, go get yo' shit... you coming home with me."

Last time, I held back. I could have fucked her to death if I wanted to. She had just fucked another nigga and was still screaming as she took the dick. The keyword was *took*. She took that shit even though she left my ass with a noise complaint. This time, though, I hoped she'd had that little pussy on ice because I was going all in.

Slapping her on the ass as she stood, I helped her down the stairs.

"Meet me at the front door." She licked her lips, and I couldn't wait to feel them on my dick. Missy just had that shit you can't teach.

I watched her ass disappear, and every man she walked past damn near begged for her attention. That shit made my dick jump knowing I was about to be buried deep in that gushy shit for the remainder of the night.

"Aye, I'm out." I slapped it up with my boys and hit the girl's booth with a head nod.

It wasn't no getting out of taking pictures with the fans because they were right outside the booth. Once I had that done and practically had to fight my way through the crowd, Missy was standing at the door, playfully rolling her eyes. She'd changed into a pink jogging suit that had her ass sitting just right. Her feet were in a pair of Ugg slides, and I couldn't wait to have her pretty-ass toes in my mouth. Before tossing my arm across her shoulder, I pulled the shirt over my head. That bitch cost a pretty penny, but someone had spilled liquor on it while I was toughing through the sea of fans. Tossing it behind me, I could hear people fighting over it. I swear it wasn't that serious. I wasn't nobody for real. Thankfully, no one was outside, so I was able to lead Missy to my rental car with no problems. This time, I'd rented a pretty-ass red Camaro. I had plans on buying myself a whip soon that would stay here in Jagoda Bay, but I was undecided on what I wanted. Once we were in the car, I looked over at her pretty ass.

"Baby..."

She batted her long ass lashes in response. All girls couldn't rock them shits, but they looked good on Missy. Every fucking thing looked good on her, as if she was the originator of that shit. I'd only seen her three times, but all three times, she was in a different element. The blonde sluterella, the brunch baddie, and now, the sexy-ass vixen. She couldn't do no fucking wrong in my eyes, and it was a shame that she had a nigga wide open after one day.

She had me low-key stuck as I looked at her. Before I could finally finish what I was about to say, she reached over and ran her finger across my new ink. "Is this new? It wasn't there when I was riding ya dick."

I loved that vulgar shit. Viv talked a good game, but she was shy with her words. Missy didn't give a fuck.

Looking down at the tattoo on my chest that I'd done on myself in Chicago, I reached over and squeezed her thigh. I ran the red light and put the pedal to the medal. We didn't stop at no fucking red lights.

"Yeah. It's new, but it was there. I had a covering patch on top of it to heal it faster."

"You did it?"

"I did, baby."

It took long as fuck for me to finish the damn tattoo once I started. There was so much detail. My kids had even fallen asleep on the bed I kept in my office for them. I was determined to finish it, though, and I did. It was the Earth with the words: *The world is my Discovery at the bottom.* I didn't know where the words came from, but they couldn't be truer.

"Crazy thing is, that little girl whose picture you was looking at... her name is Discovery."

"What?" I swerved the car looking, over at Missy. She reached for the dash to steady herself.

"Yeap. Now, don't ask me no more questions. I told you this mouth don't pillow talk. But it does some other shit."

While I was processing what Missy had told me, she was climbing out of her seat belt and unbuckling my pants. My mind was going as fast as this damn car, and Missy sliding my dick to the back of her throat may have slowed my thoughts, but it sped up the car. I needed to get her back to the condo immediately.

"Shiiiit." I bit down on my lip to prevent myself from sounding like a bitch.

I looked at her briefly while making sure we didn't crash for real. With the way her lips were feeling and the effects of the weed from all the blunts I'd smoked tonight, I couldn't even remember what it was her fine ass had just said anymore.

CHAPTER 13

NEL

"**M**an... you should have never hired that bitch! Big, bad-shape-ass hoe was jealous of you from the jump!" Yelling at the screen, I tossed popcorn in my mouth. This was the second bag I popped. The air still reeked of burned food from me overcooking the first bag. Thankfully, I was the only person at home. Pearla was in the streets, probably hitting all types of curbs and potholes. Ezio's mom had come and picked up Patty hours ago, claiming they were having a girl's night. Neltz was with Bozo the Clown, and Pia was out doing whatever the fuck it was that she did these days with her father. It was as if we were on two different frequencies. I thought we were getting somewhere at the club last night, but when she came home and turned her back to me, I took my mad ass to bed with a stiff dick. This morning, I woke up to her dressed and headed out the door before my feet could hit the floor.

I heard everything Shio was saying, but I didn't *hear* him. If Pia wanted to talk to me, she knew how to come to me. We lay in the same bed every fucking night. Still, she had her secret

231

conversations with her stripper bestie and dad, and left me in the fucking dark. Today was no exception; I woke up to an empty bed, so to keep myself busy, I cleaned Pia's bedroom and the kitchen, showered, and now I was sitting in the living room, enjoying my favorite movie. This girl had turned me into a fucking domesticated simp waiting on her by the door and shit.

"Selena, you'll still be here today if you didn't trust these hoes. These hoes will be your downfall every time."

It was sad that Selena had taken that lady under her wing, giving her a job and access to luxury, and the lady killed her ass in the end. Just imagine if my girl had never died; we would have so many hits right now. She didn't even get the chance to have any fucking kids before being murked. Shit is sad.

"Man! Why in the fuck are you always watching this sad-ass movie?"

I'd heard Neltz's badass pull up before he even walked through the door. Bozo had picked him up from school yesterday, claiming that he would be taking him to get a lineup this morning and shopping before dropping him back off. I didn't see no fucking bags in his hand, so I guess they skipped the shopping trip, but his hair was lined to perfection. The nigga was a hoe, but he had Neltz with a cool barber.

Tossing a handful of hot buttery popcorn in my mouth, I kept my eyes on the screen.

"You be acting like you deaf. All you niggas must be gay around here. Watching this bullshit every day. Put on some Power or something."

I grabbed the bottle of water from the coffee table, twisted the top, and chucked down a swallow. Taking my time, I sat the popcorn on the table and used a paper towel to wipe the butter and hot sauce off my fingers. I had to have seasoned salt and hot sauce on my popcorn. The shit wasn't good for blood pressure, but I'm a young nigga; I'll be good.

"Have you ever seen this movie before?"

Neltz balled his face up. "Hell nawl. Ion watch sh—stuff like this."

"Okay, so why the fuck it gotta be gay?"

"Cuz it is! Watching a Mexican girl sing all day, every day is gay."

"Young nigga, shut yo' dumb ass up! This shit ain't gay. And I don't watch no muthafuckin' Power because that shit is fictional. You know what fiction means?"

"Talking about like a book?"

"Yeah, like a book," I mimicked his questionable tone.

"It means it's not real."

"Exactly. Power isn't real. I'm a gangsta for real, young nigga. I don't need to see actors who wouldn't know the first rules of the streets portraying to be me. They reading from a script, but I live that life for real."

"What—"

"And don't ask me to fucking elaborate because I'm not on that with yo' young ass. You need to be focusing on getting the fuck out of elementary school because it ain't looking too good for ya, buddy."

Neltz crossed his arms, and I knew he was about to get on good bullshit from his stance. I thought he would take his ass to his room like he usually did when I was around, but his daddy must've pumped his nuts because he was on that today. He just didn't know that I could match his ignorance and would. I usually ignored his ass, but I see that talk we had a few weeks ago hadn't registered because he wanted to test me. I knew how Pia was about this jug-headed, big hair-having-ass nigga, so I tried to steer clear, but all that shit was over with. His mama already had me fucked up.

"Y'all always on me about school, but you don't even need

school to make it. Some of my uncles didn't finish high school. My daddy finished, but he didn't go to college; he gets his money outta the streets just like my uncles. My mama didn't finish school, and look, you don' upgraded her. Now, she got a rich daddy. My grandma didn't even finish school. School ain't nothing but a piece of paper. My classmates not on my level. I know what it is that I'ma do with my life, anyway, and I don't need no education for it."

I knew that my cousins and I had it hard growing up and weren't into school like we should have been, but it was merely because we were trying to survive. Our fathers, as awful as they were, cared about our education, even if we had to get homeschooled. Eventually, they sent us to physical school because they didn't want us dumb as fuck when it came to their organization. Neltz was only nine years old and worried about the wrong shit.

"So fuck being a doctor and a lawyer, hunh?"

"Hell yeah. That shit lame. I'm getting mine outta the streets. Look at you. Ion fuck with you like that, but you doing aite to me."

Sliding to the end of the seat, I rested my elbows on my knees and looked Neltz square in the eyes. I knew I didn't have much power when it came to him hanging with his daddy, but it was obvious that he was getting this shit from somewhere. If Pia could hear him talking, she would beat his motherfucking ass.

"So, what you plan on doing?"

Neltz scratched his man bun and pondered a bit. I had never felt like he looked like Rio, but right then and there, he did. It was evident that he was a product of the nigga.

"My daddy sell dope, so I'ma be the muscle. Any nigga that don't pay up—" Neltz held his arm straight and positioned his finger as if he was holding a gun. "Bloodshed."

Oh, hell nawl.

"Any nigga short... *doo doo doo.* I'm on that."

"You on that?"

"Like my mama and Tee Tee be saying... *and is.* I told my daddy I can start now, but he won't even let me shoot a gun until I'm eighteen. So, I'ma thug it out until then."

"*Doo doo doo.* That's how yo' gun gon' sound?"

Neltz pulled his trigger finger again. "*Doo doo doo.* Yeap. Just like that. Don't fuck around and be my first victim. You better be glad I lied to my daddy and told him you was gon' with my mama. I spared you. He would have come in here and laid yo' ass out. *Doo doo doo.*"

Running my tongue across my bottom lip, I nodded. I bit down on my lip, and then I smiled. Neltz was too busy running his mouth on his future as a jackboy and being his daddy's flunky to notice me pulling the gun from under the couch. Once I trained it on him, making sure to point it at his stomach, with the red dot piercing the pocket of his color-block Polo hoodie, he froze up.

"And just like that, your ass is dead."

"Y... y—you just gon' pull a gun out on me? I'ma tell my mama—"

"Un hunh! Ion wanna hear that shit. You said I'ma be yo' first victim, right? Don't tell yo' mama now. As a matter of fact, tell her about how you want to be a loser."

Neltz had his hands tucked in his pocket and was trying to play hard, but I could see the sweat on his forehead. Boy was so shook up, his knees were bucking, but he didn't shed a tear, and for that, I had a tad bit more respect for his little sucker ass.

"The difference between me and you, though, is that my daddy put a gun in my hand when I was three. By the time I was eighteen, I probably had eighteen bodies, lil' nigga. If yo' daddy really wanted you in that field, he would have been schooling yo' ass. He also wouldn't make you no fuckin' send out. He would hand over the plug to you and let you take over. But yo' daddy not cut like that. I park my car outside every fuckin' day, and yo' daddy don't do shit but pull up and use *you* as an excuse to be seen. But what he fails to realize is... nobody in this muthafucka even pays attention to his ugly ass."

"I... I ain't no loser."

"You are a fucking loser! You headed down the fucking loser path. Talking about lawyers and doctors is lame. Let me ask you this... who in the fuck gon' get yo' ass outta jail if you get jammed up?"

"Uh... uh."

"Uh uh, what?" I moved the red dot from his stomach to his thigh. His big-ass eyes bulged.

"Uh..."

"Uh, what, baby shark? You said yo' gun go... *doo doo doo*, right? Well, my gun goes... *tatt tatt tatt!*"

Neltz was swallowing so much that I was sure he didn't have no more fucking spit in his mouth. Selena's "Dreaming of you" began playing loudly as Jlo performed. This was one of my favorite fucking parts, and I was in here upping the pistol on a fucking child. The nigga had a mouth like a grown-ass man, and if he didn't get that shit in check, he wouldn't have to worry about being his daddy's wingman because he would end up being in a fucking grave.

"Uh, a lawyer. I would need a lawyer to get me out."

"Exactly. And that's if you even making enough to be able to afford one. Niggas like you would end up having to use a public defender because you don' spent the re-up on pussy. You seem like one of them loud, flashy, wanna-be tough-ass niggas." I moved the dot over to his right kneecap. "If I blow yo' fuckin' knee off, who the fuck you gon' need to get you back right, Coco Felon?"

'Uh... a doctor."

"A fucking doctor! So them lame-ass niggas you just spoke on could very well be the niggas that save your fuckin' life. Real street niggas respect men in all positions. It don't matter if a nigga the janitor, work at a wing spot, or smoke the fuckin' dope that yo' weak-ass daddy *don't* sell. Every man you encounter, unless he tryna take you out, plays a vital role in your life, even when it's not directly associated with you. Stop idolizing yo' daddy. The shit yo' daddy out here playing with has been stepped on so many times, he may as well go to the infant aisle in Walmart and buy three cans of baby powder and bag that shit."

Hobo is making it out here, but that's all his ass is doing— making it. He is not a real nigga, either, because there was no way in hell that he should have had Pia living in the hood and driving a raggedy-ass car. She's not a problematic female and she didn't ask to be taken care of. He was so busy putting her down just because she cut the pussy off that he forgot how to be a real nigga, or his ass was never one from the jump. He is the reason why Neltz's ass is so bad. He probably didn't teach him everything, but the shit he does and says around Neltz when it comes to other motherfuckers got this little nigga walking around like he's untouchable. But, look at him now —touched.

"Let me put you in on a lil' secret... I killed the last nigga yo' mama was dealing with. What's his name? Hanger or some shit... killed the shit outta that nigga." I watched for Neltz's reaction, and besides his chest swelling due to the breath he inhaled, his expression was the same; scared as fuck that I had a gun on him. "The way that niggas body shook like he was doing the cha cha slide... that shit wasn't fiction. Don't ever feel like you doing me a favor by not dropping my lo' for yo' hoe-ass daddy. Only reason why I haven't killed his ass, too, is because I like you a lil' bit. You my fucking junior—my namesake. I care about yo' feelings, even though I should put a belt to yo' ass. But a belt ain't gon' do shit for yo' ass. I see now that I'ma have to shoot you to get you to learn. Maybe I can shoot you in the foot. It ain't like you play sports or nothing."

I moved the gun to the grey and white Jordans on his feet. He jumped back. "You see how I came in and moved y'all outta the hood? Put your mama in a new whip? Let her quit that shitty-ass job? You went from being neighbors with Timonshe and Meka to being neighbors with Timothy and Miley. That's what *men* do. Real men take care of the people they love. They don't disrespect them. You'll never see me treat yo' mama, auntie, or grandma with anything less than respect. That's gangsta. One day, when you realize how much of a buster yo' daddy is for filling yo' head with nonsense, you'll try to be my son. And I'm such a real nigga that I'ma just accept you with open arms and kiss yo' forehead instead of saying I told you so."

I saw right through Neltz. Yeah, his ass was bad, but he looked at everyone's flaws and wrongdoings and felt like that's what he wanted for himself in life. He actually wanted love. I'm not saying Pia didn't show him love, but she had times when she was too busy working to provide that. She didn't have the luxury of really sitting down with Neltz and undoing all the bullshit his dad did and was continuing to do. It was cool, though; I had it. I was going to get this nigga right.

"Are... are you gon' kill my daddy?"

"Do you want me to?" I asked, serious as a fucking heart attack.

Neltz shook his head no.

Giving him one last look, I lowered my gun and tucked it back under the couch. "It depends. If you keep being mean to me, his ass is grass." I smirked.

"Why you kill Banger?"

Looking Neltz in the face, I knew I shouldn't have told his ass about a murder I'd committed, but for some reason, I trusted the young nigga. He could very well tell his daddy, but I didn't think he would. He acted like Bozo was the best thing since sliced bread, but he loved the fuck out of his mama.

"When it comes to your mama, I'm ending any muthafucka that's not good for her. I'm real stingy with Natazia Pia Cuppacio, young nigga. I shoot first and ask questions never. That's another lesson yo' ass needs to learn. Ask no fuckin' questions."

Neltz swallowed hard.

"Now, come sit yo' ass down, eat some of this salty-ass popcorn, and watch this movie."

Hesitantly, Neltz sat on the opposite end of the couch. He had his arms folded tight and that same scowl on his face. Picking up the bowl, I held it out, but he turned his nose up. Shrugging, I sat back in my seat and started the movie over. Next time, I may just have to shoot this nigga, for real, if this talk didn't work.

Two hours later

"I thought the movie was gay. Look at you over there... crying like a baby."

I thought I'd never see the day that tough-ass Neltz cried. His little-ass face was drenched. I'm talking, snot pouring from his nose and everything. If I wasn't slick in my feelings, too, I would have been laughing my ass off.

"Man... Daddy Number Two! You didn't tell me... she was going to die. Is... Is... this true or fiction? I... I think I want... that lady to be my first victim. She... did... her so wrrrrong," he cried out. He was no longer on the other end of the couch. The little nigga was right under me. I placed my arm around his shoulder and consoled him. I officially had another Selena fan. It would be a while before he asked to see the movie again, but when he did, I would be right here.

Neltz used his sleeve to wipe the back of his face.

"Let this be a lesson; you can't bring everybody in your circle when you reach a certain level of success. Unless you still trying to be the send out?"

Neltz shook his head no.

"Good."

The front door opened, and I already knew it was Pia. She'd texted and said she was on the way, plus the camera showed her pulling up. Standing in the doorway, her brow rose, and before she could ask, Neltz jumped up and wrapped his arms around her waist. "Mama. I'm so glad you not a singerrrrrrrrr."

Pia looked at me, and I shrugged.

"Wait, hold up." Grabbing his face, Pia held his head back. "Did Renello do something to you?"

It was my turn to draw my head back. Instead of going off, I stood and went to the back. I told him I would never disrespect his mama, and I meant that. Bad enough, she was coming in here with shopping bags and shit, and with the names of those brands, I knew her cheap ass didn't buy it. Pia's accounts were stacked, thanks to me. I was sure her daddy had hooked her up, but before then, I made sure she was straight. She is still penny-pinching even though I leave money on her dresser every damn day. We were at the point where I gave her all my fucking profit. That little nigga was bad, but I wouldn't do shit to his ass unless it was in her face. Earlier, I was just shaking him up.

Plopping down on her bed, I lit the blunt that was on the nightstand. The end of it had gloss on it since Pia was the last one to hit it. Without wiping the residue off, I placed it to my lips and inhaled. I needed to be high in order to suppress my feelings. Coco Felon and I had finally had our moment, and she had to ruin the shit by thinking I'd done something to him. She knew me better than that. Granted, I should have kicked his ass a long time ago, but it wasn't my place.

A few minutes later, I was high as a damn kite. I could have gotten even higher, but Pia had walked her ass in, looking like a fucking puppy dog. She was dressed down but still dressed up. I hated to admit it because I knew it had a lot to do with the glam team her father had hooked her up with, but her look had elevated. Her nails and feet were now done, her hair was styled to perfection, and she was rocking brands most bitches couldn't even pronounce. Today, she was in jeans, a cropped sweater, a crossbody Chanel bag, and white Chanel sneakers. Licking my dry lips, I watched as she placed the shopping bags at the foot of the bed.

"I'm sorry." She plopped down on the side of the bed and placed her head on my chest. She smelled so fucking good, like cherries and chocolate or some shit all wrapped in one.

"Go on, Pia. I ain't fucking with you right now."

"But, why? What I do? You been actin' funny."

"Shit, if anything... I'm feeding off you."

She propped her head up and cocked it. "What you mean?"

"Man, ion wanna get into all that. But what the fuck was that shit about? Fuck you think I did to that lil' nigga?"

She sighed heavily. "Ion know. He is bad as hell, so I thought you hit him or something. I never seen him cry like that since he was a baby. He told me he wasn't crying and that it was something in his eye. I had to pick up the remote to see that it was the movie. Why you let my son watch Selena?"

I sighed. I was tired of the surface-level conversations. Pia stayed dodging me when it was time to talk about the shit that mattered. I would admit that I had been doing the same, but it wasn't about me right now. "Wassup, Pia? What you on? What we doing?"

"What you mean?"

"You know what I mean. I told you what it is. How long we supposed to keep playin' this game?"

I wanted nothing more than to fuck the shit out of Pia and make her mine. It wasn't even about the sex. But I love the fuck out of her and wanted her in all the ways possible. She was treating me just like what the fuck Don called it—a kissing cousin. A kissing cousin that had kissed on her pussy. I'll be damn if that's where it ends.

"Renelloooo." She covered her face.

Prying her hands from her pretty mug, I grabbed her chin. "We either gon' take it there or we not, Pia. I know we was perceived to be cousins, but we both know we not. I think my mind has always known we weren't related. You gon' have to figure some shit out, though."

"What you mean *I gotta figure some shit out*? And why are you cursing at me?" Now, she had an attitude.

"Exactly what I said, and I'm not cursing at you, Pia baby." I softened my tone. This was the problem now. All she had to do was bat her lashes, and I was on my fucking knees. Pia knew what she was doing. She knew she had that power over me. But we had to establish some shit and fast.

"You are! You said shit. You don't even talk to me like that."

"Okay, I shouldn't have said that, Pia. But we got to figure some *stuff* out. We either gon' be friends or lovers. I can't even say cousins because we aren't related by blood. We not gon' be no in between, though."

"I just don't get it, though. I just—"

Pulling her lips to mine, I sucked down on her bottom lip, drawing heat from her body. Her lips were moist, and her saliva tasted like the sweet tea I knew was still resting in the cup holder of her SUV. My dick grew just thinking about how her pussy tasted just as sweet. She hesitated at first, but she kissed me back with just as much passion as our tongues wrestled. Just as she began to moan, I pulled back. Lust was written all over her face.

"That's what we can't do. I can't keep making you feel good, Pia baby. That ain't fair to me. If you not ready to take this shit to the next level, then I'ma chill out. I won't be eating your pussy. I won't be sleeping beside you and letting you dry hump me in your sleep. You won't be bouncing your ass on my dick in the club. All this extra stuff would be over. We gotta have some boundaries."

She pouted, and it was so damn cute. Still, pouting didn't pull this nut up out my dick, so it didn't mean shit. I was beating my shit down every chance I got, and my hands were tired.

She perked up. "Let's go out."

"What you mean *out*?"

"A date," she suggested. Pia hopped up and started pulling shit out of the bags. "I bought this for you. I want us to dress up and go somewhere nice."

"Were you gon' ask me this before I mentioned establishing boundaries?"

"Duh! Now, shower. I'll go shower in Pearla's room."

"I'm not wearing shit you bought with your daddy's money." I sounded bitter as hell. Pia had pulled out a LOEWE set, and even though it was fly, I wasn't on that.

A text came through on my phone, and instead of it being a text about some mob shit, it was from Essex. That nigga had been taking off with this rap shit, and his copycat ass hadn't left Jagoda Bay since the wedding. He wanted to be a Cuppacio so bad.

E-BLOCK:

Aye. What you know about Pia's stepmama?
How old is her daughter? What's their names?
Shit how old is the step mama?

YEAH, I didn't have time for this shit here.

"I used your money! Now go shower. You taste like hot sauce and weed."

Before I could reply with something smart, she ran out of the room with her bags. She'd better be glad I was high and hungry. I could go for a steak, but pussy sounded a lot more appetizing. That fucking Pia.

You and that Target hoe not finna put me in
y'all shit. Ask Vello about her. I'm not fucking
that bitch so I don't have no info for you.

EVERYBODY IS WORRIED *about that Target hoe's pussy. The only pussy I'm targeting is Pia's.*

CHAPTER 14

PIA

Life has been different recently. Just last week, I was complaining that I was waking up with nothing to do. At the time, I had money in the bank, the bills were paid up, my credit score was rising, and the whole family was good. Still, I felt like I needed something to do regularly. Now, I'd been spending the last few days meeting up with my father in various parts of the city. We'd gone from the yacht to dinner in the valley to walks in a vineyard. Rio never ceased to amaze me with the places he'd been inviting me to. Every day, I wake up at the crack of dawn and meet him wherever he requests. I'd seen so many hidden oases, places I never knew existed, all within Jagoda Bay. Seeing the way that Rio lived, I couldn't imagine growing up with all of it. It was all surreal. Gay and all, that man is a true king, and I couldn't believe that I was able to call him my father.

Today, he had the mall shut down just so I could shop. He'd given me debit cards with access to multiple accounts, but I'd been too chicken to even look at the amount each account held. Rio was loaded. People all but bowed at his feet anywhere we were. I hadn't gotten used to the way they handled me, and I don't think I ever would. There was only one person who had ever treated me like a princess, and he was sitting on my bed, looking handsome in a black and grey LOEWE outfit. His signature diamond chain hung around his neck, resting right below my name, which was etched on his skin forever.

Renello had been distant with me, and I'd also been distant with him. I wanted to blame it on getting to know my father, but Rio didn't take up that much of my time. I truly enjoyed getting to know my father, which was still so crazy to say out loud. The real reason I'd been keeping a safe distance from Renello was because of the dynamics. I didn't like the way my body reacted to him. I was delirious anytime he didn't pick up the phone, which wasn't often. I stayed away from him during the day, but at night, I needed him in my bed, only if it was just to keep the other side warm. Everything felt right when he was around. If I didn't wake up to his face, I went crazy. He was the only person I would get ignorant with, and he still handled me with care. Nevertheless, I didn't want to like him in that way.

Glancing in my bathroom mirror, I clamped the thin gold diamond necklace on my neck. This wasn't a gift from my father or Renello but from my mother. I didn't know what the hell she and my daddy had going on, but I knew his ass was gay, even though I hadn't seen him with a man as of yet. Still, my mama was constantly shopping, and even though her ass couldn't drive, she was never home. I had to catch up with her one day so that she could give me the tea.

Regardless of what Renello thinks, I was going to ask him to dinner tonight. Him eating my pussy twice felt way too good, and even though I thought about it way too often, it was still very awkward. I knew I'd been acting funny with the man, and that was some shit we didn't do. But I was at a standstill with Renello. He was attempting to put his foot down, and while I wanted to give this man an answer, I didn't have one. This shit was just all-around awkward and confusing to me. Was I worried about Renello following through on his threat of putting up boundaries? Not really. I knew that shit was all fluff. He was all bark and no bite when it came to me. If I asked him to drop to his knees right now, he would do it. I wouldn't do that, though, because I was trying my best to not send mixed signals. But I clearly was doing a horrible job since I was just ready to take him down on the bed an hour ago.

I knew we weren't blood-related, but we grew up as cousins. No matter how much time had passed, that was hard to overcome. Today, I'd almost asked my father for his advice on Renello, but I was too ashamed. Anytime we were around the family and got touchy-feely, no one questioned it, but I still felt shame. It had literally only been about three weeks since I found out the truth with concrete proof! I needed some time to process things and sort out my feelings. Since I was too chicken to talk to anyone about him, I figured it was time for him and I to talk amongst ourselves. I just had to tell my body that because she was ovulating and in heat. I'd already had to change my panties and had only been dressed for twenty minutes.

Bruno had walked me through what he called a fifteen-minute no-makeup look on FaceTime. What should have been fifteen minutes took an hour. Still, I was pleased with the results. I couldn't believe I'd done such a good job on myself, and if I could remember the steps, this was going to be my go-to. Pearla had been dabbling in makeup, too, so I would probably show her.

My phone vibrated on the bathroom counter as I ran the flat iron through my tresses. I'd gotten dressed in Pearla's bathroom but had to come in mine once Renello was done to add my finishing touches. Looking down at the screen, it was none other than fucking Hobo. He'd been calling me all damn day, and I'd been ignoring him all day. I didn't have shit to talk about with his disrespectful ass. My son was home, and even when he was with him, Neltz had a phone.

Unplugging my flat irons, I added the perfume my father picked out and then hit the light. Wanting to match Renello's fly, I was wearing a black LOEWE Anagram tank dress that was sleeveless and split on one side that stopped mid-thigh. I topped the look with black leather LOEWE mules that had the hot pink nail polish block heel. I didn't do heels, but the shoes were comfortable and were a sexier option than flats. I had the matching bag sitting on the end of my bed and tried hard not to look at the tags. I lied to Renello earlier about purchasing his items myself. My daddy bought that shit. Rio went into stores and blacked the hell out. Nothing was off-limits. I hadn't looked at the accounts that Rio had set up for me, but I'd finally peeked into my personal account Nel had been depositing into. I had over four hundred thousand dollars sitting there. My *cousin* and my daddy were both tricking on me so hard. It was insane.

"My bad for taking so long. I'm ready."

Renello looked up from his phone. He was texting what seemed to be a lot of information, and I had to mentally coach myself not to walk over there and look at his phone. I saw a heart for a reply, and that shit had my eye twitching. See, this is the shit Renello was talking about. I would nut up on his ass, but didn't want to go there with him in a sexual manner. That didn't make no damn sense. Renello's low eyes scanned my frame, and when he licked his lips, my neck heated.

Calm down, girl.

"You look pretty."

"Just pretty...?"

Renello locked his screen, tucked his phone in the pocket of his jeans, and stood with a stretch. His shirt lifted a bit, showing that dangerous v-cut of his. I had to look away so that he wouldn't catch my ass.

Stop, Pia. Stop.

"Beautiful, Pia baby. Gorgeous. Fine as hell. Sexy. All the above. You smell good too."

"Thank you." I blushed.

"We leaving Neltz?"

Hearing him mention Neltz warmed me and also embarrassed me. I was wrong as hell for blaming him for my baby's tears. But I knew how Renello was and knew it wouldn't be long before he beat Neltz's ass. My baby was bad, but he meant well. It felt good knowing they finally had their breakthrough moment. He'd already asked me ninety-nine questions about Selena that I didn't have the answers to. When I just walked past his room, I heard him scrolling on his phone, watching TikTok's about Selena conspiracy theories.

"Pearla is in her room."

It was one of the reasons why I finished getting ready in my own bathroom. Pearla had kicked me out, claiming she needed to shower. She didn't want anybody touching her stuff. She claimed we were too junky for her. She had me fucked up; I kept my shit clean.

"Aite. Lead the way."

"You just wanna see my ass in this dress."

Renello gave me a devious grin. "I been watching that muthafucka from the side since you was in your bathroom struggling with the makeup."

Hitting his chest, he weakly brushed me off with a laugh.

"You said it's cute," I whined.

"It is. It looks way better than what I thought. When you tried to put the concealer on your eyelid, I wasn't no more good."

I thought I heard his ass in here laughing, but when I looked up, he was on his phone.

"I didn't know you were paying attention. I thought you was too busy texting," I said with venom in my tone.

There I go with that crazy shit.

"Grab the phone," he told me with a straight face. It was sticking out of his jeans. I was never one to have to be told something twice, so I did just that. Typing his code in, which was my birthday, I went straight to his messages. It was a picture of Jisei's ultrasound. He and Ezio were texting back and forth about the baby shower. Renello was talking shit to Ezio in the text thread, though, and Ezio had replied back with a heart emoji.

"I told you the only thing I'm on is waiting on you, crazy girl. I'm not with that. You the one that gotta catch up."

Rolling my eyes, I locked the screen again, stuck it back in his pocket, and grabbed my purse. Turning on my heels, a loud smack echoed across the room and stung at my backside.

"I couldn't help it. That muthafucka so juicy."

"Boy, come on."

I wanted to drive to pamper Renello to the fullest tonight, but he wasn't going for it. When I told him I wanted to pay during the drive that he'd won, he nearly had a stroke. He'd even put money in my purse to reimburse me for the clothes after I tried again to convince him that I'd used his money. We spent the drive laughing and bickering and listening to Essex. I really enjoyed myself at the concert. For that to be his first performance, he had the crowd rocking. My thoughts drifted to Discover. She was in a fucked up situation with Rio, and now she was pregnant by Vello with Essex as her secret baby daddy. Vello knew about Rio, but he didn't know about Essex. Essex didn't know shit, and there was no telling what Rio knew. He could know it all, or he could know nothing. He'd been so busy building a relationship with me that he hadn't even mentioned his young wife. I wanted to check on her, but I wanted to keep myself out of that situation as much as possible. I now had some level of loyalty to my father, even though I had undevoted loyalty to the twins. Rio was powerful, but he didn't seem like he would hurt a fly. He was so kind, so hopefully, he was forgiving. I was going to play Ray Charles when that shit blew up. Best wishes to my girl, though.

"Mecanio, table for two."

We didn't have to wait but two minutes at the packed steakhouse. This was one of the most exquisite places to eat in Jagoda Bay. I'd asked my father to tell me his favorite places to dine, and this was one of the ones he had listed. It wouldn't be Rio if he didn't ask me if I wanted him to rent it out. I declined respectfully, though. Once we were seated, we looked over the menu and placed our orders. I kept it simple with steak, mac and cheese, a salad, and a Lemon Drop. Renello ordered the whole damn menu.

"We should do this more often," I said to Renello over the live musician that was playing somewhere in the distance. The restaurant wasn't dark, but it still had a romantic vibe. It almost felt like I was in the lobby of a fancy hotel in New York. I had never been to New York, but I imagined this was what it looked like.

"Pia baby, I want to do whatever you want to do. We could have been doing this. We can do it every night if you want." He took a sip of his water as he spoke with ease. He wasn't cocky in his statement, but the truth behind it had me squeezing my thighs together.

Our drinks came out along with an order of some type of fried lobster bites on a bed of white cream sauce. One bite had me damn near moaning in these people's establishment. This shit was too fresh and good. I took a few sips of my drink, needing liquor courage for the conversation I was about to have. First, I had some questions for Renello before I broke into my own shit.

"Why you so mean to the family, Renello?" The few times we'd all been around, Renello was talking shit to everyone and being mean as hell to them. Most of the time, they ignored him, but I didn't remember a time when he treated them like that. Maybe I had missed a few chapters in my absence.

"Why, Pia baby? Wassup?" Renello picked up a lobster bite and licked the white sauce that had fallen onto his lip. I cleared my throat and had to cool myself down.

"I just want to know. I mean, if you not fucking with them for real, maybe I shouldn't."

A mischievous grin spread across Renello's face. I was deadass serious, though. I was loving getting to know everyone again, but if Renello wasn't fucking with them like that, neither was I.

"You ain't gotta do that. I'm just pissed at Ezio and all them niggas feeling that shit. That's all."

"Why you mad at him, though?"

Renello ran his hand from his chin down to the branding of my name that covered his neck.

"You ready to tell me what happened when Ezio set y'all house on fire? I'm talking the days leading up to that. Don't tell me you don't remember, either. I sleep beside you every night, Pia baby. I hear your dreams and your nightmares."

An oddly primitive echo sounded off in my brain. Renello's handsome scowl was locked in on mine with a worried expression. I turned away, breath caught in my throat, as I felt my heart pounding.

"I... I don't remember."

Renello reached across the table and grabbed my hand. "Aye. Let it go."

I let out a massive exhale before inhaling and then focused back on him.

"It's cool. I'm here now. We don't have to bring it up today. But that's why I'm pissed. It's me and you, Pia baby. It's always us. Been us. Only reason why Ezio still breathing is because he didn't succeed. You being gone nearly fucking killed me, baby. I'll forgive them niggas, though... only if you say so." Renello rubbed the back of my hand lovingly. His dreads hung in his face, and they looked so good after I'd retwisted them.

"Yes. You can forgive them. I love them, and so do you. Life too short, Renello. You can't be holding onto the past."

Sitting back in his chair, he let my hand go, taking the warmth with him. "I'll think about it." He winked with a closed-mouth grin.

"For me, Renello..." I pleaded.

"You know its anything for you, Pia baby. Even when you not giving me what I want. Now, talk to me. What else on your mind?"

Clearing my throat, I got my head back in the game, trying to venture off the memory lane. I also had to ignore the second heartbeat in my panties. "You know, I've been getting to know my father, right?"

Renello placed the triple shot of Dusse to his lips and took it to the head. "Yeah. How that's going?"

"I like him. He's nice. Spoils me too much and wants to meet Neltz, but I'm taking that slow. They met at the party, but only briefly. Neltz is a lot. I love my boy, but uh, no."

"My young nigga ain't that bad."

"Oh, so now that y'all bonded over Selena, he straight? You wanted to kill his ass last week."

"It ain't off the table just yet."

I kneed Renello under the table, almost making him spill his liquor.

"Aye, watch out!" He laughed.

"You take him out, you better take me out too."

"Shidddd... well then, I'll take myself out after. Come on now, Pia baby. There ain't no me without you."

Either the drinks had me hot or his statement had me hot. Either way, I was regretting the no-makeup makeup look. I felt like I was going to sweat it off with the way my temperature was rising.

"Anyways. You know what he does. He says I'm the heir. If I don't want it, it goes to Neltz. If I do want it, it still goes to Neltz eventually. I don't even know what being a Don means. I be telling myself I want something to do, but do I want that? Running the ports? Running an empire? I could barely run my household. Neltz is bad enough, though. He don't need no damn empire, even if he won't get it until he's grown. I'm not a gangster, Renello. Then, you say you like me-like me, and sometimes, I like you too. I like you, and I like the way you make me feel, but I just got a lot to take in. I always viewed you as family when I did remember you before I blocked all y'all and the past out. To go from family to lovers is just beyond me. I have been running from you, but I also don't want you out of my sight for too long. I know I be acting crazy and insecure and giving you whiplash, but right now, I'm just confused. While I'm trying to figure this out, can you just please stick it out?" I took a deep breath as he stared a hole through me. He was so damn handsome. I'd grown used to the frizzy dread look on him, but my favorite new monster was Renello with a fresh retwist. He looked like a rowdy, well-kept, rich-ass gangsta nigga.

Shit. I should've brought an extra pair of panties.

"I want to say you don't have to do shit. But if you're bored, we get you back in school or you can start a business. You can get up and do whatever you want to do every day, Pia baby. We can take flights and go around the fucking country if that will satisfy you too. But I'm not the type of nigga to make demands on your life, Pia baby. If you want to take over Rio's organization, do it. But just be mindful of what you're getting yourself into. I'm Cuppacio, but I'm Rinaldi Mob. You're Mecanio now, but you'll be Mecanio Mob. Some things... you won't be able to confide in with me, and vice versa. But, I'm here for you. It's yo' fucking world, baby. Just make time for me in it. As far as Neltz... that lil' nigga will be ready. Our son is the Seed of Chucky. He got mo' heart than his bitch-ass daddy, that's for sure. I'm with whatever you with. Ion like it, and I wanna tell you to make that nigga Rio go fuck himself, but that ain't ever been me when it comes to you. I don't gotta like your choices to roll with 'em because, regardless, I love you. When it comes to my feelings, ain't no liking going on, Pia baby. I love the fuck outta you girl... too much."

"To infinity?"

"And beyon—"

Silverware clanked, plates shattered, and my chair flipped over as my scalp felt like it was on fire. It took me a minute to realize what was going on, but when I felt a fist pound my head, I snapped into reality.

"Bitch! You got me fucked up, hoe!" a high-pitched voice that I didn't recognize squealed.

I didn't know who it was that had gotten the best of me for ten seconds, but I was on her ass like white on rice. My eyes were open, but I'd blacked out. Even with my long nails, I delivered blow after blow. I'd come out of my shoes a while ago, and that gave me the advantage I needed. I had her ass bent over someone's table, socking soul to her ass. I didn't fuck with nobody, and nobody fucked with me. I wasn't fucking nobody's nigga, and nobody's nigga was fucking me. Whoever this hoe was, she was a straight-up hater, and now she was a hater that was getting her ass whooped.

"Whoop that hoe, Pia baby!" Hearing Renello in the distance gave me the extra boost I needed. I didn't like to admit it because it went against what I preached to my son, but I loved to fight. I was always ready for a hoe to run up so that she could get done the fuck up. The patrons of the restaurant scattered about as I slung this bitch all up and through the five-star steakhouse.

"You got my friend fucked up!" another high-pitched voice said before my hair was being yanked from the back. These hoes were trying to jump me.

"Bitch! You got my niece fucked up!"

My hair was let go with a yank, and I could feel a fight going on next to me.

Arianee?

I didn't know where she came from, but I could smell her signature perfume. Concerned customers whispered off in the distance, but nothing was stopping me from tearing into this bitch's ass.

"Is anyone going to call the police?"

"Oh, no. They are Mecanios. It's best to just let them finish with no interference," another guest suggested, and they made the wisest decision. I would hate to call Rio's ass.

"Come on, baby... y'all got them good. Nel, get Pia off that hoe."

I was lifted in the air. "Calm down, Pia baby. I got you. It's over."

My body relaxed, and when my vision returned, I saw Arianee pulling at her dress as her husband calmed her.

"Them hoes tried to jump me! Where my phone? I need to call Missy!" I couldn't believe this shit. We'd knocked over three tables, and people were either looking on in awe or in disgust. I didn't give a fuck. These bitches started with me.

Looking at the manager help the girls off the ground, the one I was fighting stood, and I tried to break free again.

"Bitch! You had my husband killed!" she screamed.

"Aye, hoe! Ion know what the fuck you talkin' 'bout, but accusations ain't safe for you," Nel spoke up.

"Hell nawl, they not," Arianee's husband added.

"Fuck that hoe! She was fucking my husband! That's why the detective looking into your ass now! You going down, hoe!"

"That dirty-ass hoe not nobody but a broke-ass, bottom-tier security guard!" Her friend had inserted her opinion, and when I looked over, it was none other than the dirty bitch I had to beat up at my old job. The one that always came with her ratchet family to beg their granny for money every week. She tried to jump in and got her ass kicked by Arianee. For her to have gotten her ass whooped twice in one year didn't stop her from talking shit, but it should've.

Reaching back, I went into Renello's pocket and grabbed a knot. "Shut yo' junkie, broke ass up! Hoe, is you still begging your half-dead ass granny for her SSI check? And you bitch! You can't get mad because yo' dead ass husband was a eater, bitch! May the limp dick bitch rest in hell!"

"Stupid bitch! Pop the rubber band and rain on them broke hoes, baby!"

I did exactly what Renello asked and tossed the money, sending twenties flying everywhere.

"Broke-ass hoes! I'll end both of you bitches! Even when I was working security, you hoes couldn't fuck with me on your best day! Every time I see you bitches, I'm on your ass!"

They were yelling and screaming while being dragged out of the restaurant. What was even more embarrassing was that the bitch from the nursing home had grabbed up plenty of the money. When they were finally gone, Renello let me down.

"What you muthafuckas looking at? The fuck! Eat!" I was

shamed but I would never admit it. I didn't start with nobody but I damn sure finished whatever was started with me.

"Aye, we apologize for disrupting yall's night. The meal is on us," Arianee's husband announced and everyone cheered. With the price of these steaks, I would be clapping too.

Arianee came over and hugged me after fixing her dress. Not a hair was out of place in her pretty little head.

"You good?"

"Yeah, I am. I appreciate you."

Nel and her husband bumped hands and chopped it up. Arianee pushed my hair out of my face.

"I needed that. I haven't fought in years." We laughed at her admission.

"Are they or what they said going to be a problem?" she asked with a content look more than a worried one. Being Rio's sister, I'm sure she'd seen, heard, and even done somethings involving people dying.

There were no cameras at my old apartment complex and there was no evidence of the crime. Now it made sense that the detective was hounding me that day. She had sent them. That bitch's husband was dead and it would be best for her to get over it.

"Hell no. She just a mad-ass hoe that's stuck with four kids. She's a cute girl—better get the fuck on. She should have been cheating back."

We laughed again as Arianee continued to smooth my hair back in place.

"I knew it was a reason I wanted to come here tonight. Come on... let's go across the street to the other steakhouse before I have to whoop one of these folks ass."

Looping my arm in hers, I let her lead the way as our guys followed behind. Two waiters were cleaning up the money and another three were fixing up the tables.

"Aye! Apply that money to the tabs too. Send us the bill for whatever's left after you apply them ten racks," Renello yelled and I knew he was deadass serious too.

Looking back at him walking with Arianee's husband, I couldn't help but swoon at how fine this nigga was. The swag. The protective nature. The fucking tattoo of my name. I needed a fucking fan or some water.

Calm down, Pia. You are not fucking this man tonight.

CHAPTER 15
VELLO

It took that nigga from our mob so long to get back with Big Mama's information that I almost said fuck the shit. He ended up sending it to me last night while I was hurled over the toilet. I told myself that I was going to get up bright and early and pull up on her ass. Unfortunately, I spent most of today over the toilet again. I was really over whatever the fuck it was that I had. I still refused to accept what my brother and Don had said about Big Mama. I had to pull myself together and make it to her crib because I wasn't letting another day go by without us talking about what the fuck was going on.

Pulling off the exit that led to Twin Peak Lakes, I looked at the dash and saw it was a little after five. I hoped she was home and not out shopping or having an early dinner. I knew she lived in Twin Peaks from our first conversation where her ass was volunteering information like I was her compadre. Twin Peaks was big, though, and had plenty of HOA neighborhoods. Big Mama's address led me to the back gate, and God was on my side because I was able to tailgate behind a

Cybertruck. Now, I was parked in front of her big-ass house. I guess she wasn't lying about not living with Rio.

Killing the engine, I hopped out of the car, leaving my spit cup. I hadn't spit in a couple of hours and prayed the ginger candy under my tongue continued to do its job. Don nem was confident that my sickness was because I had a little jit on the way. Saturday night, I took my ass to the emergency room, and after three hours was sent home and told to drink more water because wasn't shit medically wrong with me. It didn't make no fucking sense, though, because I was sick as a damn dog. I'd tried to call Ma, but her ass was back in Jamaica. She needed to learn how to sit the fuck down somewhere. She was never around when I needed her ass. But let this have been her baby, Nel, sick, she would have had her ass in the room making him all types of curry stew.

Seeing that there was a camera on the doorbell, I bent and looked directly into it. "Aye! Big Mama! You got a lot of fucking nerve. You playing too many fucking games."

I felt a wave of nausea, so I placed my fist to my mouth and took a deep breath. This shit had taken a fucking toll on me, but Google had come through for a nigga with the ginger candy. The nasty-ass hospital just sent my ass out the door; didn't even offer to pump a nigga with fluids. When the nausea subsided a few seconds later, I resumed my speech.

"A nigga been around this bitch sick as a fucking dog, man, and you playing Houdini. Bring yo' muthafuckin'—"

The door was snatched open, and a rush of warmth smacked my face. Big Mama stood in front of me, and even though it was good to see her, she matched my shitty look.

"What the hell are you doing here, Metavello?"

Her radiant chocolate skin appeared dull, bags were under her eyes, and a baseball hat was on her head as a few strings of hair hung down her ears. The oversized white T-shirt and dark grey leggings that made up her attire differed from what I was used to seeing her in. But then again, the only time I'd seen this lady was in a setting where she was dressed up. Tucked under her arm was a large Hermes bag, and on her feet were a pair of New Balance sneakers. I tried looking past her and was only able to get a quick glimpse of her home before she pulled the door shut. As the door closed, a gust of fragrance sifted into my face, and now I knew why she smelled a certain way every time I saw her. It was how her house smelled.

"I don't even have time to ask you how you got my address. I know my husband didn't give it to you." She rolled her eyes and tried to walk around me. Grabbing her arm, I pulled her into my chest.

"Aye... fuck yo' husband."

Discover looked me up and down, chuckled, and pulled her cap down as far as it would go over her big-ass forehead. "So, now you beefing with him? Metavello... if you think for one moment you'll be able to go against Rio, you're sadly mistaken. Another mistake of yours was coming to my home. Now, if you'll excuse me, I have an appointment I'm already running late for."

Everybody was acting like Rio was fucking God. Yeah, that nigga was cool at first, but if me and my brother said it was fuck him, then fuck him. She had some nerve talking shit when I had her sitting on my fucking dick every time I saw her ass. She wasn't worrying about her husband then, but I wasn't no disrespectful-ass nigga, so I wasn't going to even voice that shit.

"Look, I didn't come over here for all that. I would have never even pulled up at your house had you not blocked a nigga. I'm not here to disrespect your home. I know your daughter lays her head here. I just want to talk."

I liked Big Mama. I was cool on the bullshit and truly

wanted to talk. The reality was we'd fucked up, and even though I'd caught feelings during the process, I had to put that shit aside and figure the shit out. She didn't do this shit by herself. I was partially the blame for this shit and needed to see what the fuck the next step was.

Discover gnawed down on her bottom lip and sighed. Letting her arm go, I took a step back to give her some breathing room. I wasn't trying to set her pretty ass off. I just wanted to get to the bottom of this shit. Yeah, I was salty as fuck that she was married to Rio because I liked the fuck out of her, but I should have never taken it there. I was also salty that I could never have her like I really wanted to. I was going to have to let this girl go even though the shit was like pulling teeth. Not only was she off limits, but she acted like she didn't want my ass outside of spontaneous dick.

Instead of responding, she walked past me to my car. Jogging around the rear, I made it to the passenger door before she could and opened it. She took another look at me with those deep brown eyes before lowering herself into the car. By the time I got to the driver's door, the door was pushed open.

The engine roared as I sped out of her neighborhood. It was rush hour on a Monday evening so I knew we would get caught up in traffic if her doctor's office wasn't in Twin Peak Lakes. I had a feeling it wasn't.

"Could you please not smoke?"

We came to a red light, so I looked over at her pretty ass. It didn't matter that she looked like death was knocking on her door, she was still so damn gorgeous, and a nigga that liked to dip his dick in another man's ass didn't deserve her. If Rio's ass was in traffic, I would have run him the fuck over; that's how jealous I was. I knew her stingy ass wasn't going to ever give me no more pussy. She was too scared of how closely connected I was to her husband, so there was so much for farewell pussy.

"A nigga been too fucking sick to smoke, Big Mama. I haven't hit the blunt in... I don't know how long." The last time I smoked, I was throwing up the last ten years of my life. Since then, I stayed the fuck away from the blunt. "You gotta tell me where we going."

I'd passed at least four doctor's offices, but she hadn't pointed out one or given me directions. We were just driving and lost in our own fucking thoughts.

"Oh, my bad. But you're going the right way. The third light you come to, make a right, and then it's going to be on your left."

Nodding, I sped through traffic, holding my spit in my mouth. I had a McDonald's cup with me today with a lid. I didn't want to have another situation where I spilled my shit. There was so much that we needed to talk about, but I decided to keep the shit in until after her doctor's appointment. I had a feeling that this was where she was planning to tell me that her slick ass was pregnant. There was no way she was keeping this baby, though. She was married to a whole other nigga. I would be damned if I let his queer ass raise mine—if it was mine. But, above all, that nigga had her and her daughter set up. I didn't want to come through and fuck up anything she had going on just because I had fallen in lust with the pussy.

Turning into a dark brick building, I parked a few spaces down from a Lexus and killed the engine. I could no longer hold my spit in, so I grabbed my cup, removed the lid, and let it go. This shit was so fucking ridiculous.

"My mouth gets watery as fuck when I get nauseous. Swallowing the spit makes me throw up, so I gotta let the shit out," I explained.

"Oh..."

"Yeah, oh. You fuckin' pregnant, Big Mama, and I got all yo' symptoms," I admitted for the first time out loud.

Lowering her head, she fumbled with the string of her sweatpants. "This place is like an off-record clinic. It's free, and for mother's that's undecided. I wasn't expecting you to pop up, but since you're here, I guess I may as well tell you." She pushed her head into the seat and pulled her cap down. "I'm pregnant. It's not Rio's. It's yours. Rio and I have never had sex. I am supposed to give him a child through IVF. He already has the doctor set up and everything. I know you don't know me, and us having sex all those times was a mistake. A fun mistake that happened three times, but a mistake. I know I have to get rid of the baby. I don't want to, though." Her voice shook.

I reached over and rubbed her back. Hearing that I had made a whole fucking baby was like a punch to the gut. The signs were there; my brother told me, Don nem told me, and hell, my body told me. Still, *knowing* that she was pregnant was surreal. She was right, though. I wanted to be a daddy, too, but not under these circumstances. Nobody was going to be around here mistreating or playing with my child because of the misfortunes they were born into.

"I was going to tell you, Metavello. I just wanted to at least see the baby alone before bringing you in. I'm selfish with my babies like that. For so long, it has just been me and Discovery. I was pissed that I would have to have another baby and would have to share it with Rio. I love mothering on my own, even though it's hard. But it's selfish. It's selfish to the child and the father. I'm done being selfish. So... Metavello, would you like to go in here and check on your baby, even though I'll be terminating it soon? You can just think of this as a practice run appointment for whenever you do meet that one and have to come to prenatal appointments."

I could tell she was tearing up. She held them in, though; she was a fucking hard body. I been knew that, though. You got to be a hard chick in order to marry a nigga that takes dick every night. But, nah, the way her wanna-be-down ass was taking my dick when I knew she wanted to tap out let me know that she was strong as fuck. Grabbing her hand, I circled the back of it with my thumb and then placed peppered kisses on it. She smelled of shea butter and gourmand. It was fitting for her chocolate ass.

"Come on, Big Mama." Hopping out of the car, I went to her side and helped her out. This time, I brought my damn cup with me. I didn't want to keep getting up and spitting in these folks' garbage cans.

We stepped inside the building, and it was as if we'd jumped into Autumn's land. Pumpkin spice, apple pie, and cinnamon filled the air. It was overwhelming as fuck, and I had to fight to not throw up. The décor was nice, with wallpaper-lined walls, crème and mint green furniture, and sterile floors. Discover signed in at the front, and we were directed to a seating area. On the coffee table in front of us were pamphlets ranging from adoption options, abortions, and single parenting. Seeing the word abortion had me feeling uneasy, but what the fuck else was I supposed to do? She had her mind made up, and it was the right choice.

Would I have loved to make Discover my baby mama? I mean, yeah. I like her, her pussy is excellent, and she's beautiful. But I couldn't have her. Plus, the mob didn't play that shit. Fuck the mob, though; I didn't want no married-ass baby mama. I didn't even want a fucking baby mama, and that's why I'd skated by all these years without one. When it was my turn, my wife, whoever she was, would bear my children.

"Discover Banks?"

Discover shot up out of her seat as her name was called. There was a middle-aged Indian lady in a white coat with a soft smile and long black hair. There was a stethoscope around her neck and a folder in her arms. Placing my arm around Discover's neck, I kissed her jaw and led her to the back. I may have been a salty-ass nigga, but this shit was my fault. I had no business running in her raw. Now, she had to get a baby sucked out of her. My baby. I was just glad that shit wouldn't be happening today. This appointment was just for her to check on the baby. I didn't understand her logic in wanting to see something that she would have to get rid of, but I was curious my damn self.

I stood idle as a nurse walked up and took her weight and blood pressure. She also had to have blood drawn, and Discover acted like a whole baby. I had to all but hold her ass down. Then, she had to pee in a cup. After that, we were led to the room where she was instructed to undress from the waist down. I had to fight hard not to bend her ass over, but when she pulled her pants down, and I saw a pad with speckles of blood, I froze. I wasn't the brightest nigga in the world, but I thought when you were pregnant, you didn't bleed.

"I've been having some spotting the last few days. It's normal." She shrugged like it was nothing, but I wasn't convinced.

The doctor entered the room with that damn clipboard, so I focused my attention on her. "Hello. I'm Dr. Rasey. So, your pregnancy test did come back positive. Your blood pressure is a little high, and I want you to watch that; change up your diet and take it easy at work."

I side-eyed Discover because her ass didn't fucking work. If she was stressing it was because of her husband and the thought of getting caught. Shit had me getting pissed all over. Opening my cup, I spit inside.

"I just want to ask you a few questions. I can see that Dad is already experiencing symptoms."

"Hell yeah, I am, Doc. I can barely sleep, I throw everything up, my mouth waters all day, and I can't even keep water down. Why the hell this shit happening to me? I'm not the one carrying the baby."

"Well, we call it couvade syndrome or sympathetic pregnancy. It's more of a psychosomatic disorder, meaning that the physical symptoms are manifestation of psychological feelings."

"So, you saying it's all in my head? I didn't even know she was pregnant, though!"

"I'm not saying that, but still... it happens. Things just happen without an explanation. I don't like to involve religion and keep patient conversations aligned to evidence-based theories, but if you believe in God, I like to say... it's just the testament of the Good Lord and Savior." Her Indian accent was heavy, but in that moment, she sounded like a sixty-two-year-old black woman.

"Have you been sick?" she asked Discover.

"Yes. Very. It's hard to do anything. I used to love working out, but I haven't done that in weeks. I only keep down the soup that my daughter's nanny makes. It's the only reason I haven't lost weight. I can give you some when you take me back home," Discover answered the doctor before turning to me. I appreciated the idea, and the thought of eating something that I wouldn't throw up had a nigga a little hungry. I was weak as fuck and needed to eat something that would stick.

"It's all very normal. The first trimester is the hardest. Sickness usually goes away by the second trimester. The best thing you can do is keep yourself hydrated and get lots of rest. Don't worry about weight or anything; same with you, Dad. I have an ultrasound tech coming in shortly. Mom, are you having any doubts about the continuation of this pregnancy or having thoughts of adoption?"

"If I'm being honest, Dr. Ramsey, I want to get an abortion. It's the best thing for our... situation."

A fucking situation. That's what the fuck I was to her.

Opening my cup, I spit.

"I do, however, want to make sure it isn't twins. If it is twins, I will no longer entertain getting an abortion. He's an identical twin, and I'm not too sure if he passed that to my womb. That's why I'm here."

Hold the fuck up. She had just told me some totally different shit in the car. She didn't mention no twins or the possibility of wanting to keep the baby. I was shooting daggers at her ass, but there was also a part of me that was jumping for joy like her faggot-ass husband.

Another woman came waltzing in and cut the lights off. Discover explained to the doctor that she was spotting while the woman, who I assumed was a nurse, started messing around with the bulky machine. The doctor repeated what Discover had told me about it being normal to spot as long as the blood wasn't bright red. That blood in her pad looked bright red to me, but I elected not to say anything. As the doctor went on to explain the bleeding as implantation or some shit like that, I watched the nurse as she held up a long dildo-looking tool with a condom on it. She cut into Discover and the doctor's conversation, explaining what she was about to do before she eased it between Discover's thighs. A digital display monitor on the wall showed an all-black screen, and as she moved the tool around, white lines and shapes came into view.

"That right there is your bladder," the doctor explained. "I understand you said Dad is an identical twin. While that is amazing, identical twins aren't hereditary. Identical twins happen when a single fertilized egg splits into two. The sperm would have already reached the egg; it just decides to split, resulting in identical babies. As far as fraternal twins, those play a genetic role."

My eyes were locked on the screen as I sat in the chair placed against the wall. I glanced over at Discover, who was also glued to the screen. She caught me looking and gave me a half smile. She was so damn pretty, even though her fine ass had me sick as fuck.

"Well, I take back what I said. Look here..."

I stood in my seat as two black dots appeared side by side on the screen. Discover gasped as my heart blasted off in my ear. My nerves tensed immediately.

"What the fuck?" I stammered in bewilderment.

Alarm bells were sounding off within me, and sweat seeped through my skin. I'd hoped what I was looking at was a sick joke, but with the way the room had grown uncomfortably quiet, I knew what I was viewing was true.

"There are twins, and this here..." The doctor circled with the mouse. "This is the amniotic sac. They share a sack. Nurse, let's measure the fetuses."

I'll be damned.

I couldn't pull my eyes from the screen if I wanted to. There were two dots with no form or shape, but all I could do was picture my brother and me. I knew my brother went through his shit when Pia was gone, but I was blessed to have him all my life. I would never be alone and had never felt alone. Knowing my kids would have the same thing was heartwarming. All that abortion shit and leaving her alone shit had gone out the window. Twins changed things. Who in the fuck aborted identical twins?

The doctor and the nurse grew eerily quiet. I wouldn't have noticed if Discover hadn't called it out. "Umm, is everything okay? I can't believe it's twins."

Walking over to the bed where Discover was lying, I

grabbed her hand. She was nervous as fuck as the doctor and nurse studied the ultrasound machine.

"Well, you are measuring at six weeks and four days. How long have you been bleeding?"

"Um... it started some time after my daughter's birthday party. We had sex and... yeah. It's been spotting on and off for maybe a week in a half.

"Right. Okay. I don't want to alarm you, but we are not able to locate any heartbeats for the twins. Before you get upset, we want to give it three or so more weeks and see you back here after nine weeks. By then, we should either have a detectable heartbreak or—"

"Or what?" I asked in a strained voice. I'd just found out about the damn pregnancy and then agree to her wanting an abortion. Then we walk in this bitch and find out it's twins, jump for joy, and now the doctor is telling me my little niggas possibly hadn't made it. Had I fucked her too hard? Was this shit my fault too? She said the bleeding had started after I sexed her down in Rio's bedroom. Fuck.

"Again, we do not want you to be alarmed. Let's come back in three weeks. By then, we should either see two healthy heartbeats or a confirmed miscarriage. We did run a blood test, so when that comes back, I can check your hCG levels. The numbers should be high since you are pregnant with twins. This will give us a clearer view of what's occurring."

We thanked the doctor, and I helped wipe the gel from Discover's easy bake oven. The spotting Discover claimed was occurring was heavy blood. I could have sworn I saw a blood clot, too, but I kept my mouth shut. I felt like my chest was about to cave, but Discover was cool as hell. She wasn't crying, nor was she concerned. She was still in shock that it was twins and had repeated it a few times from the office to the car. I knew, though. I knew they were gone. I didn't have the heart to tell her that shit, though.

"You think they're dead, hunh? You think I'm having a miscarriage?" Discover snapped me from my thoughts as I turned into her neighborhood.

"Nah. I'm just shocked it's twins, baby. That's all. All that hereditary shit she was talking don't mean shit. I bet my brother gon' have twins too." I'd hope she didn't hear the resentment in my voice. I should have never fucked that girl in Rio's house. This shit was karma.

"I guess you'll see."

"I guess so," I said as I pulled into her driveway beside her AMG. I didn't even put the car in park. I had my shit in reverse and was waiting for her to make her exit.

"I'll text you with the reminder for the next appointment."

I nodded as Discover gave me one last look and got out of my car. Once she was in the house, I pulled off and let out the breath that I'd been holding. This mob shit was so fucking crazy. My babies were dead, and that shit couldn't have been a coincidence. Maybe that nigga found out she was pregnant and had poisoned her or some shit. She did say her nanny had been making her some soup. Yeah, that had to be it. He poised her. He killed my babies.

There were two things I knew for certain, though. One was that I wasn't going to that appointment. I didn't want to hear the doctor tell me what I already knew. Two, I was killing Rio. Fuck what everybody was talking about. He had something to do with this shit. The nigga was dick silly, but he wasn't a fool. I needed to pull up on my brother as soon as I could because we had to put this shit in motion and be ready for whatever came with it.

CHAPTER 16
PIA

The fight I had gotten into with those two irrelevant-ass hoes had my whole fucking body sore. I didn't feel it last night, but I damn sure felt it today. The night had been fun afterward, with Arianee and I across the street at a different restaurant, sipping Lemon Drops and laughing about beating bitches asses. Her husband and Nel just watched us and shook their heads. I didn't even have room to get upset about them making me hop out of character until I woke up this morning. Nel wasn't beside me, and being that his side was cold, I knew he had been gone for some time. To add to my irritation, my knuckles felt like they were on fire. On my son, when I saw them bitches again, it was on.

I didn't understand how a hoe was so mad at me about a nigga that was maggot food. She wasn't even considering the fact that I'd given her nigga back after finding out he had a bitch at the crib. Granted, I would be pissed, too, if my nigga was killed outside of his sneaky links house, but Banger hadn't smelled my pussy for months before he was killed. I had only planned on sucking his dick anyway for the measly hundred dollars and the pair of shoes he was bringing for Pearla. Them hoes had to see me, though. I didn't even know them weak bitches knew each other.

After handling my morning hygiene, I made my bed. Making my bed always made me feel better in the mornings, but in this case, I was still hot. Pearla and Nel were already at school. I woke up to texts from her telling me she'd gotten him ready and dropped him off at the bus stop. I slept straight through the alarm; that's how exhausted my body was. They weren't due home for hours, so I made use of the free time and organized my closet.

It was now two hours later, and I hadn't even left my room to see if Patty's busy ass was home. I was sitting on the side of my bed, calling Nel back to back. He did too much fucking lying for me. He had just told me Saturday night that he wasn't going to do this ghosting shit no more, and not even a full 48 hours later, he was pulling the same shit. Gnawing on my bottom lip, my knee jumped as my eyes scanned my room wildly. I wasn't looking for shit, but more so trying to calm my raging nerves.

Figuring he was in a meeting, I hung the phone up and shot him a text instead.

Renello! I know you see me calling you.

SITTING MY PHONE DOWN, I absent-mindedly cracked my knuckles and yelped in pain. I'd forgotten that quick that they were sore. Swallowing hard, I tried to suppress my anger. I didn't like being lied to or ignored. That shit grinded my fucking gears. I didn't even like when my weak-ass baby daddy lied to me and had been known to pop his ass in the mouth a time or two for that shit.

My phone chimed, so I picked it up from the mattress with squinted eyes.

RENELLO

Wassup Pia baby? You good? How you feeling?

WITH MY NOSTRILS FLARING AGGRESSIVELY, I tossed my head back.

"Nigga! You can't be serious? Fuck you mean, how I'm feeling?"

Instead of replying to his text, I called for the umpteenth time. Each time the phone rang, my meter climbed up a notch. When I was about to hang up and call again, he answered. His breathing was heightened, and that caused me to stand straight up.

"Wassup, Pia?"

Drawing my head back, I looked at the phone to make sure I'd called Renello and not my baby daddy by mistake. "So... it's just *wassup Pia*? No, Pia Baby...?"

Renello had the nerve to fucking chuckle. "You good? You need something?"

"Do I fucking need something? Renello, don't play games with me. You know why I'm calling! You said you wouldn't spend the night outside of the house no more! Where you at?" I'd begun pacing the room with my hand on my forehead. I could feel myself raging on the inside and was trying to calm down. "And why in the fuck is you breathing so hard? Renello!"

I could hear him shuffling the phone, whispering, and shit

in the background. With the phone still to my ear, I went to my closet and stuck my feet in the first pair of shoes I saw. I didn't even know if they were on the right foot. All I knew was that I was about to pull up and show my whole black ass.

"Pia, some shit came up. You called me in the middle of a count with Ezio n'em. I been here since around four. Do you need something or not?"

Intently listening to his background, I could tell that he'd taken a step outside. I wasn't taking his word for it, though. I was ready to pull up to his location to see for my fucking self.

"Send me your location, Renello."

"Pia ba—"

"Send me your fucking location! Right now, nigga!" I looked crazy as hell screaming at the phone, but I didn't give a fuck.

Then, he had the nerve to sigh into the phone like I was getting on his damn nerves. "Aite."

"Yeah, aite! Now!" I hung up the phone, grabbed a scrunchie from my nightstand, and pulled my hair back out of my face. Just in case he was with a bitch, I looked myself over in the bathroom mirror to make sure I wasn't too fucked up. The navy Lulu lemon skirt set would have to do, and it offered flexibility so that I could kick ass.

It was too damn cold outdoors for me to be wearing this shit outside of the house, but there were shorts underneath, so my ass wouldn't be entirely out if some shit went down. I had never gotten into a fight two days in a row, but shit, I was experiencing crazy shit these days. New daddies, talking mamas, and stalking baby daddies. One more fucked up thing on the list wouldn't hurt me.

Opening the door to my room, I halted seeing Patty standing there. I didn't know if she was on her way out or had just come in. The frown on my face softened a bit as I looked at the woman who had given me life. She didn't sit down much these days, but it was good seeing her in a new element. The jeans and sweater she was wearing looked expensive, and even the fumes spewing from her body smelled rich. Her shoulder-length hair was in big curls that framed her youthful face, and as she smiled, her white teeth could give veneers a run for their money. My mama looked like a rich nigga's baby mama, and I loved that for her.

"Good morning, Pia."

I still hadn't gotten used to hearing her raspy voice, so I giggled. "Good morning, Mama. You look pretty."

She looked me over with approval. "You look pretty too. You headed to see your dad? It's cold out there." Her smile dropped as if she already knew I wasn't going to see Rio.

Holding my phone up to see if Renello had sent me his location, I shook my head, seeing that he hadn't.

"Nope. I'm about to beat Renello's ass."

My mom's eyes ballooned, and she clutched her pearls. She was really wearing fucking pearls this early in the morning. "Oh God. Now, why are you about to put your hands on that man, Pia?"

Stomping my feet like a child, I whined, "Cuz! I told him yesterday to stop sneaking outta my house! He lied! I can't stand niggas that lie, Mama."

"Hmm... I see."

"You see, what?"

My mama walked around me and sat down on my bed while patting the spot beside her. Groaning, I stomped over until I flopped down beside her. "Mama, I gotta go."

"And you will. After we talk. I've had the chance to talk with your sister, but I haven't really sat down with you. I know you've been connecting with Rio, and outside of that, been busy with my grandbaby."

Instead of replying, I batted my lashes, trying to figure out where this conversation was going.

"Pia, what is the relationship status between you and Renello?"

Placing my head in my hand, I groaned again. "Mama, please. Not you too. That boy is my cousin. That's it... that's all."

"Hmm."

"Mama..."

"Pia... hear me out, baby. You're the strongest person I know. You stepped up when all you should have been doing was being a child. I know Niccoli didn't treat you the best, and instead of dwelling on that, you stepped up for our family when we moved to this new city. It must've been terrifying for you... a brand-new world, a baby sister, and a mama that could barely function."

Lifting my head, I looked into the teary eyes of my mother, and some of the ice in my veins for Renello and his games instantly melted. "Mama—"

"No, let me finish. I know you still hold onto a lot of pain from the past. You should have been somewhere in counseling for what we went through in Chicago. You should've been making friends and dancing or something, but you had to suppress your emotions and become the woman of the house. I let my own traumas shut me down, and I shut myself off from the world. The problem with that is I shut myself off from you and Pearla. Pearla needed me, but she was a baby, so she didn't miss out on mothering because she had you. But you... you needed me the most. And I let my head win Pia, and I will never be able to make up for that."

"Mama, it's okay. I did what I had to do," I said, having zero regrets for stepping up for my family. Dropping out of school, working dead-end jobs, and busting my ass was all worth it.

We'd survived. We'd overcome the bullshit. We made it out. I have zero regrets.

"No, you shouldn't have had to do that. When you first brought Hobo around. I knew then that I'd messed up. But, by then, I was so deep inside my own head that I couldn't even speak up. You were looking for love. You wanted to be loved, and when he came along, you thought he would give you that. He lied, he mentally abused you, he cheated, and he made you a teen mom. That was something I never wanted for you. I had you at sixteen! I didn't want you to do the same thing. But... because of me, it happened.

"I love my grandson, but I hate his father. That man knows you yearned for love and made it his mission to break you down like a fraction. Instead of loving you, he belittled you. He made sure Neltz was intolerable, and then, he left. That negro packed his things up and moved away, leaving you with not only a child but an entire household. We weren't Hobo's responsibility, but someone who loves you understands that you come with extensions. Then, you got with that other wannabe pretty boy who only wanted to jump up and down in your tail. Thank God he's dead!" She fanned her face as if she was getting hot as she expressed her emotions.

"Mama!" My mouth was wide open in shock at her admission.

"What? I am glad he's dead! He wasn't shit! But back to Hobo. That man is evil. He never loved you. He's always been jealous of you. You don't have to have materials for people to be envious of you, baby. He was in competition with your spirit. That's why he pulled the move he pulled when you dropped my grandbaby off. Now, ironically, he's here to stay since he caught wind of Renello. *Tuh!* It was all good when we were in the hood, in that raggedy car. Now, you've bossed up, and he's sticking around. I just hope and pray my grandson is prepared when Hobo breaks his heart because it's coming. But I'll be right here to pick up the pieces."

"Me too, Mama," I mumbled. I didn't like Hobo, but I prayed he didn't play with my son. Neltz loved his ugly-ass daddy, even though I hated the ground that bastard walked on. He was too fucking petty for me.

"Renello? That's a man. That boy has had it bad for you since you were children. Everyone looked at it as innocent cousins bonding, but I knew better."

"Because you knew Niccoli wasn't my dad, hunh?"

"Exactly. Around the time I became pregnant with you, Niccoli was so full of cocaine that he could barely get it up. When he did get it up, he was pleasuring the sluts they liked to keep around. Anyway, may he rest in Hell."

"Mama! You're on one today." I was holding my stomach as I cackled. She laughed, too, before grabbing my hand and looking me in my eyes.

"Renello has always loved you, Pia. He came in and upgraded us immediately. He did what a man that loves do! Hobo didn't have to be in love with you to help you. Him loving you on the strength of you being the mother of his child should have been enough for him to help you more. Renello, though? He's handled everything—no questions asked. I watch that boy walking around here like a sick puppy in love, sniffing behind you. I know you're dealing with getting to know your father, but Rio isn't going to be your whole life. And Pia, Renello will have to get married."

Scoffing, I turned my nose up.

"He will. It's just the way of their world. Your world, now, too. Don't let him get away because you're scared to let a man inside your heart. You know that boy is not your cousin, Pia. You know that. The DNA proved it too. You are using that as an excuse. I know you. You're my child, and you're afraid. You're afraid of letting a man in. You let Niccoli love you as a parent should, and he broke your heart. You let Hobo in to love you as a spouse should, and he broke your heart and left you with a baby. You let Ranger—"

"Banger, Mama."

"Ranger, Danger, bang bang... his ass is dead, Pia. It don't matter! You let him in to fill the void of the first two, and he turned out to be a fraud, and he hurt you. But don't punish Renello. He loves you, Pia. He actually adores you. You know how rare that is for a man to be utterly obsessed with a woman? It doesn't happen often, baby. And you got to stop getting mad with that man for handling his business outside of this house. You can't get mad when he leaves your side. He's not a child that needs monitoring twenty-four seven. You have to let that insecurity go, my child. If you're not mentally ready to let him in, let him go find the woman that can be that for him. He's ready to love, Pia, and he prefers it be you to receive his love. Don't drag him along. Let him in or let him go."

Sighing, I looked from my mother's beautiful face and studied the floor. She was making sense, but my mind still couldn't digest everything that had transpired in the last three months. "I asked Rio to give me time. I need time to sort this all out, Mama. You just started talking, Neltz is in a new school, we moved, I got a daddy now—"

"And you have nothing but time on your hands. You've shown and proved that you can handle a full plate. It's not fair to ask him to wait because what if he waits and you never come to terms? What if he waits and you find another man? Then, his waiting is for nothing.

"I love you, baby girl. And I'm so proud of you! You're the best thing that's ever happened to me. God knew not to give me children by Niccoli. No matter how you were conceived, you were created by a good man and a good woman. You have so much good in you, even if you don't see it. You aren't damaged. You aren't broken. You're hurting, baby. You're hurting and tired to the point that you wake up every day not knowing what to do with yourself. You're so used to having that cape on, and now that Renello has come along and removed it, you busy yourself trying to find it in the loads of freedom instead of enjoying the lifted weight. Let him in, Pia, or let him be. You hear me?"

Nodding my head, my mama placed a kiss on my forehead and then stood. "I know most of that went out the window, and you're still about to pull down on him. Call your daddy if you get locked up. He has connections."

Looking at my phone, I saw that Renello had sent me his location and flew out of my room. The cold air smacked me in the face, but before I could shudder, I was in the front seat of my truck and making the sixteen-minute drive. With the heat blasting, I let my mother's words linger. I did love Renello. But a part of me still felt like it was weird.

My heart pounded as I spotted Renello's Porsche. His car was one of six cars along the side of the street. The duplex home had no driveway, and even though the house was dead smack in the middle of the hood, the grass had been maintained, the green shudders on the house looked as if the paint was fresh, and the wrought iron door securing the house was beautifully crafted. There were also bars on the windows, ensuring no one would be able to break in. Parking on the curve behind what I recognized as Jisei's Rang Rover, I knew Ezio must've been in it because I knew her pregnant ass wasn't on this side of town. Still, I didn't know what the fuck Renello had going on.

Leaving my car running, I hopped out on ten, not giving a fuck if I would catch pneumonia up the ass. I'd applied lotion after my shower, but I was sure I would be ashy again soon.

Before I could get halfway through the yard, Renello was walking out the door. Seeing that he wasn't in the clothes from last night had me running up on him, but he caught my ass mid-jump.

"You got me soooo fucked up!" I screamed. Renello smelled like pure fucking soap. My legs were wrapped around his waist as he held my arms behind my back and walked through the yard with me trying to bite his face. "You're handling business! Well, why in the fuck are you in different clothing? Hunh? Then you on the phone calling me Pia, and not Pia baby!"

I was trying to bite his fucking nose off since he had me restrained, but all his ass was doing was moving his face. When he laughed, that shit did something to my soul. I was damn near foaming at the mouth.

"Aye, Renello! What the fuck y'all got goin' on out here?" Shio was standing at the door with a frown on his face.

Renello pecked my lips with a grin before looking behind him. "Go back in the house, cuz, and finish up. Pia just being Pia. I got it."

Looking over Renello's shoulder, I yelled, "You may as well call this nigga an ambulance! Allll y'all got me fucked up!"

Shio waved his hand and closed the door.

With my hands still secured behind my back by one of his, Renello used his free hand to pull the handle on the passenger side door. This gave me the opportunity to bite his ass, so I leaned in and took a chuck out of his neck.

"Aye! Stop that shit, crazy-ass girl," he shouted while still laughing. He tossed my ass in the passenger seat and jogged around to the driver's side. Not wanting to touch him while he was driving because I loved my life, I sat there and pouted while he jetted out of the neighborhood.

"Man, you crazy for real." He side-eyed me after a few minutes of silence.

"No! You play with me too much. What I just say at the restaurant?"

"Pia baby—"

"Oh... so, now I'm Pia baby again!"

"Pia, you always been my baby. You threw me off... that's all." He licked his lips while zooming through traffic.

"You said you wouldn't leave like that again."

"I did. But when counts and shit come up short, I gotta get to it, Pia. You want me to keep bringing home the money, right?"

Instead of answering him, I tsked. "That don't explain you changing clothes!"

Renello rubbed his hand down his face. "I had to shit. That fucking leftover mac and cheese tore my stomach up. So I showered in the count house and put on the extra clothes I had in the car. Come on now, Pia baby. Why you trippin' on a nigga? I thought we was good? You told me to give you time, and I agreed."

Blowing out a long breath, I put on my seat belt and rode in silence, with the exception of pouting. Renello reached over and grabbed my thigh but hurriedly snatched it back. For some reason, him removing it annoyed me. I didn't let him know that, though. When I didn't notice the house we'd pulled up to, only then did I speak up. "Who's house is this?"

The house was made of a similar style to our house. It sat in a middle-class neighborhood with a well-manicured lawn.

"I gotta check the count here to make sure it's thirty stacks of money. It's another count house, Pia *baby*." Renello snickered and turned the car off.

"Stop playing with me," I sassed.

"Man, come on, crazy girl." I followed Renello into the home. It smelled of bleach and Fabuloso, and I could tell it hadn't been lived in. "We've only stepped foot in here about three times. We have to keep our shit spread out, and in the case that it's raided, we got it furnished so that it looks like someone lives here."

There was so much that I didn't know about Renello's world, and that angered me. There was once upon a time that we knew everything there was to know about each other. The house was warm and had furniture and TVs in every room but no other décor. It was a four-bedroom house with identical bedroom sets in every room. As we walked through the house, the smell of new timber from the beds and dressers drowned out the cleaning supplies. Black comforters decorated the mattresses, and basic lamps sat on the nightstands. With the right décor, the house would be really inviting, but by it being a count house, I knew décor was the last thing on their minds. I was shocked they even furnished it, but Renello's logic made sense.

"Sit down." Renello's command had me growing warm. My body was reacting to him again, and he was oblivious as he went into the closet of the master bedroom. I heard him type in a few codes, and then an iron door popped open. I couldn't see him from where I was sitting, but I could hear him shuffling money around.

Looking around the room with my legs crossed and arms folded, I was happy that the heat was on because I had no business wearing this skirt in forty-degree weather. I'd thought Renello was up to some bullshit, and that was still up for verdict. I didn't like calling folks, so having to call back to back without an answer didn't sit right with me. Anytime anyone called me, I picked up, with the exception of Hobo, because all he wanted to do was argue these days. Our child was nine years old. There was no point in us fucking arguing.

I could hear a beeping sound again, and seconds later, Renello emerged. Stress covered his face, and I knew whatever it was that he'd counted in the closet wasn't right.

"You good?"

Licking his lips, he grabbed at one of his locs and twirled it. "Yeah, ain't shit. But—" He took a few paced steps toward me and didn't stop until his torso was in my face. "Why you trippin' on a nigga, Pia baby?"

Shrugging, I turned my head, arms still crossed over my breast.

"Aye... it's okay to love me, Pia. We grown as fuck, baby. I ain't gonna keep repeating myself because you know what it is. Even though I like when you do that crazy shit, you don't have to."

"What crazy stuff, though, Renello? I just don't like when you sleep away from me and don't answer the phone." I let my arms flop to my sides with a huff.

Renello stared at me intently. His sharp nose was shiny at the tip, matching the rest of his chocolate skin. Renello took very good care of himself and had a whole skincare routine. Sometimes, it made me envious because I knew he'd learned it from somewhere. We had been out of touch for seventeen years. I was always his person before then, and the thought of him replacing me during that time made me sick to my stomach. He gave me another look before taking a seat next to me. The mattress dipped as he lay back on the bed. I was still sitting upright, so I watched the rise and fall of his chest as he stared at the ceiling.

"I'm in the streets, Pia baby. And I'm in them bitches heavy. Sometimes... duty calls. If I'm called to report, ain't no way in hell I'ma wake you up outta your slumber so you can be up worried about a nigga. Just know I'm not fucking with no hoes. And while I have no reason not to, I'm not on that type of time. You gotta believe in me, Pia baby."

"I... I'm damaged. I know I am," I admitted.

Renello's gaze fell on me again, and he chuckled. "Hell yeah, you are."

Punching his chest, he tried scooting away, but when he realized he wasn't fast enough, he grabbed my fist. "Watch out! I'm just fucking with you, Pia baby," he exclaimed.

"No, you're not. You being for real!"

"Aye..." Renello pulled me toward him so that I landed on his chest. I could smell the blunt and candy on his breath that had his tongue a hue of red. My breathing hitched as we stared at one another. "You don't think I'm scared, Pia baby? I'm scared as fuck. Ion know shit about relationships or love or none of that shit. I basically shut the fuck down when I thought you had died. Now that I got you back, I run myself crazy thinking about the possibilities of what could happen to you when you're not in my presence. I find myself mad at your fucking daddy because he taking up all your time."

"Now, Renello..."

"Nah, that's real shit. Make me want to do sum'n to that old-ass nigga for hogging my baby."

Baby.

His eyes clung to mine, and I could tell he was studying my reaction. I tried playing it cool, but I knew he could feel my beating heart through my chest onto his. I could certainly feel his breathing change in pace.

"That's my father, Renello."

"And! Ion like sharing you, but I have to suck that shit up. I hate to say it like this, but... I have to give the streets some of my time just like I gotta give the mob some of my time. But you always come first. You, Neltz, Pearla, and Patty. Before I left, I slid money under everyone's door and made sure Neltz badass was breathing."

"What?"

"Hell yeah. That young nigga sleep on his back with his

287

eyes halfway open. That shit low-key be having me spooked, so I have to place my finger under his nose and shit."

My stomach clenched as I shook with laughter. I remember his first doing that as a newborn. It had me scared to fucking death. I thought his ass was gone. The whole time, it was just how he slept. It was like he didn't trust anybody, so he had to sleep with both eyes partially open. That boy has been giving me hell since day one.

"But for real, shit ain't gon' go how you like it all the time... just like shit you do not gon' go how I like it. We our own fucking people, Pia baby. We can't do that jealous and controlling shit. I been having to check myself these last few weeks for feeling just like how you feeling now. It ain't healthy. We got to trust each other. You hear me?"

"Ummhmm."

Renello stared wordlessly and then shook his head. "You don't hear me, but it's cool."

Reaching in, he pecked my lips once, twice, and then a third time. My body temperature went up a few notches at the feel of his pillow-soft lips.

No Pia!

He laid back down and folded his forearm on his face. It was obvious that he had something going on with his count, and here I was, being a damn brat. Looking him over, my eyes stopped at the tattoo on his neck. Seeing Pia etched in large letters never seemed to get old. My heart turned over anytime I focused on it. My name was branded on him.

"You love me?" I asked him after a couple minutes of silence.

"I do, Pia baby. Give me a minute, though. We can leave in a second. We'll be home before Neltz gets off the bus. I gotta take him to Game Stop. A nigga just tired and need to rest my eyes for a second."

My mother was right. I was afraid to get my heart broken. Niccoli was supposed to be my father, but he was a monster. Hobo was my first, and ended up stomping and jumping all over my heart. Banger was supposed to be my escape, but he turned out to be a fraud and an embarrassment. Renello, though; he'd been my first love. First loves comes in many different forms; that's what Pearla told me. It doesn't always have to be in the form of romance. Renello was that, and somehow, in these last few days, I'd gone from loving him in a hearty and platonic way to really loving him.

But it didn't feel right. On top of that, every man that had ever loved me hurt me. We'd been apart for nearly two decades. I didn't know what Renello was capable of anymore. Even though everything in me told me that he was the only one capable of handling me properly, I was just so damn conflicted. I used to say my focus was on getting myself in a better financial position, taking care of my family, and getting my mama back to talking. I now had all of that, plus some, so there was nothing holding me back from love. Real love.

Still, I was reserved. But I didn't want to let him go. I didn't want him to be with another woman and wanted to cry happy tears about him not having a baby mama. Had he had one, I would have probably been jealous of the bitch and her baby. It wasn't fair, but that's just how I felt. This man, this amazing man, hadn't ever told me no. Even when we were kids, he found a way to grant my requests. Those days, his father worked him to death, and he would still carry his exhausted little body to the garden with me and smell roses.

He was my best friend, my partner in crime, and my escape. Even now, I'd come back into his world with baggage, and he hadn't complained once. My mom was right; it wasn't fair for me to ask him to wait. I was giving myself whiplash with my conflicting emotions and thoughts, but one thing was evident. I loved him. Even if I didn't want to in this way, I did. And it almost pained me to admit it.

Throwing logic out of the window, I swung a leg on the side of Renello and straddled him. With the way his breathing had changed, I knew he was asleep. I'm glad he was because if he was coherent, I would have chickened out. Taking a deep breath, I pushed the built-in shorts aside, and air hit my bald box. Lifting a bit, my knees drove into the mattress, and I reached into the black sweats he was wearing and gripped his tool.

"Fuck," I drawled. He was not only hard but thick and long. I hadn't been with many men, nor had I felt all of him, but I could tell he would be the biggest dick I'd ever had. That said a lot because Banger nor Hobo had small dicks. They were both packing in their own right.

"Shit," he slurred, but by the way his arm was still folded over his face, I could tell he was still asleep. I slept beside this man every night; I knew when he was in the land of the dreamers.

Bracing myself, I placed him at my sloppy, wet hole. My pussy felt like she had a pulse with the way she was thumping, ready to receive him.

"Ahhhhh," I winced as I let him fill me up. Thank God I was Super Soaker wet because it would have been a struggle.

"What the fu—" Renello's eyes bounced open, and the red in them let me know he was indeed asleep. His hands shot to my waist, and I could tell he was confused by the way he was looking around. My face was contorted because his dick was resting uncomfortably in my guts, and I needed to move in order for it to start feeling good.

I lifted my body and lowered it back down slowly on his meaty stick.

"Pia baby," he croaked. His eyes squinted, and then he

closed them and mumbled, "Wet as this pussy is... this shit bet not be no fucking dream."

"Renellooooo." It was hurting to slowly ride him, but with the way he was gripping my hips, I knew it felt good to him.

His eyes shot open again, and when he realized I was really riding his dick, his lids lowered. "C'mere."

I lowered my chest onto him, trying to keep the rhythm. He smothered my lips, taking my mouth with demanding savagery. The kiss was so intense and so sloppy that it set off a burning desire and aching need, and it made me even wetter. He'd packed me to the fucking brim, and I still wanted more of him. I needed more of him.

"What you doing this here for, Pia baby?"

Be... because... I—I need you."

"Fuck, baby." He breathed on my lips. "I need you too. You riding that dick so good, you know that?"

I nodded my head as I slowly winded my hips.

"It's hurting?"

I nodded again. I thought the uncomfortableness would succumb, but it didn't. Still, I didn't want to stop. I'd never felt so close to him—to my person. I felt more locked in now than we'd ever been. I could feel all of him, even the frustration from the count. I guess this was what they meant by soul ties.

"How you want it, Pia baby?" Renello began unzipping my jacket as I kept making love to his body. Once the jacket was off and the sports bra was over my head, he leaned in and took my breasts in his mouth.

I moaned in satisfaction as he gave them equal treatment, and I thought I couldn't get wetter. The way he was sucking on my breasts mimicked the way he'd eaten my pussy. He was a dangerous man with his tongue. It was a wonder that this man didn't have twenty kids running around with the lethal combination he possessed. During sex, most men forget all about the titties. But I liked my sucked just as much as I liked the kitty slurped on.

Renello used his strength to flip us around, and once he was on top, he pulled his dick out of my warm snatch. He stood and looked down at me, reaching for the waistband of my skirt. I helped him pull it off me and was now lying here as naked as the day I was born.

"You so fucking gorgeous."

Pulling his shirt over his head, he stepped out of his pants and then his boxer briefs. He wasted no time lowering to his knees and putting my pussy dead smack in his face. I felt my legs weaken as his warm mouth sucked in my clit with a slurp.

"Ohhhhh!" I squealed as my hips bucked in his face as he was taking his time devouring me. Throwing that shy shit out the window, I grabbed a handful of his dreads and drove his face further into my kitty. My body arched toward him as he feasted as if he hadn't eaten in weeks. When his eyes locked in with mine, my stomach clenched.

"You... 'bout... to... cum? Hunh... Pia baby?"

Nodding my head in a frenzy, I nearly ripped his dreads from his scalp.

"Pussy taste so good... I can eat it all day. Is that what you want? You wanna wake up to me sucking on this pretty pussy? Cuz on foe nem, I will."

"Yasssss! Yessss! Yeahhhhh!"

"Cum tastes good too. Cream in my mouth, Pia baby."

My breast tingled and my back lifted from the bed as I became undone. My legs vibrated, and my eyes rolled to the back of my head. It looked like I was having an exorcism in here when all I was doing was coming. Coming for my person. Coming for Renello.

"Good girl, Pia baby."

With my chest still heaving and eyes now low, Renello

placed kisses on my inner thigh and trailed them all the way up my belly. He went to work back on my breasts before sucking my lips in. Tasting myself was never something I enjoyed, but with Renello, it was as if I craved it. Getting lost in his kiss, he positioned himself at my entrance and slid back in. This time, it felt much better.

"Ummmmm shiiiit," I moaned.

"You so fucking tight, Pia baby. I love this pussy already. It's mine, right?" Renello's thrusts weren't fast, but they weren't slow either. They were perfect. My body squirmed beneath him as an icy cold feeling came all over me. I was about to come again, and I had barely come down from the first organismic high. I tried pressing his chest to get him to ease up some, but he wasn't having it. He placed both of my hands above my head and held them down to the mattress. "Take this dick. You can do it."

Renello's body was so fucking nice. Not only was he tatted up, but his rock-hard abs made me want to get my ass in the gym. He was a walking fantasy. He was a walking wet dream with dreads that trapped and mobbed for a living, and he was all mine. With my arms pinned, all I could do was take it—take everything he was giving me.

He captured my lips in his again, and that was when I let my body give in to the second orgasm. He fucked me through my orgasm, not once switching up the pace, and when he felt me come down, he flipped my ass over.

Slap Slap

"I want to keep making love to you, baby because that's how much I love you, but I owe you an ass-whooping in the form of fucking." He pressed his hand on my arch, driving me into the mattress while keeping my ass tooted. I felt him slap his dick on my ass cheek, and that motherfucker was too heavy. I wanted it in my mouth, but I'd save that for when I found myself in trouble.

"I'm 'bout to fuck the shit out of you, Pia baby. I'm 'bout to fuck you like I picked you up in the club for a one-nighter. You made me wait too long, baby." He teased my entrance with his dick, and it felt so good. "You held out knowing I'm the only nigga that's gon' fucking treat you right. I'll never hurt you, Pia baby. But I'm 'bout to hurt this pussy."

"Ohhh!"

Whap Whap

He slapped my ass two more times. "Didn't I drop the lo' for you?"

"Ye... yesss!"

"You trust a nigga?" He was still playing with my hole, and it was driving me crazy with anticipation.

"I... I do!"

"Nah, you don't, but after this, you will. You bet not fucking run, either. Take this dick with yo' tough ass."

Renello rammed his dick inside of me, and that shit had my knees giving out. He had a trick for my ass, though, scooping me up by my stomach and holding me right back in place.

"Un hunh! What I just tell you?"

"You... you said... Shiiiit. You... no runnnnn!"

"Yeah, no run! With yo' good pussy having ass!" Renello was fucking me so hard and fast that if I didn't believe he loved me, I would have been questioning it. It hurt so good. The immense amount of pleasure I felt was indescribable. He was fucking me so good that I felt him everywhere, even in my hair follicles. "Tell me sum'n, Pia baby. I ain't in this shit alone, am I? If so, I'll never fuck you again."

"What? No! I... I love youuuuuuuu! To in... infinityyyyy!"

His balls slapped my pussy repeatedly as he rearranged my organs. It didn't make no sense how good this man could fuck. My knees buckled again, and this time, he pulled me by my neck. I'd never been fucked like this before. If I wasn't crazy already, his ass had just flicked on the crazy switch for sure. The grip on my neck tightened, and his pounding intensified. This man was fucking me like he didn't have no sense.

"And beyond. Fuck! Pia baby, if I nut in this pussy, you marrying me. So where you want it?"

"I... I—" I was too dick dizzy to speak.

"Where you want this nut?"

"Don't... don't nut in me," I said, trying to sound confident in my plea.

"Too fucking late. Praying for twins."

Squeezing my eyes shut, another orgasm rocked my body like I was placed in the electric chair. I felt Renello empty his seeds, and when I tried to move, the grip he had on my neck tightened. He was choking the fuck out of me from the back. "Gotdamn! Fuuuuuck, Pia baby. Shit!"

My body gave out, and I fell forward on the mattress. Renello's heavy ass landed on my back too, but I didn't mind. I was trying to catch my fucking breath. He eased out of me, and at the same time, his warm nut gushed from my womb onto the black comforter. With his dick lying against his thigh, he stood.

"Turn back around."

I'd turned on my back, and his ass was trying to get me back on all fours. My shit had gotten beaten out of the frame. The work he put in was evident because both of our bodies glowed with a sheen of sex sweat.

"Renello, no—"

"Turn back around," his voice boomed, and I wasted no time giving in to his demands. He brushed my ponytail out of the way, and I felt his index finger trace the back of my neck. "When you get this?"

Renello wasn't the only person branded. I had his name

inked into my skin on the back of my neck. "You like it?"

"I love it, baby. Stay bent over like this." Before I could protest, Renello had stuck his whole tongue in my asshole.

"Huuuuhhhh." I had never felt no shit like this before.

"You crazy as fuck if you think you not 'bout to marry me, girl. Now ride my tongue."

I don't even think Jagoda Bay was ready for the dick spell this man had put on me. He was going to have to lock my ass up in the crazy house if I even saw a bitch sneeze on him.

CHAPTER 17
PEARLA

"I can't believe we finally got you outside, little Miss P.R," Mahzeyah voiced from the back seat. She and I had been hanging out all week after school. Bella had been so damn busy with work that she had been pushing us to the side.

"Right, you know we the three live crew," I added while watching my phone that was mounted and displaying the directions.

We had three minutes until I turned into the parking lot of our destination. The dazzling lights of the city shone inside of the car as I did five miles over the speed limit. Tonight, we were all spending the night at Bella's house, so Mahzeyah would be able to stay out all night if need be. My sister had my location, but hopefully, she wouldn't be watching it tonight. Bella was in college, so technically, she didn't have a curfew, plus her mama was cool as hell. All of the Cuppacio women were down-to-earth. I guess whatever they had gone through had left them with carefree spirits. All my mama told me was to not bring a baby home. She didn't have to worry about that, though, because I wasn't even sexually active.

"Y'all haven't been missing me. Y'all been all over the city." Bella rolled her eyes and then smirked while replying back to whoever was on her phone.

"Pearla's ass be in her own world. You know she's the cool-calm one out of the crew. I love her, but you my turn-up partner."

"I'll remember that when you want company, and she's too busy to answer."

We giggled before Mahzeyah yelled out to Bella, "That nigga better be paying you good!"

I still couldn't believe that she was Essex's social media manager. He was a grown-ass man, but Lord, he was fine and talented. Whoever got him would be one lucky lady, for real. I didn't do grown men because I was only seventeen and liked to stay in a child's place, but if I was hot in the ass like Bella, it would be a go. I was shocked that she wasn't on him. When she told me he was like a big cousin to her, I thought it was cap, but Bella never brought Essex up. It was always Mahzeyah or me.

"Hell yeah, he is. He knows how I rock. Plus, now that he has Ekon, my workload has lessened. My job is easy as hell. But managing his social media shows me how much of a groupie these hoes can be out here. It's sickening at this point. I hope you ready for that shit." Bella looked at Mahzeyah in the back seat.

Mahzeyah fanned Bella off as she looked out the window. As always, my girl was iced out. Her jewelry was shining under the lights. My mama bought matching necklaces for my sister and me. It wasn't shit like what Mahzeyah had on, but it was cute and real. Bella was even rocking a chain, thanks to her new salary. It was her name engraved on a diamond-encased plate hanging from a platinum rope. As always, we were coordinated in our new Jordans. We weren't dressed alike, though, keeping it individualistic. I kept it simple in a Fashion Nova Velour jogging set that showed a bit of my waist. I was thick but confident in my body and didn't mind showing skin. Bella was in ripped jeans and a cropped hoodie, and Mahzeyah was in a Prada hoodie dress. My girl kept that shit on, but with a daddy like hers, I expected nothing less.

"Damn! This bitch packed. Is it the club or the studio?" I asked as I parked beside a black Charger.

"Un hunh, bitch... park over there beside that Benz. This Charger look like a bunch of YN's gon' be hopping in it. Niggas might rob us. I just got my chain! I'm not trying to get my shit snatched," Bella complained as she pointed to the spot she wanted me to park.

"What's YNs? I always see that in the captions on TikTok."

"Girl, even my ass knows what that means. YN's means young niggas. It's an abbreviation. Knowing Flexer, it's plenty of them up here too," Mahzeyah answered. "And to answer your question, Bella, I'm not ready for shit. Flexer is fine and all, but he's my mama's favorite rapper, not mine. He cool to kick it with, but he be having too much going on. He not the only nigga in my phone... trust me. Also, I'm in my senior year of high school. I'm not trying to have my name attached to no drama."

"Period! That nigga don't know who the fuck your daddy is. You don't need these niggas."

"And don't. What Latto say? Fuck I look like asking him about anutha bitch?"

"Ahhhh! On foe nem! But no lie, I'm asking!" We all laughed at Bella as I removed my seatbelt. We were now in the new spot, far away from the YNs.

"Let me text that nigga and tell him we outside. If it's too many bitches in here, we leaving." Mahzeyah's fingers got to pecking. I removed my phone from the mount and went to my messages. I had one from my nine-year-old daddy, also known as Neltz, asking me if I wanted to watch Selena tomorrow when I got back. It was a weeknight, but school was out for today and tomorrow. With the way this parking lot was set up, you would have thought it was the weekend. Choosing to not reply back to Neltz because I wasn't trying to watch that sad-ass movie, I paused seeing Grind had texted me. The night we chilled at his apartments, we texted the whole next day, and I hadn't heard from him since then. I told Bella about it, and she told me not to chase no nigga and to wait for him to text me. My ass had been waiting so seeing his name all these weeks later had my heart pumping like an 808.

GRIND

What are you doing?

GRIND WAS as hood as they came, but he always used correct grammar when texting. I thought it was too attractive, even though it was odd. He didn't use any abbreviations or anything, even though he talked with plenty of slang. The night we texted, we had a fire conversation, and after that, nothing. I liked him a lot. Too much. Even still had him as my screensaver. But I wasn't chasing anybody. So, I left him on read, and yes, my receipts were on.

"Lip gloss check!"

Bella had done all of our eyebrows again and added strip lashes. I added gloss to my already glossed lips and sprayed more perfume in my key areas. I'd brought the travel size with me. My bro Nel had bought me a Speedy Louis bag,, and I already knew I was going to carry the LVs off of it.

"He sending his security down. Y'all ready?"

"Damn! That nigga ain't that famous! He could have come down!"

"Bella, stop. You know damn well he is. He cannot be just coming outside, even if this is downtown. You know the hood only three blocks over."

"Much as that nigga rap about guns, he better not be scared of the hood. Nah, I'm just playing. He doing the right thing. Can't be moving like no crash out. Is that the big nigga right there?"

A guy in all black, who looked to be the same build and height as Shaquille O' Neal, stood in front of the black building. If it wasn't for his long blonde locs, he would have blended in with the building.

"Yeah, that's him."

We all filed out of the car, letting Mahzeyah take the lead since this was her dude. My friend was playing it smooth, but she had pulled a whole rapper. This past week, Mahzeyah had me everywhere, and I got to really see how the rich live. She was that fucking girl, but she didn't try to put others down just because she had a lot. Her daddy kept her blinging, fresh to death, and with a pocket full of money. Unlike the girls at my school, Mahzeyah treated everyone equally. She had a smart-ass mouth at times, but she meant well. Smart mouth and all, I ain't never seen her pop heavy. She was the same girl that chilled with me in the hood with jewels on worth thousands and didn't complain, not one bit. It could have been because her dad had eyes on us, but she was comfortable. I loved me some her. Bella was my bitch too.

"Y'all here for Flexer?"

"Nah, nigga, we here for the boogie man," Bella sarcastically replied.

"Man... bring yo' young ass on inside."

We all snickered as marijuana smacked us dead in the face as we entered the building. The lobby was nice, with crystal chandeliers and a black marble desk with a security officer in the same uniform Pia used to wear sitting behind it. Her security days seemed so far away, even though they were literally weeks ago. So much has happened since then.

The security guard leading us swiped a badge at the elevator. We all filed in, and once the door opened, I got nervous, like I was meeting Flexer. I'd never been to a studio before, but hanging with these two, I went places and did things I never had. We hadn't done anything bad outside of smoking weed and taking a shot here and there, but I loved the experience.

"How I look?" Mahzeyah asked.

"Like you belong on that niggas side and out of his league at the same damn time. Girl, you a bad bitch. You better run his pockets too. It don't even matter what the fuck you got in yours, he not sending you off without shit. He got it."

"Girl, I'm not doing shit with him. We just here to chill. You know these dudes not putting out when you not giving it up. We just here for the vibes."

I wanted to say that Grind had put a few hundred in my pocket, and I didn't give out shit but a hug. I kept my mouth shut, though.

The elevator dinged, and the security grunted. "I'm so fucking glad ion have no daughters."

Bella looked back at him with a frown. "I'm glad too. You don't need to make no big-ass Helga's. Stick to making wide receivers. Come on, y'all."

The studio was nice as hell and crowded as fuck. YN's, as they called it, were posted up on the walls. There were at least two dice games going on, and girls were dancing with red cups to their mouths. In the middle of the room were two men sitting behind a table that had many buttons and dials. Beyond that was a glass wall that showed Flexer standing in a booth with earphones on his head. There was so much smoke coming from his mouth, you could barely see his face. I knew it was him, though, because of the dreads.

"Damn. This my type of carrying on. I should have made myself available sooner," Bella stated and clutched her chain with glee in her eyes.

"Aye. Hol' up... stop the beat." The beat stopped, and all eyes were on the glass that Flexer was standing behind. "My baby. Bring yo' fine ass in here. Y'all make her friends feel comfortable. Don't be on no weird shit, to the niggas ion know. My camp would never."

Bella nudged Mahzeyah. Clearing her throat, she pulled her dress down and switched to the booth.

"They fine ass hell."

"They fly as hell in the new J's."

"They iced out too. Where Flexer find them?"

"You know he keep the low-key bad bitches."

I tried to ignore all the chatter around me, but that last remark was going to stick. I was telling. I'm glad Mahzeyah kept her options open. Flexer is a famous rapper and all, but my friend wouldn't be one of the bitches he was fucking and ducking. I hoped she wasn't all talk and was more like me. Soon as Dalton got to running off at the mouth and acting weird, I got rid of his ass.

Bella and I found a corner to post up at, and the security guard ended up bringing both of us a black bar stool. I was grateful that Bella's smart-ass mouth hadn't swayed his kindness. Her mouth was ruthless. Mahzeyah was just as bad.

Taking our seats, we heard the beat drop again. Flexer started spitting over the beat while looking directly at Mahzeyah. The song sounded dope, and I knew it was going to be a hit.

We not no regular niggas
We don't fuck regular bitches
We getting hella dem riches
Ayeeeeeee
She was iced out when I met her
Had mo' rank than me when I vetted her
All this fame shit, don't impress her
Fuck a first class, gotta jet her

Bella and I looked at each other and did a silent scream. Not he made a whole song about friend! Oh, the summer was for sure ours, baby! We were about to make so many Snapchats to it.

"Here... I wanted to get y'all your own bottle. I know y'all too young to drink, though." The security guard handed us a bottle of Patron, and before I could reach out and grab it since Bella was too busy making a selfie video, a tattooed hand grabbed it for me.

"They not old enough for this shit, big dawg."

Letting my eyes trace the tattooed arm, I had to catch my balance from almost falling out of the chair when I realized who it was.

Security held his arms up. "Just following orders from the boss, homie."

"That's my cue to roll." Bella stood. "Hey, phone thief. Bye, phone thief."

Chuckling, Grind rubbed his chin. How was it that this boy got finer by the day? He had grown out a goatee and was in his usual attire: a crisp white tee, sweat pants, and white forces. Still, he looked so fucking fine. Whew.

"Sup, Bella."

Bella disappeared in the crowd, and when I noticed Italian over in the direction she was headed, I felt much better about being here. We had family in the building.

I could feel Grind staring a hole in my face, but I looked everywhere but at him. He made me so nervous that it was almost embarrassing. "You left me on read. Why?"

"Damn, Grind... how you doing?" Turning my head, I gave him my attention, but that was the wrong thing to do. The way he was eyeing me had me ready to do things my mama wouldn't be proud of. "You left me on read so long ago. I thought you wasn't interested."

"Nah. That's where you wrong. Come on now... I told you wassup the night of the show."

"Um, no. You told me to stay in school where it's safe at. Remember?" I snaked my head.

"And I meant that shit too. Why you not in bed getting ready for school, no way?"

"Cuz you not in it."

Yeah, you're being bold tonight, Pearla.

"Prettiest Pearl in the clam... in your bed is the last place you want me."

Fuck. Not he called me the nickname my mama uses.

Grind licked his lips, and I had to break eye contact. When I did, I got more dirty looks from the girls than Mahzeyah when she went into the booth.

"There you go telling me what I want again. If you must know, school is out tomorrow."

"And the studio is where you decide to spend your time?"

"It's where you spending yours, ain't it?"

"If I'm here, it's cuz—"

"The money here."

"And you know that, so why you trippin' on a nigga?"

"I'm not, Grind."

"You are. Why haven't you hit me?"

Because Bella said not to chase you.

"I don't know."

"If I haven't hit you it's because I'm getting to it. It's not because I'm out here with no hoes, Pearla."

"You not out here with me, though."

"Nah. That's cuz you 'pose to have your ass at that school, getting your people's money worth for that expensive-ass tuition."

"I know how to juggle you and school, Grind."

"That might be true. But until I get my shit together, I'ma let you be. That don't mean we can't talk and I can't see if you straight."

My phone vibrated in my hands.

THEM GIRLS: (MAHZEYAH)

I'm about to go with Flexer real quick. I'll get dropped off at your house, Bella.

THEM GIRLS: (BELLA)

Girl why in the fuck is Vello on the way. He told my ass I better not leave. Somebody done snitched on a bitch. I think it was Italian's friend. He mad cuz I don't want his ugly ass. If you don't wana get caught Pearla you better gone head to my house. I can walk you out.

Girl wow!

THEM GIRLS: (MAHZEYAH)

Yeah let me tell Flexer. Vello would snitch on my ass quick. And you know Italian friend not ugly he fine as hell!

THEM GIRLS: (BELLA)

He also too damn young!

Y'all the same age, Bella.

THEM GIRLS: (BELLA)

Again too young.

I'll get Grind to walk me out.

THEM GIRLS: (MAHZEYAH)

Wait my fine ass friend here. Where? Tell him to wave at the booth.

HOLDING my phone up in Grind's face, he read over the text, smirked, and tossed his head at the booth. "Y'all wild. Come on, so I can walk you out."

"Un hunh. If I'm leaving, so are you. I see how those girls are looking."

Grind looked across the room at the culprits. "Man... come on. Ion even know shawty and them."

Grind helped me stand, placed the unopened bottle on the stool, and walked me toward the booth instead of the exit. I couldn't help but peek once more at the haters while Grind held onto my hand, guiding me through the numerous bodies packing out the studio. He knocked on the booth door, and seconds later, Flexer was opened it. Mahzeyah had head-phones on her ears, bobbing her head. When she noticed me, she bent over and twerked. She was too silly.

"Wuz good," Flexer spoke to me. Trying not to fan girl out, I waved. I didn't want to be disrespectful to my friend or Grind, even though Grind wasn't my man and wasn't trying to be.

"Yo', I'm out," Grind said before Flexer slapped hands with him. Flexer had on so much ice; he and Mahzeyah were defi-nitely on each other's fly. That could either be a beautiful thing or a disaster.

Flexer grabbed a backpack and handed it to Grind. "I put it all in there. Man, get up with me and answer the fucking phone. You harder to get in contact with than me, trapstar!"

Grind took the backpack. "I got you. Stay dangerous nigga, and make sure that one ain't out too late."

Flexer looked back at Mahzeyah, who was now eating a Laffy Taffy. Her ass loved candy. She kept snacks and nibbles on her. "That's bae right there. I ain't gon' get her in trouble."

They slapped hands again, and Grind pulled me through the studio.

"I'm snitching!" Italian yelled over the music, and I tossed up the middle finger to him.

In no time, we were out of the sound-proof studio, on the elevator, and walking through the parking lot. Just when I thought we were in the clear, I ran dead smack into Vello. I only knew them apart because of how they styled their locs.

"Grind hard! I can't believe yo' ass ain't on the block. First, the concert, and now, the Yo. I thought you was scared to let the money go."

They slapped hands as I stood still as a statue. "You know I'm everywhere the money be."

Vello's eyes traveled over to me, and he turned his lip up. "Y'all asses is too hot to trot. Prolly got y'all panties in these niggas pockets. I know you Three Musketeers bet not bring no babies home cuz, on foe nem, I'm on y'all asses.

My face flushed red from embarrassment.

"Nah, ain't none of that goin' on. We ain't having no babies 'til I see her down that aisle in white."

"Yeah. I said the same shit. Shit didn't happen like that, though. Go on, Pearla, for I hit my brother up. He bought you that damn car, and you ain't sat down since."

I tugged Grind away from Vello, and Grind's ass was still

trying to talk. When we got to the car, Grind shook his head. "Get on the passenger."

He was doing that thing he did when he watched his surroundings. Instead of questioning him, I got on the passenger side as he sat his bag in the backseat and started the car. He pulled his gun from his waist and placed it on his lap.

"Next time, park close to the exit. This shit too blocked in."

That spot would have been the one next to the YN's charger that I was at first, but Bella's ass made me move.

"You kept trying to talk and stuff." I huffed.

Grind pulled into traffic, going above the speed limit but not dangerously fast. He was trying to push me away, but I felt a magnetic pull anytime I was around him. I liked Grind—too much. He wasn't what I needed, but he was what I wanted. We lived two different lives, with him hustling and me having my head in the books. He was out here grinding to make it to the next day when all I had to do was ask my sister or her man-cousin for some money. Hell, now, I even had my mama to beg from. He was dodging the robbers and the police while I was just praying I passed my chemistry test. We couldn't relate, but he was so relatable. It was crazy.

"What you talm 'bout? With Vello? Shit, you was already caught. That nigga not gon' squeal."

My phone vibrated in my hand again.

THEM GIRLS: (BELLA)
Vello already snitched.

So much for that. Thankfully, Pia wouldn't trip. Nel may give me the side-eye, but that was it. Mahzeyah had her daddy wrapped around her finger, so she was good.

"You passing your turn, Grind." He was watching the rearview mirror more than he was watching the front. This man was so damn paranoid, but I would be too if I lived the life he did.

"I'm making a few blocks. And I'ma have somebody follow you to the crib, too, when you pull off."

"You always saying you not where it's safe, but I feel the safest when I'm with you." I sounded so pitiful, but I couldn't help myself. "I like you, Grind."

With one hand on the steering wheel, he ran the red light, and at the same time, reached over and tugged at my necklace. "I'ma have to ice you out."

"Grindddd! I'm for real."

"I'm for real too. Can't have my girl not on the same wave as her friends. I got you." He winked, and my panties were ruined. "I told you... you the star of the show, baby."

"I shol' don't feel like it. You don't even call me."

"If you wanna talk to me... call."

"Even Flexer said you don't answer..."

"Cuz that nigga don't be wanting shit. But for you, I'll always answer."

"So, I'm supposed to chase you?"

"What? Hell nawl. You know what I be out here doing, though. So I get a lil' side-tracked sometimes. If you want to get at me, call me, baby."

Grind pulled up to his apartments that was live, as always. The girls should have rode with me; they loved it out here just as much as I did. Grind picked up my hand, examined it, and locked it in his. His fingers felt so good resting in mine. His handsome face told so many stories that I wanted to sit down and hear, but I knew that was a no. It was insane the way this boy hadn't left my mental since the day at the dental office. I couldn't even brush my teeth without thinking about him. Every time I caught a glimpse of my braces, he was on my brain.

"Why were you at the studio? Were you... selling drugs. Or, you rap?"

"My nigga that was killed... that rap shit was his dream."

"You know who killed him?"

Reaper's murder was still hurting his fans all over the internet. It wasn't an hour that I didn't scroll where his face didn't pop up. It was so sad that his baby mama had been killed with him. With the way she was always with him, she probably wouldn't have made it without him.

"No. I'ma find out, though."

I couldn't imagine losing a person I loved to murder. That had to feel like a death sentence all in one. The trauma that the murder of a loved one left had to be one that left a lasting impression. It was one I didn't wish on my worst enemy. Just thinking about if Grind left me the same way his friend did made my stomach flip. I didn't even know him, but I wanted him to be here forever.

"Aye... fix yo' face. I ain't going nowhere. Even if I do go somewhere, I know where to find you. Don't focus on me right now. Keep yo' pretty-ass head in the books. I'll stack the money, baby. You hear me?"

Lifting my head, I made eye contact with Grind and nodded. I had to hold back my emotions. Getting teary-eyed, I chopped it up to my period. Today was the last day I was on, and even though it was a light one, I had been irritable all day.

"Aite. You can't sit out here tonight." Grind reached over and swiped my chin. "Pretty ass."

He opened the door, and I switched seats as he got out.

"Gon' pull off. My nigga in the challenger gon' tail you. Text me when you get in. Even if I don't reply back... I'll see it."

"It's late, Grind. You not about to go to sleep?"

He closed the door and leaned in the window. "No sleep. Niggas like me is up 'til morning to provide for pretty girls like you that's supposed to sleep. Go get yo' rest, baby. Call me in the morning."

Looking behind Grind, I caught the looks of a few niggas that were peering at us, looking like they were up to no good.

"Maybe you should just come with me. My sister won't know. I can sneak you in. I don't like you being out here. Your friend, Reaper, was killed out—"

"Pearla. While it's unfortunate that he died... I'm not him, and he definitely wasn't me." Grind looked behind him, staring at the other guys for a few seconds before focusing back on me. "I'm good out here."

"When can I see you again? You not gon' answer, and then I'll just have to hope I run into you on a different day." I sighed.

"Aye." I looked up at Grind with watery eyes. "I'ma set something up for us, pretty girl. You'll see me soon. Now, pull off."

Grind hit the hood, and I drove off. I didn't want to, but I did. I was so in my feelings that I drove the whole way home in silence. Every so often, I looked in my rearview mirror and saw the Challenger following. When I got to my exit, he finally pulled off. I appreciated it because I didn't want him coming to the house. Nel was there, and I didn't know Grind's friend. Grind knew Vello and all, but still. I didn't want random folks to know where we lived. We kept money in the house, and Nel had just as much jewelry as Flexer. I had to be cautious. I planned on going to Bella's house, but since we were caught, home was where I wanted to be.

Pulling up in the driveway, my phone rang as soon as I parked.

"You made it home?"

"Yeah."

"Why haven't you gotten out the car?"

"I'm about to." Reaching into the back seat, I grabbed for my overnight bag but clutched Grind's backpack instead. I pulled it in the front seat with me.

"You left your backpack."

"It's cool. Hold on to that for me." I was smiling like a kid on the phone. I could be holding a damn murder weapon and was smiling and agreeing to keep it. "Pearla... go in the house. I gotta go."

"I'm calling you in the morning, Grind."

"You better. Or I'ma call you."

"Byeee."

"Goodnight, Pearla."

When he hung up the phone, I screamed like a mad woman. Once I gathered myself, I unzipped his backpack. There was a notebook and stacks of money. It was also a chain that I'd seen before. Opening the notebook, I flipped the pages, and at first, I thought it was poetry. Ten pages in, and I saw it wasn't poetry—it was lyrics. Not just any lyrics, though, but lyrics to Reaper's songs. All his trending songs were right here in the notebook—word for word. The chain he wore, which was missing from the crime scene, was also in the backpack.

I was at a funeral.

My nigga that was killed. That rap shit was his dream.

You know who killed him?

No. I'ma find out, though.

Dropping the notebook like it was hot, I zipped it back into the backpack. Hopping out of the car, I left my own bag in the car and rushed inside the house. I didn't stop until I got to my room. Opening my closet, I shoved the backpack deep into it.

What the fuck?

Plopping down on my bed, I buried my face in the pillow.

Shock and anger rested behind my eyelids. A weight seemed to press on my chest, even though I was lying on my stomach. My blood curdled as a tendril of panic seized my chest.

The world was hurting behind Reaper, and Grind, his friend, was the one to kill him? But why would he kill his own friend, though? That thought alone had me hopping out of bed and running full speed to my bathroom. I dropped in front of the toilet and let my dinner splash into the water.

"Grandma gon' fuck you up if you pregnant."

Not even looking up, I slammed my door shut, closing me in the bathroom. I didn't have time for my nephew's bullshit.

After getting my breathing under control, I sat against the sink, swiped my mouth with the back of my hand, picked up my phone, and blocked Grind's number. I was going to make sure he got his stuff back, but I wouldn't be the one to take it to him.

I had to stay in my lane.

Bad boys were cool and all, but murderers were where I drew the line.

CHAPTER 18

PIA

"Bitch, you should have called me! You know I don't live far! Oh, that hoe got to see me!"

Holding up an obnoxiously green sweater so that I could get a better look at it, I placed it back on the rack. I didn't give a fuck what brand it was; there was no way I was paying six hundred dollars for the Grinch's attire. Fuck that. I didn't care how much money I had now, there were limits.

"Girl, I had that hoe by myself. I could have handled them both, but they were lucky that Arianee was there. I didn't want Renello having to catch a charge for killing two women in the middle of a restaurant, but he damn sure would have."

Missy held out a Rick Owens dress that I already had in my closet. I thought it would look cute on her, but she put it back. I invited her out on a shopping date courtesy of the mob. My bestie, being the shop-a-holic she was, obliged. I had been rotating payment methods as we shopped. I would use Renello's cash in one store, and my father's card in another. Rio had me set up nicely with accounts I still hadn't looked in, but yesterday, he handed me his black card. This was our sixth store, and bestie babe had done some damage. I didn't mind, though. Missy was there for me when I had no one. I wasn't really good with blurting my feelings out, so I wanted to show her how much I appreciated her versus telling.

I was having a great time shopping with my bestie, and even though I was telling her about the fight, I couldn't stop smiling. I wanted to slap the fuck out of myself for holding out on Renello. That man had fucked me from the window to the wall. He rotated between making love to my body to fucking me like a slut. I didn't know which one I liked more and was itching to go home and get some more. Outside of that time in the count house, we hadn't had sex again, but he hadn't slept another night outside of the house.

"Still! That hoe is out of her mind putting her fucking hands on you! Her nigga been dead for how long? That shit don't have nothing to do with you!"

Clearing my throat, I picked up another shirt but quickly put it back down. I already had it. I'd gone from not having any clothing to not being able to fit anything in my closet. My mama was the one with the walk-in since she had the master. I was going to have to store some things in hers if I kept on shopping—well, if Rio and Renello kept on forcing me to shop.

"Wait." Missy looked around for eavesdroppers, and when she saw a few, she pulled me to a secluded part of the store. We were in Neiman's, and even though it was a weekday, there were a few shoppers scattered about. "Why did you make that face?"

Holding my nails out, I pretended to inspect them. "What face?"

"Bitch! The face you made when I said Banger's death don't have nothing to do with you."

Flopping my hands, I pushed out a breath. "It was nothing, Missy. Just know, the hoe gotta get her one every time I see her, and that other bitch do too!"

I barely knew them hoes names, and they had the nerve to try to jump a bitch. It had been days since it happened, and I was still mad. One of them had pulled a plug of hair out of my fucking head. It was in the lower middle of my cranium, so you couldn't see it, but still. I couldn't stand a hair-pulling ass bitch.

"Umph. Let me find out. I know you gotta keep your secrets. Plus, you was smiling all hard and shit when you said that?" Missy paused and eyed me. "You look different. Pretty as fuck... but different."

"Thank you. You look cute too. Didn't you say you wanted some Balenciaga boots? Come on." Balenciaga was at the other end of the mall. With how slow we walked and talked, it would take an hour to get down there. Missy looped her arm in mine and led the way.

I was dressed simple today in a tan jogging set that I didn't know the name of and gold Air Max Venmos. Missy never did simple. She was done up even when she was simple, and she always had to show some skin. Her jeans had rips under the butt cheek, and the white bodysuit she paired it with had a deep v-cut showing the girls just right. She, too, was in Nikes but was rocking Dunks. We'd had lunch at Pappadeaux and shopped until we dropped, and only now was I telling her about the fight. It had slipped my damn mind initially. I was still replaying our count house sexcapade. Nothing else mattered at the moment. I saw a girl I thought was Candace, the poor bitch from the nursing home, and that's what prompted me to tell her about the fight. That Candace hoe had better been glad I wasn't petty. I had half a mind to call the nursing home and get her ass fired since the bitch had taken my position as security. Thankfully for her, I wasn't into bitches losing their job. I knew how important your bread and butter could be. Plus, I was still on a dick high.

While in my own thoughts, Missy continued vocalizing hers out loud. "I'm trying to figure out how them bitches even know each other?"

I, too, had been wondering the same shit. But mad hoes linked up, so I shrugged. Before talks of the fight, we'd been discussing what's been going down in the club. It was always some entertainment at Missy's workplace. She also told me about her neighbor, and I wasn't surprised. That old lady was too bossed up and sassy. I couldn't wait till I saw her again.

"I can get used to this, friend. Let me find out my bestie is my new trick. I feel like I gotta bust the pussy open for you now or something."

"Please keep the pussy, boo."

"You sure? It's real good," Missy kidded.

"I'm sure it's Super Soaker good. I'm straight, though. Speaking of tricks... I haven't heard you mention not one today, nor did you bring up Railroad. I thought you was trying to be the next baby mama?" Every time we talked, Missy had a story about her trick of the week. Railroad had been the recent favorite, but she hadn't brought his name up once.

"Girl, I cut all them niggas off, him especially. The nigga called himself getting all aggressive with me."

"He put his hands on you?" Stopping in my tracks, I waited for her reply. I was already on one; Railroad's short ass could get it too.

"Fuck no. He knows better. He was just salty as fuck. Ms. Covington threatened the nigga, and he left. I blocked him after that. She made me realize that maybe I'm selling myself short. Fuck these niggas, friend. I told you... I'm over the club too. I'm getting too old for that shit."

"Well, what you wanna do?"

"Ion know yet. I accepted a booking the week before your

birthday in Orlando. I'll see how that goes, and if it's as easy as I think it is, I'll do that for a while. Long-term, though? I don't know."

Missy tugged me along so that we could resume our walk through the Galleria. Billie Eilish played over the sound systems, freshly baked pretzels watered my mouth, a carousel was turning in the distance, and associates stood outside their stores to try to draw in the few shoppers here.

"I've been thinking about what it is I want to do. Maybe we could figure it out together," I voiced. I was no longer bored since I'd been spending all my days with Rio, but I knew he was a busy man and would have to get back to running his empire soon.

"Friend, you know I'm all for it. You have been working since you were sixteen. You have always hated your jobs. Take this time to just relax. We can figure out what it is that we want to do later on, but right now... life is beautiful. Let's spend this money and enjoy this shit."

I stopped again. "Wait, bitch."

"What?"

"Who the fuck you fucking?"

"Nah! I need to be asking you who *you* fucking?"

"Answer the question, Missy!"

"I shouldn't tell you shit. You haven't told me shit, and I saw you and Renello in the club. Plus, you glowing! I know when a bitch done got Grade A dick."

And Grade A it was. Rolling my eyes, this time, I resumed our walk. I had to turn my head to hide my smile.

"He's not your cousin, friend; I told you that. The man crazy as fuck about you. Just gon' give him the pussy before you give him blue balls. You be in your head too much. If anybody feels like what the fuck y'all doing is nasty, they slow. Lock your man down."

My phone vibrated in the crossbody Chanel I was wearing. I didn't even bother to look at the phone because I knew it was Hobo. He'd been blowing my phone the fuck up to the point he was calling Neltz and asking him to hand me the phone. The nigga didn't want shit but to complain about another nigga being around his son. I didn't have time for his shit. He needed to take his ass back to Chicago. He'd gone from saying he couldn't keep Neltz like that to picking him up from school every day. I wasn't trying to deal with Hobo. Baby daddy drama was not on my Bingo card for the year. I used to be the one blowing up his damn phone for petty shit. My my my, have times changed.

"It's just kind of weird. Well, it *was*. But he loves me so much, Missy. I love him too. He takes care of me, and bitch... I don't feel right when I'm not around him. I mean, I let him breathe when I'm spending time with my father, but other than that, I be losing my damn mind when he's not in my presence. I was tired of his ass looking like a sad puppy every day. I thought the sex would just be cool, but *bitch*!"

"Not COUSIN PETE done knocked your shit loose!"

"COUSIN PETE KNOCKED MY SHIT LOOSE, FRIEND! What them niggas be saying?"

"On FOE NEM!" we chanted in unison.

We were cracking up, laughing in the middle of the mall.

"Oh, friend! I love this! I'm team Renello, but friend, you gotta do right by that man. You know I love you, but you can get crazy and abusive. Let him love on you, and you love on him. I can tell the way he be eyeing you that he was gon' pound that lil' pussy into a coma."

"Girl, and did. I still feel conflicted because of how I always knew him as family... but damn. I can't stop thinking about that session."

"Ooo wee! Shat, Pia! I'm glad you took it there, friend. That nigga came in and applied major pressure. Try staying out of that big-ass head of yours. You just scared of getting hurt. That nigga not Banger, nor is he Hobo. Enjoy your man, boo. Ride that dick until you can't no mo' and get up and ride it some mo'. You deserve big dick and big bankrolls."

"Yeah, I do." I grinned, finally agreeing with Missy as she stated the same thing my mama had the other day.

Renello had nutted in me each time he'd fucked me that day. I had so much of his nut in my guts that I was still peeing it out days later. Thankfully, my peak ovulation was a day or two before we had sex, so I wasn't too worried about getting pregnant. The last thing I needed was another badass Neltz running around. And Nel's crazy ass wished twins on my womb. Lord knows I didn't need that. I was still trying to accept the fact that a person I thought was my cousin was now my man. We had to move in baby steps. He had a handful of days left to give me more dick, though, before I would take it again in his sleep.

"You do. You are in a much better place, friend. Don't feel guilty for letting a man take care of all your needs, especially a man with pure intentions. I know you got a lot coming at you, but you can juggle it all. You been the goat when it comes to having a full plate. You better than me... I would have had one twin eating the pussy and the other licking my ass."

"Ew! Gross! I definitely don't look at Vello like that!"

"Girl, them niggas are the same person. They literally have the same DNA. Like I said! Chooo Chooo!"

"No fucking thank you! Anyway... who you fucking? I need to give out a new nickname?"

Missy's face flustered, and I knew right then that she liked this new dude. "I shouldn't tell your secretive ass shit."

"Don't even do that! I told you a whole lot! You act like I'm just keeping you in the dark. You know who my daddy is, who my family is, and how I feel about Renello. Come on now, bestie. Who is the new trick?"

"Ummhumm. Anyway, you know ion like to kiss and tell. I only tell you about the tricks when I feel them out a bit more. But this ain't no trick; he's a sponsor. At least that's what he told me to label him as."

"Wait! He told you that?"

"Hell yeah! He was like, 'this pussy so good. Can I sponsor it?'" Missy mustered up the deepest voice she could, and I fell out laughing. "Just know he got a big ole elephant trunk for a dick. He fine as hell. *And* he rap."

Drawing my head back, my eyebrow rose. "He rap?"

"He do."

"What he rap?"

"Aht aht! That's all I'ma say."

"What happened to *I don't do famous niggas?*" I mocked her before feeling my phone vibrate in my purse again. This time, I pulled it out and saw I had three texts. I opened the one from Neltz's first.

SON-SON

> Ma please call your baby daddy. He keep getting mad at me because you not answering.

HOBO WAS RIDICULOUS. Now, I was going to have to pull down on his ass and curse him out about my son. He put Neltz in our business too much, knowing he was already grown as fuck.

I'll call him.

THE NEXT TEXT was from Renello, and that had my frown turning into a smile.

> RENELLO
>
> What we eating tonight, Pia baby?

I WAS STILL full from earlier, so it was hard for me to choose what I wanted to eat. I knew I would be starving later, but I would let him pick.

Surprise me.

> RENELLO
>
> Ima pull down on my brother and burn one then I'll grab something.

Remember to be nice.

RENELLO PROMISED he wouldn't be mean to the family anymore, and I found myself reminding him every chance I got. I'd even reminded him on my second attempt of riding his dick. He was holding a grudge about something that happened seventeen years ago. I'd buried it, and he needed to do the same.

The last text was from Pearla. Hers wasn't words, though; it was three screenshots. I had to halt in my steps for a third time. We would never make it to Balenciaga if I kept this up. I zoomed in on the pictures to be certain that my eyes weren't deceiving me.

"What now! I'm 'bout to pick your ass up and carry you!" Missy stopped, annoyed that our walk was taking longer than it should. She had other shit to worry about, though. With a shit-eating grin, I chuckled, knowing these screenshots were going to piss her all the way off.

Flipping my phone around, I made sure I had the most raunchy picture on display. Missy squinted her eyes, and then the color drained from her face. "Ahaaaaaa! You nasty little slut you! You really wasn't gon' tell me Essex was the rapper you were just talking about?"

Missy snatched the phone to get a better look at the picture. She looked like she'd seen a ghost while I was trying hard to catch my breath from laughing uncontrollably. Missy did not do public relations at all. Now, her face was all over the internet. I didn't want to laugh, but her reaction was comedic gold. I was too tickled.

"Haha! Look at all three of them. Matta of fact, go directly to Celeb Gossip page. Hell, it may be on the front of every blog! Y'all so nasty! They had to blur your lap out. My favorite picture is him licking your juices off his finger. I don't blame you, though, friend. He fine as hell!" I was laughing so hard, I had to bend over to stop from peeing on myself.

Missy was looking too busted. I don't know why she thought she could fuck with a famous person and keep that shit on the low. She was on my ass about twerking on Renello when she was getting fingered one booth over. Whew, chile. Essex was a hot damn commodity around these parts. I wasn't going to tell her Discover's business, though. Missy is my bestie and all, but if he had an elephant dick as she claimed, her ass would be singing like a bird, telling that man Discovery was his child.

"Ugh! See! This why I don't date famous niggas! My phone in the car, but looking here, these folks is tagging me in the comments."

Missy had placed her phone on the charger in my truck when we went to take all the bags before going to Neiman's. I knew they were blowing her ass up. Her followers were probably going up by the minute. Hell, Essex already had three million followers, and his page was new. We really were going to have to whoop these hoes asses.

My friend was at such a loss for words that she had to sit down on the nearby bench while she read the comments. I couldn't see what she was reading because I was too busy trying to cease my laughter and push my pee back up. Looking behind her, I spotted a restroom.

"I'll be right back. I'm 'bout to pee real quick."

"*He licking his finger after sticking it in a stripper hoe. They love the hoes that's ran thru. Damn he too fine for her. Maybe it was for a video shoot. I thought he had a bitch? The one he got the two kids by. She not cute. She nasty looking.* These bitches got me so fucked up! Friend, I can't wait to get to my phone. I gotta go off using yours!"

"Do you, boo. Be right back," I called out as I ran to the restroom. Not having the strength to hold it any longer, I pushed open the door on the first stall. The bathroom was empty and smelled clean. I sighed with relief to see that the toilet was up, indicating that no one had used it yet. Once my pants were down, I relieved my bladder. It was that liquor coming out of me from the swamp thing I'd drank at Pappadeaux.

Hearing the door open as I wiped myself, I knew it was Missy's ass. "Friend. I got the perfect name for him. Bars! Cuz that nigga fasho got them bars. I wonder if you can get a spot on Love and Hip Hop. The stripper and the rapping tattoo gangsta."

Flushing the toilet, I pulled my pants back up. Missy was upset, but she would be cool when I gave her the last surprise I had. In the trunk, I had a backpack full of money for her. It was forty thousand dollars. I had collected all the money that I had in dressers around the house. It took me so long to count it because I'd never counted that much money before. Hell, I've never had that much to count. Money was now plentiful, and I was going to see to it that my best friend was straight for life. But shit, she was a rapper's wife now. She didn't need my money.

"We can—"

The last time I checked, which was only a few minutes ago, Missy was black and fine; not white, male, and bald. That same damn detective from my apartment complex weeks ago was standing at the sink in that worn leather jacket. I had my Taser and mase in my purse, so I wasn't scared, but him being in the women's restroom pissed me the fuck off. Knowing that Banger's wife was the one who put the bug in his ear about me further irritated me. I still hadn't told Renello about the detective, but now that he'd popped up a second time, I was going to tell him and possibly my daddy too.

"You breaking at least ten laws by being in here unless you identify as a *she*?" Squirting soap on my hands, I watched the detective through the mirror.

"All I want you to do is tell me what happened to Banger. Who was it that killed him? I have a witness that says a man with dreads and tattoos has been linked to you and he is also linked to Banger's murder."

Running my hands under water, I didn't break eye contact. "Look, I know who the bitch-ass witness is. It's Bangers wife.

And I'ma tell you like I told her, I don't know shit. Her nigga wasn't shit to me. As far as who you link me with, ion know what the fuck you talking about."

He smiled, showing stained teeth. I could smell the cigarettes and coffee from where I was standing. On his jacket was pink icing, indicating his fat ass had a sprinkled donut sometime prior to walking in here and fucking with me.

"You are going to make this difficult. I can take you down to the station—"

"Okay... take me now." I held my wet hands out, ready for the cuffs. His smile expanded, but he didn't make a move. "Exactly. You can't because there is no fucking case, and you don't want me to sue the socks off this city."

"You're making this harder than what it has to be."

"You just gon' have to do your fucking job. If you approach me again about what that tired, thrown-off pH balance-ass bitch of an eyewitness you got, I'ma beat her ass worse than I just did. Now... good fucking day."

Walking around the detective, I held my breath as I approached Missy, who was still on the phone with her mouth wide open. The old me would have been shaken up, but I watched Law and Order. I knew my rights. That nigga was fishing, and he wasn't a threat. Tonight, I was going to enjoy dinner with my person and worry about this shit tomorrow. Tomorrow, though, I was going to tell Renello. I should have been let him know, but to be honest, Banger, his death, his wife, and this diabetes-having-ass detective were the last things on my mind. However, he'd approached me twice, so that meant he wasn't going to stop until he had something. Plus, the thought of him following me didn't sit right with me. I didn't want Renello doing something to the detective and actually catching a case for real. From what it sounded like, they didn't know who Renello was. It was a million niggas in the city with dreads. Like I said, he had to do his job. But if this information made Renello hold out another day of giving me some more dick, I was going to be pissed.

CHAPTER 19
DISCOVER "BIG MAMA"

M etavello had given me the nickname Big Mama, and even though I hated it when I first heard it, I couldn't help but feel like it was a subtle foreshadowing. Standing in my floor-to-ceiling mirror, I rubbed my hand in circular motions on my pudgy belly. Yes, I was carrying twins, but it was far too early for me to be showing. My appetite had picked up in the last few days, and I still hadn't resumed my workouts, so I was blaming the bloating on my poor eating habits and lack of movement. In just a few months, though, I would be a big mama for real.

I hadn't heard from Metavello since the appointment. I hadn't called his ass, either. I still had two weeks until I reached the nine-week mark, so my next appointment wasn't until then. I saw the look on the doctor's and the nurse's faces when they didn't detect heartbeats. They thought I was experiencing a miscarriage. I should have been afraid, but I wasn't. I knew the babies were alive. I was still wearing a pad because, after a week, I hadn't stopped bleeding yet. Something was telling me that this wasn't a period, though. I was a teen during my first pregnancy, so I wasn't an expert on pregnancy, but I knew my body. I wasn't having a miscarriage. Miscarriage may have been the best thing for our situation, but that wasn't happening.

I had every intention of getting an abortion at first. I was only going to the appointment to confirm what I already knew —I was pregnant. The medical clinic had already told me, but I needed to see the baby. I told myself the only way I wouldn't get an abortion was if it was a twin pregnancy. In my wildest dreams, I wouldn't have predicted it would be multiple babies for real. What were the fucking odds that I would be having two kids at the same time?

God had dealt me a bad hand. Then, he turned it around. When I first figured out that Rio was the head of a mob, I thought I was going to be some kind of slave for him to live out all of his weird fetishes. It turned out that he was kind. He was honest. He was one of the best people, if not the best person, I'd ever met in my life. He made it clear that I could live my life as long as I was available when he needed me for appearances. He'd also told me that I had to give him a baby. Now, here I was, pregnant with not one but two children, and neither one of them belonged to the man who had changed my life.

Standing in this five-hundred-square-foot closet loaded with brands and labels, I should have felt bad about what I'd done, but as the days passed, the guilt did too. Now, I was in survival mode. I was praying that the babies had survived, and I was busy formulating a plan so that my children and I could still live the good life, even if Rio put me flat on my ass when he found out. At first, I thought he knew. I thought he knew because I hadn't heard from him or his doctor. But then, I remembered Pia. There was always the possibility that she could rat me out, but something told me she wouldn't. Pia was a special girl. She'd texted me the other day to check on us when she didn't even have to. I know I put her in a tight spot with her holding my secrets while building a relationship with her father, but I appreciated her loyalty, even though I had no right to it.

I hadn't been sick lately, and my days had been filled with scrolling on TikTok. I became obsessed with all things twin pregnancy. I wasn't looking at the cute videos of round bellies and nesting, though. The ones of the women claiming that they received negative pregnancy tests or their doctors didn't detect heartbeats, and weeks later, there were their twin babies on the ultrasound machine healthy and strong was my current obsession. I knew that would be my outcome. I was waiting to hear about my hCG levels, but they still hadn't come back. The numbers in my blood should be extremely high due to the twin pregnancy, according to my social media research. If I was nervous about anything, it would be the numbers. If they were less than five, it meant I did indeed have a miscarriage. If they weren't in the thousands, it could mean either one of my twins died, or they both were dying. Not wanting to go down the rabbit hole of negativity, I finished getting dressed.

Slipping an olive-hued, long-sleeved shirt over my head, I snatched the tags off the sleeve once over my burgundy lace bra. I wanted to be comfortable, so I paired the top with flared olive sweatpants. My olive sneakers had already been taken out of the box, so I grabbed a pair of socks from the island draw, slid them on, and stuck my feet into my shoes. I didn't have any plans for today, but I had gotten my hair done yesterday when I took Discovery. I figured I would at least put on clothes today. I was going to change the sheets on my bed to the fall plaid ones that I'd ordered from Belk. I'd also ordered Discovery some that were pink leaves, but I would see how I felt after changing my own before committing to doing hers. I wasn't sick, but I was still heavily fatigued. That was how I knew I was still pregnant despite the blood leaking in my pad.

In the last week, I'd thought about Metavello more times than I liked to admit. This pregnancy had been giving me vivid dreams, and he was in every last one of them. Even the ones that didn't make sense, he was in them. Some nights, I would wake up in cold sweats because I would witness him doing some absurd shit like being chased by a wild animal. Then, in others, I would be moaning because he would be wearing the soul out of my body. Metavello controlled my dreams, but by morning, I would snap back to reality. He wasn't mine. He never was. I was married to another. Even if our union wasn't a traditional one, Rio had been way too good to my daughter and I for me to be playing with Metavello behind his back. It was bad enough that I'd gotten pregnant.

Grabbing the sheets from the shipping box, I unzipped the plastic and removed them. I should have washed them since that's what the girls on TikTok did, but these babies were going straight on the mattress. Hell, they were brand-new, so I knew they were clean. I was bougie now, but I remember the days when I slept on a piss-filled cot without a single sheet. A little factory germs wouldn't kill me.

By the time I was done making my bed and tossing my old sheets in the washer, I was slumped. Josephina had made me breakfast a few hours ago before taking Discovery to school, so I wasn't hungry. With nothing else to do, I sat at my vanity and did a light beat on my face. I guess that I would bless Instagram with some selfies in my story. I'd gotten so good at my makeup that it took me less than thirty minutes. I'd done such a good job that it made my simple look appear as if I was headed out of the house. I wasn't going any damn where, though. I was staying right in this house, waiting for my baby. She had piano lessons after school, so she wouldn't be home until about six-thirty. I missed her sweet face.

When she came home from the concert, talking about all the fun she had, I immediately felt bad. I'd left not only because I was sick but because I was a coward. I should have never taken Metavello up on his offer in the first place. However, seeing Essex with Metavello by my side didn't sit right with me. I had one niggas' baby on my side and the other niggas' inside of me, and at the time, neither of them knew. I felt like I was suffocating. I felt like I was being set up. Then, we had backstage passes. I had to get the fuck out of there. Discovery hadn't mentioned Essex at all, so when I saw that she had put the caption "Treacherous Twins" up with a picture of her and Essex the other day, I nearly fainted.

Most parents would brush it off as nothing. She and the rapper were dressed alike, so the caption worked. Me, though? I knew my daughter. She was smart as hell and was the type to know things but held it in until she felt like releasing it. That was something her damn therapist hadn't been able to work through with her. She knew something. Yet, I wasn't saying shit if she wasn't. If she came to me asking if he was her father, of course, I would tell the truth. But other than that, my lips were sealed. What the fuck would I even say to Essex? Hey... this is your child? Fuck, no! The man was rich and famous now. There was no way I was going to approach him like a fucking groupie. What would he even have to offer to my child? I gave her any and everything she wanted and more. She probably ate better than he did. I was already caught up with Metavello and Rio; I wasn't trying to get caught up with Essex too. It was all too messy.

Picking up my phone, I took a few selfies and uploaded them to my story. I had been neglecting my followers. Social media did nothing for me other than feed my boredom. I'd been invited to the creator fund and signed up a while ago, but the money was nothing compared to what I already had access to. Instead of hopping off Instagram like I should have, I went ahead and scrolled my timeline. I commented on a few of my favorite people's posts and even liked a couple of pictures.

Rapper Essex is handsy with a Stripper.

Gasping, I examined the slideshow of pictures of Essex with a girl on his lap. They had even had to blur her lap out because he was clearly fingering her. The pictures were sexy as hell, and the girl had a body to die for, but that shit was tacky. I hadn't even realized I was frowning until my face started hurting. See, that was some other shit I wasn't ready to expose my daughter to. His being with a woman didn't faze me; I didn't even know the man. It was the way the media hawked celebrities down and exposed their most private moments to the world that I wasn't feeling. My daughter shouldn't have to see her father tonguing a naked woman down on the net. Clicking off the picture, because the thoughts of me having to face Essex made my damn head hurt, I continued to scroll through Celeb Gossip page. I needed to see what I'd missed out on. My time had been spent sleeping, reading, and on TikTok, trying to ease my nerves about this pregnancy. I hadn't even been worried about Instagram, so I knew I missed a lot.

Saying I missed a lot was an understatement. These famous niggas, especially athletes, had been cutting the fuck up. They were having babies week after week. Hell, they all passed the same damn girls around, so many of these NBA and rapper baby mamas' kids would be half-siblings. That was crazy. I couldn't even talk, though, because I had babies by friends my damn self. Scrolling from the baby mama drama, the last picture on the profile was of a cute, light-skinned girl. It was also a slideshow, so I swiped the next picture and saw that it was of the same woman Essex had been fondling with, except she was dressed. Barely, but she was dressed. She and the first girl were actually dressed identically.

Tea sippers, you know we had to do it. As you know, the first Picture is of Vivian Green a.k.a. baby mama of the rapper Essex. The two share two sons. The second picture is of the young lady he seemed to like the taste of. She is none other than Passion, a top stripper in Jagoda Bay, but was born as Missy Arther. They were both spotted wearing this seventeen hundred dollar, two-piece Diesel set. You know we had to ask, who wore it better?

Both ladies looked damn good. Missy's look just appealed more vixens-like on her, whereas Vivian's looked sort of classy. I hated when they pit two beautiful women against each other over dick. I mentally took a tally of another reason why I didn't want Essex to know about Discovery. My picture would be in the slideshow because, unfortunately, I had that same outfit on somewhere on my page. I wore it last summer in New York when Arianee came to visit.

The comments, as always, didn't disappoint.

I'm putting my money on the stripper. She looks damn good.

Viv! Classy is always timeless.

Y'all love siding with the baby mama. Newsflash, these baby mamas mostly be mistakes out here to these niggas! Passion looks great and she get her own money.

Yeah she a stripper but she not linked to nobody but Essex. She wore the outfit better.

His baby mama live in these comments when it comes to her baby daddy. Where her ass at now? LOL but both ladies look cute. That man gone get y'all. He already said in that interview that he not with the media shit.

The caption asked who wore it better, and instead of people just giving their answers, they attached think-pieces on who they liked better. It was crazy. Having seen enough on the tea page, I checked my notifications. I was already getting likes and messages for the two photos I'd uploaded to my story. I saw a blue check in my notification, and the name Essexchi had me throwing my head back. He'd liked my story. Wasting no time, I clicked on his page. The last post was a snippet of him laughing during a video of him at The Morning Club. The Morning Club was the number-one radio show on-air, and they often did interviews with different stars. His being on there with the three hosts was huge and meant his career was skyrocketing.

I hated to admit it, but the man was fine. If his baby mama was beefing over him or whatever the media claimed, she better have a big appetite for beef because the ladies were going to be on him. No matter how fine he was, though, I still saw him as the Essex I was in survival mode with. He held a special place in my heart because he was not only my first but my daughter's father.

You're his baby mama too.

That fact had me groaning.

I combed through every last one of his pictures until I came across one of the oldest pics on his profile, which had only been uploaded weeks ago. The picture was of two little boys. They looked like Essex. Not Essex now, but the Essex when he was living in foster care. If you didn't know him back then, you wouldn't see those features in his sons. They were their mother's twins, though, down to the skin complexion. I smiled involuntarily. They were extremely handsome, holding their dad's mixtape. These were Discovery's baby brothers. When this shit was all over with, my daughter would have four siblings.

This shit is crazy.

Scrolling back to the top of his page, I saw that his profile picture was highlighted, indicating he had something on his story. He'd already watched mine, which made me uneasy, so I might as well watch his. He was flirting at Target and trying to rekindle an old flame that was not there. I was not into Essex on any level. As a matter of fact, the only man I was into was walking around here with a spit cup. The babies making Metavello sick were comical. His ass ought to be sick; he was the one to impregnate me with two kids.

In Essex's story, it was just professional pictures of him rapping on different stages. Ole boy was booked and busy. He looked like a natural in the various locations. I was hiding a secret from him, but I was proud of him. He'd made it out. The kids that no one wanted almost always turned out to be somebody. Essex was doing his thing. The next sequence was a clip with a link attached. Clicking the link took me to my YouTube app. Raising the volume on my phone, I impatiently watched the ads until the timer went down so I could press skip and go straight to the video.

Welcome to The Morning Club. We have none other than the rapper Essex here. His mixtape Gunned Down has been taking social media by storm, and he's been topping the charts. Essex! How are you?

Man, I'm blessed. 'Preciate y'all for having me.

'Preciate you for being here. I know you're booked and busy. So you were, or you are a successful tattoo artist. You've done some big-name artist tattoos as well. Is that how you got started rapping?

Yeah. I was tatting up that nigga Frost, and they dared me to get in the booth. I stepped in, and when I came out, my mixtape was born. Shout out to Frost for that shit. Shoutout to Flexer for giving me a shot and letting me open for him at the Fall Ball. Frost and Flexer are my guys, for real.

That's dope. Did you ever see yourself rapping?

To be honest, all I ever saw myself doing was getting money. I was a foster kid. I grew up in the system. I knew I had to do whatever to get out. I knew I could draw, and I wrote a lil' poetry too. The drawing, though, was my passion. I started selling my pictures, and my nigga Ezio asked me if I could do it on skin. I didn't know what the fuck I was doing, but him and his people gave me a shot. Shout out to the Cuppacio boys. They not with the media shit, but them my guys. Outside of my kids, they my only family.

Another ad popped up, and I wanted to toss my damn phone.

I always love people's success stories. Looking at you now, you wouldn't even think you came up in foster care. That's amazing, man.

Yeah. Them were some crazy-ass times. I damn sure wouldn't go back, though.

Everyone shared a laugh.

You look like a tattoo artist, but you look like a rapper too. How many tattoos do you have?

Shid, no telling. I actually inked myself not long ago.

Let us see.

He lifted his shirt, and there was a vibrant display of the world.

The words at the bottom say 'The world is my Discovery'.

What does that mean to you?

Essex looked off into the distance. My stomach was doing flips, and my armpits itched from being sweaty.

It means a lot of shit. I have to watch what I say on here because they make shit bigger than what it is when I do speak or post or even like a fucking comment. A nigga can't even go watch no ass in peace.

They laughed again.

But nah. This tattoo shit has put me in doors I couldn't even fathom. I went from starving to really eating out here. I was content —I'd made it. But God said fuck no, nigga, I got more for you. This rap shit... this rap shit is showing me that it's so much more out there in the world. More people to love. More places to see. More goals to reach. More money to make. The world is a big place, and I'ma Discover it all. It's an ode to some other shit, too, but I ain't gon' get into all that.

No, tell us! We been on your side! All we been doing is boosting your music!

Essex rubbed his hand down his face.

It was a girl. I guess you can say she was a nigga's first love. She was the first person outside of my niggas to show me real love. I saw her recently, and shit, but she had a big-ass rock on her finger.

What was her name? Gon' and tell it all!

Y'all on some other shit. But her name Discover.

"Oh shit!"

Pretty name. So we got Discover, Passion, the dancer, and Vivian, the baby mama. You a busy man.

They all laughed again, and here I was about to pass the fuck out.

Nah. It's nothing like that. Me and my baby mama not together and haven't been for a long-ass time. Discover living her life, man. I haven't even had a conversation with that lady outside of seeing her at the store. She look good as fuck, though. But Missy? Missy... that's my baby.

Missy is the stripper, right?

Yeah. That's her.

He smiled.

How you gon' say the stripper is your baby, but in the same breath say another woman look good. You rappers can do whatever. I wanna be you when I grow up.

Ha! Nah, it ain't even like that. I'm just giving Discover her props. She showed a nigga love when no one else did. I would take just being her friend or handing her some bread just for my appreci-ation. That's it. Missy not tripping, though. If Discover with that, we can take her down together.

I clicked out of YouTube fast as hell. First of all, he was wrong as hell for even bringing my name up. Secondly, eww. I wouldn't touch Missy with a ten-foot pole, and it had nothing to do with her being a stripper. My husband was gay, not me. My phone rang.

Eater.

Seeing the FaceTime from Metavello, I jumped up. "He—Hello?"

His face on the screen was mellow, but I could tell he was anything but that. "Y'all just grew up together, hunh?"

"I... I... We did."

"Discover. Stop fucking playing with me. So, now, I'ma have to kill my homie and your husband... is what you telling me?"

"What?"

"*What?*" he mocked. "You heard me."

The interview had only been live for twenty minutes, according to YouTube, and here Metavello was on my line.

"How can I control what he says? I don't even know him like that!"

Metavello pointed to the screen. "I'ma show you better than I can tell you."

"Whatever. Are you coming to the appointment in two weeks? That's what you should be calling my phone asking me."

"Nah. Ask your husband. You do too much lying and secret-holding for me."

"Fuck you, Metavello!"

"Shid! When you stop bleeding, I gotchu. Matta fact, start setting them panties to the side for me once you stop. I've been rotating the few pair I got and they ain't enough."

Hanging up the phone, I went to block his ass because I was sick of his foolishness. Before I could, it was ringing again. This time, an unknown number displayed on my phone screen.

Fixing my face, I answered, "Hello?"

"Hi... Discover Banks?"

"Um, yes, this is me."

"This is Life Cycle Clinic. We have your hCG results back. I want to move your appointment up to this week. Based on your numbers, you are still very much pregnant. These numbers are too high. Of course, we would have to take another look to confirm and maybe draw more blood. Can you come in on Thursday? It's important that we see you as soon as possible, especially with you bleeding."

Gasping, my hands went straight to my belly. I knew that the babies weren't dead. I just felt like I was still pregnant. "Yes! Yes, I can be there!"

I had one nigga mad, the other nigga reminiscing, and the last nigga trying to knock me up, even though I already was. And, now, a confirmed, viable twin pregnancy. My life couldn't get any crazier. What I did know was that since Metavello's petty ass wanted to say he wasn't coming to my other appointment, he wasn't being invited to this one.

"All right. Thursday at 10:45 in the morning."

"See you there." Hanging up the phone, I placed my face in my hands, not even caring that I'd done my makeup. What the fuck was I about to do with two more kids? Reality was slowly starting to kick in.

My phone pinged, and I hoped it wasn't anything else to send my poor heart into a frenzy. It couldn't take anymore. Pulling my face out of my hands, I tapped my screen to see what it was. It wasn't a what, though; it was a who.

Going straight to my IG messenger, I groaned in response to the message. This shit couldn't be happening.

EssexChi: Aye. Call me Discover!

HE'D EVEN GONE ALL OUT and attached the two pictures of Discovery and him to the message. My baby daddies were doing too fucking much.

CHAPTER 20
VELLO

The day before watching the interview

My day had been going great. A nigga wasn't feeling sick no more, and my mouth was watery, but not from throwing up. I was craving a blunt after I'd successfully eaten a full meal without barfing the shit back up. If that wasn't proof enough that Discover was having a miscarriage, then I didn't know what was. At first, I was down about it. We didn't need a fucking kid together, let alone two, especially with her being married to that fag. My kids dying, though, didn't sit right with me. It must've been meant for Nel and me to be the only twins in the family because Jisei and Ezio had lost their twins as well when she overdosed. I didn't know what the fuck God had against twins in our family, but he was offing them motherfuckers, pregnancy by pregnancy.

Ding Dong

Our count was off by a few thousand dollars, and that shit

had never happened before. Granted, the nigga who it was off by gave us the difference immediately, so we were chilling for now, but after the bullshit of counting everything from all the spots, I was at the house thugging. I'd even had plans on chilling and playing the game for the next couple of days.

Instead of looking at my Ring camera, I walked to the front door and opened it. "Superstar! What the fuck do I owe the pleasure, nigga?"

Slapping hands with Essex, I stood back so that he could come inside. He'd been to my house before, but his coming by without calling let me know something was on his mind. He had been having a hard time coming to terms with the fact that he was a famous-ass nigga now, and that shit was funny, but I understood him. We were the same niggas that had made a way out of no way and were now living a street nigga's dream. Granted, I was still in the streets and seemed to be getting even deeper, but Essex had ventured from that lane and was successful in his own right.

Leading him to my game room, he fired up a blunt and took a pull.

"I know this rap shit ain't got you that stressed."

Chuckling, Essex exhaled the smoke and then passed me the blunt. I hesitated. The last time I tried to smoke, I threw up everywhere. Holding the wood to my nose, I took a quick sniff and sucked in a bit of smoke. Smacking my lips, I waited for the effect it would have on me.

"What the fuck?"

"Nigga, I'm trying to make sure this shit don't make me sick."

"Weed, nigga?"

"Yeah, weed. It's a long story." I waved him off and took a deep pull.

When my body didn't react in severe nausea, I chilled. If

this shit did me right, I was going to pull down on the block and buy some more weed. I'd thrown all mine out that day I damn near threw up to death. I wanted that shit far away from me as possible. Now, sitting here smoking with my man had me ready to fill my weed jar.

"Anyway, back to you. What the fuck going on?" I took another pull before passing it to Essex. I could tell he'd gotten that weed from back home. Jagoda Bay had that Jungle Kush, but I knew Chicago weed.

"I might be chasing nothing, but lately… a nigga been feeling something weighing on me. Not this rap shit either…" he stated as he choked out a cloud of smoke.

He passed the blunt again, and I anticipated the high. Damn, I missed this. "Aite… wassup then? What's on yo' mind?"

"That lil' girl. The one you brought with you to the concert. What's her mama name?"

My shoulders tensed. I was already side-eyeing Discover's ass due to my brother revealing that she'd talked to Essex at Target. Then, she claimed they grew up together. Now, he was asking about Lil' Chef. I was slick relieved that her pretty ass had a miscarriage, but only because I didn't want a gay nigga raising my seeds, and I knew she wasn't leaving that nigga. She was *my* bitch. Even with her tripping on a nigga, Discover was mine. Soon as that pussy stopped bleeding, I wanted to dive back in. Fuck the risks. I was just going to glove up.

Hell nawl, I wasn't gloving up. I would just pull out. I needed one more for the road, anyway.

"How you know she came with me? She was with Pia half the night."

"Nigga, I asked yo' brother first. He told me, and I quote, 'he not fucking that bitch nor is he getting in our shit and that I should ask you.' So…" Essex handed me the blunt. "I'm asking you."

Taking another pull, I shrugged. "Shit, you tell me, nigga. She claim y'all grew up together and shit."

"Who? You gotta be specific. This shit been driving me fucking crazy, man. Let me know sum'n. Everybody tiptoeing and shit... scared to pillow talk."

"Pillow talk? Nigga, what?"

"Forget it. Just let me know wassup. Are you fucking Pia's stepmama, and is her name Discover? I want so badly for you to say nawl nigga, but I got this feeling..."

Sweat lined my forehead, and my heart crumbled in my chest. What the fuck was this rapping-ass nigga about to say about my bitch?

"You got what fucking feeling? If you think you still in love with my woman after some childhood crush shit, you can dead it."

"So her mama's name is Discover Banks? Pia's stepmama is Discover... that's what you saying?" Essex's elbows rested on his knees as he swiped his nose with his thumb.

"Why, though, nigga? You tryna fuck my bitch?"

"Nigga! She married from the looks of that big-ass rock on her finger. She not yo' bitch."

Standing, the chair I was sitting in slid back, and Essex matched my height. I would hate to have to do that nigga dirty, but he was worried about the wrong shit. He was a newfound rapper now. He better snatch up one of these groupie bitches.

"Married or not, that's my pussy! She pregnant with my babies."

"Nigga, what? Man, fuck that! She had my baby nine years ago! I got the firstborn, nigga."

I felt a punch to the gut. Bending over, I grabbed my stomach, but Essex's hands were still at his side. He hadn't touched me, but his words were enough to take me off my feet.

"Man, you tweakin', G. On foe n'em, ion give a fuck what y'all got going on. But I took her virginity back when we were living in a group home."

My mouth watered while I clutched my stomach. "Oh shit! I need my spit cup. I'ma be sick."

"Look, I just want some answers. I know you can see the resemblance. I wasn't sure at first, but when lil' mama tagged me in her pics, I just had this feeling. I left the group home, and apparently, our foster mama put her out when she found out she was pregnant."

"So—so—so... you abandoned my bitch? You raising them light-bright leprechauns, but Discover had to get with a gay nigga to support y'all child? Nigga, you ain't shit! Ugggh! My stomach hurt."

It felt like I had to throw up. My heart was racing uncontrollably. I was sweating like a fat nigga running two miles on a hot day, and he'd casually just delivered some news that had me ready to ball up in the corner and suck my thumb. Why had all these niggas fucked my girl? Why, Lord, why? I should have stuck to the original plan and married all three of my hoes I had at first. This married-ass girl had too much going on.

"I just told you... I didn't know! You know me! Had I known she had my daughter, I would have stepped up. I know Discover. She not gon' reach out because she got pride like a muthafucka. Fuuuuck! I should have never left. Look, give me her number."

Standing, I pointed at Essex and hit the blunt that was pinched in my fingers again. "You don't know shit about mine. Talking 'bout... you know her! I ain't giving you shit! Fuck I look like... Maury? Dr. Phil? Matta fact, she not 'bout to be tussling with Viv's ass. She too pretty for all that. Just forget you even figured the shit out, Blues Clues-ass nigga."

Discovery being Essex's had never crossed my mind once.

Now that he said it, she looked so much like that nigga that it made my mouth water, and not in a good way. I was ready to puke. Shit had me sick to my stomach.

Essex turned his nose up at me as I tried to hand him back the blunt. "Ion want that shit... all the slobbin' you doing over there." Running his hand down his face in frustration, he sighed. "Look, I'm not trying to come in between whatever the fuck it is y'all got going. I just want to know wassup. I just want to know if her daughter is mine. Fuuuuck! This shit crazy!"

Damn right, it was crazy! I bet Don n'em FBI-ass niggas knew about this shit too. Them niggas were probably sitting back laughing at me. What are the odds that the woman I like was connected to me in more than one way. Then, they shared a child while my babies were floating in her uterus, all dead! Fuck that! My nigga couldn't have one up on me. I was getting her ass pregnant again.

"Man! Ain't shit wrong with you. I thought Nel was the love-sick twin. I'm out."

"Adios, muthafucka! I'm not telling you shit! Call a fucking lawyer or something."

"You still my dog, Vello. You foul for not giving me her lo' but, I get it. My baby mama is bad." He teased, and if I wasn't a moment from throwing up, I would've decked him in the throat. Have his ass rapping like Pop Smoke.

"You doing a lot of smiling for a deadbeat dad. I would hate for the blogs to find this out."

"You a snitch?"

"You had the pussy. You know how good it is! Damn right, I am." I couldn't believe my own words, but was blaming it on the weed.

"I thought your brother was the ignorant one."

Holding up my middle finger, I smirked. "We the same

person, goofy."

Essex returned the middle finger and walked out of the room. I followed him to the front door, and before I could slam the door in his face, he paused. "I did an interview that's going live tomorrow that you ain't gon' like. I'm a real nigga, so I'm givin' you the heads up. I can see that you like Discover, so for your sake... I'ma back off. I just want to get to know my daughter and make sure they straight. The same as I do for Viv."

"Nigga, you still feeding Viv dick on the low. Fuck outta here."

"I just told you what it was. I love you, bruh."

Slam!

Closing the door in his face, I raced to the toilet and emptied my guts out. "Uhhhh. I'ma kill him and Rio! They got me fucked up. *Blarggggggghhhhh!*"

My throw-up was green like the weed. That had to be from the kale smoothie I had earlier. This shit didn't make no sense. I needed to talk to my brother and let him know we had a new victim added to the kill count.

CHAPTER 21
NEL

Pia told me that she would be home in two hours, so that gave me at least an hour to chop it up with Vello's upset stomach ass. Then I'll have another hour to pick up dinner and make it home at the same time as her. So, here I was, sitting in the car outside my brother's crib. Looking over at my own house, I made note of the growing weeds and burned grass, which was abnormal for me. As kids, Pia and I stayed in the gardens and shit. When she *died*, yard work became my therapy and was a way for me to feel close to her. Wherever we lived, I made sure the yard was always maintained to perfection. Now that she was back, I hadn't even been in the damn yard. Hell, I paid a service to maintain her yard.

"Yeah, I gotta get my shit right."

Doing my yard and tossing that cheap-ass furniture out of my house was on my priority list when it came to my home. At this point, selling it needed to be at the top of the list since I was never there. Pia acted a damn fool anytime I tried to come here for a night or so, and to keep the peace, I just gave in to her demands. She wanted a nigga, and with the way that pussy was hitting, I would give her sexy ass the world if she asked for it. Fuck it; she could request another planet, and I would put on my space suit and go conquer Jupiter for her pretty ass.

My baby was not only a beast in the bed, but she had fucking hands. When she whooped that hoe's ass the other night for the first few minutes, I was stunned. I couldn't believe someone had actually run up on us. It was like those hoes had been given the location on us because they weren't even dressed for the fancy steakhouse. Those hoes looked like they belonged down the road at the chicken coop. But Pia had held her own. Before the other bitch even jumped in, I was going to snatch that hoe off Pia. Her auntie coming out of the woodwork worked out well because I wasn't going to play with them bitches; I was shooting their asses.

No lie, though; Pia should have taken her ass to the pros for MMA. She was too damn pretty to be fighting the way she did. That lady didn't even have a chance. With the way Pia drug the girl, I knew it wasn't the last we would see of ole girl. When Pia told me she was the nigga I shot up wife, I knew I would have to kill her ass too. I was trying to lock down my own fucking wife. I didn't need all these fucking distractions popping up and stopping her ass from focusing on the mission, and the mission was Pia and I walking down the fucking aisle. She thought I was playing about making her my wife after shooting buckets of cum in her. I keep on telling her ass, I had to have a wife. Now that I had the pussy and rubbed my fucking face all in it, she was going to be the one. It was Pia or nothing. I would die behind that girl, and her finally giving me the pussy sealed the deal.

"Oh, so you back smoking now?"

A cloud of Kush hit my face as soon as I walked into the spare room that Vello had turned into a game room. He had his basement set up as a man cave like everybody did except me. My mama didn't even bother to furnish the damn basement. Shit made me mad every time I thought about it.

Plopping down on the black leather couch next to Vello, I snatched the blunt from his fingers and placed it to my lips. "This shit bet not have no throw up on it, neither."

"Well, even if it did... you don't care because the shit already in yo' mouth. Can't believe you over here. I thought Pia had a vice grip on your balls."

"Shid! She do." Blowing out a wad of smoke, I took another choke.

Vello shook his head and picked up the controller. The nigga looked depressed as shit. He was playing Call of Duty, and he rarely played this shit, so I knew he was just doing some shit to occupy his mind or time. He mostly had the room set up for when our little cousins came over. I didn't have the patience for their little, young asses, so they favored up to Vello.

"She still got you in the cousin zone, hunh?"

"You still lusting after that married pregnant hoe, hunh?"

Vello snatched his blunt out of my hands, and I snatched the game controller from him. I was a real shooter in the virtual world and the real world. He couldn't fuck with me on either. I wasn't about to kiss and tell, though. What Pia and I did was our business. She'd been begging for the dick since that day, and I was holding out. It was some shit I needed to do first, and step one to my plan was talking to my brother. He wasn't going to like what I said, but fuck it; Pia had me by the balls.

"For yo' information... she not pregnant no more, goofy-ass nigga. She had a miscarriage."

"Good for her."

"What? No, nigga, not good. She was pregnant with twins.

Identical twins..."

Shrugging my shoulders, I tapped the buttons on the controller, trying to take the fucking zombies out. There were too many games and movies indicating that the world would be riddled with these shits one day. Good thing I had an extensive gun collection. I was apocalypse ready.

"Man, see... that's why I barely tell you shit. You would have had nephews or nieces out here, and you don't care."

"Shid, you look like you don't care, either. You in this bitch smoking and playing the game."

"Fuck else I'm supposed to do? She married any fucking way. That shit was for the best. I wasn't letting Rio's ass raise my kids. Hand it here." Vello took the remote and handed me back the blunt.

I didn't know where the hell he got this Kush from but it was lethal. It had my body relaxed as fuck off three hits, and my eyelids were heavy. That nigga didn't do shit right, but he came through on this.

"I'm just happy I'm not sick and shit no more. That experience had me rethinking having kids. I couldn't be sick as fuck like that for nine ass months. I'm over that, though. But you a fake-ass nigga."

"Man, I'm not finna play with yo' ass today. How I'm fake?"

"Cuz, nigga! Fuck you tell Essex me and her fucking for?"

"I told that nigga I'm not fucking her and to ask you about her. Ion know the broad. Plus, I wasn't trying to get in y'all's shit."

"You still wrong! Fuck her!"

"So, now it's fuck her. You was just crying and shit."

"You the one was crying over Pia. *Oh, she keeping me in the cousin zone*, sick-ass nigga."

"Fuck you!" I spat.

"Anyway. She fucked Essex. Then, she married to Rio. It's

one thing for her to be married to a dick eater, but she fucked my dawg. Her pussy so good... she got me ready to take Essex out. Fuck! I'm still thinking about killing my nigga. He all on interviews confessing his love for her and shit!"

I heard the interview with Essex, but I could have been told Vello that it was something between them. She liked Vello more, though, because she wasn't studying Essex ass when she thought I was my brother. He was talking to her, and she was looking upside my damn head.

"You know what, brother? Be glad you haven't got the pussy from Pia. What y'all got is pure as fuck. Puppy love type shit. Just let that shit happen naturally. Sex fuck shit up. We already some fucking crash outs, and pussy just takes us further out there. You haven't experienced that yet, but I'm you... so I'm telling you. Man, I was on the way to Rio's house earlier, ready to take his ass out just because. Cuz... who told that nigga to even marry her to begin with?"

Vello was so damn high, it sounded like his words were slurring. If he only knew I had the pussy, sucked the pussy, fucked the pussy, nutted in the pussy, and was praying for a positive pregnancy test. Still, I let him cook.

"Then, she so damn pretty brother. Her pussy? Shit so juicy and tight. She so fucking soft and smell so good. The three hoes I was fucking could all be morphed into one bitch, and they won't hold up to Big Mama. She had me ready to empty my fucking wallet out for her. Man—" He rubbed his hand down his face, and I passed him the blunt because his ass needed it. "She perfect, nigga. She's too fucking perfect. I was around here talking so much shit, saying Ezio was going about it all wrong and that all he had to do was just go at Jisei without the cat-and-mouse shit, but I get it. It's like... I wanna be with her, even though I can't have her. I wanna stay away, but then I wanna snatch her ass up. Me and this girl haven't even had a conversation that lasted longer than sixty minutes, and she got me outside my fucking body. Ion even know myself no fucking more. Then, Don n'em coming at my head and shit about her. Just be glad you haven't got the pussy yet."

Swooshing my tongue around my mouth, I was starting to feel like I had popped a pill. I had cottonmouth like a mother-fucker, but was too damn high to get up and get a bottled water. I needed to tell Vello the real reason I'd come over here. I wasn't going to kill Rio. Pia had made me promise to talk to her pops while I was deep in the pussy, and I didn't lie to my baby. I was going to talk to that nigga and let him know I was marrying his daughter. I wasn't asking him for her hand in shit. He hadn't been her daddy that fucking long to get permission. Plus, he needed to get ready to fork over that wallet to pay for our shit since he wanted to spoil her so bad and flaunt his riches. Our shit was going to be way better than Ezio and n'em's historical-ass underground railroad wedding.

"Aye, bruh. About that lil' mission—"

Hearing sniffles, I leaned up because I knew damn well I didn't imagine one of the zombies crying. I wasn't that damn high. When I confirmed that the only thing the zombies were doing was grunting and moaning, I turned to my right. Vello had his eyes closed as tears ran down his face. The blunt was perched in between his lips as he sat up here and cried like a hoe.

"Bro, what the fuck!" Snatching the blunt out his mouth because he'd damn sure had enough of this shit, I let the smoke suffocate my lungs. "Fuck is you crying fo'?"

"Man... I love that girl. How the hell can I love somebody ion even know? Hoes just be so evil! Why the fuck she married to a gay man fo' anyway? She... she... she Essex baby mama! He came over here yesterday and told me that bullshit. Hoes just doing that shit for the moneyyyyy."

I wasn't expecting him to say that, but then again, that little girl of hers was hyped as hell during Essex's performance. They looked alike too.

"Bruh, that lady grown as hell. Rio was before you. Essex was too. Yeah, just leave that shit alone. You tweakin' behind that bitch when you was the main one saying you was gon' buy your wife. What you wanted to do before you fucked her is the same thing Rio did. I'm sure Essex was some young teenage shit. Didn't he grow up in the system?"

Vello opened his eyes, and more tears streamed down his face. His lips were dry and ashy white as a motherfucker. He looked like Pooky from *New Jack City*.

"So, now you team Rio and Essex? He baby mama'd my bitch, and Rio wifed my bitch! You just said you had my baaaaaaaack?"

"Nigga, I do got your back! But... but..." I found myself getting emotional my damn self. Holding the blunt out, I had to examine the shit, but before I could get a good look, tears sprang free. "I do wanna kill that nigga, bro, but Pia... she love that nigga. She really not gon' fuck with me if I kill him!" I cried out.

"See! You see what these hoes do to us?"

"Don't call her a hoeeeee!" A nigga was crying like someone had beat my ass. I put the blunt out in the ashtray on the side table next to me, but it took about three attempts because I couldn't see through the tears. "Man, why the fuck is we cryinggggg?"

Vello poked his lip out as his shoulders sagged and chest heaved. I don't think I've ever seen my brother cry like this. "Ion knowwww! But this shit hurt so bad, brooo! Is we love sick... or naaaaah?"

"We... we gotta beeeee! Oh shit, you right... it do hurrrrt. Pia baby, I'm sorrrrryyyyyy."

"Discoverrrrr! I'm sorrryyyyy tooooo!"

I didn't know why I was sorry, and Vello had no reason to be sorry about anything except for fucking Rio's wife.

"Just think about it, bruh. R... Rio really coooool. He was good to us."

"Y... yeah. Yeah, he was. We was really gon' kill that niggaaaa? For what?"

"Ion knowwww, shit. I can't stop crying, brother," I wailed.

"I think you was gon' chicken ouuuuut."

"Bitch, I just killed a nigga a few weeks ago. Yo' scary ass was gon' be the one to back ouuuuut."

Vello used the back of his hand to wipe the never-ending tears, but it was no use. The top of my shirt was drenched.

"So, we not killing him no more?"

"N... no. Like you said. Pia love her daddddyyyyyy."

"She dooooo. I fuck with Pia so hard. I wish Neltz was miii-iine. I hate her baby daddddyyyyyy." I cried hard as hell at that. It was the truth. Neltz was my homie now. I wish he'd come from my nut sack.

"Well, at least he named after youuuu. My twins deaaaaad! Damn, I should have been there for her during the miscarriage! I'm a deadbeaaaat."

"You can't be a deadbeat to kids that's already deaaaad."

"You riiiight!"

We were in this bitch tore up. If this is what girls did on wine nights with their friends, they could keep this shit. Not only was my mouth dry, but my eyelids were sore from crying like a gotdamn baby.

"So, we forgive Rio?"

"We... we... we ain't got no choiiiice!"

"You riiiiight!"

Leaning back on the couch, I folded my arm across my face. I need to calm myself down. As long as we kept talking and shit, we would keep crying. Just like with babies, when you calm them down, the tears stop.

"It feels so good to cry, bruh. I love you. I know you love Pia mooore, but I'll die for youuuu."

"You gotta re... relax. That's the only way the tears gon' stop." It felt like my chest was hiccupping.

"O-oh-kay. I'ma laydown."

Our sniffles and the sounds of zombies filled the room. The darkness from my arm got to me because, before I knew it, I was knocked out.

Pia had it bad turning the fan and air on, knowing good and well the temperature was constantly dropping around the city. At the beginning of the month, you didn't know if it was November or August, and now, it was finally feeling like December. Still, Pia made it her business to keep the fans and the air-conditioned, and sometimes the window cracked. I didn't understand that shit because she was always fucking cold. With my eyes still closed, I reached for the comforter. Swiping my hand in the air, I groaned in frustration when I couldn't find the cover.

"Who the fuck got it so cold in here?"

Stopping my hand in mid-air, the sound of my brother's voice had me sitting up. I opened my eyes but was met with darkness. I couldn't even see in front of me. I must've fallen asleep at his house. Grabbing at my pocket, I tried locating my phone but couldn't feel it.

"Damn, nigga! Why the fuck you didn't wake me up?"

I could feel Vello sitting up beside me. This nigga must have black-out curtains on the widows because I couldn't see shit.

"And where the fuck my phone at?"

"My bad, Twin. Shit, I can't find my phone, either."

I was never smoking with this nigga again. I could still feel the tightness of my eyes due to all the fucking crying we'd been doing. I cried so much that I didn't have another tear to shed as long as I was on this earth. Whoever was selling that weed needed their asses kicked. That shit was worse than Ezio binging on pills.

"Aye. Why the fuck is my ass wet? And why in the fuck are we on the ground? We was sitting on the couch."

Feeling around me, my palm lay flat against something fluffy and wet. Now that Vello mentioned it, I was soiled. "Wait, nigga... did I piss on my fucking self?" Still not being able to see in front of me, I grabbed my crotch to see if I'd pissed on myself for real. It was dry. Some shit wasn't adding up, though, because the hard surface underneath my ass was soaked and wet.

Hearing crunching, I figured that Vello had stood, but I was confused on what the crunching underneath his foot was.

"Turn the fucking light on and turn the air off. Nigga, it feels like Alaska in here! You might have fucked around and busted a fucking pipe! That's probably why it's wet, goofy-ass nigga."

Crossing my arms, I tried warming myself while waiting on my brother. After a few agonizing seconds of him crunching around, I could feel my dick turning into an icicle.

"Bro! What the fuck taking yo' goofy ass so long?"

Where the fuck is my phone? Fuck! Pia is going to be on my ass. I told her I wouldn't miss any more of her calls if I could help it, and I knew I'd missed several of them depending on how long I'd been asleep.

"Man, I can't find the light!"

"Nigga! What the fuck you mean you can't find the light?"

"I mean, I can't find the fucking light! I keep swiping my hand to where I think the wall is, and all I keep getting is fucking air! My feet wet and cold, nigga! What the fuck going—"

Blinding light impaired our vision all of a sudden. Holding my palm out in front of my face because the shit caused me to only see white, I blinked repeatedly to get my sight back.

"Am I the only one seeing white?" Vello asked.

This weed had to have some fucking crack in it. We'd fucked around and smoked ourselves into the fucking game. That fucking zombie war we were just playing in—we were now inside of it. Blankets of stark white snow stretched on for miles. Looking up at Vello, since he was standing, snow damn near covered all of his dreads and continued to fall. Reaching my hand up, I pulled at my own hair to see if snow was on my head. Pulling my hand back, I saw a few white speckles before it melted.

"What the fuck was in that weed?" I questioned as I stood. We were both standing in the middle of a fucking snowstorm with fog coming from our mouths with each breath we took. There was even ice at the tips of Vello's eyelashes, making them bitches look wispy. I was in a hoodie and coat, but it still wasn't enough to shield me from the weather. What the fuck was this?

"Nah, this ain't no fucking weed." Vello looked around, and I knew that nigga was cold because he had on short sleeves, baller shorts, and socks. At least I had on shoes and was covered. "On God, Don play too fucking much! Aye! Ayeeeee! This shit ain't funny!"

Looking up at the blue sky, my heart thumped against my rib cage. It fought for space in my chest with the frozen air in my lungs. I had never been more colder in my fucking life. Vello's shoulders tensed as he tried to process what the fuck was going on. I could tell by the wondering expression on his face that he didn't want to believe our circumstances. Me though, I was mentally kicking my own ass because I should have never even brought my ass over to his house, and I damn sure shouldn't have smoked his weed.

"You see that up ahead?" Vello pointed as he shook like a fucking tambourine. His fucking lips looked purple, and that couldn't have been a good sign.

"Nigga... I can't see shit but snow! Fuck is you saying right now?"

I knew damn well Don hadn't snatched us up and put us in Preston's virtual bullshit. I was so motherfucking tired of them and these climate-aligned missions and shit. That Demise nigga needed to be the Don of the fucking Discovery Channel because it was always a habitat or a fucking animal. Thankfully, though, it wouldn't be no animals here because it was too damn cold. Not even a fucking abdominal snowman could survive this weather here.

"Look! A few miles ahead! That's a tent!"

Squinting my eyes, I could see a small black dot, and if that was what Vello considered a few miles ahead, that nigga needed to re-measure. It looked like it would take us a few hours to get to that shit. Not only was the snow heavy, we were cold as fuck, the winds were harsh, and the snow was falling so hard that you could barely see in front of you. We had to elevate our voices while talking because of the wind.

"Nigga! How the fuck you gon' make it all the way up there in short sleeves?"

Vello's lips went from purple to blue. Rolling my eyes, I shimmied out of the bubble coat that I had on top of my hoodie and tossed it to him. I couldn't afford to lose layers, but my brother couldn't die out here. Even if this was a damn dream, I still didn't want to be stuck in this bitch by myself.

My twin slid the coat on, zipped it up to the neck, and looked down at his feet.

"Nigga... I'm not that fucking generous! Why the fuck would I give you my shoes, and then I get frostbite in the fucking toes?"

"Come on now, Twin! Give a nigga one shoe, and you keep one shoe."

"Hell naw, nigga!"

"Stop being low-down! It's obvious we being tested! We gotta work as a fucking team! That's the only way we gon' make it out; you know how this shit goes, Nel!"

"And I know I want my fucking toes! I gave you the fucking jacket!"

Vello smacked his lips. Looking down at my feet, I couldn't see them because they were already covered in about four inches of snow. Reaching down, I grabbed my left foot and snatched the Jordan off of it. Pushing it into his chest, I didn't wait for him to put it on as I pushed my stiff limbs toward the tent.

"Beg too fucking much," I mumbled as my teeth chattered.

"Aye, Twin! Wait the fuck up, nigga."

Vello was crunching behind me, and I was trying hard to not let my anger take over. I'd been mad quite a few times in my life, but this shit here was the angriest I'd ever been. I would have never guessed that I would get high and wake up in the middle of the fucking North Pole. I tried to steer my thoughts away from my circumstances because the more I thought about it, the colder I got. Who did some shit like this? I wanted to see the numbers at the end of the year. Ain't no way Don was wasting his money on shit like this. He was having us train as if we were going to war against the whole world, the supernatural, and the fucking aliens. I was over this shit, though.

Just when I thought my body was about to freeze over and shut down, we made it to the tent. Or at least what we thought was a fucking tent. This shit was beyond fucked up. We had trekked for what felt like miles to a portable dog house that neither of us could fit in. However, there were two big-ass backpacks in it. One was black, and the other was brown. Reaching in, I snatched them both out and never thought that moving my arm would feel like death. It felt like we had been sitting in an ice bath overnight. This shit was beyond inhumane. I was beating the fuck out of Don, Matteo, and Preston's big ass when this shit was all over.

"I don't even think I can unzip it. I needs help, brother," Vello croaked. Ignoring him, I opened the black backpack and almost praised God, seeing a snowsuit. Instead of sliding it on, I handed it to Vello. He didn't have the strength to open his backpack, but he damn sure had the strength to slide the suit on. Rummaging back through the backpack, I found goggles, gloves, and big-ass moon boots. Passing it all to my brother, I picked up the second backpack and started dressing my damn self. By the time I was dressed, I barely felt like I could move, but I was warm. It was still cold as shit, but it was tolerable.

"Where the rest of them niggas at? They split the squad up?" Vello muttered as if he was just now realizing it was only us enduring this torture.

Bending as much as I could, I looked inside the dog tent to see what else was left. There were two Stanley-looking cups and two objects stacked on top of each other that I couldn't make out. Grabbing it all, I passed Vello one of the cups. He struggled to open the top with the gloves but eventually got it open.

"This shit hot as hell, but it feels good." As Vello slurped on whatever was in the container, I tuned him out. If I wasn't in such a disarray, the white noise the winds caused would have been therapeutic. "Drink your shit. It tastes like chicken or somethin'. I think it's broth. I feel good as hell now."

Ignoring him, I looked for something that would give us instructions. Usually, there was a video or some shit with Don or Scarlett, but there wasn't shit left in the fucking tent. I didn't want anything to drink or eat. I was just ready to get the fuck on and get home to my Pia baby.

Picking up one of the iron subjects, I held it up to my face to observe it. It looked familiar, but I didn't know what the fuck it was.

"Oh, give me one," Vello asked as he picked up the identical object. "Man what the—"

Grrrrrrrrrrrrr

We both froze and looked around us. I couldn't see shit, but I damn sure heard it. "Nigga... was that a fucking zombie?"

With furrowed brows, Vello adjusted his goggles. "Ion know. I hope the fuck not. That shit sounded bigger than a zombie."

"Man, where the fuck you get that weed from?"

"Shit from Chico's ass! You think we just too high?"

"Nigga, you better hope we too high!"

Grrrrrrrrrrrrr

"Oh, shit! That ain't no fucking zombie! That's a bear!"

Looking to the left of me, I saw a big-ass ball of white fur running toward us. "Run, Twin! Run!"

Swiping the Stanly from the ground, I tried running but slipped. Vello grabbed my shoulder and pulled me in the opposite direction of the polar bear. He still had a ways to go before he reached us, but with the way we were restricted in the big-ass snow gear, he was going to catch up with us in no fucking time.

"I saw on TV one time when I was chilling with Scarlett that if a polar bear finds you... that means it's been tracking you for some time. They... they said them niggas the only animal that hunts humans. Hurry the fuck up before he eats the fuck out of us!"

Using all the strength I had, I ran beside my twin. Both of my hands were occupied, but I refused to drop this shit. It could be useful later down the line.

"Aye! There go something right there!" I pointed at a shadow. Turning around, the polar bear was closer and baring his sharp-ass teeth.

"It's a snowmobile! Get on the passenger!"

Running to the passenger side, I hopped in as Vello got in the driver's seat.

"How you crank this bitch up?" He panicked. It was all over; the bear had caught up to us.

"Bitch-ass nigga! You the one hopped on the driver's side like you know what the fuck you doing! Ahhhhhh!"

Opening the top of the Stanley-looking cup, I tossed the hot liquid in the face of the polar bear who had come up to my side. Using his big-ass paw, he swiped at his nose, and at the same time, Vello pulled off. We slid a few times because he didn't know how to drive the fucking thing, but finally got a comfortable distance away from the bear.

"Whoooo hoooo! Oh, shit! I gotta get me one of these bitches! Ayeeeee!"

The engine purred as Vello drove like a bat out of hell with no direction. The polar bear had begun to chase us again, but his red eyes told me he was hurt.

"Really, nigga?" Vello side-eyed me.

"What?"

"You used chicken broth on a fucking bear!"

"Fuck you wanted me to do? Help the fucking bear kill your ass?"

"Nigga, he was on your side!"

"On God, that's the last time I give your ass a shoe! You'd be a block of ice if I didn't save your groggy-belly ass. Slow this bitch down! We can't even see in front of us! What if we drive off a fucking cliff or something!"

"Nigga... this nothing but flat land! And you was supposed to use the bow."

"The what?"

"The bow and arrows. Here..." Vello reached down on his side and pulled out what I knew now was a weapon.

"I didn't know what the fuck that was game playing-ass nigga!"

Vello smirked, and I knew then he was about to do some shit to get us killed. I should've let his ass freeze and dealt with Ma's crying on the back end.

"Ahhhhhh!" My stupid-ass big brother did a fucking U-turn so that we were facing the polar bear and shifted the snowmobile in reverse. "You just didn't know how to start it, and now you done turned into a fucking Eskimo! Turn this shit back around!"

Instead of listening, this hard-headed-ass nigga pushed the gas, sending us driving in reverse. Lifting his bow that was already loaded with an arrow, he pointed it at the bear, who dodged the arrow like his ass was a ninja. He had to weigh over a thousand pounds and was mobbing like he'd been trained in Jiu-Jitsu!

"Nel, shoot!"

Lifting my own bow and arrow, I lifted it and pulled the bowstring.

Grrrrrrrrr

I hit the polar bear in the shoulder, and that slowed him all the way down. Red blood seeping from his fur let me know this shit was real. It wasn't like back at the school.

"Shoot his ass again, but aim for the face this time. My shit not hitting!" Vello was missing shot after shot while driving in reverse like we were in the Alaskan version of *Fast and the Furious.*

Raising the bow and arrow, I drawed again, hitting the polar bear near the same spot.

"Yeahhh! My brother a real fucking shoooooooterrrrrr—ahhhhh!" Vello screamed as my stomach dropped to the pit of my ass as we fell.

"Brotherrrrr!" Vello grabbed at my arm, and I pushed his ass off as I screamed to the top of my lungs like a bitch. I had never been a fan of heights, and here we were falling to our fucking deaths. The polar bear stood at the top of the ice cliff, watching us fall. I could have sworn that white furry nigga was smiling.

"Least I get to meet my twinsssssss!"

When I thought our bodies would spatter on ice, I felt a shock as we fell into a body of water. This time, I kept my eyes open as my brother swam through the clear blue, ice-bitter-cold water. This shit could not be happening.

Vello's eyes bucked as he pointed behind me. He reached down and fumbled with his bow while I prayed that another bear wasn't about to eat my ass up. "Duuuuuuck, Twin!" Bubbles spewed from his mouth as he lifted his bow and arrow. If I had to depend on his bad shooting ass, I knew I was doomed, but I did as he instructed and swam toward the bottom of what looked like nothing but blackness.

Zoop zoop

Instead of seeing blue, red flooded the water instantly. I could no longer hold my breath, and it was hard to swim in this snowsuit. Plus, I couldn't feel my legs. Fighting my way to the top, my lungs sucked in the frosty air as I made it to the surface. Vello was already leaning over a block of ice, catching his breath and choking.

"Nigga! I told your ass not to drive in reverse! I knew it was a fucking cliff!" My heart was beating so fast that my fucking head was hurting.

"Fuck that! You was about to get eaten by a big-ass seal. Look!"

To the right of me, a dark grey, shiny-ass mass with spots and long-ass whiskers floated. Where the fuck did they get all these fucking animals from? As half of our body was on land and the other still in the water, we could hear the crunching of something else coming near us.

"On God... ion even want to look. I can't take shit else. I'm just accepting my fate at this point!"

"I ain't accepting shit!" I had Pia to get home to. I made it this far; I was making it out of this shit, even if the lower half of my body suffered frostbite. I'd gotten the pussy and would just have to reminisce if my dick didn't work no more after this.

Looking up, my eyes landed on a pair of brown animal-skin boots. Scanning the tall figure, I saw that it was also in a snow-suit. His legs were too damn small to be Preston's round belly ass.

"Ah, fuck naw!" When Vello realized who it was standing over us, he smacked his chattering teeth. My whole body was shaking, but it damn sure wasn't from fear.

Squatting, he swiped his gloved hand across his nose. "I have shown you two nothing but respect. I let you in my home and in my heart. Still, you betray me. This is just a glimpse of how fucking cold my heart can get when you plot against me." Rio looked both of us in the eye before standing. "I'm not the motherfucker you make enemies with. I made myself accessible to you, but if you can't even rumble with a fucking bear, you have no chance to even stand next to me. Get the fuck up. We got shit to talk about, and I intend on talking before you turn into human popsicles."

Rio's gay ass may have had some balls all along. He walked off, leaving us to struggle with getting out of the water. I should have just talked to Rio before I pulled up on Vello. I had to start following my first mind!

"On God... I ain't never smoking with yo' ass again."

Vello pulled himself out of the water and laid on his back. "Shut the fuck up. I told you we was supposed to been kill that nigga anyway."

It was going to take me three days of defrosting to get feeling back in my circulatory system. Instead of going back and forth with my dumb-ass twin, I remained quiet. I needed to conserve my energy for this talk so I could make it home to Pia.

CHAPTER 22

RENELLO JR. (NELTZ)
(MAN-MAN)

riiiiinggggggg
B Not even waiting for the teacher to dismiss me, I hopped up from my desk and scooped my backpack from the ground. Mr. Gates side-eyed me but knew better than to stop me. The class snickered as I opened the door, and the cool breeze from the hallway rushed my face. The first time I left without the teacher dismissing me, he called himself standing in front of the door. I pushed his ass out of the way. As he lay on the ground, beet red in the face, I stepped over him and went to the bus lane. My bus driver was petty as hell and wasn't trying to wait on anyone who wasn't sitting behind her once she closed those doors. Today, though, my pops was picking me up. As a matter of fact, he'd been picking me up for the last few weeks unless he got caught up making a serve. Anytime he couldn't make it, he usually texted me by recess. I hadn't received a text, so I expected him to be parked outside in his rental.

My dad was cool. Both my parents were straight as long as they were apart from each other. For so long, I didn't understand why they always fought. Everyone else's parents got along and loved on each other, but mine were always at each other's throats. My mama was forever cursing his ass out, and he matched her energy every time. A few months back, when she put my ass on a plane and dropped me off at my dad's doorstep, it was then that I was able to see why my mama was angry all the time. On that plane ride, I watched her battle with herself on if she was doing the right thing. I had planned on running and hiding in the airport, but when I saw the worry in her eyes on top of my auntie crying the whole ride, I knew to just go peacefully. Living with my dad was okay. His wife wasn't my mama, and she stayed out my way and didn't say shit to me. After the first month, I started missing my mama, and when I realized my daddy wouldn't let me call her and was rejecting her incoming calls, I started acting the fuck out.

I knew it was wrong, but disrespecting his pregnant wife and kicking ass at the schoolhouse was going to be my ticket back to Jagoda Bay. I proved my theory right because my dad snatched my ass up and booked us a plane ticket back home. The day I stepped off the plane, I knew things would be different. Stuff just felt different. I couldn't explain it. Then, my daddy, who once didn't care anything about what my mama had going on, all of a sudden started to care. I used to love spending time with him and was glad he'd extended his time in Jagoda Bay, even after hearing him say he didn't want to keep me anymore. Then, I noticed the way he would talk shit about my mama at the barbershop. He made it his business to fuck with her and treat her like shit. I was young, but I knew that my dad was jealous. He was cool with my mama cursing him out and living in the ghetto. He used to ignore her over the years unless she caught him in a bad mood, and only then would he roast her back. Recently, though, she'd been ignoring him, and he'd been knick-picking. The shit was starting to be annoying. If he kept on talking shit about my mama, though, Dad or not, I was cursing him the fuck out.

School had been dismissed for three minutes, and most of the teachers still had their doors closed. They were petty as hell. I was basically in the hallway by myself. They had me messed up if they thought they were keeping me hostage past dismissal. They weren't going to give nobody a ride for missing the bus.

"Jacoby! Move! Leave us alone!"

I'd almost made it out of the front doors when I stumbled across Jacoby doing what he did best—fucking with folks. He had a shit-eating grin on his face as he stood over two girls that looked like they were about to piss themselves. I recognized one of them as Romana. She wasn't in the same class as me, but we had lunch together, and her class always took P.E. with us. Usually, her teacher, Mrs. Barker, would flirt with my teacher, even though both of their cheating asses were married. They were no better than my daddy. He had a whole wife back in Chicago but was forever pulling up at bitches houses. Sometimes, he left the door cracked when he went over, letting me take a peep.

I didn't know Romana had a big sister, though. The two girls were on the ground while Jacoby stood over them with his fist balled up. If Jacoby wasn't such a hoe, I would give the nigga his props. He didn't have hair like me, but his folks kept his shit in a low fade with designs on the side that he changed out weekly. His scalp wasn't going to be no more good once he got older if he didn't ease up. Before I came to the school, he was the flyest. Now that I was here, he wasn't seeing me. The two fights that I'd gotten into had been with his flunkies. He sent them out to, I guess, get the new boy in check, but I showed both their asses. I'd been itching to kick Jacoby's ass. I told my mama I would be on my best behavior, though, but the day he popped shit, I was laying his ass out.

"Aye, y'all get up."

I used to think it was normal to see men and women go at it, but when I got into a fight with a girl two years ago, my mama kicked my ass after explaining to me the importance of protecting girls. After that conversation, I cooled it. I didn't put my hands on girls. I was raised by women who were once girls. Yeah, my daddy had been in my life, but he was more like a big brother. It was my mama, auntie, and grandma who had shown me love and nurtured me even when I didn't deserve it. I respected girls because one day they, too, would be women. Jacoby, standing over the girls as they cried, had my trigger finger itching, but since I didn't have a gun, my fist would have to do if he protested.

Jacoby looked at me with his mug on, still standing over the girls. The big sister was trying to protect her baby sister. I could tell by the way she was covering Romana's body with hers, but they both were scared of him. He was weak as hell, though, so they had no reason to be afraid.

"Man, this is my business! Go get your ass on the bus!"

Ignoring him, I walked up and looked directly at the girls. "Come on, y'all... get up."

Reaching my hand down, Romana's tear-stained face pierced my heart. She was too pretty, reminding me of a doll with her big, wet eyes. Her curly hair had been ruffled, probably from this nigga shoving them down, and her knee was scraped up.

Without hesitation, she placed her hand in mine, and when I helped her stand, I reached down and pulled her sister up.

"Why the fuck you in my business? You think you all that because your non-driving ass hit the curb in that Porshe!" Jacoby laughed.

"Aye, go clean her up, and hurry up and get to the bus line before y'all end up getting left."

Romana's big sister put her arm around Romana and ushered her to the restroom, which was only a few feet away. By now, students were starting to fill the halls. Jacoby was fuming as he watched them walk into the girl's restroom, and when I saw that he wanted to go after them, I pushed him into the trophy case.

"So, you about to go in the girl's restroom? Nigga, leave them the fuck alone before I beat yo' ass out here. You know you can't whoop me!"

With flaring nostrils, he tried pushing me off him, but I held him to the glass with my forearm. "That's not none of your business!"

"Nigga! They not none of your business, either! They not no kin to you, plus, they girls!"

Jacoby smirked. "That's where you wrong. Our families got us arranged to be married. Romana gon' be my bitch! So, I can do whatever the fuck I want with her."

Shaking my head, heat flushed my face, and I didn't know why. "Nigga, what?"

"I forgot... you just a product of a single mama. You don't know nothing about my family. You don't know shit about legacies."

Pushing his ass again, I let him go because I didn't have time to get sent to the office. I didn't want to hear my daddy's mouth if he had to come inside the building and get me.

"You don't know shit about me! Whatever the fuck yo' weak-ass family got going on don't mean shit to me. Next time I see you put your hands on her, we gon' see whose bitch she gon' end up being. I'll take yo' bitch, nigga... soon as I turn eighteen."

I didn't even know Romana like that, but I wanted to get

under Jacoby's skin. With the way he was red in the face, I could see it worked. "I wish you would. You couldn't go against the Ernesses even if you tried! Who gon' help you? Yo' mama and her fat-ass sister?" Jacoby laughed.

Looking around to make sure none of the teachers were looking, I cocked my fist back and knocked him dead in the jaw. When he hit the ground, I squatted near him since he wasn't trying to get back up. He just sat there holding his jaw. He thought he was the shit because he had on some Off-White sneakers, but he just didn't know that my dad had bought me those same ones last year for my birthday. I played in them now.

"Stop speaking on my family. I don't give a fuck about no Ernesteins or whoever the fuck y'all is. Stay away from Romana and her sister, like I said. Ion need no help to go up against y'all. I'll do it by myself."

"Yeah, we gon' see."

Standing because my phone was vibrating in my pocket, I gripped the straps on my backpack. "Yeah. We are."

Walking backward because I didn't want him to sneak me, plus I wanted to see if Romana and her sister had gotten to the bus lane safely. Once I was in the clear, I jogged down the stairs and stood at the end of the car line. I knew my daddy was going to be late because he'd called and then texted as I walked to the line, informing me that he was running fifteen minutes behind. It was cool. As long as he had me some food as soon as I got in the car.

The line had started to clear out, and just when I was about to play Monopoly Go on my phone, an all-black Maybach pulled up in front of me. All I had been seeing was fancy cars since moving to our new house and starting this new school. My mama had even upgraded to AMG, which I loved. I hated when she drove that damn Honda and had avowed that soon as I turned eighteen, I was buying her a car.

When the car stopped directly in front of me with its heavy tint, I crossed my arms in front of myself. I didn't know who the fuck was behind the tinted windows, but they could get these hands too. I beat up grown people too. I fought a seventeen-year-old one time and hadn't regretted it. Pearla's old boyfriend, who had spread that rumor about taking her virginity, had been the victim. That preppy-ass bitch wasn't seeing me.

The window rolled down, and when the face came into view, he was met with a deep scowl. "Who the fuck is you, old-ass nigga?"

A white man with grey hair and a neatly trimmed grey beard peered at me. I knew there were plenty of people at that stuck-up girl's birthday party we'd gone to, but I didn't recognize this man. I made it my business to memorize faces everywhere I went just in case I had to come back and *doo doo doo* when I was eighteen.

"Who the fuck is I? I would say who the fuck is you, but by your attitude, I already know."

A broad smile spread across his tanned face and revealed chalk-white teeth. He looked crazy as shit, but still, I wasn't scared of his ass.

"My son has done something right after all. I'm Rionardo Mecanio Sr. Your great-grandfather."

"So, you the gay dude's daddy?"

Chuckling, her stroked his beard, showing an expensive-looking watch. "I'm the gay dude's daddy. But... I think he would prefer it if you called him Grandpa. Same as me."

"Yeah, nah. I'm good on that shit. I went nine years without a grandaddy; I can go nine more. Unless you got somethin' for me. Money make me reconsider, Paw Paw."

He tossed his head back, a deep laughter erupting from

him. "You'll do just fine in the family. With the future in your hands, we'll be alright."

I didn't know what the fuck he was talking about, so I just stood there staring at him.

"Your grandfather is a very important person. He had the position handed down from me, and one day, the position will be yours."

I didn't know why the fuck he was telling me this on elementary school yards. But it made me smile. "On some gangsta shit or some business shit?"

"Both."

We wore matching grins.

I caught a glimpse of Jacoby from my peripheral, so I tossed the middle finger at his ass. He rolled his eyes like a hoe and hopped in his daddy's Benz.

Bitch boy.

"Aye... Paw Paw, you know the Ernesses?"

"Maybe. You have grievances with them?"

"Nah, but one day I just might."

He laughed again. "My great grandson, you'll do just fine. I gotta go. I see your father pulling up, but we will meet again."

"I guess we will." I shrugged.

He rolled his window up and pulled off. At the same time, my daddy took his spot, and as soon as I opened the door to the rental, smoke from the weed he was burning spilled out. My principal was going to be emailing my mama again. He was going to have to chill out with this shit, at least until I was in the car and we were off the premises.

Closing the door, I pulled my backpack off my shoulder and placed it between my legs. My dad didn't even wait till I had my seatbelt on before he was pulling off.

"Aye, who that was?"

My daddy pulled from the weed before handing it to me.

He'd been letting me get high with him for about a year now. It was another reason I didn't mind him picking me up from school, even though his questioning me about my mama's business was starting to irk me. Pulling from the weed, I let it suffocate my lungs, and just when I thought I had it, I started coughing my organs up.

"I told yo' ass you got to do the shit slow. Give me my fucking weed." My daddy snatched the blunt out of my hand and placed it to his lips.

As always, Hobo was fly. He was always dressed in the latest, but his problem was he wore too much of it at one time. Like today, his jogging suit was red, his shoes were red, his hat was red, and I bet his socks were red too. He had chains on his neck that I used to think were the shit until I got sight of Renello's necklaces. Even his brother and the whole family were icy. They made my daddy's stuff look fake as hell.

"Aye, call yo' fucking Mama. She with that nigga?"

Pulling my phone out, I pretended to call my mama while still trying to control my breathing. I could already feel the effects of the drugs, so I wasn't too irritated. "She didn't even answer."

Making a U-turn in the middle of the street, he headed in the direction of the nearest McDonalds. That McFlurry was going to hit.

"That bitch think she's so smart. Aye, what you know about that nigga? Y'all got the same name for real? I know you mine because the test came back 99.9."

That was another reason I was side-eyeing my daddy. He had a bitch that he was fucking swab our mouths a day after he found out I was named after another man without telling my mama.

"Dad, I really don't know. Him and Mama be gone or in their room with the door closed. I don't know much about him."

Renello and I had gotten close after he pistol-played me and made me watch that sad-ass Selena movie. If that Yolanda bitch was still alive when I turned eighteen, it was on. I was taking her ass out. I was still mad that I walked in on him doing nasty stuff to my mama, but he put a lot of things into perspective for me. My daddy wasn't rich, but he wasn't broke, either. He could have easily helped my mama get another car or helped her out with the bills more. He lived in a nice town-home in Chicago, whereas before Renello came along, we lived in the hood.

A man takes care of what he loves.

My daddy had no love for my mama at all, even though he made her a mother. Renello had come through, and my mama hadn't stopped smiling yet.

"So, now she fucking on a nigga instead of being a mama. I ought to take you back to Chicago since she wanna be trifling."

The weed had gotten to me, so I laughed. My mama was far from trifling. She did plenty of stuff with me as long as I did right in school. Even when we were poor, she made sure we created memories, whether it was having a movie night or going to Dave and Buster's. He had my mama fucked up.

"What the fuck you laughing at?"

My dad wasn't the best-looking man, so the steam coming from his flat-ass nose made him look like the gorilla my mama liked to call him when she got mad. I was glad I took after my mama's people. I loved my ugly daddy, though.

"Nun, pops."

"Answer the fucking question—"

One of his three phones rang, halting him from continuing. My dad picked his phones up one by one from out of the cup holder. He was shuffling the phone and trying to drive; some-times, he sacked up dope while driving. One day, his ass was going to crash, and I hoped I wasn't in the car on the day it happened. Seeing that it was one of his flip phones that was his trap phone, I diverted my attention out the window. I was almost dizzy watching the trees pass by.

"Didn't I tell you I was fucking working on it? Stop calling my phone! When I got more info, I'll call you. Look... I got my son in the car. I'll ask him about the shit!"

He tried to whisper the last part, but I'd heard him even over the music. High and all, I was always attentive. One of my teachers told me a long time ago that I had ears like a bat. I heard him flip the phone closed. I didn't know who he was on the phone with, but he wasn't getting anything out of me.

"Son... look at me."

Turning my head, I gave him my attention. "Wassup, Pops?"

"You know, when you turn eighteen, I'ma put you on, right?"

Renello had made me sound like a fool when I told him about my future with my daddy, and now that I had time to analyze it, he was right. My daddy wanted me to be his flunkie, but Paw Paw just told me I would be handed down the business, whatever it was. He looked like a Cartel nigga, so I would take Paw Paws proposition over my daddy's. Especially if I could go after Jacoby's weak-ass family with it.

"Yeah. I can't wait," I lied.

"Aite... aite, cool. Look, that nigga yo' mama be with... the one she claim as her cousin. Did you hear anything about him killing somebody?"

My body went rigid, but I played it off.

Why he asking me that for?

"What you mean?"

"I mean, that nigga tried to shoot me back at the strip club when I brought you here. A nigga yo' mama used to fuck with was killed right outside her old apartments. Did you hear if that nigga had done it?"

Renello had looked me square in the face and told me he killed Banger. Why the fuck my daddy wanted to know was beyond me, and why someone on the phone was asking him about it was beyond me too.

"Dad. I don't know that man. All I know is that he be making sure Mama straight. He put her in a house, bought her a car, and he takes care of all of us. He makes her happy. That's all I know. You know they don't talk around me. Half the time, I'm with you."

I didn't know what type of police-ass shit my daddy was on, but he and whoever on the phone was going to have to do their job without me. I wasn't no snitch. Besides, I fucked with Daddy Number Two. I wasn't sacrificing my mama's happiness for a man who didn't care if she had transportation—father or not.

"Who was that in the Maybach?"

"Shit... ion know. They asked me what the name of the school was and drove off. Some old-ass black man." Again, another lie. That man was very much white with a heavy accent.

My dad eyed me skeptically while speeding down the streets. When he purposely passed McDonalds, I knew he was in his feelings.

"So, you don't know the niggas last name or nothing? Your mama talking 'bout he her cousin, but she don't have no family like that."

Shiddd. My mama got plenty rich-ass family.

"I told you, Dad... I be with you. You know people don't go around broadcasting their last names."

"He get mail at the house? Matta fact? You been to his house? Can you give me instructions?"

"I don't even think the nigga got a house, Daddy. He be over ours too much." Another lie. He had a big-ass house, and I knew exactly where it was at. Shit had tiny-ass rainbow furniture in it, but it was big, and his brother owned an even bigger house next door.

"Fuck! I need you to start listening. I hope you not trying to side with yo' mama. She dropped your ass off to me for five months and didn't call or visit once. Fuck her! I'm all you got. That nigga don't take care of you, I do! Matta fact, don't take shit from him or wear shit he buys. That's why I take you to the barbershop myself. He not finna be playing Daddy to you."

Too late. Renello my Daddy Number Two.

My mama was right. My daddy was so bitter. "I hear you, Daddy."

"Yeah, hear me loud and clear! And call me Pops. These bitches call me Daddy! That shit gay!"

"Okay." I couldn't wait to get out of this damn car.

"I'm changing your name too! You should have been named after me, anyway."

I would die before I sported the name Hobo. That shit was weak. I was really going to be kicking ass with a name like that. My dad parked next to my mama's new truck, and when he acted like he wanted to hit it, I laughed and hopped out before he could even shift gears.

"Aye... wait. I'm coming in with you. I gotta talk to your mama."

I didn't have the energy to argue with him. If he wanted to get cursed out by my mama, he could be my guest. I knew the only reason he was even attempting to come in was because Renello's car was not parked in the driveway. I had the munchies, so I had a date with the refrigerator. Making sure to use my key instead of the code so that my shiesty-ass daddy didn't have it, I let myself in. The vanilla plug-ins greeted me, and the smell of Pine Sol let me know my mama had cleaned up. Our house was always clean, and she had it decked out too. I loved it here.

"Mama! Come to the living room! Daddy here!" Looking back at him as he stood in the living room with a scowl on his face, I cleared my throat. "I meant, *Pops* here."

Not waiting to witness them argue, I slipped my backpack and shoes off and headed straight to the kitchen. I thought about Jacoby's ass as I pulled the leftover pasta from the stainless-steel refrigerator. I didn't know what he meant by Romana being his, but I felt sorry for her if she had to be stuck with his ass. I saw myself stomping his ass out before the school year was over. He made me appreciate the fact that I didn't have a sister. I would kill something behind my sisters. My daddy's wife had lost her baby, and that shit was for the best. Placing the Tupperware on the island, I went to grab a spoon and plate when I heard something shatter.

Pulling my pants up on my waist, I rushed through the living room, and when I saw my dad wasn't where I left him, I hustled to my mama's room. The door was closed, but I could hear tussling.

"Aye! What y'all doing in there?"

"Get the fuck off me, Hobo! Why the fuck you in here questioning me on some police shit? And then you gon' put your fucking hands on me!"

That was all I needed to hear. Twisting the knob, it was locked, but I knew how to pick it. Jumping up, I swiped the tools I used last time to pick the lock. It took me less than five seconds to get the lock open, and when I saw my dad on top of my mama as they wrestled, I ran full speed. They were fully clothed, but I didn't care. He had Pia fucked up.

"Aye! Get the fuck off my mama! What the fuck wrong with you, nigga?"

I reached for his back, and at the same time, my mama screamed.

"Renelloooooo, noooooooooo! What the fuck did you do, Hobo?! Ahhhhhhh!"

A loud popping noise went off, and I felt my breath leave my body. My daddy froze, and my mama used that time to push him off of her. When her eyes grew big, I looked down at my chest and placed my hand on the hole in it. Blood covered my fingers, and there was a loud piercing in my ears. I would have beaten Jacoby's ass had I known this was how my afternoon was going to play out.

The horror on my mama's face frightened me, and before I could tell her I was okay, everything went black.

To Be Continued...

PART 3 WILL BE the finale of the twins book. I hope y'all are ready for the smoke! Things are turning up a notch in the next installment! All these secrets will be revealed! Also, if you didn't catch this on the order of the books page, here is the link to read Big Boss. That is the book that introduces Mahzeyah's family and Rio's sister.

Big Boss

MORE BY THE AUTHOR

Yayo: The Beginning
  Yayo:Riot's Revenge
  Riot 3 (Yayo)
  Death of a Nawf Memphis Trap King
  Boostin' around the Christmas Tree
  I choose you boo 1&2
  Annihilate your love
  You're My favorite Mistake 1&2
  Peek it's boo 1-3
  Bossed Up
  Bayb
  If Cupid was a Thug
  Giving it a try with a street Guy: The Valentines
  Forever Good in his Hood
  Bound to a Bandit
  Dreaming of Spring
  Big Boss
  Humbled by a Real n*gga 1-3
  Humbled on Christmas Day- lani & Rut

Just like I taught you
Honey, I f*cked the Plug 1-3
Daddy's Lil Baby
Pregnant by a Muthaf*ckin Don 1&2
A Winter Crest Christmas: Pure & Luxe
A Winter Crest Valentine's: Snowy & Sphere
Wealth over riches & bad b*tches
Paradise Bay: Coastal & Bliss
Exhilarated 1-3
Put it on The Mob: Ezio and Jae
On The Mob: The Cuppacio Twins

Get your signed Paperback of Put it on the mob 2! Features an autographed copy, matching bookmark, and stickers!

Put it on the Mob book 1
 Put it on the Mob book 2
 On the Mob book 1

KEEP UP WITH ME

Join my Facebook group and mailing list for exclusive sneak peaks, prizes, book gossip, and never before released short stories! Also, follow my Amazon Author page for first dibs on new drops!

ABOUT THE AUTHOR

Lisa Austin is an award winning, National best selling, independent Author who often creates tales about the grit and grind of the streets but with a romantic twist. Born and raised in Memphis, TN, the on the rise Author has been penning stories her entire life.

www.ingramcontent.com/pod-product-compliance
Lightning Source LLC
Chambersburg PA
CBHW020931020726
47495CB00002B/440

* 9 7 9 8 9 8 9 8 3 6 3 5 2 *